180° MAGNETIC

REPEL ALL BOARDERS

JIM SCHOENDALLER
JEANNE C. STEIN

James Schoendaller Publishing

ACKNOWLEDGMENTS

Whereas this book took a fraction of the time of book one, there are several individuals that I wish to recognize.

My wife Amy and daughter Natalie - Thanks for your patience, understanding, and encouragement.

Jeanne C. Stein - Thanks for investing your time and writing prowess, especially with all of the changes that were made. Like you say, "Writing is 10 percent writing and 90 percent rewriting."

Deanne Conte, mom #2 - Thanks for your feedback and support.

I wish to thank my self-publishing support group - Stuart Smith at Avant Studios; Deborah Dove, editor; and Leslie Waara for the artwork.

I wish to thank my subject matter expert for his valuable assistance. Jim Cook, the founder of the Victoria Sailing School.

I also wish to thank my beta-readers for reading part or all of the various drafts and providing their honest feedback - Steve Bohn, sailing and ballroom dancing friend; Sharyl Davis, ballroom dancing friend from California; Kimberly Schmitt, friend who was my wife's roommate in college and they kept in touch; Shirley Yook, friend and lead singer for the dance band Perfect Harmony.

Jim Schoendaller

I'd like to add a quick thanks to Jim for sharing his work with me, and to his wonderful wife, Amy, and daughter, Natalie (my unofficial goddaughter and tennis partner.) They are more than friends to me—they are family.

Jim mentioned all his contacts who added to the accuracy of the book—to that I want to add my thanks as well. And to my own husband, Phil, and daughter, Jeanette: you have always encouraged me to spread my writing wings. I couldn't do it without you.

Jeanne C. Stein

CHAPTER 1

I was sitting alone in the Bermuda Customs Office. The dingy hallway was hot and reeked of cigarette smoke, making me long for fresh air. Pat and Tracy had already been interviewed and had left for *The Lady Anne*. I was the last one. And it seemed like hours before a slender man in a crisp white shirt finally called out my name.

I stood up and followed him, finding it amusing that he had practically shouted out my name even though I was the only one left in the entire building except whoever awaited me behind that closed door.

He opened the door and gestured me inside, then took his place beside his comrades. The men sat at a folding conference table, each with a notebook in front of him. In spite of the heat, they were dressed in white, long-sleeved shirts, ties, and dark slacks. There was an old-style cassette tape recorder on one end. They faced a solitary metal folding chair—mine presumably. Judging from their expressions and how hot it was in this room, I figured that they were likely to be grumpy.

No one moved to make introductions. Each man wore a badge and name tag, and from the varying amounts of braid on their shoulders, I surmised the burly guy in the center was the ranking officer, and the one who ushered me in, the most junior.

"Please be seated, Mr. Adams," said the man in the center, Taggart, confirming my guess that he was the chief.

I did as instructed.

The man on the left switched on the tape recorder and said, "State your name for the record."

"Reid Adams," I replied.

"Which vessel brought you to Bermuda?"

"*The Lady Anne*, sir."

"What type of vessel is that?"

"She is a sixty-eight-foot sailboat, sir."

"What was your position on *The Lady Anne*?"

I knew I couldn't tell them I was hired by the owners, Pat and Tracy, to help sail *The Lady Anne* from the US Virgin Islands back to Florida. Admitting that I was a sailing instructor working in a foreign country without work permits or visas might get me into trouble. And since Pat, Tracy, and I had discussed how best to explain our presence here, I'd keep to the script.

"I'm a friend with extensive sailing experience, sir," I said simply.

"Extensive sailing experience?" Taggart echoed, looking me in the eye. "Tell us, then, why you are in Bermuda if you were headed from the Virgin Islands to Florida via the Dominican Republic, Turks and Caicos, and the Bahamas? The Bahamas are roughly one thousand miles to the south."

His skepticism about my abilities was obvious. I'm sure he asked the same question of Pat and Tracy. And we had an answer prepared. "We got caught in a bad electrical storm that severely damaged all electrical systems," I said. "With no way to navigate or communicate, we simply got lost, sir."

He thumbed through a few pages of notes and then asked, "And what about Pat Taylor? Did she have extensive sailing experience too?"

"What he's asking," the second man, Bowman, interjected, "is if this Pat Taylor is qualified to be the captain of a sixty-eight-foot sailboat?"

The way he asked his question made it sound like he was pursuing some type of insurance angle. Then a thought flashed through my mind that he might be looking for a scapegoat to pin *The Lady Anne's* disappearance on. And to charge someone for what would have been an enormously expensive search.

I formed my answer quickly but carefully.

"Pat is qualified to be the captain. She has recently completed sailing classes, passed exams, and holds sailing certifications for basic keelboat, coastal cruising, and bareboat chartering. In addition, she has completed the open water classes for offshore passage making as well as for docking certification and multihull certification. Pat is completely qualified to be the captain."

"What about Tracy Palmer? Is she qualified to be the first mate?"

"Tracy has the same sailing certifications as Pat so yes, not only is Tracy qualified to be the first mate, she is qualified to be the captain as well, sir."

"To the best of your knowledge, do either of them have their captain's license from the United States Coast Guard?" The second man seemed determined to press the issue.

I smiled and answered calmly, "They are fairly well prepared to take that exam if they choose to, but they'll need more time on the water as they don't yet have enough documented hours at sea, sir."

Bowman shook his head. Taggart glared slightly at me. I made direct eye contact. I could tell he was judging the adequacy of my answer about Pat's and Tracy's qualifications. Then the questions started coming faster. "Tell us about the storm."

"We were engulfed in fog, encountered a ferocious electro-magnetic storm the likes of which I've never seen before, lost power, and then sailed around, looking for an inhabited island."

"Why didn't you use your emergency EPIRB locator beacon?"

"Its battery was dead, and when we eventually restored power, it couldn't get a signal. All of our GPS units quit working after the electromagnetic storm. We couldn't get a satellite signal."

"Where did you get the dog?"

The change of subject was like whiplash. "We found Buster at the site of the wreck of *The Obsession* from Nova Scotia, sir."

"Who killed Bonnie's husband, Carl?"

"He was killed by Tracy, in self-defense, when he boarded and tried to pirate *The Lady Anne*, sir."

My throat had gone dry. I wanted a sip of water, but I didn't see any and the questions kept coming.

"Who killed Captain Rick?"

"He was killed by Bonnie after he assaulted her. He also killed the husbands of the other three women—Angie, Ashley, and Donna—and he assaulted them as well."

"Where are the bodies of these men?"

"They were buried at sea, sir."

The man on the right of Taggart thumbed through his papers. He hadn't yet asked a question, but he did now. "What happened with Captain Pincus in the Virgin Islands?"

I swallowed. That was a question I hadn't expected. "After Pat and Tracy acquired the yacht, *The Lady Anne*, they fired her former captain, Captain Pincus. He snuck aboard and pirated the vessel, kidnapping both women."

The man who asked me the question wasn't looking at me but was looking at his notes instead. I continued, "Fortunately I saw *The Lady Anne* leaving her slip, snuck aboard, and tried to rescue the women. Captain Pincus overpowered me and was seconds away from raping Pat when the Coast Guard arrived, having been alerted by the marina guard."

"Why didn't you return to St. Thomas to complete the police report?"

"Since the Coast Guard couldn't find Captain Pincus after he fled by jumping overboard, we were concerned with our safety and sailed to Puerto Rico instead."

"Where did the electrical storm hit you?"

"Between Provo and Eleuthera, sir."

"Why did you sail northeast into open water and not west toward the Americas?"

"We were uncertain of our position, our main compasses were broken, we had no communications or GPS, and we feared sailing through the shallow Bahamian waters. We were very lucky to spot Bermuda."

"You may have not been aware of this, but Captain Taylor's vessel, *The Lady Anne*, was the subject of an intensive Bahamian search, even making the news up here."

"No sir, I was not aware of that." But my suspicion was confirmed.

"Had you stayed in the area of the storm, your vessel would have no doubt been spotted by the rescue effort."

That wasn't a question so I didn't respond. There was a brief pause.

"A person with extensive sailing experience would not have left the area. Why did you?"

"Like I said, that storm blew us way off course. Without GPS or a compass, we had no way to ascertain our position. Our clocks had stopped working. We had no way to know the exact time so we couldn't ascertain our position using celestial navigation. We were completely lost, sir."

"Where did you find the catamaran, *The Aquaholic?*"

"She found us when Captain Rick wanted revenge. She was lost as well. We decided it was prudent to stay together, sir."

"What happened to *The Day Dream*, Captain Rick's vessel?"

"She was anchored by a deserted island the last time I saw her," I replied. I didn't mention I had disabled her in an attempt to keep Captain Rick from chasing after us.

"Why doesn't Gertrude Kohler have a passport?" Bowman asked.

Once again, the change of subject gave me pause. I had expected more grilling on where this deserted island might be. I replied, "She told me she lost everything when the vessel she was on sank, sir."

"Where is Mr. Morris's airplane?"

"The last time I saw it, it was wrecked on another deserted island," I answered.

My last answer seemed to stop the questions. All three men looked at me, staring intently. Had the roles been reversed, I would have been watching for any nonverbal signals that might indicate the truth or not. They looked at me for an entire minute. I remained calm and still. They finally exchanged glances with each other and, judging by their facial expressions, I was fairly certain my answers had matched everyone else's.

Finally, Taggart asked, "What are your plans now, Mr. Adams?"

I knew what Pat wanted to do—tell Charles, *The Lady Anne's* previous owner, everything. But I remembered the warning that public discussion of what had happened would cause alien intervention. I, for one, had no wish to be incinerated the way our documentation confirming their existence had been.

I wasn't sure Pat would keep quiet, though.

I didn't realize how long I had been thinking until the question was repeated. "What are your plans now, Mr. Adams?"

"Our first priority will be getting medical attention for those that need it."

"And then?"

"And then those who want to will leave Bermuda. I plan to stay to oversee needed repairs to both vessels."

"Will you be staying less than ninety days, between ninety-one days and one hundred eighty days, or more than one hundred eighty days?"

"Less than ninety days, sir. Probably less than thirty."

"Will you be sleeping aboard or ashore, Mr. Adams?"

"My intention is to sleep aboard *The Lady Anne*, sir."

"Will the others be leaving by air?"

"I would guess," I replied, thinking that was a stupid question. If the boats they had arrived on were staying for repairs, how else would they leave?

"Then consider yourself under watch and restriction," Taggart continued. "Don't leave the marina area and keep the dog aboard *The Lady Anne* with you at all times. We will send a local veterinarian over to inspect the dog. If the dog passes, it can stay; if not, it will have to leave. You will have to pay cash for the visit. Is all that clear?"

"Yes sir, it is." As the man on the left switched off the tape recorder, I finally relaxed, knowing my interrogation was finished. Taggart opened my passport to the page he wanted and stamped it.

"Go ahead and move your vessels from the customs docks and make your own arrangements at the marina of your choice. We'll find you if we have any further questions. Thank you for your cooperation. Ms. Taylor has already paid your required taxes and fees. Welcome to Bermuda."

I rose and offered my hand, but no one got up or extended a hand to shake it. Instead, my passport and paperwork were shoved toward me. I retrieved my items and briskly exited, not sticking around for any more questions.

CHAPTER 2

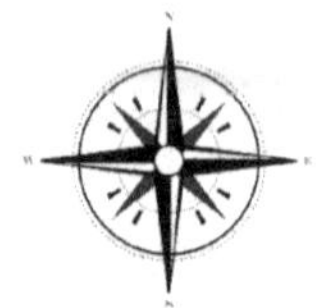

Tracy was waiting for me at *The Lady Anne*. As soon as she saw me approach, she ran down the dock to meet me.

"Can we go now?" she asked. She looked around nervously, as if afraid I was being tailed by a customs agent.

I nodded. "It's all right. They've given us clearance to leave." I paused. "Any news from Charles?"

She shook her head. "He may know we are here in Bermuda, he may not. Regardless, Pat used the radio and reserved two slips at the Royal Bermuda Yacht Club in Hamilton."

"Let's go," I said cheerfully.

Mo and Gert were aboard *The Lady Anne* with Bonnie and her kids, Max, and Joey. Pat shot me a look when she saw me approach. I gave her the thumbs-up. "Let's get out of here," I said.

She grinned and set to untying *The Lady Anne* and then went aboard with Tracy. Tracy steered the boat away from the dock. I tossed Pat the bow line.

Mo and Gert waved. They were still showing signs of serious malnourishment, having barely survived alone on a deserted island for months, but as always, they were in good spirits. Bonnie, Max, and Joey had gathered at the bow. The kids were excited to be in Bermuda and looking forward to spending some time on land—land that offered shopping, gaming, and bike riding instead of little food, dangerous terrain, and a psychopath for a skipper. Their mother, Bonnie, looked worn out but was managing a smile.

I instructed Angie to get the *Aquaholic*'s engines started. Angie had been very pleasant since reaching Bermuda. I was glad she had no memory of her ordeal with the monster, Captain Rick. He had beaten her unconscious, tied her up, and raped her.

The other two women aboard *The Aquaholic* had not been as fortunate. Ashley and Donna had been awake for their bondage and repeated assaults. All were happy to be in Bermuda, but I knew they would be plagued with nightmares for a very long time.

I got *The Aquaholic* untied, and with Angie at the helm, left the customs office on Ordnance Island in our wake.

We followed *The Lady Anne* to the marina. As I joined

Angie at the helm, she told me all of our firearms had been confiscated, even the flare guns.

That surprised me since I remembered we had all agreed to deny having any firearms if the question came up. She could tell from my expression I didn't know.

"The customs inspector asked if there were any firearms aboard *The Aquaholic*. I told him there was. He impounded my shotgun and its ammo."

I shook my head.

"Would you have wanted me to lie about firearms in a foreign country?" she asked.

"I thought we agreed to say nothing about the guns," I snapped. "After all we've been through, I would think you wouldn't want to lose our only means of self-defense."

Color crept up Angie's face. "I have a receipt for the gun, ammo, and even the flare gun, which I didn't expect to be a restricted item. They will all be returned when we depart."

"And what about *The Lady Anne*'s weapons?"

She looked away. "Those too. Your shotgun, Mo's rifle, all the ammo, and also your flare guns. I believe Tracy has the receipt."

My shoulders tightened. "I wish you hadn't said anything."

Angie shrugged. "I'm sorry. I was afraid if I hadn't told them about the guns and they were found aboard, we'd be in more trouble than if I just admitted we had them." She touched my arm and pointed. "But we shouldn't need weapons here," she said. "It looks like a very nice marina."

Ahead of us, Pat radioed which slips she had reserved for

us. The marina was bustling with lots of masts jutting skyward. We located the slips, one for *The Aquaholic* and one for *The Lady Anne*, farther down the same row.

Ashley, Donna, and I had scarcely gotten *The Aquaholic* secured in her berth when Pat appeared, tapping me on the shoulder.

"I'm going to the office to sign in and pay for the slips," she said. "Do you need anything?"

I shook my head, so she gave me a hug and walked away.

As Angie shut off the engines, I headed for *The Lady Anne* to see if they needed any help. Mo was assisting Tracy with the dock lines. They were doing everything correctly, smiling and laughing. Gert was topside with Bonnie, Max, and Joey. The kids were playing with Buster.

It felt comforting to be back in civilization. I knew I owed Tracy our lives. Hell, we all did. If she hadn't been able to convince the aliens to return us to the present time, we'd all be stuck 25,700 years in the past.

That Angie had gotten our weapons confiscated rankled me. Still, overall I was pleased with everyone's statements to the authorities. With even one wrong answer, we might have been refused entry, and the US coast was several hundred miles distant.

I turned to check on Pat's progress. She was near the end of the dock and barely in sight but there was a small group of people passing her, headed in our direction. I could see at least two large television cameras.

"We've got company," I said softly to Tracy. "Reporters."

Mo noticed them too, and as he climbed back aboard *The Lady Anne*, he asked, "How do you want to handle this?"

"Get everyone belowdecks," I said. "I'll get rid of them as quickly as possible." Then, "Oh, and Tracy, radio *The Aquaholic*. I don't want them getting blindsided. Everybody just stay out of sight until I give the all clear."

Tracy nodded and followed Mo. In a flash, the decks were deserted.

At the rate the reporters were closing in, I barely had time to make sure my shirt was tucked in. I drew a breath and turned to face them.

CHAPTER 3

An attractive young woman with nice legs and a pretty face introduced herself as Brenda Bishop and asked me if I was Reid Adams.

"Good guess," I replied. She seemed friendly enough, but I reminded myself she was a reporter out for a story and not to get distracted by her looks.

"It wasn't a guess." She smiled. "Pictures of this vessel, Reid Adams, Tracy Palmer, and Patricia Taylor have been all over the news. The mysterious disappearance of *The Lady Anne* and her crew prompted a massive search centered in the waters in and around the Bahamas."

I didn't say anything but knew immediately what the questions were going to be about.

"Do you mind if I ask you some questions when we go live?"

I exhaled slightly and replied, "Okay."

She led me forward on the dock, toward the bow. Obviously she wanted *The Lady Anne* in the background. Her cameraman took up position where he had a good angle. A young man with long hair and a headset stood beside the cameraman.

Another cameraman stood a few feet past them. A female reporter with a Channel Seven microphone stood by him. I surmised that Brenda had gotten here first and the other network was being professional by letting her interview me first.

"Three minutes," the headset man announced.

Brenda looked at me and smiled. "I'm going to ask you about how your vessel arrived in Bermuda when it was last spotted in the Bahamas. I'm going to ask you about Patricia and Tracy."

"Call her Pat," I said quietly. "She goes by Pat."

"Is Pat or Tracy available to go on camera with you?"

"Two minutes."

I shook my head. "Pat isn't here right now and Tracy wanted me to speak for her."

She looked a bit disappointed but nodded. "We'll just see how the interview goes. Try and speak clearly and just be honest. Follow my lead. I'll close by asking what your plans are now. Will all that be okay with you?"

"Sounds fine."

"One minute."

The pronouncement at my shoulder made me jump. I

laughed. "I don't do this very often," I said. "I'm a little nervous."

"Don't be." She smiled again. "You'll do fine."

I waited by her side. I wondered if Tracy and the others were watching us from inside *The Lady Anne* but I didn't turn to look. A little red light on the front of Brenda's camera came on. A few seconds later, a red light on the other camera turned on as well. The second reporter whispered something to her cameraman, who nodded. I couldn't hear what she said.

"Five, four, three. . ."

Brenda turned to face the camera. "This is Brenda Bishop, with Channel Nine News, live from the Royal Bermuda Yacht Club in Hamilton, Bermuda. I'm standing in front of *The Lady Anne* which, as you have no doubt heard, was declared missing at sea in the Bahamas."

She turned to face me and continued. "With me is Mr. Reid Adams. He is a sailing instructor from Colorado, USA and was delivering *The Lady Anne* from the Virgin Islands to Florida with two of his former students, Tracy Palmer and Pat Taylor."

I kept my face carefully neutral. My profession, which I had successfully kept from the customs inspectors, had just been broadcast on live television. I hoped there would be no repercussions.

Brenda faced the camera again. "*The Lady Anne* was reported missing in the waters between the Turks and Caicos and the Bahamas and magically reappeared today in Bermuda, nearly one thousand miles away."

"Mr. Adams"—she turned toward me—"could you please tell us what happened and how your vessel came to be in Bermuda?"

She placed her microphone close to my face. I knew the camera had zoomed in. I swallowed and spoke.

"We sailed through a violent electrical storm that damaged our navigation and communications equipment and we simply got lost. We were fortunate to spot Bermuda. It was simple luck; there was nothing magical about it."

"From the reports about *The Lady Anne*, wasn't she equipped with the proper gear to cross oceans, including GPS, EPIRB locator beacons, paper and electronic charts, and a satellite phone? And wasn't there a radio and multiple cell phones aboard?"

"The electrical storm damaged everything electrical. None of those things you mentioned worked."

"Mr. Adams, could you please explain how you managed to sail nearly one thousand miles to Bermuda without being spotted by the large number of search and rescue vessels and aircraft that were searching the area?" Brenda was still smiling and looked nonthreatening, but I knew she was going to be persistent. Very persistent.

I shrugged. "I can't explain why nobody spotted us," I answered, hoping she would ask something else.

"So you sustained electrical damage in a violent electrical storm and made your way here, undetected by the flotilla of search vessels out looking for you. Is that right?"

"Yes."

She looked at the camera and raised an eyebrow. I gritted my teeth, waiting for a follow-up, but instead of what I expected, she asked, "What are your plans now?"

My shoulders relaxed. "Get the boats repaired and then resume course to Florida." It sounded like my thirty seconds of fame was over. I smiled for the camera.

Suddenly the other reporter hustled forward, brandishing her Channel Seven microphone like a weapon. I gulped.

"Mr. Adams, you said *boats*, as in plural. Are our viewers to understand that you are not alone?"

I gulped. Oops. That was dumb. I was so close to being finished and now I had more explaining to do. Brenda was looking at me, waiting. The other reporter wasn't backing down either.

"We sailed here with others who were lost in the same electrical storm that hit us, leaving them without navigation as well. It was safer to travel together."

"Who are they? Where is their boat?" Brenda asked, looking around.

"Who are you referring to?" the other reporter asked at the same time.

There was no way I would answer those questions. I didn't have permission to release names, not to mention that two of our passengers were minors.

"We have all been cleared by the customs office," I said after a moment's hesitation. "But not everyone has had a chance to contact their families. After they do that, they can decide if they want to speak with you."

The other reporter turned and motioned her cameraman to stop filming. She headed back down the dock, I imagined heading for the customs office. If Bermuda had an open records law, the names I avoided mentioning would no doubt be all over the news in a short time.

But Brenda didn't follow suit.

"I would really like to come aboard and speak to the others with you. You have to agree that their families and friends would no doubt be relieved to know they are safe and sound in Bermuda. We could do that for them right here and now."

I shook my head.

She persisted, smiling. "Ahoy. Request permission to come aboard and interview all of *The Lady Anne*'s passengers?"

I barely hesitated. "Permission denied."

I noticed the headset man gesturing with two fingers in a circular pattern. I guessed it meant for Brenda to conclude.

"While *The Lady Anne* has arrived in Bermuda, nearly one thousand miles from where she was reported missing, there may be more to *The Lady Anne*'s disappearance." She was looking at the camera. "We will keep on top of this developing story. This is Brenda Bishop, Channel Nine News, live from the Royal Bermuda Yacht Club in Hamilton, Bermuda."

CHAPTER 4

After Brenda lowered her microphone, the red light on the camera went out. I figured we were off the air, but I wasn't one hundred percent certain so I reminded myself to watch what I said.

"I'm disappointed you won't let me break the story about the other storm survivors," Brenda said.

I didn't reply.

"Would you at least go aboard and ask if any of them want to be interviewed?"

She had a valid point. I was assuming no one wanted attention called to our arrival here in Bermuda. Maybe I was wrong. Maybe the others *should* decide for themselves whether or not to be interviewed.

"Stand by," I told her. She smiled and backed away a few feet.

I climbed aboard. From my higher vantage point, I looked toward the small crowd that had gathered at the end of the dock, drawn by the television cameras.

I spotted Pat. Her height and short blonde hair made her stand out. She was watching from a safe distance. But who was that standing next to her?

It was Charles.

"Is there a problem?" Brenda asked.

Having Charles and his vast wealth and resources so close suddenly changed my mind about asking the others if they wanted to go on live television. But what to do about Brenda? Charles had worked hard to remain anonymous. If his name came up, it would be inviting disclosure.

I rejoined Brenda on the dock. "Why don't you let me talk to them after you and your cameraman have left? If anyone agrees to be interviewed, I'll call you."

Brenda looked toward the end of the pier as if trying to ascertain why I had changed my mind. I held my breath. Pictures of Pat, Tracy, and I had been plastered in the local papers but she didn't appear to recognize her. She turned back to me and dipped a hand into her jacket pocket.

She held out a card. "Promise to call me first. Don't give anyone else an interview, okay?"

I nodded.

Brenda smiled and turned to leave. I noticed the cameraman lower the camera. It had been pointing at me the whole time. Even if he had been filming with the red light off, I didn't say anything I would have wanted to retract.

I returned aboard, watching. I knew Brenda might notice if I suddenly left the boat and ran over to talk to someone. Charles and the others had their anonymity intact, but Brenda might recognize Pat if I approached her.

The people who had gathered to watch the interview dispersed. Pat and Charles slowly meandered away, and not in the direction of *The Lady Anne*. I figured they were playing it safe as well.

Tracy poked her head up through the hatch. "Are they gone?" she asked, glancing around.

"Yes, but stay below a bit longer," I said softly. "We're still visible from the other docks if they decide to keep filming."

"Would you do me a favor?" Tracy asked. "Would you please connect the shore power and then find out the marina's Wi-Fi password?"

I nodded. After connecting the shore power and making sure it was working, I left the dock, looking for Pat. I knew she had the paperwork showing the Wi-Fi password, but right now I was more concerned with what she might be telling Charles.

It was no surprise that he found us. The tracking device Charles had installed on *The Lady Anne* would have started transmitting again once we returned from the past. Pat had tried unsuccessfully to contact him on the passage to Bermuda. We kept waiting for one of his planes or boats to meet us en route. I was curious why they had not.

I had truthfully told Brenda that no ships or planes had spotted us. What I didn't say was that we hadn't spotted any other ships or planes either. I hoped it would be accepted that it was a vast ocean and we were two very small sailboats.

Pat found me before I found her. She was alone in front of the Gosling Brothers Limited spirit store on Main Street.

"How did it go with the reporters?" she asked.

"Fine." I looked around. "Where is Charles?"

She took my arm and steered me toward the side of a building. Then she whispered, "I told him everything."

I sighed, wishing I'd had had a chance to talk to her before she spilled *everything* to Charles.

She grinned. "Relax. I told him about everything but the aliens."

"So what's he going to do?"

"First off, he feels totally responsible for what happened. Had he not made his outlandish poker wager, we never would have been aboard *The Lady Anne*. Never.

"Second, when he heard about Mo's and Gert's condition, heard that Angie, Ashley, and Donna had witnessed their husbands' murders and then been viciously raped, and that Bonnie had been widowed and then sexually abused, he insisted on meeting us at the nearest hospital. He already left and is probably waiting for us there now."

"That was nice of him," I replied. "But why—"

As if Pat could read my mind, she answered the very question I was about to ask.

"The reason he didn't meet with us sooner," she said, keeping her voice low, "is that he and several of his associates were searching in Venezuela."

"What? Why Venezuela?"

"Because that's where Daniel and Sam Pincus would have gone had they had killed us and taken *The Lady Anne*'s gold. Which was what Charles thought had happened when *The Lady Anne* completely vanished from his tracking software. Charles assumed the worse."

She glanced around and, satisfied we were alone, continued. "He had teams of two, all over coastal Venezuela, looking for either the Pincus brothers or looking for any transactions involving large numbers of Canadian Maple Leaf gold coins."

I nodded. That all made sense. Had the Pincus brothers found and killed us, Charles's transmitter would have stopped working when the ship was scuttled, but they would have had a large quantity of gold to dispose of in a nonextradition country.

"The more he couldn't find any traces, the harder he looked. He really does feel responsible, terribly responsible."

CHAPTER 5

Using two cabs, everyone except for Bonnie and her two kids and myself made their way to the nearest hospital. Bonnie was adamant she was okay and insisted that she fly back to Houston on the next available flight. I told her to wait until everyone returned because I was sure Charles would arrange transportation that would not expose her to the press if Brenda was watching the boat. As it was, he managed to spirit the others off by having them slip into rowboats and bringing them into Hamilton and waiting cabs without attracting any attention.

According to the customs man, I wasn't allowed to leave the marina area, so I used the time to wash the salt off of *The Lady Anne's* decks. I would have enjoyed some company, but Bonnie took my advice and stayed below with her kids and Buster.

When I finished *The Lady Anne*, I walked over to *The Aquaholic* and hosed her off as well. During my washings, I made a mental note of items to address.

I put the hose away and went back to *The Lady Anne*.

Bonnie was below, closing a duffel bag. I didn't see the kids or Buster, so I figured they might all be taking a nap or resting.

"Are they back yet?" Bonnie asked, keeping her voice low.

I shook my head.

"So who exactly is Charles T. Williams?"

"He is the former owner of *The Lady Anne*."

"Did Pat say she won *The Lady Anne* in a poker game?"

I nodded.

"And Charles is a very wealthy widower?" Bonnie didn't seem interested in him, just curious, and there was more inflection on *widower* than *wealthy*.

I nodded again. "And he feels very responsible for what we all went through."

She didn't ask anything else, but I could tell she was worried about something.

"Are you okay?" As soon as I asked, I realized it was a stupid question. With all that had happened to her, how could she be okay?

She sighed. "You're sure Charles can arrange transportation for me and my family back to Houston?"

I nodded. "It won't be a problem."

She sank down on the edge of the bunk. "I'm sorry Carl attacked Pat and Tracy, but I really do miss him. I've had enough time on a boat to last a lifetime. I just want to put these horrible events behind me and get back to Texas. My family is there and they can help me." She wiped her eyes, looked at me for a split second, and then nodded. "You don't have to babysit me. I'll be fine."

"Are you sure?"

She nodded and shoved the duffel bag over. "I'm going to take a nap. You can go."

I went topside, found paper and a pen, and began making a list of things that I noticed earlier would need attention. I added buying cell phones. None of us had one. Mine had gotten wet when I snuck aboard *The Lady Anne* the night Captain Pincus tried to kidnap Pat and Tracy. Gert had lost hers when she abandoned a sinking whale-watching vessel. I wasn't sure if Max and Joey had cell phones at their age.

The rest of our group had thrown their phones into a blazing hole of fiery heat the aliens had created as a condition of returning us to the present time. That part was forbidden to discuss.

CHAPTER 6

The kids complained it was boring being stuck belowdecks and asked if there was anything to eat.

I was sure there were places within walking distance, so I took some cash from Pat's secret stash and told them I'd be back.

Nearby was an Italian restaurant that was pretty crowded, so taking that as a good sign, I ordered lasagna, two pizzas, and three salads to go. I had a little trouble getting back to the dock since Pat had the gate codes, but an exiting couple let me in.

Back onboard *The Lady Anne* there were a lot of people. Pat, Tracy, Angie, Ashley, and Donna were all waiting down below. Pat explained that Mo and Gert were being kept at the hospital but that everyone else had been examined, treated, and released.

"Are Mo and Gert okay?" I asked.

Tracy answered. "They are suffering from severe acute malnutrition and have been admitted. They'll probably be there at least a week or two to stabilize them, and maybe longer for rehabilitation."

Pat added, "The doctor was agitated they weren't seen sooner, but his prognosis for a full recovery was very optimistic."

"They both have to 'drink' three scoops of room-temperature ice cream every day. Now that's my kind of diet." Tracy chuckled.

"Is Charles here?" I asked, glancing around but not seeing him.

Tracy looked inside the top pizza box, swiped a piece of sausage, and then closed the box, looking guilty.

"Charles has invited all of us to dinner at the yacht club," Pat spoke up, giving Tracy a stern look.

"Is that wise?" I asked. "There may still be reporters waiting to interview the *storm survivors*." I put air quotes around storm survivors. "In fact, how did you all get back aboard? No one waiting to ambush you?"

Pat shook her head. "Nope. I think Charles worked some more of his magic. Sent them on a wild-goose chase, I bet. In any case, we're expected at five."

"As much as I need to talk to Charles," Bonnie said, also helping herself to a chunk of topping, "I just don't feel like leaving the boat. The kids and I will stay here. It looks like Reid bought plenty of food, so we'll be fine."

I nodded. "Besides getting you a phone and a flight to Texas, is there anything you want me to ask him?"

"Tell him I'm happy to meet him; it's just tonight is not good."

I nodded again.

"Let's clean up and go eat," Tracy said, peeking inside the other pizza box.

The women separated, some going over to *The Aquaholic* to change and Tracy and Pat heading to their stateroom. I followed, changing from shorts to slacks. When I returned topside, Pat and Tracy were having a glass of wine on deck.

I whistled.

Pat was wearing a short, sarong-type dress, her hair slicked back and fastened behind one ear with a silver barrette. Tracy, ever the exhibitionist, had changed into a bikini top and low-slung cropped pants. She'd gathered her hair into an arty bun, letting strands fall around her face and tickle her collarbone.

I eyed the outfit. "What if they have a dress code?" I asked.

She laughed and pointed to a shawl draped over the cockpit table. "Then it's their loss."

Pat was shaking her head. She was watching me looking at Tracy and I could see the question in her eyes.

I had the same one.

Things had gotten pretty hot and heavy between the three of us when we were lost. I loved them both. I wondered how our relationship would play out now that we had returned to civilization. I hadn't made love to either of them since we were sent back to the present. There was an awkwardness that had never been there before.

Pat looked toward the dock. Ashley, Donna, and Angie waved up to her.

"Time to go," I said.

Tracy plucked her shawl from the table and wrapped it around her shoulders.

It was a short walk to the yacht club. Charles had reserved a small private room and was waiting by the door to greet us. He shook my hand.

"Nice to see you," I said.

"Better to be seen than viewed," he responded with a grin.

The first server had a tray of Dark 'n' Stormy drinks, the second had Rum Swizzles. Both servers boasted these were the national drinks of Bermuda. After we each had a cocktail, we took seats at a long banquet table.

I sat between very sexy, blonde Tracy and distinguished Charles T. Williams, who looked every inch the commodore of a yacht club in his blue blazer and dark slacks, the picture of casual elegance. He took the end seat, closest to Pat, who was across from Tracy and me. Next to Pat was Ashley. She looked a little like a cute, impish Tracy, but with bobbed brown hair. To her left was model-thin Donna, her purplish-red hair standing out like a beacon and matching almost exactly the color of the shirt she was wearing. Angie was next to Donna. She was as tall as Pat but a bit heavier. It was the first time I'd seen her in anything other than shorts and a T-shirt. She wore a dress and heels, and I didn't think it my imagination that she looked a little uncomfortable.

Truth be told, I think we all felt that way.

The other three chairs were empty. Charles had known that Mo and Gert were hospitalized, but he no doubt expected Bonnie, Max, and Joey, not knowing until now they had declined his invitation.

Looking around, my thoughts flashed back to the decision Pat, Tracy, and I had made to let Captain Rick go free after his foiled attempt to take *The Lady Anne* from us. I had foolishly left behind a radio, enabling Captain Rick to get onboard *The Aquaholic* and begin his reign of terror. That radio led to the death of three men and the assault on their wives. Not something I'd ever forget. I owed these women a lot.

Charles brought me back to the present when he clinked the rim of his glass.

Having our attention, he proposed a toast. "This one is for Reid Adams, who teaches sailing for a living."

I glanced at him, uncomfortable after my introspection of moments before. I hoped he wasn't going to call me a hero. That was Tracy's role, not mine.

He continued. "And who followed the axiom of sailing instructors everywhere: Keep the students in the boat. Keep the water out of the boat. Well done, Reid."

Relieved, I laughed along with everyone else. I had never heard that one but made a mental note to remember it.

Tracy squeezed my leg under the table. I leaned close and whispered, "We should all be toasting you for getting us back."

She squeezed my leg again, this time a little higher up.

I met her eyes.

She leaned close to me. "It's been too long," she whispered.

I looked up to see Pat staring at us. She raised her glass. "And here's to Tracy."

"Here's to Tracy," everyone else echoed.

I noticed that Charles raised his glass too but shot her a puzzled look.

I wondered if I was the only one who caught a tinge of sarcasm in Pat's toast.

CHAPTER 7

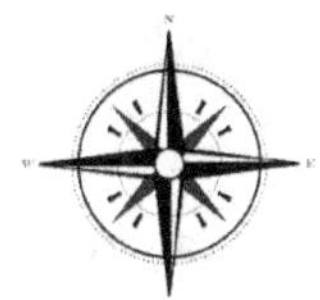

The rest of the dinner conversation went pretty much as I feared—Charles pressing us for the details of our disappearance, us keeping the details vague. If he was getting frustrated, it didn't show. I chalked that up to him being a poker player.

After awhile, he began asking what he could do for each of us to make our transitions back easier. He took a small notebook and pen out of a pocket and looked around the table expectantly.

Tracy, Donna, Angie, and Ashley asked if he could get them cell phones. I added that Bonnie needed one as well.

"None of you have cell phones?" he asked, glancing at both sides of the table.

I tensed up, wondering how to answer that.

Fortunately, Pat broke the awkward silence. "Almost all of

our communication equipment was damaged during the electromagnetic disturbance I told you about earlier, including cell phones."

Charles nodded, accepting her explanation. He jotted a note. "That will be easy. What's next? What are your plans now that you have safely found Bermuda after being lost at sea?"

I knew what Bonnie wanted; I had no idea what the others might say. Tracy squeezed my leg again, moving still higher, a not-so-subtle expression of what her immediate plan was.

I shifted away, reaching under the table to move Tracy's hand back into her own lap. "Bonnie wants to go back to Texas, Houston I believe, with her two kids," I answered.

Pat spoke next. "Bonnie, Angie, Ashley, and Donna all need to return to their homes to make funeral arrangements for their late husbands." She paused while Charles kept writing. "I also need to get back to Denver to reassure my friends and family that I'm not dead." She chuckled. "And to pay bills which are getting more overdue by the day."

Tracy said, "Ditto." So did I. Charles was silent but continued writing.

"Then what?" he asked. "What's after that?"

"Then I guess I'll get on with my life," Donna said, taking a big sip of her drink and looking sad.

Charles put his pen down and stood up. "The last time I saw Pat, Tracy, and Reid was in San Juan," he said. "I wanted them to forgo their voyage to Florida via what the press is calling 'the mysterious Bermuda Triangle' and take *The Lady*

Anne south, through the Panama Canal and on to Hawaii instead."

I remembered that conversation. It was a very generous offer. Had we not declined it and gone to Hawaii instead, we probably wouldn't have spotted the alien UFO and would have been drinking piña coladas instead. . .

My thoughts continued: instead of being transported through time where we were able to rescue Mo and Gert and also eventually rescue Bonnie, Angie, and the others, albeit at a high personal cost to all of them.

Charles continued, "Since I feel partially responsible for what all of you have gone through, I would like to at least try and make things right."

I jumped as Tracy put her hand on my crotch. I shot her a sideways glance, but she kept looking at Charles.

"I propose furnishing manpower and resources for each of you to handle funeral or other arrangements as you see fit," he said.

Before anyone could respond, he continued, "Then I propose the use of my compound in Hawaii for any of you who want it. You can go there and take whatever time you need to deal with your losses."

As if sensing the uneasiness that had wafted over the table, Charles took his seat. "Let's have another drink and talk again in the morning. Let me know where you need to go and let me know what kind of cell phones you want."

Angie threw Charles a speculative glance. "I was running a charter business with my catamaran *The Aquaholic*," she said slowly. "Do you suppose I could continue that business in Hawaii?"

Charles nodded, smiling. "Of course."

"I never want to be on another boat again, never ever for the rest of my life," Ashley exclaimed softly.

"Me either," Donna agreed. "In fact, I'd be real happy to move to a hotel room until I can leave Bermuda, if that's all right with you."

Again Charles smiled and nodded, writing something down.

"But after the funeral, a few weeks of privacy in Hawaii might be just what I need to clear my head," Ashley added, squeezing Donna's hand above the table.

Donna looked at Ashley but didn't say anything.

"Would you consider a joint venture?" Pat spoke up, looking at Angie. "Would you want to be a part of a charter service that offered both monohull and catamaran vessels?"

I was surprised at Pat's suggestion. We'd never discussed what came next. I only knew there was no way that Angie, Pat, Tracy, and I could sail both boats all the way to Hawaii by ourselves.

But if Charles could provide crew, it might work.

"The boats would need repairs before a passage of that magnitude," I said.

Again, Charles offered his resources.

"I like the idea," Tracy said.

I looked at her and she looked back. She was grinning.

I knew why. It was her slow rubbing of my crotch that had given me the boner she was feeling.

Charles spoke. "Like I said, let's think about the future and talk again in the morning."

He stood, offering Pat a handshake. She stood and accepted.

Charles moved around to shake my hand. If I stood, I knew my erection would be visible. So I didn't stand, shaking his hand and then quickly reaching for my drink. Tracy removed her hand long enough to give him a hug, then she sat back down and resumed her hand job. She was slow enough to not be noticed but steady enough to be effective.

Charles made his way to the other side of the table and Pat came around to sit next to me.

"How about it, big boy?" she said. "Do you want to take *The Lady Anne* to Hawaii?"

As she moved her left hand underneath the table, I quickly stood up and slowly walked away, saying, "I need to use the restroom."

I was glad to get away from Tracy before I had an accident. I felt like a horny teenager. I wondered if Tracy was going to follow me into the men's room. I wondered if she did, whether I could relax enough to have sex in a public place.

I wondered how I was going to resolve the situation if both women showed up in my bed tonight. In spite of how close the three of us had become, Pat was adamant about not wanting to take the next step to a three-way. She was content with the way things were—she and Tracy taking turns.

I found myself grinning. How many men would envy my position? Loved by two beautiful, sexy women.

It was either the best or worst thing that had ever happened to me.

My worries about how to sort out the situation if both women appeared in my cabin tonight resolved itself. Charles asked Pat and Angie to accompany him back to his hotel room to talk with them further about the possibility of a start-up charter company out of his compound in Hawaii.

They both accepted.

On the way back to *The Lady Anne*, Tracy let the others walk ahead, whispering what she had in store for me once we tucked the others in for the night.

She didn't disappoint.

CHAPTER 8

Three days later, Pat, Tracy, Buster, and I were the only ones left in Bermuda. The others had gone back home. Reporter Brenda Bishop had returned with all the passenger's names and Ashley had given her a vague interview but everyone else managed to stay off camera. Brenda eventually stopped coming by.

Bonnie, Max, and Joey were going to remain in Texas. The kids promised me they'd keep quiet about seeing aliens, and while I wanted to believe them, I knew they probably wouldn't be able to keep it a secret.

Ashley and Donna had accepted Charles's offer to go to Hawaii after the funerals.

Angie had gone home, promising to rendezvous in Hawaii again after her husband's funeral. She would then return to

Bermuda to sail *The Aquaholic* to Hawaii via the Panama Canal.

Buster had been cleared by the local veterinarian and could now leave the boat, on a leash of course. We got him some real dog food instead of table scraps. He seemed very happy.

I went to see Mo and Gert at the hospital every day. Their condition was slowly improving and they were anxious to get released. They both had affairs to wrap up stateside but then wanted to help get the boats to Hawaii.

Angie had proudly shown *The Aquaholic* to Charles. When he asked about the unusual paint job, she told him that her mom's great-great-aunt Luverne, an artist, designed razzle-dazzle paint schemes for the Navy to confuse U-boat commanders. The ships with Luverne's designs, which were basically optical-illusion camouflage, were never torpedoed.

The Aquaholic's razzle-dazzle paint scheme was in Luverne's honor. Angie explained a modern-day benefit: her customers absolutely loved it.

However after seeing both boats up close, Charles pulled Pat and me aside for a very serious conversation.

He had noticed the blackened rigging, burned sails, charred metal fittings, and busted compasses. He demanded to know what had really happened. When Pat replied she couldn't tell him, he got even more suspicious.

"Can't or won't?" he pressed. She turned away and didn't respond.

After several futile attempts to get the truth, he dropped it, promising to send people to repair the boats. Pat and Tracy agreed to visit the others in Hawaii, via a pitstop in Denver. I insisted I remain in Bermuda to first oversee repairs and then to keep an eye on *The Lady Anne's* cache of gold. Charles understood.

I gave Tracy my basement apartment key and a limited power of attorney so she could make deposits and pay my bills. I also ordered a new cell phone online with an international calling plan and listed her as the pickup person. We agreed she would then express it to me in Bermuda.

Charles offered to put a property management company in place to run the small strip mall I had inherited. He was adamant he pay their fees. I agreed.

He also offered to have a moving company pack and ship all of my stuff to Hawaii, again at his expense. I told him I'd think about it. He made the same offer to Pat and then to Tracy.

As for Pat, she agreed to let Charles get contractors to finish her current and pending remodeling jobs. He would then give her employees a generous severance check and help them find other employment if necessary. She refused his offer to pack and ship her belongings to Hawaii, but she did agree to put everything in a storage locker, again at his expense. I sensed she was ready for a change.

Tracy agreed to let him cover her monthly expenses but wasn't ready to move to Hawaii just yet.

Mr. Charles T. Williams had been very busy arranging all of these things. But he was a man of his word, very methodical and very generous, both compassionately and financially.

The evening before Pat and Tracy were to fly to Denver, we left Buster aboard and went out to dinner. We had driven by a restaurant that was an easy walk from the marina, so we decided to try it. I told them it was my treat. They both giggled.

We were all holding hands, making our way down a narrow sidewalk bordering the water, when Pat suddenly stopped. She squeezed my hand so hard it almost hurt. She started backing away, nearly dragging me with her.

"Pincus," she uttered, her eyes wide. Her face had suddenly gone pale. She was so terrified, I could feel her trembling.

I looked at where she was pointing and sure enough, there was Captain Daniel Pincus. He was slowly coming toward us, ominously blocking our path.

"Back up," I said, letting go of their hands. "Back to the marina."

Pat and Tracy turned to retrace our steps while I kept my eyes on Pincus. He stopped dead center on the sidewalk, watching me watching him.

"We've got another problem," Tracy said.

"What is it?" I asked, backing slowly but still watching Pincus.

"There's another man behind us. He looks serious. I've got a bad feeling."

CHAPTER 9

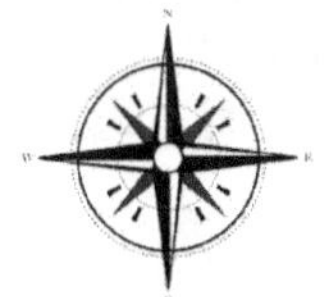

I quickly checked my six. We had been cut off. However deserted the sidewalk was at the moment, it was still daylight and I was confident others would pass by. I just didn't know when.

"Did either of you bring your phone?" I whispered. Charles had trouble replacing some of our phones in a foreign country so he offered everyone a rental. I had accepted his offer, but since the three of us were together, I left my rental phone aboard.

"Mine's in the charger," Tracy answered.

"Mine's in my purse," Pat said. "When you said you were treating, I didn't bring it."

"You don't happen to be carrying your whistle?" I asked Pat hopefully.

"No," she answered sadly. "It's in my purse, next to the phone."

Captain Pincus slowly closed in on us, finally stopping about five feet away.

"Let's all go back to *The Lady Anne*," he said. His voice was calm and quiet. "We don't want to make a scene." After finishing his last remark, he lifted his shirt, revealing the black, finger-gripped handle of a dive knife.

Judging by the size of the handle, he had a pretty stout knife.

I turned away very cautiously only to see the other man behind us was less than six feet away. The man smiled and then flashed the handle of another big dive knife.

"How did you find us?" Pat questioned. In spite of trying to hide her fear, her voice trembled.

"After I jumped off *The Lady Anne*, I stayed mostly submerged and avoided the Coast Guard's searchlights," Captain Pincus replied. There was no emotion or hostility in his voice. He was calmly stating facts.

"After you sailed away, I began the long swim back to St. Thomas, using the lights ashore as a landmark. I was only a few miles offshore when a local fishing boat saw me and took me aboard. Needless to say, I soon had their boat and both of the fisherman were shark food."

Again, his voice was void of emotion. He glanced around and, satisfied nobody was coming toward us, continued.

"I went back to St. Thomas and grabbed the bags I stashed after being fired from *The Lady Anne*."

He looked directly at Pat. She tightened her grip on Tracy's hand, causing Tracy to wince.

"Then I took my new fishing boat over to St. Croix and retrieved Sam. Say hello Sam."

From behind us the man said, "Hello."

Pincus continued, "I figured that we'd have to lay low, knowing you three would have filed a police report. But you never returned to St. Thomas; you never finalized the report. Better yet, you never filed a complaint and you never pressed charges. Since our pictures weren't in the news, we bided our time, waiting for any word of *The Lady Anne*."

He had a good point. Without a completed police report, the Coast Guard's report would be laying on some detective's desk. Charles had been able to see it, but that might have been as far as it went. Without the proper paperwork, the authorities would not have taken action. Not returning to St. Thomas had an unintended consequence.

"I heard from a captain friend of mine at the Blue Haven Marina in Provo that *The Lady Anne* had stopped there. Sam and I figured you would stop next in the Bahamas. Sam guessed you'd go to Nassau, but I concentrated on the marinas in Eleuthera."

I was partly impressed he had correctly guessed our next destination after Provo and was momentarily thankful the aliens had changed our plans. Had he spotted us first, the two of them might have been successful at their second attempt at piracy.

Pincus continued, still speaking matter-of-factly and still

keeping his distance. "Since you never finalized a police report, Sam and I weren't on any No Fly lists, so we took a commercial flight from there and waited at an all-inclusive resort.

"The resort had a complimentary vehicle rental, so we checked marinas and kept our eyes and ears open. I bet *The Lady Anne* would show up and Sam indulged me.

"We had almost given up on Eleuthera when *The Lady Anne*'s disappearance made the news. She was the object of a large-scale search, and we were ready to make our move as soon as she was found."

It was obvious Captain Pincus was obsessed with finding *The Lady Anne*. Maybe it was more than greed; maybe it was payback. Had he found us, I knew it would have been the end of our lives.

My mind raced. An image of Ashley and Donna, naked and bound aboard *The Aquaholic*, was replaced by a vision of Pat. I saw her on *The Lady Anne* naked, tied up, and screaming. That image changed from helpless Pat to Tracy. She had been beaten so badly her face was raw and dripping blood.

The image vanished the moment Pincus resumed speaking.

"Sam and I were reevaluating after *The Lady Anne* was never found. With her gold bounty lost, we figured we'd have to go find another rich yacht owner to work for, without a reference from Charles."

I looked back toward Sam. Like his brother, he was prob-ably in his late thirties or early forties. He wasn't a large man but looked very fit. He didn't look nervous and he hadn't moved any closer.

"Then *The Lady Anne* mysteriously made port in Bermuda. Sam and I watched your interview with that cute reporter. Actually we weren't watching you much. We were fixated on *The Lady Anne* in the background."

I remembered how Brenda had me stand by her bow, the name clearly visible to the camera.

"So we flew to Bermuda, easily found you, and then watched and waited for the perfect time."

Sam startled me a little when he spoke. "The five of us are going back to the boat. If one of you screams, I'll cut your tongue out. If you run, I'll catch up and cut your eyes out. If any of you fight back, you will all suffer. That's a promise."

His voice was calm. His message was clear. He was serious. Deadly serious.

"We're not going anywhere with you," Tracy blurted.

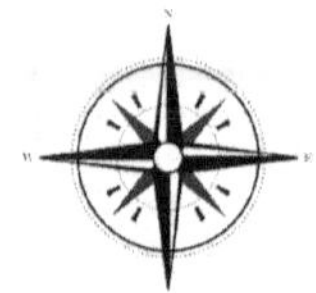

CHAPTER 10

"How much gold do you want to just walk away?" Pat asked.

"What?" Pincus replied, his eyes still on Tracy.

I watched intently as he slowly raised his shirt and grasped the knife handle. He didn't pull it out of his pants; he just held on to it.

I deliberately moved closer and repeated the question, "How much gold do you want to go away and not come back?"

He glanced toward Sam.

I made my move.

I stepped closer and grabbed his knife hand with all the force I had.

He looked at me, startled.

I raised my other hand but instead of making a fist, I

extended and then tightened my fingers together, keeping them rigid. As I felt him trying to draw his knife, I thrust my fingertips into his throat. He gasped and his eyes got big but he didn't let go of the knife.

I quickly glanced backward and saw Sam advancing, his weapon drawn. Pat and Tracy stepped aside, but instead of running away, they moved toward the water.

I figured I had two or three seconds before Sam reached me.

I bent my fingers up and back, out of the way, and using the heel of my hand, delivered a palm strike to Daniel's nose. Blood spurted out and he staggered back a foot or so but he still didn't let go of his knife.

Figuring Sam was now close to slashing distance, I whirled in behind Daniel and applied a one-arm choke hold, still holding his wrist, still trying to control his knife.

Sam was nearly on top of me but he stopped short when he saw his brother had become a human shield. I used his hesitancy to try something that had just crossed my mind.

I was holding Pincus's wrist and hand, which was holding his knife. It was in his waistband, handle end up. That meant the pointy end was aimed at, or close to, his manhood. I suppressed a grin and then forced the knife downward, trying to angle it toward his body.

"You motherfucker!" he screamed as the knife hit home. He tried to jerk it out of his pants but I had the better angle and forced it downward again.

I let go of his knife hand, released the choke hold, and

shoved him right into his brother. His brother had his knife pointed at me and nearly stabbed him by accident.

I stepped forward diagonally and stomped the side of Captain Pincus's knee, trying to drive my heel clear through.

But I was little low and hit more leg than knee. Regardless, he fell, hollering more obscenities. Sam was trying to steady his brother and was off-balance. That gave me another opportunity.

I stretched my arms out, turned my palms in, and then drove my cupped palms into the side of Sam's head, right over his ears. As expected, the incoming rush of air damaged his eardrums. He lowered his knife and shook his head, trying to focus.

He took a wild swing with his knife but he telegraphed his move, allowing me to lean back out of the way. As the blade passed harmlessly by, I moved back in, grabbed Sam's knife hand, and then redirected the blade, driving it deep into his chest. Sam collapsed, stabbed by his own weapon.

Daniel Pincus saw his brother fall and hobbled to him, screaming Sam's name.

Sam didn't respond. Daniel rolled his brother over. Sam didn't move. Daniel dropped to his knees. He felt for a pulse then leaned over to rest an ear on his brother's chest. From the look Daniel gave me, I knew Sam was dead.

Daniel slowly raised up, pulling the knife out of Sam's body. His eyes were intense, and I could practically feel his fury. I backed away, getting some distance.

I was more mobile but he had two knives, one in each

hand. Daniel approached and I retreated, glancing around for something to even the odds.

Just then, I heard a *thud*. Daniel winced and spun around. He had been hit in the back by a rock. I looked past him and saw Pat and Tracy.

They were right off the edge of the sidewalk, on the rocky shore. As Pat bent down to pick up a rock, Tracy wound up and threw one like a pitcher. It would have been on target, but Daniel moved out of the way.

By the time Tracy's rock hit the ground, Pat had thrown again. Two rocks this time, one right after the other. The first one missed but the second one hit Daniel in the arm.

He cussed and moved away from me, toward them.

Knowing he could get there before I could, I shouted, "Hey, asshole. Who's got a pink ass now, you fucking pussy? Leave the women alone and pick on someone your own size."

He turned back toward me, glaring homicidal anger. Then he got hit by another rock, right in the shoulder. He dropped one of the knives.

Another rock landed a few feet away from him but bounced toward me. I picked it up. It was grapefruit sized and fairly heavy.

There was a loud *smack* as Tracy fast-pitched a rock directly into the middle of Pincus's back. That one must have hurt, because the rage in his face was replaced by a flash of pain.

I stepped sideways, out of the line of fire, looking at the

knife he had dropped. A rock whizzed by his head. Had that one hit him, it would have probably knocked him out.

He twisted to face his rock-throwing assailants. That gave me an opportunity to throw my rock. I hurled it overhand. I traded power for accuracy. It hit his lower back with another *smack*.

He doubled over, grabbing his kidney area but still not letting go of his weapon.

Pat must have seen my throw, because her next rock went way over Pincus's head and landed near me. Daniel watched as I picked it up. His expression changed. He looked beaten.

Captain Pincus dropped his knife and stood up, raising his hands high. I raised my rock to a throwing position and waited to see what he would do next.

Without another word, he ran past me, away from Pat and Tracy. He sprinted down the sidewalk, moving faster that I would have expected with his injuries. For a millisecond I debated picking up a knife and giving chase. I didn't expect I could catch him, but I thought I could probably keep him in sight. If I passed any people, I could ask for help.

"We make a good team," Pat said, trotting up behind me. She was carrying two large rocks and looked pretty formidable.

Tracy walked past Sam's body, hesitated a moment, and then joined me and Pat. "I hope we're not in trouble," she said softly. "After all, it was self-defense—again."

CHAPTER 11

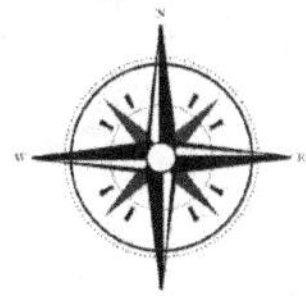

I wobbled a bit, the result of adrenaline dissipating. One threat was neutralized, the other threat had retreated. The women were safe. The mission was over. Tracy grabbed my arm and steadied me.

"That was amazing," she whispered. "You were a whirling buzzsaw."

"Oorah," I answered, the Marine Corps battle cry an automatic response.

"Was that Marine training?" Pat asked. She still had rocks in her hand. She tossed them away and brushed her hands together.

I nodded. Although I hadn't used hand-to-hand fighting techniques since basic training, it had all come back to me. Sam's body on the ground was testament to that.

"I couldn't have done it without air support." I chuckled. "Tracy, where did you learn to pitch like that?"

Before she could answer, a young man came jogging toward us. Upon seeing the body lying on the sidewalk, he stopped short and said he was going to call the police.

"Thank you," Tracy said.

"Yes, please call them," Pat added. "Call them now."

He produced a phone from his pocket and made the call. He kept his distance, though, and didn't say anything else to us.

I walked a few steps to a big flat rock and sat down. Tracy sat down next to me. I took a series of deep breaths. She squeezed my hand. Pat joined us. We waited for the police.

My mind raced as I waited. Would an unsympathetic jury hold me responsible for defending myself and the women? Since I had stabbed Sam with his own weapon, did assault with a deadly weapon carry the death penalty under Bermuda law?

The questions just kept coming. What would have happened had our counterattack not been successful? Once aboard *The Lady Anne*, would Daniel and Sam have killed me or just tied me up?

The flashback was raw and real—Pincus standing tall in *The Lady Anne*'s salon. He had Pat bent over the table, her face bloody, her hands tied, her panties pulled down around her ankles.

The image turned red, as if colored by the blood that was oozing from her injured face.

Tracy squeezed my hand and the image vanished. The Bermuda Police Service had arrived. A motorcycle cop drove his bike up to Sam's body. He checked for a pulse and then radioed for backup. He pulled a notebook from his shirt pocket, removed his helmet, and walked over to where we were sitting.

"What happened?" he asked.

Pat spoke first. "We were walking to dinner. We were attacked by a former employee, Daniel Pincus, and his brother." She pointed to Sam's body.

The officer looked up. "Where is this Daniel Pincus?"

"Gone." Pat wiped a hand over her face. "But he can't have gotten far. He's injured. They had weapons. Knives. We didn't. Reid saved us."

Another Bermuda Police Service squad car arrived, followed by a coroner's wagon. Before long, the crime scene was very crowded. I wondered how many homicides they had to investigate. We were separated then, and interviewed separately. I noticed one officer talking to the jogger that had phoned, though I wasn't sure if he had seen anything that could help us.

While I was being questioned, an older couple emerged from a wooded area just beyond where the attack had taken place. The man urgently waved the closest officer over. I couldn't hear what was being said, but the man seemed very insistent about something.

I finished answering the detective's questions. He was called over to join the new arrivals. The detectives interviewing

Pat and Tracy went over as well. Whatever the old couple was saying had drawn a crowd. I began to feel hopeful when the man cued something up on his cell phone and showed it to the detectives.

The officer who appeared to be in charge made his way back to us and told us our story had been confirmed.

He gestured behind him. "They are birders and they saw the whole thing. Videoed it. We have your contact information, and if we need anything else, we trust we can find you aboard *The Lady Anne*. You are not under arrest, but I suggest you not leave Bermuda until given clearance. Is that understood?"

I felt incredibly relieved. Looking at Pat and Tracy, I could see we all did.

Not wanting to repeat an earlier mistake, I got the detective's card. "We will want to press charges against the attacker who got away, Captain Daniel Pincus."

He understood and said he'd send someone over with the paperwork in the morning. We told him where our vessel was berthed and he jotted it down. He wanted our phone numbers, but none of us could remember the phone numbers that came with the rental phones. He accepted that and left.

We decided to pass on dinner and made our way back to *The Lady Anne*. I feared that reporter Brenda Bishop would be there waiting for us, but we were all by ourselves.

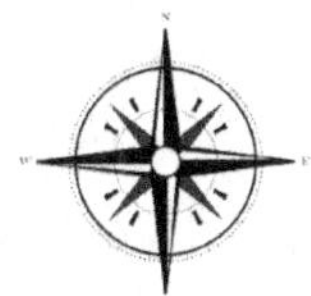

CHAPTER 12

Pat immediately called Charles. He was at the airport, waiting for the Clarriage field engineer to arrive. She gave a brief description of what happened with the Pincus brothers but told him we were safe at the boat. He said he'd be over as soon as he got his guest situated at his hotel.

Now that we were out of danger, I realized how hungry I was. Assuring me they would be okay, I left Pat and Tracy and went for more Italian takeout. We had just finished eating when Charles's arrival was announced by Buster's barking. Pat met him topside and led him below.

"What happened?" he asked, quite anxious to hear the details.

Tracy answered first. "Pincus and his brother attacked us. They wanted to take us back to *The Lady Anne*. They had knives." She put a hand on my arm. "Reid kicked their asses."

"But they got away?"

"One of them," Pat said softly. "Sam is dead. He won't be bothering us again, ever."

"And Daniel?" Charles asked hesitantly, as if afraid of the answer.

I understood his concern. In spite of what Pincus had done to us, he had been a loyal employee to Charles. At least that's what Charles thought until he learned Pincus had planned to scuttle *The Lady Anne* and make off with her treasure as soon as Charles had left for home. He had no idea how dangerous the man was until that fateful poker game exposed what could have ended tragically for Pat and Tracy.

After a moment, I answered that question. "Daniel ran away like the coward he is."

Charles looked at me, shaking his head. "I thought I knew the man. How could I have been so wrong?"

Pat spoke up. "I don't want to sound ungrateful, Charles, but what happened to the men you had keeping an eye on us?"

That was a good question, and if she hadn't asked it, I would have.

Charles took a seat and cleared his throat.

"This is going to sound like a poor excuse, but one of my men is keeping watch over Mo and Gert at the hospital. All of the others are accompanying the survivors back to their homes."

"Escorts," Tracy said.

"Escorts. They have instructions to help to clear any obstacles the women may face from local officials."

"When will they be back?" Pat asked.

"One is heading back from Houston today. But Ashley, Donna, and Angie asked that my men stick around as long as they were needed. I, of course, said yes."

"Please don't feel bad that your men weren't here," I said. "It was lucky that Daniel and his brother didn't have guns. This time, we'll press charges against Daniel. Hopefully he'll get picked up before he's able to leave Bermuda."

"When my men return, they'll find him," Charles said confidently. "I'll post men at the airport and have the others check all the motels on the island. He has to be sleeping somewhere. It's just a matter of time."

Charles left, apologizing again. He looked sad and angry. We each assured him that we were okay and not to worry.

Then Pat and Tracy finished their packing. They were both flying out tomorrow morning. I wondered which one would be sleeping with me tonight. I hoped it was Pat. Last night with Tracy reminded me of the differences between the two. Tracy was a demanding lover, impatient to please, but even more to be pleased. She never let up until she was completely satisfied. Pat, on the other hand, always pleasured me first. As a result, I could concentrate on her fully. Her orgasms wracked her entire body—I'd never been with anyone like that before —which often led to my body responding far more quickly than with Tracy.

I started to laugh. What in the hell was I thinking? Two

beautiful women servicing me. In an age wary of sexism, I had to be the luckiest man alive.

My hubris didn't go unpunished. Regardless of whatever discussion Pat and Tracy may have had amongst themselves over the final night's sleeping arrangements, neither showed up at my cabin door.

I was disappointed.

The next morning, I arose before the women and took Buster for a quick walk. I figured his prowess at relieving himself directly into the water was frowned upon. Nobody at the marina had said anything yet, but I noticed other pet owners headed for a spot nearby and it seemed prudent that I do likewise.

I returned to a note saying Pat and Tracy were taking their showers at the marina's bathhouse and would be back soon. I wondered how they had gotten past me and Buster unnoticed, but obviously they had. I started making coffee when there was a knock on the hull.

Pat and Tracy wouldn't have knocked, so I expected it was either Charles or someone from the police department.

I was wrong.

Brenda Bishop announced her presence and asked permission to come aboard.

I glanced through a porthole and saw her standing with her cameraman and someone else a few feet away.

Shit. Was she here to get details about what had transpired between the Pincus brothers and me or to ask more questions about our "storm survival" story?

I went to grab my phone and call Pat, warn her not come back to *The Lady Anne,* when I realized we hadn't yet programmed our new cell numbers.

Shit again.

I called out that I'd be right up, told Buster to stay, and headed topside.

CHAPTER 13

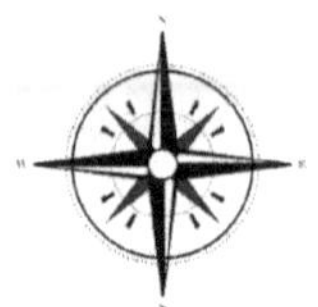

I forced a smile. "Good morning, Ms. Bishop," I said cheerfully. "What can I do for you?"

"We're not going live right now," she said. "But I have several questions to ask you, on camera, to be broadcast later, if you agree."

"Depends on the questions."

She raised an eyebrow. "What do you think I'd be asking you about?"

The way she said it made me wonder if she'd heard about the Pincus incident last night. I hadn't seen a local newspaper, but I'd assumed it would be all over the front page. After all, how many fatal attacks happened here in Bermuda?

"Give me a minute," I said, more to stall for time than anything else. I ducked back below, quickly splashed some water on my face, ran a comb through my hair, glanced in the mirror to see if my shirt looked clean, and then returned topside. I stepped off of *The Lady Anne* and joined Brenda on the dock. She pointed where she wanted me to stand. She didn't introduce me to the newcomer accompanying them.

The cameraman counted down and then Brenda looked into the camera. "This is Brenda Bishop, with Channel Nine News, at the Royal Bermuda Yacht Club in Hamilton, Bermuda."

The camera slowly followed Brenda as she moved closer to face me. "With me is Reid Adams of *The Lady Anne*. As you may remember, when we last spoke, Mr. Adams said his vessel had gotten lost and eventually made its way to Bermuda with some other survivors of the same storm that had blown them hundreds of miles off course and left them stranded with no means of communication. Does that sound right Mr. Adams?"

The way she said it and looked at me, I knew this wasn't about Sam Pincus.

"That's what happened," I replied.

"But isn't there a lot more to this story?" Brenda turned to face the camera. Her tone was serious, almost threatening.

"Our network has obtained a survivor manifest from the customs office. There is additional information about these *survivors* that we have uncovered."

I felt my shoulders tighten, but there was nothing I could do but wait and see where this went.

She was holding a notepad. She glanced down at it before continuing. "The sailing yacht, *The Lady Anne,* arrived in Bermuda with another vessel, *The Aquaholic. The Lady Anne* is owned by Pat Taylor and Tracy Palmer. You, Mr. Adams, were also aboard that vessel."

She didn't wait for confirmation or denial.

"Now *The Aquaholic* is a charter catamaran, operated by Oscar and Angie Pepper, out of Eleuthera, in the Bahamas. Angie, who is also *The Aquaholic's* cook, is one of the survivors. Her husband Oscar was allegedly killed by Captain Rick Howard, who ran a fishing boat, *The Day Dream*, out of the Turks and Caicos."

I looked away. Brenda had been busy. She knew things I didn't know. I never knew, for example, Captain Rick's last name, or Angie's late husband's name. I hid a smile at the irony that a cook's last name was "Pepper."

Brenda wasn't looking at me, though, but at the camera. "Now allegedly Captain Howard also killed the husbands of Ashley Morgan and Donna Kincaid, who had booked *The Aquaholic* for a crewed charter. Ashley and Donna arrived in Bermuda with Pat, Tracy, Mr. Adams, and Angie. Now if you viewers are confused, stay with me, because it gets better."

Another glance down at her notes. "We discovered that *The Day Dream* was booked by Carl and Bonnie Buckman to take their family deep sea fishing. How interesting that Carl was allegedly killed, in self-defense, by Tracy Palmer of *The Lady Anne*. Bonnie is another of the survivors."

Brenda turned to face me. "Captain Howard wasn't one of the survivors because allegedly he was killed by Bonnie after sexually assaulted her and the other three women I mentioned earlier: Angie Pepper, Ashley Morgan, and Donna Kincaid."

Then Brenda smiled at the camera. "But wait, the story continues. Another of the survivors is Morrie Morris, whose plane disappeared en route to Cat Island, also in the Bahamas. The last survivor is Gertrude Kohler. She was on a whale-watching boat, *The Splashy*. *The Splashy* was reported missing with all hands presumed dead, lost at sea. Apparently not all hands were lost. Gertrude survived and arrived in Bermuda with the others."

I had easily followed all of that and Brenda was surprisingly accurate. So much for wanting to keep a low profile and not draw attention to what had happened. I tried to hide my nervousness. I knew Brenda would start asking me questions, impossible questions that I couldn't honestly answer without divulging the alien encounter that had precipitated all of the events she was going to eventually broadcast.

"So Mr. Adams, now that you've heard what you already knew but failed to mention at our first interview, how do you explain how some of the passengers, from multiple vessels, were reported missing over the span of months in an area nearly one thousand miles south of here, and all happened to arrive in Bermuda, together, in two of the vessels that were reported lost at sea?"

The camera slowly shifted from aiming at Brenda to pointing directly at me. I have no idea why, but an old military adage suddenly popped into my head: *The best defense is a good offense.*

I looked directly at the camera and said, "Brenda, I'm very disappointed that you chose to release the fact that so many had died before the recent widows had a chance to make proper notifications."

I did not look toward Brenda for her reaction; I stayed focused on the camera.

"I'm also disappointed that you mentioned several of the women had been sexually assaulted. Surely you knew that Bonnie and Carl had their underage children with them. Now the children will hear their mom was sexually assaulted from the national news. They will probably hear it again from other kids at school who happen to be watching, not from their mom, in her own words, and at a time of her choosing."

Then I faced Brenda, trying to look sincere. "I ask you, as a woman yourself, to please be a little more sensitive in your reporting. Chalk up what happened to another *unexplained Bermuda Triangle incident* and please give the people you mentioned some privacy and time to grieve their losses."

I paused for a moment. She was looking directly at me. Her expression conveyed I had caught her off guard. I turned back to face the camera, raised my hand, waved goodbye, and said, "I've got to go."

I returned to the illusion of safety aboard *The Lady Anne*. As I made my way below, out of camera range, I heard Brenda saying, "This is Brenda Bishop, signing off from Hamilton, Bermuda."

Her voice had lost some of the bravado she exhibited in front of the camera. I smiled and sat down to pet Buster, hoping that Brenda would be gone before Pat and Tracy returned from taking their showers, gone before the police arrived to take my formal statement about Daniel Pincus's armed assault, and gone before Charles arrived and found himself on camera.

CHAPTER 14

A short while later, Pat and Tracy returned. Brenda had gone. They joined me in the galley and helped themselves to coffee.

I filled them in on what Brenda had discovered.

"How do you think she managed to piece the story together so fast?" Pat asked.

I shook my head. "I suppose once she had the names of the passengers of our two boats, it wasn't hard to do a search. The fact that they all were reported lost at sea would have made all the national news outlets."

"Shaming her was a good tactic," Tracy said. "I wonder how much of that story she'll use now?"

I shrugged. "What really surprised me was that she didn't ask about Pincus."

Charles arrived and I briefed them all on what had happened with the reporter.

"As soon as your men return, will you have them watch over *The Aquaholic* and *The Lady Anne?*" Tracy asked. "It seems more important than ever now that the story is about to break. Even though everyone has left except us, I'd feel better knowing the boats are being protected."

Before he could respond, Pat said, "Armed, too, I hope."

"Yes," Charles said. "The men are licensed to carry firearms, and when they return, they'll present the proper documents to the local authorities. In the meantime, I'll hire someone local to stand guard."

Charles left soon after, saying he had arrangements to make and that he'd be back as quickly as he could. He said his goodbyes to Pat and Tracy in case he didn't make it back before they had to leave for the airport.

A little later, I was helping Pat and Tracy load their bags into a dock cart when a police detective arrived. He was an older man, and very soft-spoken.

He checked our IDs and then took our statements on the dock. Tracy wanted to know if I was in any sort of trouble for permanently stopping Sam Pincus. So did Pat.

The detective assured them, and me, that we had all been vindicated by the video the older birding couple had taken. I then signed the paperwork formally pressing charges against Captain Daniel Pincus.

Pat asked if the police had a picture of Daniel and if they

didn't, said she was sure she could get one from a friend. I knew she meant Charles, and he probably did have one.

But the detective declined, saying they already had circulated Daniel's picture, having gotten it from the video. The police were watching hospitals, the airport, and the tourist docks and had circulated the picture to all of Bermuda's marinas and hotels. He was confident our assailant would be located.

I didn't say anything, but I wasn't so sure that Daniel Pincus would try and leave via any predictable exit point. I was pretty sure he wouldn't be checking into a hotel either. Judging by the look Pat and Tracy gave me, they too had their reservations the police would find him.

After some more routine questions, the detective was finished. Pat and Tracy were ready to go and he graciously offered them a lift to the airport. They accepted, and after some hugs and kisses, Buster and I watched Pat and Tracy follow the police detective down the dock, taking their loaded dock cart with them.

"It's you and me for a while," I told Buster, climbing back aboard. He looked toward where Tracy had walked away, looked at me, and then walked over to his water bowl and loudly slurped a drink.

I left Buster below and went over to *The Aquaholic*. The mattress that Ashley and Donna had soiled during their captivity needed disposing of, badly. I couldn't wait any longer for workers to show up so I decided to do it myself.

Despite the open hatch, the cabin smell was rank. I

couldn't stay inside for more than a few minutes at a time. The mattress was larger than I could handle alone, so I just cut it up.

Using a kitchen knife, I quickly removed the ticking. I put it in a trash bag and headed for a dumpster. On the return, I stopped at *The Lady Anne* for her bolt cutters. The metal frame cut easily, and I soon had half a dozen pieces I could manage. After a few more trips to the dumpster, I smiled as I washed my hands. "One smelly job done," I told myself.

I traded the bolt cutters for cleaning supplies and then returned to *The Aquaholic*, bringing Buster with me. Leaving him topside, I started cleaning under and around where the mattress had been. The smell of orange cleaner slowly replaced the stench of captivity.

I found a dead spider. It had died underneath the mattress. I made a mental note to check all the other berths. I made another mental note to remove drawers and cushions and everything else that could conceal dead bugs as well.

Going through the alien's time portal had killed every bug aboard. If I had the time, I wanted to dispose of any remaining. I didn't want any observant workers asking questions as to why there were only dead bugs but no live ones.

Buster's barking brought me topside. Charles was standing on the dock with three other men and one very attractive woman.

CHAPTER 15

Charles came aboard first. "This is Reid Adams. He has remained in Bermuda to keep an eye on things."

"I'll try and stay out of your way," I answered with a smile.

The next man aboard introduced himself. "I'm Ed Browning, Senior Field Engineer with Clarriage Yachts."

Ed had a firm handshake and handed me his business card. He was about my height and slender, and was holding a clipboard. He was wearing a Clarriage polo shirt. His mustache was neatly trimmed but graying.

The man following him introduced himself. "Chet Burgess. I'll be the project manager and your liaison with the local tradesmen. Welcome to Bermuda."

Chet was a local, shorter than me, of slight build and much younger, probably in his late twenties or early thirties.

He had a welcoming manner and was also holding a clipboard.

The woman came aboard next. She was very pretty in a sexy, understated, educated, businesslike way. She passed the Buster sniff test and then introduced herself. "I'm Elouise Ryall and I've been requested by Charles to take care of all things financial relating to this project."

As Elouise and I shook hands, Charles added, "You should all be nice to her because she's the one with all of the money."

She smiled and looked slightly embarrassed but didn't comment.

The last man came aboard. He was about my height but much heavier, wearing a plaid, unbuttoned sport jacket, pale green slacks, a bright yellow shirt with a narrow red tie, and tan snakeskin cowboy boots. His sunglasses had dark lenses and bright purple frames. I guessed him to be in his seventies. He was carrying a shiny aluminum briefcase. The man looked completely out of a place on a dock in Bermuda.

"I'm Tommy Kraft. Charles Williams hired me to assist you in getting whatever products you need. I own a chain of competitively priced, well-stocked marine supply stores. If you're into watercraft, you probably know Tommy Kraft. Our motto is: *If it's fore or aft, just call Tommy Kraft.*"

I had never heard of his stores but thought his motto was clever. He was an outlandish dresser but seemed pleasant enough.

Tommy opened his briefcase and handed each of us a business card. Then he set out some swag, all imprinted with his "fore and aft" motto. He had leather coasters, bottles of hand sanitizer, gray metal LED flashlights, some pens, and some buoy-shaped key chains that floated and held your boat's registration papers.

I took a flashlight and a pen.

As Tommy finished putting the untaken swag back in his case, Charles cleared his throat to get everyone's attention.

"I want to thank everyone for coming with such short notice. One of you is a local, the rest of you flew in. I appreciate it."

I glanced around. Everyone was listening intently.

"The reason you're here is that this catamaran and my old Clarriage have suffered damage from an electrical storm and need repairs."

Charles made eye contact with Chet. "Now no offense to the local repair facilities, and I'm sure Chet and his people could do a fine job, but time is of the essence as both vessels will be departing for Hawaii in two weeks."

Chet spoke. "I thought you said I'd have a month for repairs." He sounded politely agitated.

"I said a month *or less*," Charles replied. "Two weeks is less than month."

"I'm intimately familiar with Clarriage products," Ed said, raising his hand. "I'm not familiar with this catamaran."

"I tried to get the catamaran's builder to send someone but they wouldn't," Charles said.

He sounded aggravated and I could guess why. I imagine not too many people said no to him.

"So, what exactly needs to be done?" Ed asked.

Tommy retrieved a clipboard and one of his logo pens from his case. Elouise pulled out her phone.

"I'm so glad you asked that." Charles grinned. Looking at me, he continued, "I've got to go and arrange for some additional security so I'm going to defer your questions to Reid Adams."

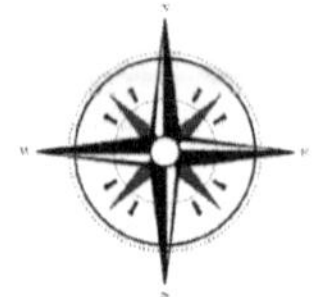

CHAPTER 16

Charles excused himself and I took over.

"Both vessels went through an electromagnetic storm. All of the standing rigging is blackened, as are most of the metal parts topside and below."

Chet and Tommy looked at the closest wire cable and saw what I meant by blackened.

"Besides the obvious charred sails, broken compasses, and questionable electronics on both vessels, the biggest challenges will be on *The Aquaholic*."

"What else is wrong with her?" Chet asked, glancing around.

"*The Lady Anne*, a Clarriage sixty-eight, is designed to cross oceans. *The Aquaholic* is not."

I saw Ed nodding, then he spoke. "Despite a really cool paint job, *The Aquaholic* is a sailing barge, no offense, intended for weeklong charters in protected waters. This multihull was never designed for what, five, six thousand miles of open water?"

"Closer to seven," I corrected. "Maybe more if we make any detours."

"Why don't you just put *The Aquaholic* on a freighter and ship her from here to Hawaii?" he asked, shaking his head as if he already knew my answer.

"The owners of *The Lady Anne* are sailing her to Hawaii. I'm going to accompany them. The owner of *The Aquaholic* wants to sail her boat along with us."

Their expressions betrayed what Ed and Chet were thinking, so I added, "And no, she won't sell her and replace her with a cat that's already in Hawaii."

"What kind of security is Charles arranging?" Elouise asked, taking me by surprise.

I knew I couldn't mention the rolls of gold coins *The Lady Anne* had hidden in her grab rails. My mind went blank for a second, stumped by her delayed question. Then it came to me.

"The former captain of *The Lady Anne* is making himself a serious pain in the ass, pardon my French."

I chose my words carefully. "After Charles fired him, Captain Daniel Pincus committed piracy, broke my ribs, and was seconds away from sexually assaulting the new female owners. He escaped from the Coast Guard and then tracked *The Lady Anne* here to Bermuda. He and his brother attacked the three of us last night and I killed the brother in self-defense. Daniel Pincus, the coward that he is, ran away.

Charles is concerned that Daniel may want revenge, so until the police find him, Charles doesn't want to take any chances."

"That's quite a story," Elouise said. "No wonder you want security."

"And it's why we need to get these repairs done quickly. The sooner we leave Bermuda, the safer we'll all feel."

"You don't happen to have a list of needed repairs, do you?" Chet asked, getting back to business.

"Yes I do, and when we're done here, if you'll all follow me over to *The Lady Anne*, I'll show you what I've come up with."

Before leaving *The Aquaholic*, I gave them a quick tour below, purposely leaving the aft cabin where Ashley and Donna had been held captive for last.

Despite me having disposed of the rank mattress earlier, the stench lingered, even with the open hatch and my liberal use of orange cleaner.

"Where's the mattress?" Chet asked, seeing the empty space.

"Did somebody die in here?" Ed asked.

"Can you answer those questions after we leave?" Elouise asked, holding her nose and backing away. Tommy was right on her heels and looked like he might get sick.

I followed them out, Ed and Chet close behind.

"No." I shook my head. "Nobody died. As for the mattress, I disposed of it earlier, so, Tommy, we'll need a replacement, along with new linens. In fact, replace everything in there that isn't screwed down."

"If nobody died, what the hell happened in there?" Tommy asked, still looking a little pale.

I didn't want to tell them the truth so I lied. "One of the charter guests had a medical problem and was very sick and had ungoverned incontinence."

Nobody pressed me for details.

Elouise and Tommy hustled topside, anxious to breathe some fresh air. We all left *The Aquaholic* and then headed over to *The Lady Anne*.

Neither Tommy nor Elouise had ever seen a Clarriage sixty-eight up close before and they were both impressed.

Chet briefly examined the blackened standing rigging but didn't say anything. Ed asked what the filmy residue was. I thought we had managed to clean the decks of the residue from sailing through the electromagnetic time portal pretty well, but Ed had a well-trained eye.

"It's some kind of baked ozone or something, compliments of the electromagnetic storm we encountered. It comes off with hot water, degreaser, and elbow grease."

"Chet," Ed spoke while writing on his clipboard, "be sure the decks get pressure washed, both vessels."

Chet nodded and noted something on his clipboard too.

"And when you've got a pressure washer here, you might hit that stinky cabin on the catamaran as well," Ed added.

I went below and everyone followed, introducing themselves to Buster one by one.

I retrieved my fix-it list and took a seat at the salon table.

Elouise sat next to me. Chet, Ed, and Tommy took a few minutes to look around.

"Chet," Ed spoke again, "both vessels, but especially this yacht, will have to be decluttered before any serious work can begin. Can you get a rental truck, moving boxes, and some men?"

Chet nodded and wrote something.

After everyone took a seat, I began reading from my list.

CHAPTER 17

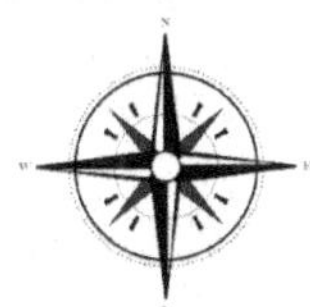

"Let's start with basics for both vessels," I began, speaking slowly so they could take notes.

"You've seen the blackened rigging, fittings, and metal railings and supports. Rather than assume the blackening is strictly cosmetic, let's just assume the metal has been stressed and fatigued. That all needs to be replaced if possible. You've also seen the charred sails, so replace those as well."

I looked at Tommy and added, "Name brand, first quality, please; no cheap imports." He smiled but didn't comment.

"Have a technician check all of the electronics. If any equipment looks suspect, replace it.

"Replace all of the running rigging, both vessels.

"All compasses are broken. Replace them. I also want spares for each vessel, both main and hand bearing. Get the kind with shipping screws so the needles can be locked down." I paused, waiting for them to catch up.

"Replace all batteries. Service the engines, even though it may not be time."

"Should the dinghy's outboard motors be replaced?" Tommy asked.

"Yes, and since you brought that up, *The Aquaholic* needs dinghy davits. Towing her dinghy for several thousand miles isn't practical."

My phone chimed. I paused a moment to read a text from Tracy. They were through security and waiting to board their plane. I sent a thumbs-up. She replied with a bunch of hearts.

"I also want a survival kit that fits inside a five-gallon plastic bucket. Desalinator, water filter, fire starter, cooking pots, knife, emergency fishing gear, shade tarp, space blankets, nylon rope, signal mirror, flare gun, signal whistle, chainsaw chain, hatchet, battery-free flashlight, you get the idea. One bucket for each vessel. And one more bucket each full of assorted freeze-dried meals."

I read through that list again, making sure they hadn't missed anything. Then I added, "We plan to transit the canal but get paper charts for the long way around, just in case."

"In case of what?" Tommy asked, making direct eye contact with me. "Is there something you're not telling us?"

"We got in a bad way once when a freak electromagnetic storm totally disabled us. I want to be fully prepared for any contingency the next time we go out."

"Anything else?" Tommy asked. His tone betrayed the

huge amount of items that needed to located, possibly shipped, and then installed. Although he kept smiling and nodding, the reality was there was an enormous amount of work to be done and to be done quickly.

"Add one small pull-start, gasoline-powered generator for each vessel. I prefer Honda."

Ed interrupted. "*The Lady Anne* has a built-in diesel generator. Why a gasoline backup?"

"Because that diesel generator is a bitch to start when the batteries are dead," I replied. "I want a generator that's quick and easy to start. *The Lady Anne* has a portable battery charger. *The Aquaholic* needs one too."

"Is that it?" Tommy asked, scratching his head.

"Don't forget celestial navigation materials, including backup sextants. *The Aquaholic* has cheap snorkeling gear. Upgrade all of that. Her tools aren't the best either, so upgrade those too. I also want a basic weather station for each vessel—thermometer, barometer, wind speed, stuff like that. It can be wireless but not one hundred percent Wi-Fi."

"You mentioned paper charts earlier," Ed said. "You do know *The Lady Ann* has a chart printer onboard?"

"Yes, I do, but since you mentioned it, I want each vessel to have a complete set of electronic charts and backup paper charts for the entire journey. Throw in a set of round-the-world charts and a pilot chart atlas as well."

"Anything else for *The Aquaholic?*" Chet asked.

"Good question," I replied. "Now I personally sailed *The Aquaholic* from the Bahamas to Bermuda, through a gale, and she handled the conditions very well. But sailing all the way to Hawaii, even cutting through the Panama Canal, is an entirely different matter.

"Let's upgrade her winches, increase her tankage, increase her solar panels, add radar, upgrade her water maker, strengthen the hull, add redundant systems, and give her at least two extra propane tanks."

I paused and looked at Tommy. "Can you get the same brand radar as *The Lady Anne*, to minimize the learning curve?"

He said he would see what he could do.

"*The Aquaholic* also needs a life raft, a drogue, a second anchor, and a set of offshore life jackets," I said.

"How many life jackets?" Tommy asked.

"Better get nine," I answered, silently counting cabins.

Ed suggested adding fiberglass, carbon fiber, and resin in strategic places to reinforce *The Aquaholic's* hulls and stiffen and strengthen some of her cross members and structural supports. Chet said he had a top man, skilled in that type of work. I cautioned them to be cognizant of adding a bunch of weight. They both smiled but agreed.

"While your man is here," I added, "have him repair the scratched floor near *The Aquaholic's* galley. You'll see it."

"This much work is going to have to be completed on another dock," Chet said. "And Charles's timeline of two weeks is impossible."

"Why is it impossible?" Elouise asked.

"The parts that we can't buy locally will have to be shipped in. Besides shipping time, all those parts will have to clear customs, which will take a week."

Tommy frowned.

Chet continued, "Now I can get plenty of skilled workers, but they are going to be in each other's way."

"How much time do you want?" Elouise asked.

"Two months," Chet stated.

I noticed Ed was shaking his head. "Do you agree with that?" I asked.

"If your men are as good as you say they are, working in small crews, in separate areas of each vessel, around the clock, I believe the work could be done in half that time. Four, maybe five weeks."

I hoped Charles would accept that. I also knew that Chet was right about needing another dock, one where we could make noise all day and night and not get complaints.

"Regarding another dock, what have you got in mind?" I asked Chet.

"There's a closed pier that's awaiting redevelopment. I'm sure I can get permission to rent it for a month or two, but it might be expensive."

"Don't worry about the money," Elouise interjected, smiling.

"We'll move both boats and set up shop as soon as I can make it happen," Chet continued. "A lonely pier will make Charles's extra security much more effective."

Chet made some calls while Ed and Tommy looked around some more, still taking notes. Elouise took a seat out of the way and Buster joined her. I got everyone a bottle of water and answered questions.

I wondered if Ed's timeline was feasible. Now that I had covered everything, the amount of work to be performed seemed daunting. Eight weeks seemed reasonable. Five or less seemed unrealistic.

Ed reassured me a little when he told me there was a Clarriage sixty-eight currently in production at the shipyard and we could "borrow" some parts if necessary.

CHAPTER 18

A few hours later, both vessels were tied up at a closed pier. It was only about thirty minutes away by water. Ed and I had moved *The Lady Anne*. Chet and two of his workers followed us with *The Aquaholic*. I texted Charles where we now were so he didn't panic, returning to empty slips.

A short while later, Chet introduced me to one of his best workers, Dwayne Outerbridge.

"Call me Onion," Dwayne said, his white teeth looking like a toothpaste endorsement. "Wopnin?"

"We're doing fine," Chet answered for me. "By the way, have you replaced your broken cell phone yet or should I keep calling your brother?"

"Keep calling him, man, he always knows how to find me," Onion replied, smiling hugely.

Onion was tall and very lanky, probably in his forties, and had an infectious, friendly smile and easygoing attitude.

Since the pier was concrete and easily wide enough for a vehicle, Chet ordered a rental truck to use as storage during the decluttering. We could park it nearby for loading and then move it out of the way, still keeping it close enough if we needed to retrieve anything. And a rental truck could be locked.

While waiting on the truck, Onion began emptying the trash. After the truck and moving boxes arrived, he and two other workers started decluttering. *The Aquaholic* had mostly food, which I planned to eat. *The Lady Anne* had a lot of food plus all of the supplies we had purchased in bulk.

I thought it was a good thing I'd be sleeping aboard with the dog. Onion and his guys were ready, so I told them to start with *The Aquaholic*. I still had to separate out what I needed from my cabin. They agreed.

Before putting my clothes and toiletries in a duffel bag, I took the liberty of gathering all of the clothing that Pat and Tracy had left aboard. I didn't want a stranger handling the women's clothes and underwear.

Later, Charles returned, followed by a van containing four security guards and one guard dog.

"What's with the dog?" I asked, hoping the new dog wouldn't have a problem with Buster.

"Bermuda law requires firearms be surrendered at the customs office. This is the next best thing to armed security,"

Charles replied. He looked a little tired but pleased with his resourcefulness.

"There will be one guard and one dog, around the clock, until the work is completed."

His assurance, plus the fact that the dog pretty much snarled and barked at everybody except his handler, made me relax about Pincus and *The Lady Anne's* gold.

The guards followed Chet up and down the pier so they could see the area they would be protecting. Then three of the guards departed, telling me they'd be back for their shifts.

Before dark, Onion and the two workers had pretty much cleaned out both vessels. I had them leave the perishable food and some galley equipment, but other than that, both vessels were decluttered. The three men departed. They looked tired but happy.

Ed, Chet, and Tommy inspected everything, took detailed notes, and discussed at length additional repairs. The plan was to buy everything that was available locally and then have Tommy order the rest.

Elouise had gone back to the hotel, telling me to call if I needed anything.

"I'll stop by in the morning and then I'm headed to Hawaii," Charles told me as he, Ed, and Tommy waited a short distance away, past where the dog was patrolling. "We'll keep in touch, and keep me posted if any problems arise."

"You'll be back in two months, maybe sooner?" I asked.

"I'm planning on four weeks, five at the latest."

As he turned to leave, I grabbed his arm and in a low voice

said, "Based on what happened to Angie, and what almost happened to Pat and Tracy, do you suppose you can get an all-female crew on short notice?"

His expression told me he hadn't thought about it. I could see my request had caught him completely by surprise. After a brief moment, he nodded and said, "Good idea. I'll see what I can do."

With that they left, leaving me on a lonely pier, accompanied by one unarmed security guard and one, foul-tempered, very loud guard dog.

CHAPTER 19

There weeks later, I took Buster for a leisurely walk away from the concrete pier. As he pulled at his leash and sniffed the new areas, I paused to reflect on what all had transpired.

Mo and Gert had been released from the hospital and although I only saw them briefly, they looked much better.

They had flown their separate ways to put their home affairs on hold. Then they rendezvoused with Charles in Hawaii and were waiting for everyone else. They were adamant to be a part of the long passage from Bermuda to Hawaii and insisted they would return with Tracy and Pat when the boats were ready.

Tracy had sent my new phone via FedEx, so I returned the rental phone to Elouise, who said she would handle it. Tracy and Pat were leaving Colorado tomorrow, having gotten things in order.

Charles had arranged for a property management company to run my strip mall in my absence. Tracy's accounting business only had one client, Pat, who was winding down her construction business. Both women were able to easily clear their calendars.

The three of us agreed not to relocate to Hawaii permanently, at least not yet.

Bonnie and her kids were staying in Houston and weren't communicating with the rest of us very much. I was sure that Bonnie had a lot of baggage to deal with, having been coerced into having sex with the monster, Captain Rick.

Ashley and Donna hadn't headed for Hawaii yet but, according to their texts, they were planning to do that after the funerals for their late husbands.

Angie had arrived in Hawaii, accompanied by her mother. Apparently the mom planned to sail with her daughter on the upcoming voyage. Her mom's name was Jane. That's all I knew about her.

Pat had disturbing news. According to her, Tracy had too much to drink one night and confided she was hearing alien voices. Tracy having too much to drink didn't surprise me. Hearing alien voices was something else. I hoped she was just reliving the event that nearly got her stranded back in time . . . and that there had been no one around except Pat to hear.

As for the boat repairs, things were progressing nicely.

Since there were no nearby marina facilities, Elouise had

ordered four portable toilets and had them placed away from the boats. I used a solar shower, hung from the roof of the furthest portable toilet, to take my daily shower. Elouise and Tommy had both offered their hotels rooms for me to use for showers but I wanted to stay near *The Lady Anne*.

Chet had hired the necessary workers, craftsmen, laborers, and mechanics, and repairs were progressing well. Ed was directing the workers so that they weren't in each other's way, at least not too much. Onion was always available to assist where necessary.

One night Buster and I were awakened by the guard dog barking like crazy. After five minutes of listening to the dog going berserk, I left Buster in my cabin, pulled on a pair of shorts, and rushed topside, my heart pounding.

The guard and his dog were over by the trash bin. The small floodlight that normally illuminated the area was off. The guard was holding the dog back while shining his flashlight all around.

"Do you see anything?" I asked, having to shout to be heard over the dog's frenzied barking.

The guard pulled the dog back and walked over to me. "Whoever it was is gone now. I've called for backup. I'll keep looking."

"Did the light pick now to burn out?"

He shook his head. "It was deliberately switched off. But like I said, I'll keep looking. Go back to sleep."

I thanked him and retreated below. Half-naked and unarmed was not the way I wanted to confront whoever had turned off the light. The dog barked for another forty minutes before it finally got quiet enough for me to fall back to sleep.

When I checked the next morning, the guards hadn't found any traces of an intruder. I thanked them again. Maybe it had been a four-legged rat that set the dog off and not a two-legged one. There were always rodents around docks.

We were still waiting on dinghy davits to be custom fabricated for *The Aquaholic,* but both dinghy's new outboard motors had arrived and ran well. *The Lady Anne's* was electric start but *The Aquaholic's* motor had a manual pull start.

All of the masts had been blackened but the metal didn't appear to have been weakened, so I agreed with Ed's decision not to replace them. He just had the blackening buffed out as much as possible.

We were also waiting on new sails, but Tommy was confident they would arrive any day.

The police had stopped by to inform me that Daniel Pincus could not be located. They were certain he had somehow managed to leave Bermuda without being spotted. The case would remain open but inactive.

I wasn't so sure Pincus had left, but the guards were working out well and I felt pretty certain that Daniel wouldn't be able to get close. Whatever had riled up the dog hadn't been able to get closer than the trash bin.

Onion asked me if I was in trouble with the law. I smiled and shook my head.

I had counted six different guard dogs that were rotated through every twenty-four-hour period. I finally asked if the noisy guard dog could be replaced with one that was calmer. The handler laughed when he heard my question but did as requested. After that, being aboard was much more pleasant for me and for Buster.

As the days passed, I kept Charles informed of our progress and he seemed pleased. I knew he was spending a lot of money but of course, he never complained. Neither did Elouise.

I thanked him for arranging for a property manager for my strip mall. He replied that it was his pleasure and that no thanks was necessary.

He also told me that Ashley and Donna were interested in overseeing Pat's and my business affairs, along with some of his, long distance from Hawaii. Pat wanted to wind down her business, but Charles had a retired contractor friend who was going to keep her business going, at least for a while.

Ashley and Donna had both confided in him that they needed something to do besides cry themselves to sleep or mourn their late husbands. They agreed that a fresh start with a new job in a different location sounded like a really good idea. They both told Charles it would give them purpose.

Charles asked me how many crew I wanted and for how long.

Using the charts that Tommy provided, I had already calculated some approximate distances and theoretical times. I retrieved my notes.

To get from Bermuda to the Panama Canal via Jamaica was over 1,600 nautical miles. Going through Puerto Rico,

Aruba, and Cartagena added another two hundred fifty nautical miles.

With favorable winds and twenty-four-hour watches, at eight knots, it would take a minimum of ten days with a stop in Jamaica, thirteen or fourteen days with stops at the other two islands and Cartagena.

Based on some online sailing forums, I estimated another week to transit the canal but most of that was waiting time.

From the Panama Canal to Hawaii via Mexico was over 4,400 nautical miles. Another twenty-three days, minimum.

Tracy had texted me she wanted to detour to the Galapagos Islands and possibly Easter Island. Pat talked her out of sailing to Easter Island, saying she didn't want to go 2,000 nautical miles out of the way and be at sea that much longer. I agreed. Angie wanted to see the Galapagos as well so the decision was made.

From the Panama Canal to the Galapagos Islands was around eight hundred fifty nautical miles, or another five days, minimum, plus time for exploring. Then on to Hawaii, adding 4,000 nautical miles and another twenty-two days, minimum.

When I told Charles that detouring to the Galapagos would add a week, he replied that the Galapagos were worth seeing and he'd be happy to see them with us.

"Are you coming along?" I asked, wanting to confirm what I had just heard.

"It's okay with Pat and Tracy, so if it's okay with you, I'd like to accompany you onboard *The Lady Anne*, at least from Bermuda to the Galapagos."

I did a quick headcount. Pat, Tracy, and I made three. Mo and Gert were two more. Adding Charles made a total of six on *The Lady Anne*. No problem as far as vessel capacity or personal space.

As for *The Aquaholic*, Angie and her mom made two. There was plenty of room for up to six more, but I figured four experienced crew would be sufficient. Again, no capacity issues.

As for time, we were at about nine or ten weeks, depending on route selection. To allow for weather or delays, I added three weeks more. I was finally ready to answer his initial question.

"You better get four crew for twelve or possibly thirteen weeks."

He repeated what I had said and then added, "No problem."

One by one, workers finished their tasks and left, seeing Elouise for payment before departing the pier. Chet, Ed, and I inspected their work and all of us were very happy. There was no shortage of skilled workers in Bermuda.

When the sails finally arrived and were installed, Ed told me the work would be finished in a couple of days and to notify Charles.

Chet concurred and asked Elouise if she could cover the cost of a party for the workers. She agreed. I gave Charles a status update and he was ecstatic, saying he would begin making travel arrangements forthwith.

I asked if he had managed to locate a crew. He replied that

he had indeed and that I would be pleasantly surprised. He wouldn't elaborate on their qualifications but I could tell he was very pleased with whomever he had hired.

He also told me that Tracy got hammered at a luau and said she heard alien voices. I didn't respond and he let it go. I hoped this wasn't becoming a habit.

CHAPTER 20

Late in the afternoon before the "good job getting the work done" party, I was onboard *The Lady Anne* with Buster. I double-checked everything on my list.

The work had been completed, neatly and professionally. And ahead of schedule. I was sure that equated to over budget as well. Thankfully Charles didn't have a budget and just covered everything.

The Aquaholic looked more up to the task of an ocean crossing, thanks to strategic reinforcements and other upgrades.

The Lady Anne had been refreshed as well. There was an occasional spot of blackened metal, but you really had to look to see the souvenirs from going through the electromagnetic portal.

Neither boat had had a test sail but all electronics were

working, as were the engines. I was hopeful we could move the boats away from the pier within a few days.

I was tired of the noise from our reliance on a rented, large diesel generator for shore power and was looking forward to quieter evenings. I was also tired of the commotion caused by dozens of workers. I bought some earplugs and that helped me sleep, but the generator was still loud.

I finished my final inspection of both vessels and returned to *The Lady Anne.* I wanted to look at tips on transiting the Panama Canal.

I opened *The Lady Anne's* laptop and used "history" to go back to an earlier search. That's when I noticed something strange.

I spotted several searches that I hadn't made. I stared at the screen and read the following: Recent vessels missing in the Bermuda Triangle; Disappearance of *The Day Dream* fishing boat; Disappearance of *The Aquaholic* charter boat; Disappearance of *The Lady Anne, a* Clarriage sixty-eight luxury yacht.

I looked at Buster and said, "Somebody is curious about us. Very curious." He looked at me, and when I didn't get him a dog treat, he slowly walked away, lay down, and closed his eyes.

I looked at the search histories in more detail. *The Day Dream, The Splashy,* and *The Obsession* all came up as missing, without a trace. *The Aquaholic* and *The Lady Anne* had been reported missing as well, but later articles confirmed both vessels had mysteriously been located in Bermuda, a long distance from their expected locations.

Since the incidents had occurred in the Bermuda Triangle, there was a lot of speculation but nothing definitive. How could there be? No one knew that aliens were involved in each of these instances. If someone did suspect aliens, they had no proof, at least not any that wasn't 25,700 years old.

I realized I had a nosy worker. The more I thought about it, the more I began to suspect Onion. He was the only one who didn't have a smartphone. He also seemed to come and go as he pleased, not being held as accountable by Chet for his time. He could easily slip below unnoticed and access the computer.

I vaguely remembered him always being close enough to listen to what Ed, Chet, Tommy, and I were saying about the required repairs. Yep, I was pretty sure it was Onion.

"But no matter," I told Buster. "So what if Onion watched the news, snooped around, and knows we went missing in the Bermuda Triangle? He doesn't know about the aliens. He doesn't know about the gold and he doesn't know what Captain Rick did to Ashley, Donna, and Angie after murdering their husbands. Considering the rank cabin, he may suspect foul play, but he doesn't have any proof. He probably searched on *The Day Dream* because he heard that name on the news and saw the same name on some of the fishing gear. I think I'm just being paranoid."

I let it go at that, telling myself Onion was inconsequential. But with a few clicks I cleared the search history.

I did have a fleeting thought that *The Aquaholic* appeared to be the last vessel listed as a casualty of the Bermuda Triangle. I wondered if the aliens had actually incorporated some of Tracy's suggestions about not being spotted so easily when they transited back and forth to our planet.

I started bringing loads, one dock cart at a time, from the rental truck and began putting things away, slowly and carefully. So far I hadn't seen any damaged items, and nothing appeared to be missing.

Buster and I heard the guard dog barking and a few minutes later, there was a knock on the hull.

I hustled topside after Buster. I figured it was Ed, Chet, or possibly Elouise.

I was surprised, shocked, and dumbfounded, all at the same time.

CHAPTER 21

Standing on the pier right next to *The Lady Anne* were five beautiful women. Had they been wearing sashes, they would have passed for pageant finalists.

"Elouise told us you were Reid Adams," the one closest to me said, "the person in charge."

"That's correct," I stammered. "I mean, I guess I'm in charge."

She was medium height, slender, and had short brown hair, a cute face, and nice legs. She looked young, but I've never been great at guessing women's ages. Her black skirt was tight and short. Almost too short, I thought, but I wasn't complaining.

The two standing next to her could have been twins. They were tall, like Pat. They had long blonde hair, slender builds, nice chests, even nicer legs sporting really high heels, deep tans, and beautiful smiles. They were probably close to Tracy's or Pat's age. Both women were attractive enough to have been actresses or models.

I did a double take at the sight of the fourth woman. She had flaming red hair and a big chest. She reminded me of a woman I used to date. She was tall and slender and could have also passed for a model. The cut of her red dress displayed her ample breasts. It was obvious she was proud of them.

The last was the shortest of the group. She had black hair cut in a ragged pixie with a white streak on one side. Unlike the other four, this one was wearing spandex leggings and a neon purple halter top. She was very muscular and in fantastic physical condition. Her face was hard and she wasn't smiling. I guessed that she was either a professional athlete or a personal trainer. Her outfit screamed that she worked out, a lot. I wondered if men found her muscles and abs sexy or intimidating, or both. I made a mental note not to arm wrestle her, ever.

Elouise had been talking to the guard but now joined the rest of us. She had traded her business professional attire I was accustomed to seeing her in for a bright-blue dress that accentuated her nice figure. For the first time I could remember, she was wearing heels.

On a lark I looked down and around. All of the women, except the athlete, wore high heels. I almost chuckled at one of my old sayings, *The higher the heel, the more single the girl*. If that was true, at least four of these women were single and the twins were very single.

The one with the short black skirt spoke. "If you're done staring, request permission to come aboard."

"Sorry," I answered. "But you have me at a disadvantage."

Elouise stepped forward. "Didn't you tell Charles you wanted an all-female crew for *The Alcoholic?*"

I had indeed. This crew was indeed female . . . almost too female. I gathered my wits. "You're the crew that Charles hired? I wasn't expecting you until tomorrow. Permission granted."

They all liked Buster and he liked them. I forced myself not to stare as they bent over or knelt down to scratch his ears.

Ms. Black Skirt spoke first. "I'm Captain Veronica Kline, but please just call me Vee. Sorry to get here a day early, but we wanted to see what we'll be sailing on for the next three months."

"Don't apologize," I said. "I would have done exactly the same thing. I'll show you around *The Lady Anne* and then we can go over and see *The Aquaholic*, a catamaran."

She nodded.

"I'm very familiar with Clarriage Yachts," she said. "We've all sailed on the Clarriage ninety-five."

If I remembered correctly, that was the next-larger model in Clarriage's offerings. I was impressed.

"Having a Clarriage," she continued, "is one of the reasons we took a gig as long as this."

I didn't want to curb her enthusiasm, so I didn't mention that they would most likely be spending most of their time sailing *The Aquaholic.*

"I have a question," I said after a moment. "Aren't you awfully young to have a captain's license?"

"I get that a lot, but I'm older than I look."

She didn't offer her age and I knew better than to ask.

The second woman introduced herself. "I'm Beverly Thompson. I also have my captain's license. Call me Bev."

"Are you two sisters?" I asked, looking at the third woman standing beside her. "Or twins?"

They both laughed and Bev said, "We are not related."

Number three introduced herself next, interrupting my train of thought. "My real name is Candace Glover, but everybody calls me Candy. It's very nice to meet you, Reid."

It was going to take some work to remember who was who. They really did look like twins. I knew I would be confused and get the names wrong at least a few times.

The fourth woman gave me a hug and introduced herself as Dreamgirl.

"Dreamgirl? That's your name? Dreamgirl?"

Vee answered for her. "That's what everybody calls her."

The others started chuckling. Dreamgirl didn't say anything. She just smiled. I didn't say anything either, figuring her real name would be revealed in time and wondering where Charles found this exotic collection of "sailors."

The athletic woman stepped up next. She held out her hand to shake, but when I put my hand in hers, she pulled me into a hug. She was as hard as a rock. I could feel her muscles. She was more solid than most men I knew, and definitely in better shape than I was.

"My name is Marta Kowalski," she said with a touch of an accent.

I backed away slightly. She definitely gave off a different vibe than her companions. And I was curious about the accent.

"What kind of sailing experience do you have, Reid?" Vee asked before I could pursue it.

Once again, I was caught off guard. It was almost as if they were interviewing me when, in fact, I should be interviewing them. I released a breath. "I've done quite a bit of offshore racing and I teach sailing."

"Where?" she asked.

"Colorado."

"You teach sailing in Colorado," she said, almost sarcastically. "A landlocked state."

I had heard that several times before and had a ready answer. "Wind is wind, tacking is tacking, and knots are knots," I answered. "You don't need an ocean to have wind."

"How many people will there be on this voyage?" Candy asked.

That was an easy enough question, and I must have paused longer than I thought because she repeated the question before I had finished counting.

"Charles Williams, the former owner of *The Lady Anne* will be coming, at least part of the way. So will her new owners, Pat and Tracy. There will be myself, our friends Mo and Gert, Angie, who owns *The Aquaholic*, and Jane, her mom whom I haven't met yet."

"So there will be thirteen of us sailing from here to Hawaii? Is that correct?" Marta asked.

"You're not getting superstitious on me, are you?" Vee cheerfully responded.

"Thirteen is thirteen, an unlucky number," Marta replied. "I'm just saying."

"Well, we have our dog too," I said, smiling. "If we count Buster, that's fourteen."

Marta didn't respond. There was an uncomfortable moment of silence so I changed the subject. "I assume you five have duffel bags somewhere?"

Dreamgirl nodded. "Excess baggage all the way. They're in our rooms. Same hotel as Elouise."

"Elouise met us as we checked in and told us about the party tonight," Bev said.

"So we stowed our bags, freshened up, changed clothes, and followed her here, wanting to see the boats and meet you before it got dark," Candy continued.

"Reid, could we please have a quick tour of both vessels?" Vee asked.

"Absolutely," I replied. "And while we're touring, you can tell me your sailing experience."

It's what I said, but my thoughts were really racing ahead to what Ed, Chet, and all of the workers would think when I walked into the party flanked by beautiful women named Candy and Dreamgirl.

I couldn't help but smile.

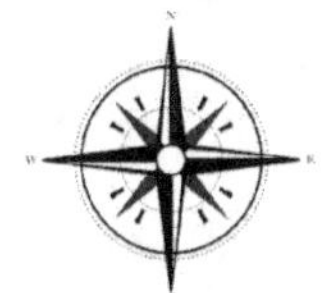

CHAPTER 22

I gave the five women a quick tour. When I asked where they sailed *The Lady Anne's* big sister, a Clarriage ninety-five, Vee responded, "We delivered a Clarriage ninety-five from Hawaii to Vancouver."

Bev chuckled a little, telling me of the wealthy Canadian couple that had purchased a Clarriage ninety-five and sailed it to Hawaii. It was only when the weather offshore got rough that they realized they got seasick. They flew back to Canada, had their boat delivered, and now it was for sale. That was amusing but, in my experience, more common than she probably realized. Ocean crossings were not for the faint of heart, or stomach.

"Are you all licensed captains?"

"I am a Coast Guard licensed captain," Vee replied. "So is Bev. Dreamgirl and Candy are studying the course materials and are now accumulating enough hours at sea to qualify for the exam."

"What about you, Marta? Are you going to take the captain's test as well?"

"No," she replied rather quickly. "I'm not much of a sailor yet. I met Veronica and the others in Europe, but now I live in the US." She backed away, and I got the feeling she was done answering questions.

"Where do you normally sail?" I asked.

"Besides occasional ocean-crossing deliveries, we have crewed on both US coasts and have sailed fairly extensively in the Mediterranean," Candy answered.

"We normally crew on motor yachts but we all really like sailing," Dreamgirl said.

"Between us, we speak nine languages, can repair almost anything that breaks, have some medical training, are accomplished cooks, and can intelligently converse on many subjects," Vee said, smiling.

I wondered again where in the world Charles found these women. I couldn't wait to ask him.

We had made our way clear forward on *The Lady Anne* and were passing back through the rigging station when Vee picked up a piece of line and asked which knots I knew.

"All the ones required to get sailing certifications," I replied. Seeing an opportunity to tell a joke, I decided to see what kind of a sense of humor these women had, or didn't have.

"Do any of you know the dragon bowline?" I asked, taking the line from Vee.

They all shook their heads no and moved in closer to see. In the confined space, their perfume was intoxicating.

I tied a normal bowline in the end of the line and quickly showed it to them. They didn't say anything. Then I dropped the knot and walked away, dragging it behind me.

I went a few feet and then turned to face them. It took a few seconds but they all erupted in laughter when they figured out I meant *draggin a bowline*.

I was pleased they had a sense of humor.

We finished the tour below and then I gave them a quick tour topside.

Due to their Clarriage ninety-five experience, *The Lady Anne* didn't present much of a learning curve.

Elouise asked how much longer I was going to be, so before concluding the tour aboard *The Lady Anne,* I excused myself to change my clothes and spray on a hit of cologne. I was underdressed compared to the women, but my wardrobe was *practical sailor*, not *head-turning knockout*.

I sent Buster topside to do his business on the stern. Candy watched him and told the others she had never seen a dog trained like that before. We then headed over to *The Aquaholic*.

The women seemed pleased with the cat's pristine, ship-shape condition. Even the cut marks in the galley's sole had been repaired to the point they were invisible.

I hesitated slightly when entering the cabin where Ashley

and Donna had been held captive. I tried to avoid it as much as possible, and I was afraid it would still smell of the foul odor of rape and captivity.

However, it smelled fresh and clean, like the rest of the cat did. No one that hadn't seen it before would have recognized it as the same place. Chet's men had certainly done a fine job. They deserved a great party.

"There are some boxes of gear that need to come over from the moving truck, but she's almost ready," I said.

The seven of us exited *The Aquaholic* and headed toward the party. I offered Elouise and Vee each an arm, which they easily accepted. The rest of the women followed behind with Marta bringing up the rear.

The guard dog growled but didn't bark. The guard gave me a discreet thumbs-up as I passed accompanied by a harem of beautiful women.

CHAPTER 23

Elouise had arranged for two vehicles to take us to a local yacht club.

"Elouise told us the party was for all of the workers who have been refurbishing the boats," Vee said while sitting next to me in the first vehicle.

"That's right," I replied. "They really did a first-class job."

"What needed to be repaired?" Bev asked. "And why?"

I told her about going through an electromagnetic storm and getting lost. I said that most of both vessel's systems needed repair or replacement.

Vee gave me a questioning look, but before I could elaborate, we had arrived.

We met Onion on the way into the club.

"Hey, Mr. Adams, wopnin?" he asked, smiling his big

smile. When he looked at the beautiful women accompanying me, he uttered, "Chingas!"

"We're doing fine and on our way to the party," I replied.

"This is really nice of you to have this session and buy us workers a big greeze and all the Black we can drink," he said.

Thanks to being around him and the others for a month, I had learned a lot of local phrases. "Wopnin?" was a Bermuda greeting that translated, "What's happening?" "A big greeze" was a big meal. "Black" was the island's favorite rum. "Session" meant party or celebration. "Chingas!" meant wow.

I had learned that an "Onion" was a native-born Bermudian, named when sweet onions were Bermuda's chief export.

"You and the others deserve this party for getting the work done on time," I replied.

Onion waved goodbye and went to use the restroom. When he was out of earshot I translated for the women what he'd said.

"Nine languages," Vee said with a laugh. "But it's the dialects and the slang that can trip you up."

The party was held in a private room at the yacht club. Elouise had arranged for a buffet and an open bar. A local band was playing.

I recognized all of the workers. Most had dressed up and many of them had their wives or girlfriends with them. They all came by and thanked me. I thought they should have thanked Elouise; after all, it was she who was footing the bill.

When I introduced my group to Ed, Vee seemed very interested in meeting the senior field engineer for Clarriage

Yachts. They visited quite a while and I believe I saw him give her his business card.

I went over to the buffet line and followed Marta, Beverly, Candy, and Dreamgirl. I found it interesting to see that Marta took mostly protein, carbs, and desserts while Beverly, Candy, and Dreamgirl took a little salad and some fruit. I wondered how menus would be handled once we began our long voyage.

I was hungry and quickly filled my plate. Everything looked wonderful. The chefs had obviously been very busy. Their presentation was flawless.

I smiled, following Dreamgirl. She couldn't see me staring at her boobs each time she turned to take a serving. They were almost popping out of her bright red dress. "Chingas!" I chuckled to myself. Chingas indeed.

There were limited tables so we ate standing up. Vee was still talking to Ed. Chet was working his way through the buffet line with Tommy. Tommy was wearing different shades of blue and was really easy to spot. Onion was across the room, talking to some men I didn't recognize. When he saw me spot him, he smiled and waved but didn't come over.

A club waiter brought over a tray of drinks that looked like inverted tequila sunrises, with the red color at the top. "Rum swizzles," he proudly announced. "The bartender's favorite."

It tasted like straight rum flavored with a little fruit juice and another ingredient I couldn't quite place. It was so strong, it was probably flammable. I made a mental note to only have one. I noticed that Candy, Bev, and Dreamgirl passed but Marta took one.

With Elouise looking hotter than usual, and with Vee and her sexy crew kind of following me around, I didn't need to get drunk and into trouble. I rubbed my homemade gold coin pendant, reminding myself I was engaged to two women.

I missed Pat and Tracy. Besides missing their company, this was the longest I had gone without sex since getting involved with them and I was more than anxious for their return. It was going to be interesting to see their reaction to their new crewmates. Especially Tracy, who who has proved to be possessive where I was concerned.

There was a loud voice across the room, loud enough to be heard over the music. I looked and saw Chet near the two men Onion had been talking to. Chet was holding his buffet plate with one hand and pointing with his other hand.

I immediately stopped eating and headed in that direction. Marta followed me. Candy and Bev followed her.

CHAPTER 24

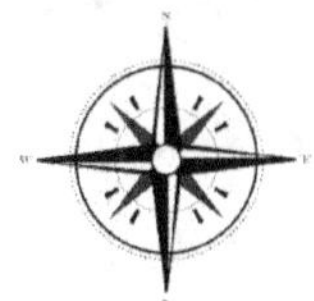

We hustled over, not sure what was happening.

"I've got your back," Marta said on the way.

Ed, Dreamgirl, and Vee joined us. I glanced behind me and saw that all of the workers had backed away, watching but keeping their distance.

"These men weren't invited and won't leave," Chet exclaimed, exasperated. "They were not on the work crew."

"Private party, guys," I said softly. "Let's not have any trouble."

The two men looked at me but didn't move. One was short and really skinny; the other was taller and broad shouldered. They looked like locals. The short guy had a dark mark on his face, like from a burn. The taller man had a scraggly black beard.

"We be friends of Mr. Onion and he invited us," the short man said.

"Workers, spouses, and girlfriends only guys," I said. "Maybe another time."

They didn't budge. Onion didn't say anything to them or to me.

Elouise joined us, bringing the manager with her.

"Is there a problem here?" the manager asked.

"There be no problem. We just having drinks with our friend Mr. Onion here," the short man answered.

The manager told both men they had been asked to leave and to please do so. He was polite and soft-spoken, but his tone was firm. They didn't move.

I stepped forward. "Guys, we don't want any trouble. Finish your drinks and just leave. No trouble."

"Who are you?" the taller, bearded man said harshly, sticking his finger about an inch from my chest.

I tensed up and clenched my fists, suspecting a fight was imminent.

In a flash, Marta swooped in from behind me, grabbed the man's pointed finger, and bent it backwards with such force I heard it pop. Everyone heard it.

The tall man winced, cussed, and cradled his damaged finger in his other hand. The shorter man stepped toward Marta, fists clenched.

I stepped in front of her. "Are you going to punch a woman?" I asked, trying not to raise my voice and escalate the situation.

I watched his fists. I told myself to move when he swung and counter with either a throat strike or a kick to his balls. If the tall man moved on me, I was going to attack his broken finger and let his pain force him to stand down. My breathing increased.

Onion stepped in between his friends and me, putting his hands out.

"We don't be wanting no trouble, Mr. Big Boss Man," he said to Chet. "My friends was only here for a drink and now they be leaving." He smiled and escorted his friends out. When they passed Vee, Dreamgirl, and the twins, the women watched them intently. The bearded man with the broken finger watched Marta all the way to the exit.

Chet followed them. Marta and I followed Chet. The manager, Elouise, Ed, and Vee followed us. Vee's crew, some of the workers, and some of the club staff followed them. I hoped it was over and not simply a change of location.

On the way out, Chet said, "Onion, you never should have brought those guys here. You know what they did. You're fired. Get your tools tomorrow."

Onion stopped walking and looked directly at him, giving me and Marta time to stand alongside Chet. Onion looked at each of us and smiled, but didn't say anything. He turned and followed his friends out the door, shaking and then nodding his head as he went.

The manager and one of his staff followed them as they left and then stayed near the door, probably to make sure they actually did leave.

"What was that all about?" I asked Chet.

"Those guys are nothing but trouble," he replied. "They used to work for me." From his tone and his glancing about, I could tell Chet was obviously upset.

"What happened?"

"Stuff used to come up missing, which is fairly common, but they went too far once and got blacklisted from working the docks. Nobody legitimate will hire them."

I walked toward a window, motioning for Chet to follow.

When we had some space I asked, "What did those guys do? How far was too far?"

"They were stealing from one of the boats when the owner and his wife caught them. They beat the crap out of the man, sending him to the hospital."

I shook my head, thinking immediately of what Captain Rick had done to Angie.

"I don't know for certain, but they must have frightened the poor wife so bad that she wouldn't talk to the police."

I shook my head again. I felt sorry for her. It wasn't hard to imagine those two guys scaring her.

"Well, the hospital staff got the old man's story and, needless to say, when word got out what had happened to him, a war veteran no less, nobody would hire those creeps for anything. I haven't seen them in over a year and figured they had gone elsewhere. Moved on."

"What was that all about?" Vee came over and asked. Marta and Bev were right behind her.

"Disgruntled ex-employees," Chet said simply and walked away.

"When your crew is ready to leave," I told Vee, "I'd like to escort you back to your hotel."

"That won't be necessary," Vee replied, shaking her head and grinning a little. "You just got a peek as to how Marta can handle herself. But truth be told, any of us could have handled those two losers."

I looked at Marta and Bev.

Marta smiled and shrugged. "Maybe I should escort you back to the boats?"

I then wondered what kind of training Vee and her friends had. Vee didn't seem at all concerned about those two men, even calling them losers.

"Thank you for the offer, but I'm going to thank Ed, Chet, Tommy, Elouise, and the workers and then I'll make my own way back to *The Lady Anne*."

Neither woman commented, so after I made my rounds, I took a taxi back to *The Lady Anne*.

I glanced around the pier but didn't see Onion or his two friends. The guard confirmed that nobody had been around. I told him to stay alert, that there had been a problem with Onion and two other guys at the party and that Onion had been fired.

He seemed surprised to hear that. He asked if the pretty women were okay. I smiled and told him they were all fine. I didn't mention that Marta had probably broken one of the bad guy's fingers.

CHAPTER 25

I took care of Buster and then checked my text messages. There were several from Pat. I cursed myself for not bringing my phone to the party. Then I laughed, telling myself I was distracted by Veronica Kline and her beautiful crew.

Pat texted that Angie's mom, Jane, was brilliant but that Pat had a feeling Jane didn't like her. She didn't elaborate, so I responded I was sorry they weren't getting along but I looked forward to meeting her.

She texted that Ashley and Donna both woke up from nightmares involving Captain Rick raping them. I didn't respond but I understood. I had one nightmare about Bonnie beheading him. It was in color and seemed very real.

Pat's last text was that Tracy was hearing alien voices when she drank but then added LOL, short for laughing out loud. I wasn't sure if she was serious or not, but what if she was?

After giving it a little thought, I replied to tell Tracy that the next time she thought she heard alien voices she should: one, say hello; two, thank them for returning her friends; three, thank them for returning her. Pat acknowledged with: okay, if you say so.

Tracy's texts were upbeat. She bragged about all the shopping she had done. She mentioned Charles had a great place in Hawaii. She confirmed that Ashley and Donna were smart workers and caught on quickly and should be able to handle our taxes with no trouble, e-filing everything.

I had completely forgotten about taxes, but it was that time of the year. I was glad I had followed Charles's suggestion and given all of them a limited power of attorney.

Tracy didn't comment on Angie's mom but said Angie was almost as good of a cook as I was.

Tracy reminded me to hug Buster for her.

Her last text said to rub myself while thinking of her. She attached a selfie. She was wearing revealing black lingerie.

Before turning in, I Googled Marta Kowalski. Her name didn't come up on the first few screens.

I asked Buster why Marta's name wasn't there. He wagged his tail but didn't answer. Talking to the dog made me realize just how lonely it was without Pat and Tracy around.

I then Googled Captain Veronica Kline. She had a simple website offering all-female, crewed yacht charters and deliveries, both motor and sail.

I remembered I had one thing to do for Charles. He had

asked me to take inventory of how many gold coins would be needed to replace what Pat and Tracy had spent.

I closed the hatch and the curtains and got the tools I needed from the workroom. Buster watched as I accessed the gold, sniffed a coin, and then lay down.

After a quick count, I texted Charles the number. I apologized for taking so long or not calling him sooner but he understood that I had been busy. I was glad for the six-hour time lag between Bermuda and Hawaii. I replaced the gold coins in the grab rails, put the tools away, checked topside one more time, and then hit the sack.

Ed stopped by early the next morning to make one last inspection of the upgrades to *The Aquaholic*. He would be leaving before Charles arrived as he was needed elsewhere for another valued customer. He reminded me to make the fuel dock the very first stop as *The Aquaholic's* tanks were really low from having to be emptied to be cleaned.

"First stop, fuel dock, check," I told him.

I thanked Ed for all of his hard work and expertise. He was very modest but wanted me to tell him how his upgrades to *The Aquaholic* handled the first storm. I told him I'd let him know.

He gave me his room key to give to Elouise. He said someone from Hawaii would be using his room. We shook hands and he departed, saying, "Fair winds and following seas."

Chet arrived shortly thereafter and passed Ed on the pier.

They talked a few minutes and I saw them shake hands. Chet came over to me and apologized for ruining the party with his outburst. He looked stressed, really stressed.

"Are you okay?" I asked.

"Those thugs last night really upset me. I didn't sleep well worrying about them coming back."

"Don't worry about those two," I reassured him. "The guards are doing a fine job and we'll be leaving within a few days."

"Has Onion been around?" he asked.

"Not that I've seen."

"Well if he shows up, don't let him aboard. I don't trust him anymore. Call it guilty by association."

I was disappointed to hear that but fully understood. I tried to think of what I would say if Onion did come by and wanted to come aboard for some of his tools or something. Nothing came to mind.

"Do you want my men to bring all the boxes from the

truck to the boats?" Chet asked. "They can help you put everything back where it goes."

"Yes, but just have them stack the boxes alongside."

I had thought about unboxing everything myself and decided it might be best to have Vee and her crew help put things away. Then they'd know what was onboard and what additional items might be needed for a three-month passage.

Chet agreed with my thinking and started texting for some workers.

Elouise was the next to stop by. She smiled and informed me that all workers, vendors, and contractors had been paid or were scheduled to be paid. She was going to brief Charles when he landed and would be staying until the boats departed in case any last-minute expenses came up.

I guessed she had spent a small fortune on parts, expedited shipping, repairs, equipment rentals, general laborers, craftsman, etcetera. Part of me wanted to know what these repairs and retrofits had cost but it really wasn't any of my business. I kept quiet and just thanked her for all of her assistance.

The next one on the pier was Tommy. He left his bags by the guard and made his way over. As per usual, he was wearing another loud outfit that clashed. But he had done a tremendous job. I knew that if Charles had not engaged his company and procurement contacts, we would likely still be waiting for parts, at least *The Aquaholic* would be.

Tommy asked me to be sure and tell him how we liked the new sails. They had arrived in time and been attached, raised, furled, and unfurled but were as yet untested away from the pier. The sails looked really nice, and I was sure we'd be very pleased with their performance.

The Lady Anne had spare sails; *The Aquaholic* didn't. I kept all of the old sails, just in case.

We then shook hands, and before Tommy departed for the airport, he told Elouise that his room was now available for whoever would be needing it. He handed her his room key and she thanked him.

Two of Chet's workers arrived. They immediately thanked me for the party and told me they had a fine time. Again, I thought they should be thanking Elousie but graciously told them they were most welcome. They began bringing boxes from the truck, stacking them on the pier between the two boats.

Vee and her crew arrived. All but Marta were wearing matching shorts and striped tops. Marta had on short shorts and a white T-shirt. Her black sports bra showed through.

Her muscles were clearly visible. She looked very formidable. I wondered how'd she'd find time to work out over the next twelve weeks at sea.

Even dressed casually with no fancy hairdos, and either a ponytail or a hat, this all-girl crew was spectacularly attractive.

"It's a pity," I said softly to myself, "that all of these beautiful women will be sailing *The Aquaholic* and not *The Lady Anne*. Talk about eye candy."

As soon as that thought crossed my mind though, images of Tracy and Pat popped up. Neither would be as appreciative of their charms as I was.

Marta went to help Chet's workers move boxes. But instead of using a two-wheeler or a cart, she just carried them.

Vee and I started with *The Lady Anne's* boxes while Bev, Candy, and Dreamgirl worked on *The Aquaholic's* boxes. Both teams fashioned an assembly line, eventually getting all boxes onboard the vessel they were marked for.

Chet got a text that one of his workers had spotted Onion nearby so Chet left to look for him, reminding me not to let him onboard either vessel.

By lunchtime, the truck had been emptied and all gear and boxes moved aboard. Except for the guard, a few miscellaneous tents, the generator, the rental truck, a large trash bin, and the toilets, the pier was nearly empty.

At my request, Elouise delivered lunch. After lunch, Chet and his men left to return the truck. I moved back and forth between vessels, supervising as the women unpacked the boxes and put items away.

Vee took some notes for things she wanted and left to talk to Elouise about getting some shopping cash. Marta followed Vee.

Bev got a text and almost immediately, the women left to meet up with Vee and Elouise to do some shopping. That left me and Buster alone aboard *The Lady Anne*.

He and I were taking a break topside when a delivery truck stopped near the guard, unloaded two boxes, and then drove away. Buster followed me over to the boxes. He was very happy chasing after the seagulls on the pier. If he could have jumped a little higher, he might have caught the first one he went after.

The boxes were from Tommy Kraft's store. I carried them back to the boats one at a time. They were heavier than I expected. I chuckled at the thought that it would have been easier with a two-wheeled dolly, or with Marta. Unfortunately, the dolly had gone with the truck and Marta had gone with Vee.

Each box contained all the cruising guides we might need on the way to Hawaii. I put the set for *The Aquaholic* away first. As I squeezed the second set into the bookcase onboard *The Lady Anne*, I found a phone, wedged way in the back between shelves. I didn't recognize it, and its battery was dead.

It hadn't been there when the workers emptied the book-case or one of them would have said something. Maybe it belonged to Charles or even to Pincus. I tried to charge it, hoping for a clue as to its owner, but my power cord didn't fit. I put the mystery phone on the galley counter, not sure what to do with it.

There was a knock on the hull and Buster barked and then scampered topside. I secretly hoped it wasn't Dreamgirl back from shopping early. If it was her, I hoped she wasn't alone. Dreamgirl reminded me of an ex-lover and she was looking more and more attractive with every box she bent over to empty.

Maybe looking at Tracy's lingerie selfie was more arousing than I realized. I took a deep breath and headed topside. But it wasn't Dreamgirl or any of the other women; it was Onion.

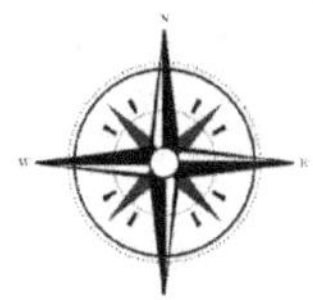

CHAPTER 27

"Have you seen a phone belonging to me onboard?" he asked, smiling. "I don't be finding my new phone nowhere. I get killed if I come back without tit."

Remembering Chet's stern warning about Onion I answered, "Wait right there. I think I found it."

I went below, grabbed the newly discovered phone, and returned topside in less than sixty seconds. Onion was waiting on the pier, and when I handed it to him, he shook my hand so hard I nearly lost my balance.

He thanked me and strutted away, obviously happy.

I tried to envision Onion leaving his phone on the book-shelf. I wasn't sure how it would have ended up there because no one had been doing any work in that area, at least not within the last few days. But if he had misplaced it and left the light on, that would explain why it was dead. It might also explain that mysterious history I found on the computer. The desk and bookshelf were close to each other. I quit thinking about it then, glad that he was happy to have found his phone and quietly hoping he wouldn't come back.

I thought about making some tentative menus but quickly dismissed that idea. There was no way to plan menus for more than one week, much less three months. It would probably be better to just get everyone's input on provisions and decide specific meals as we were sailing.

I googled where I could get a survival rifle like Mo had. Our shotguns were lethal but only at close range. A rifle, even a small caliber, collapsible model, might be a good idea. Plus if we had another one, we could keep one on each boat.

Firearms were illegal in Bermuda and severely restricted in Jamaica. But they appeared to be easily available in Puerto Rico. That made my route selection from Bermuda to the Panama Canal much simpler. We would go through Puerto Rico, not Jamaica.

On a lark, I Googled violent crime rates. Jamaica had the highest while Puerto Rico's was much lower. That sealed my route choice. Puerto Rico would also make Pat happy as I knew they had a Costco where I planned to purchase most of our needed provisions.

I got a long text from Pat. They were in Sanford, North Carolina, refueling the jet. Bermuda was the final stop. They were planning to arrive around seven p.m., Bermuda time, assuming they left the Raleigh Executive Jetport on time. They would all be served dinner on the plane. She signed off that she missed me and that she had a surprise.

Tracy texted next. It was short: *Arriving Bermuda later tonight. I'm tired, don't wait up. I owe you one.*

Just as I was replying to those texts, Elouise texted they were done shopping and would bring dinner back to the pier.

I took the time to break down the moving boxes and get them off of the boats. Corrugated cardboard boxes often contained cockroaches and I didn't want any stowaway critters. The boxes had only been used one time, so rather than toss all of them into the trash bin, I stacked them neatly between two of the toilets, hoping they wouldn't blow away during the night. I was sure somebody would have use for them.

As before, Buster enjoyed chasing the birds around the pier. I was glad to see him get some exercise. I noticed he gave the guard dog a wide berth.

Two minivans arrived and began unloading passengers and purchases. Based on the number of tote bags that were unloaded, Vee and her crew had been busy. Marta and I carried pizza boxes and salads back to *The Lady Anne*. Buster suddenly quit chasing birds, opting to follow us and the pizza aroma instead. "Smart dog," I said with a chuckle.

The rest of the women carried everything else, taking most of it to *The Aquaholic*. If I'd been thinking, I would have had them take the cardboard moving boxes along on their shopping outing. That way they wouldn't have had to purchase all of those totes. Oh well, the totes were brightly colored and appeared pretty sturdy. I knew they would make great grocery bags later, especially at the Costco in Puerto Rico.

When everyone was aboard *The Lady Anne*, I asked, "What's in all of those totes?"

Vee waited to see if any of the other women would answer, and when they didn't speak up, she did. "We normally wear really cute, nautical uniforms. You'd like them, but we're usually in more enclosed areas aboard luxury yachts."

Having seen these women in their party attire made me fairly certain their uniforms were just as flattering.

Vee continued, "This gig is going to entail a lot more offshore sailing than we packed for. Most of our purchases are practical, like fleeces, water-repellent layers, offshore rain gear, warm hats and gloves, extra footwear, extra sunscreen, lip balm, etcetera."

Some of us ate pizza and salad. Some of us ate pizza topping atop salad. I found it slightly amusing that Dreamgirl, Candy, and Bev scraped off the pizza topping and set the bread part aside.

Those three women wasted more pizza than they ate, but I guessed they didn't keep their gorgeous figures by eating a lot of bread.

Marta, on the other hand, probably ate as much pizza as I did, crust and all. I equated her solid body to her workouts.

"Are there any dietary restrictions I should be aware of on the upcoming passage to Hawaii?" I asked.

Marta was closest to me and the pizzas. She answered first. "If I maintain my workouts at sea, which I plan to do, I can eat almost everything." A second later she added, "I don't like creamed corn."

I wondered how she would work out at sea; after all, we wouldn't be on a cruise ship with a fitness room and a walking track, but I didn't say anything.

Bev looked back and forth between Candy and Dreamgirl and then looked at me. "The three of us eat mostly fresh fruit and veggies and a little lean protein. We try and avoid fried foods, baked desserts like cake or cookies, or heavily processed foods like cereal, bread, cheese, hot dogs, bacon, and sausage."

"I probably ate more cheese tonight than I've had all month," Candy said. She looked at Elouise and quickly added, "But the pizza was really good."

"I usually grill quite a bit, especially dinner, when anchored. Will that be okay?" I asked.

"Grilled vegetables, chicken, fish, and occasional red meat are okay. A grilled cheese sandwich is definitely not okay," Bev replied.

"That just reminded me of a sailing joke." I chuckled and grinned.

"Please tell it," Bev said.

"Yes," Dreamgirl added. "Especially if it's a dirty sailing joke."

Dreamgirl's comment surprised me. Most women didn't care all that much for dirty jokes. I suspected she was flirting. Maybe she had noticed me staring at her, thinking about my past lover. As Tracy and Pat could attest, I told a lot of sailing jokes, but mainly the kind that wouldn't get complaints from the sailing students or get me fired.

"Yes, please tell us a joke," Candy pleaded. "All we ever hear are Vee's jokes."

I waited for Elouise and Marta to get another slice of pizza and then I told my joke.

"A group of sailors went to a brothel after months at sea. All of his shipmates were asking for an attractive woman and a bottle of champagne. One sailor said he wanted a very unattractive woman and a grilled cheese sandwich. The sailor in line behind him overheard his request and asked, 'Why would you ask for an unattractive woman and a grilled cheese sandwich? Aren't you horny?' The sailor replied, 'I'm not horny, I'm homesick.'"

There was a slight delay and then everybody started laughing. I was happy my joke had been well received.

"Okay, it's my turn," Vee said, rising up.

"You're not going to tell that good news-bad news joke, are you? You know that men don't like it," Candy said, sounding slightly annoyed.

Vee looked at her and smiled.

"Yes, she is," Bev said. Then looking at me she added, "Don't get mad when she tells this."

Intrigued, I replied, "I can dish them out and I can take them. Go ahead, Vee, tell your joke."

She did.

"The husband came home from work and his wife said, 'I've got some news. It will either be the greatest news you've ever heard or it will be the worst news you've ever heard.' The husband asked what her news was. The wife replied, 'Of all of your friends, you have the biggest penis.'"

I had never heard that one, and I wasn't immediately sure if it was funny or not. It was sort of funny, maybe. I smiled and looked from woman to woman. They were watching for my reaction.

Candy looked at Vee and said, "I told you men don't like it."

Finally I shook my head and laughed. "That's funny," I said.

Dreamgirl and I cleaned up the dishes and put away the leftovers. We all then walked over to *The Aquaholic* to wait for our shipmates to arrive from the airport. Buster came along.

To pass the time, Candy and Bev sorted their earlier purchases, cutting the price tags off and making separate piles.

None of us were certain what the cabin assignments would be so Candy neatly folded and stacked their new purchases on the salon table. I wondered if Angie would pick the cabin she had been victimized in, but I kept my thoughts to myself.

I asked Vee if she wanted to wash all of their new clothing before wearing it. She looked surprised; in fact they all did. I don't believe she, or any of them, had thought that was an option.

I offered to run *The Lady Anne's* washing machine, but

Elouise offered to take the laundry to their hotel and let hotel services wash, dry, and fold everything, and everyone accepted. They repacked their washable purchases back in the totes to take to the hotel when they returned there for the night. I was secretly glad since using the washing machine would have put a lot of wastewater into *The Lady Anne's* holding tanks.

Vee, Bev, Dreamgirl, and I were looking at a large chart covering the waters all the way to the Panama Canal when I got a text from Pat.

They had landed in Bermuda but anticipated a delay getting their firearms secured and not to expect them for another hour or two.

Upon hearing that, Elouise, Vee, and the others decided to call it a night. Marta gathered up the totes and away they went. Candy smiled and told me she expected another joke sometime.

"No problem," I said, smiling back.

Buster and I went back to *The Lady Anne*. The dog seemed to know something was up. He'd lie down for a while and then jump up and prance back and forth before lying down again.

I debated feeding the seagulls the discarded pizza crusts. I finally decided it would be wrong to draw the birds in with food scraps, only to have Buster chase them away.

I was resting in the cockpit, enjoying a cold local pale ale, when the guard dog started barking.

Pat and Tracy had found the pier but the guard didn't

know them. He waved me over. I told Buster to stay and went and explained the situation and who Tracy and Pat were.

After he let them pass, Tracy kissed me passionately. So did Pat, just as passionately. Tracy's kiss was a little more invitational while Pat's was more romantic, but both kisses were appreciated. I had really missed them.

Pat was wearing black pants and a red Honolulu zippered hoodie—not overly flattering but very functional for traveling. Tracy's hair might have been a little shorter, but I wasn't sure so I didn't comment. She was wearing a short Hawaiian dress that was white with blue leaves.

I noticed the guard grinned at me and then managed another peek at Tracy's legs. He probably wondered how I managed to have a veritable harem of beautiful women around.

"Where's everyone else?" I asked, looking down the deserted pier.

Pat answered. "Charles and the others have gone to the hotel."

"It's just us tonight," Tracy added. "We want to sleep aboard with you."

I was sure the guard was smiling at that comment but his head was turned, like he was pretending to ignore us.

"Is this all of your stuff?" I asked, glancing at a collection of wheeled carry-ons and duffel bags.

Pat nodded.

I retrieved Chet's loaned dock cart and helped them move their luggage to *The Lady Anne*. Buster was so glad to see

Tracy, he wagged and wiggled so hard I hoped he wouldn't pee himself.

Buster's welcome gave Pat a moment to explain their late arrival. After landing in Bermuda, they had to wait behind the passengers of some other private planes.

Then when it was their turn, the agents who secured firearms were all on break so they had to wait for them to return.

She then opened her carry-on bag and removed two plastic bags, keeping one and handing one to Tracy. Buster stopped climbing on Tracy and sat patiently, watching and waiting.

The bags contained flowers, or more accurately, Hawaiian leis. They were very fragrant. Pat placed her lei around my neck, kissed me, and said, "Aloha. I missed you." The flowers were purple and white. It was very pretty.

Tracy was next. She got up, kissed me, placed her lei—a yellow one—around my neck, and kissed me again. She grinned and then whispered in my ear, "If you want to get lei'd later, let me know. Get it, get laid?"

I got it.

"She didn't waste time propositioning you, did she?" Pat asked, looking slightly bemused.

"You could hear that?" Tracy asked, pulling away and looking guilty.

"You need to learn to whisper quieter."

"Is it coincidence that your leis are the same colors as the flowers I bought you the first night I arrived in St. Thomas?" I asked. "Is that your surprise?"

"I'm impressed you remembered, but that's not our surprise," Pat replied, grinning.

"We took a resort course and now we know how to scuba dive," Tracy exclaimed proudly.

"We're not fully certified scuba divers, but we know enough to be dangerous," Pat said. "If we have to dive again, we'll be ready. We even have our own masks now."

They looked happy.

"What's with the toilets?" Tracy asked, gesturing toward the portables on the dock.

"Until we can dump or pump our holding tanks, the heads are for emergency purposes only."

"What about showers?" Pat asked, looking around.

"I've been using a solar shower over there, between the toilets." I pointed. "But I'm sure that Elouise would let you shower in her room."

Pat and Tracy exchanged glances, eyebrows raised.

"Who's Elouise?" Pat asked.

CHAPTER 29

The next morning found me topside. I had awakened first, alone in my berth, and took Buster for a walk on the pier.

Based on Tracy's suggestive comments last night, I was sure she would make her way to my cabin. I waited for a knock on the door that never came. I guessed the long day's travel had worn her out. Still, it was very unusual for Tracy to miss an opportunity for sex, especially after the time apart. As for me, being in such close proximity to Dreamgirl and the others, I would have been easy to arouse.

Pat came topside first, followed a few minutes later by Tracy. They went to the toilets together and then came back aboard and quickly washed their hands.

"How long do we have to use those gross toilets?" Tracy asked.

I raised my palms and shrugged.

"Since we're all here in Bermuda now, what's the plan?" Pat asked.

I'd been thinking about that a lot over the past weeks.

I pulled out the chart I had marked up previously and opened it on the salon table. "It's almost nine hundred nautical miles from here to Puerto Rico through open water," I said, tracing my penciled course line with a finger. "There are no landfalls on the way unless we make a substantial course change to the west. Since that's an awfully long shakedown cruise, I believe we should take the boats out for four or five hours every day before we start and make sure that all systems are working."

"That's smart," Pat said. "I agree."

"Me too," echoed Tracy.

"That gives us actual sailing conditions to make sure everything is working. Only sailing for a half day would give Chet and his men time to repair any problems. It would also give us time to refuel, provision, and shop for whatever we think we'll need between here and Puerto Rico."

"There's a Costco in Puerto Rico," Pat said, smiling.

"Not Costco again," Tracy moaned, then started laughing.

"Yes, Costco again," Pat said, sounding serious. "I looked at Reid's plotted course and distance calculations. We've got easy ports between here and the canal. Once we transit the canal, it's a long way to Hawaii, and the Galapagos don't offer much in the way of services."

"How far is a *long way*?" Tracy asked.

Pat looked at me, so I answered. "From the canal to the Galapagos is about nine hundred nautical miles."

"About the same as from here to Puerto Rico?" Tracy confirmed.

"Yes, but that's the easy part. From there to Hawaii is over four thousand nautical miles."

"If we make two-hundred-mile days, that's twenty straight days," Pat added, doing the simple math in her head.

"Correct, but remember that two-hundred-mile days require sailing nonstop and assumes the weather conditions remain favorable. In the event we run into problems out in the middle of the Pacific, we'll need to be prepared for any repairs and any contingencies, including adequate provisions."

"Haven't all the systems been repaired? Don't we have new compasses? Did you replace the charred sails? Did you—"

I held up my hand, stopping Pat's question marathon. "It's not *The Lady Anne* I'm worried about," I said. "It's *The Aquaholic*. She's a sailing barge, a crewed charter boat designed for parties in protected waters, not ocean crossings."

"But you told me her hulls had been reinforced and her systems upgraded," Pat said.

I nodded. "She should be ready, and if things break on the way to Puerto Rico, we'll get them repaired there"—I smiled—"when we reprovision at Costco."

"Costco it is," Tracy announced.

I was thinking of something clever to say about returning to Costco when the guard dog started barking.

"Does it do that all the time?" Tracy asked, glaring in the dog's direction.

"Think of it as kind of like a doorbell," I replied. "But's it's way better than the first dog they had. That bastard barked at his own shadow."

Tracy and I watched as several people made their way past the guard and walked slowly toward *The Lady Anne.*

Pat ducked below for a minute and returned with the two leis from yesterday. She winked at Tracy and then quickly tossed them around my neck.

CHAPTER 30

Charles was in the lead, escorting Gert by her arm. Elouise followed, holding Mo's arm with one hand and a white paper sack with her other hand. Following closely behind them were Angie and another woman that I guessed was Angie's mom.

"Ahoy. Request permission to come aboard?" Charles called out loudly.

Tracy granted his request and then I offered Mo and Gert a hand to assist them climbing aboard. They were moving a little slowly but were smiling and appeared to be in good spirits.

They were still thin, or else they had purchased Hawaiian shirts that were two sizes too big. Fortunately, their faces didn't look as hollow as before. Gert was holding a white lei, which she promptly placed around my neck. I thanked her. Mo said he was glad to see me again and thanked me for allowing them to come along.

Charles shook my hand, saying he was glad to be back aboard *The Lady Anne*. He was wearing a flowered Hawaiian shirt and was dressed the most casually I had ever seen him.

"What's this?" I asked as he handed me an envelope.

"It's a veterinary certificate for the dog," he answered. "A friend of a friend completed it for me."

I thanked him and slipped it in my pocket.

Next was Angie. She looked happy, wearing a black and green jungle-print dress. She gave me a hug and then placed her blue-and-white flowered lei on top of the others.

Angie's mom was next. "Jane Smith," she said, limply shaking my hand. She then handed me her lei, which had pale orange flowers. I draped it over the other four.

She was slender, about Tracy's height, and had short, straight, unstyled, brown hair. She carried a large brown purse. She was wearing a conservative brown plaid dress that came just below her knees, old woman brown shoes, and a light brown long-sleeve top buttoned at the neck and wrists. I'd guess brown was her favorite color. I wondered what her sailing outfits would look like.

I saw no resemblance to Angie. I also didn't see any obvious indication that she didn't like Pat.

Jane smiled and moved out of the way when Tracy came over and said, "Five leis by five women in twelve hours. I'm impressed."

"Were those leis your idea?" I asked, smiling.

"I thought it was very clever," she replied.

"I did too," Pat added.

"Tracy said it would make you smile," Angie chimed.

"I'm impressed you could get lei'd three times in such quick succession and still be standing," Charles said with a laugh.

Jane didn't say anything. Her face reflected her distaste at the suggestive nature of Tracy's idea. Plain and prude flashed through my mind. I reminded myself to be careful with any jokes when she was in earshot. A second thought was that maybe Jane's distaste had nothing to do with the leis but might have been her close proximity to Pat. I let it go.

"Well, thank you all very much," I said. "It's nice to meet you, Jane, and it's great to have the rest of you back."

Buster had jumped off of the boat and was intently sniffing the paper bag Elouise had placed on the pier.

She picked up the bag and handed it to me. As if reading my mind, she said, "It's breakfast for the three of you, courtesy of the hotel."

Pat thanked her and placed the bag out of Buster's reach.

Just then, the guard dog barked again.

We all looked toward the guard. I saw Chet and Marta, and what looked like four naval officers.

But as they got closer, I could see it was Vee, Bev, Candy, and Dreamgirl, all wearing nautical white uniforms complete with captain's hats, white with a black brim and anchor design. I wondered if they happened to have bought them from Tommy Kraft's store.

They wore white shirts and ironed white slacks. I did notice that Vee and Bev had four-stripe epaulets on their shoulders while Candy and Dreamgirl's epaulets had only one stripe. That jibed with Vee and Bev having their captain's license.

Even their belts were the same, sporting a nautical flag design. I could tell the flags weren't in alphabetical order but I would have had to really examine one to see what the flags said.

I silently chuckled, thinking that offering to read a woman's belt might be quite an icebreaker.

They made their way aboard and I introduced everyone. Charles's expression betrayed the fact that he had not known how attractive the female crew was that he had hired. He was too much of a gentleman to stare, but I saw him discreetly admiring them, especially Dreamgirl.

Her white blouse was too tight to contain her breasts, literally bursting at the seams. Chet was deliberately looking away, but I noticed Mo was staring. Even Pat and Tracy had done a double take.

"Dreamgirl." Charles smiled. "Is that one word or two?"

"One word," she replied, smiling right back at him.

"Mr. Williams, it's an honor to meet you." Vee cut in between them, shaking his hand.

"No, the honor is mine, Captain Veronica Kline," Charles said.

"Call me Vee."

"Marta, was it? Is she with you?" Charles asked, looking at

Marta, who was wearing spandex and another neon sports bra, not a nautical white uniform.

Vee nodded.

"But didn't I hire two captains and two female crew?"

Bev responded, "Marta doesn't sail much, but we're a team so we cover her costs."

"We won't leave the dock without her," Candy echoed.

Charles looked Marta up and down. He nodded slightly. I could see he was impressed by her physique. "Then the least I can do is to cover her expenses." Charles added, "I insist."

Angie wanted to show her mom her boat so most everyone went over to *The Aquaholic*.

Elouise's bag contained three coffees, three juices, six ham and egg biscuit sandwiches, and three fruit pastries.

While I enjoyed a breakfast sandwich, Tracy said, "Pat and I will have a lot of competition with those five aboard."

"Candy and Dreamgirl. Where did they get those names?" Pat said.

"I'll bet you a boat her passport doesn't say Dreamgirl," Tracy added.

While finishing my breakfast, I explained. "Candy is what she goes by. Her real name is Candace Glover. I don't know Dreamgirl's real name, but, Tracy, you're absolutely right; that can't be the name on her passport."

Tracy and Pat looked at each other but didn't say anything right away. Finally Tracy muttered, "Those breasts can't be real either, and she colors her hair."

"So you've been alone with that crew these last few days?" Pat said. "And where have they been sleeping?"

"Relax," I said, putting down my juice and moving in between them. "They've been staying at the hotel." I put an arm around each of them. "You two have absolutely nothing to worry about. You're kryptonite, remember?"

Tracy laughed and kissed me. She tasted like coffee. Pat kissed me as well. She tasted like pastry.

About that time, I heard Charles clear his throat. I hadn't heard him return to *The Lady Anne,* but it was obvious that he and all of the others with him had been close enough to see me kiss both Tracy and then Pat.

I figured I was probably blushing but turned to face them anyway, and said, "Elouise, thanks for the breakfast. It was delicious."

Then I added, "Now that we're all here, let's go sailing."

CHAPTER 31

Since *The Aquaholic's* first stop would have to be the fuel dock, Chet offered to take the lead.

I had read that Bermuda had over three hundred ship-wrecks. I was fine with Chet taking point. I had no desire to be number three hundred and one. I did want to go with *The Aquaholic*, at least as far as the fuel dock. That was fine with Angie.

Chet, Angie, her mom, Captain Vee, Candy, Dreamgirl, Elouise, and I went to *The Aquaholic*. That left Tracy, Pat, Charles, Mo, Gert, and Captain Bev with *The Lady Anne*. Chet told Tracy to follow right behind him. She nodded.

Angie took the helm while Chet directed her. Jane and Elouise stayed out of the way while the rest of us stood by the dock lines and waited. Once underway, we were shadowed by *The Lady Anne* the whole way.

Angie docked *The Aquaholic* near the last fuel pump. Vee, Chet, and I secured her. Out of habit, I glanced at Vee's knot. It was a cleat hitch and tied properly. I noticed *The Lady Anne* kept her distance and slowly circled, waiting.

Angie was showing the other women the process for fueling the catamaran so Chet and I just stayed on the dock, out of the way. I can't speak for him, but I was enjoying the view.

A voice behind me made me jump. "Aren't you that young man who got into a fight a few weeks ago?"

An older man was standing behind me. I didn't recognize him. He pointed toward a woman, an elderly one, who was fueling a sailboat. The name on the hull was *Mockingbird*. It was probably a forty footer, maybe forty-five. I didn't recognize her or the boat. She waved.

"Excuse me?" I replied.

"I'm sure it's you," the old man said. "And where are the two women that were throwing rocks?"

That did it. Now I knew who he was, sort of. I offered him my hand and said, "You're the couple that showed your video to the police."

He smiled, nodded, and introduced himself. "Bob Johnson, Sarasota, Florida. And that's my wife, Fern." As he pointed at her, she waved again.

"I want you to know that the video you took saved my ass."

"Who were those guys?" he asked, finally letting go of my hand.

"Disgruntled ex-employees."

"The one you stabbed never got up, did he?"

I shook my head no.

"Did the cops catch the other one? The runner?" He looked and sounded very concerned.

"Not yet," I replied. I noticed Chet had moved slightly away but was listening intently.

"And the rock-throwing women?"

"They're both fine. In fact, they're out there circling while we fuel this cat." I pointed at *The Lady Anne,* but she was too far away for him to make out Tracy or Pat.

"Are you leaving Bermuda today?" he asked.

"Probably in a couple of days," I answered. "How about you?"

"We're crossing to North Africa with a stop in the Azores. We're ready to go and now just waiting for a favorable weather window. Topping off the fuel tanks is the last thing on today's list. Fern and I want to be ready to go at a moment's notice."

Angie had finished fueling and Elouise had gone to pay the bill. Chet slowly went over to his dock line. I figured it was time to wrap up.

"It looks like we're done here, but I want to thank you and your wife again for coming forward with your video."

Bob smiled and I continued, "Saying thank you seems inadequate. Your video got us exonerated. Without it, the three of us might have been in a heap of trouble."

"Anytime," he said, shaking my hand again. Then he walked back to his boat.

I helped Chet and Dreamgirl cast off *The Aquaholic* and Angie headed us toward the channel, following Chet's directions. Almost immediately, *The Lady Anne* fell in behind us.

CHAPTER 32

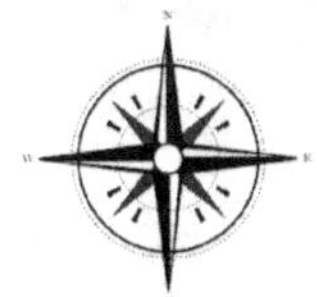

We followed the channel through the reef and headed toward open water. The wind was favorable so we hauled out the sails, shut down the engines, and watched as *The Lady Anne* got further behind us.

The catamaran was fast. Angie surrendered the helm to Captain Vee. As she called out trim adjustments, it was obvious she knew what she was doing.

Candy and Dreamgirl had no issues with the winches and, after a bit of fine-tuning, coaxed even more speed from *The Aquaholic*.

"Hey, where are you guys going so fast?" Tracy called over the radio.

"Somebody needs a radio lesson," Vee said. Her smile betrayed the sternness in her tone.

Using proper radio procedures, we switched to a working channel and told *The Lady Anne* our plan was to go twelve miles offshore and then dump our holding tanks.

By the time she rendezvoused with us, Angie had completed emptying the holding tanks.

Vee let Candy and Dreamgirl take the helm and execute a few sailing maneuvers while we waited for *The Lady Anne* to finish macerating her tanks.

Chet and I looked around, checking fittings and upgrades. No problems were evident. I directed Vee to slam our twin hulls through *The Lady Anne's* wake while Chet and I went below to check the hull's reinforcements.

There were no vibrations or signs of stress. We were both pleased and shortly returned topside.

We sailed for another hour and then headed back. Candy steered with Chet seated next to her. The rest of us just enjoyed the sail.

We returned to our pier and secured the vessels. There was nothing to do to either vessel repair wise so I called a quick meeting.

"Since the possibility exists that crews may get switched several times between here and Hawaii, I propose we all go shopping."

"Shopping for what?" Tracy asked.

"Shopping for a complete set of clothing and toiletries to last three days. Each of us should make a spare bag and stow it onboard the other vessel."

"Great idea," Charles added. "I was thinking the exact same thing."

"So was I," Pat echoed.

During our shopping excursion, Charles announced he would buy our last night's dinner in Bermuda. He obviously had a plan since he didn't ask, he told us.

Angie, walking next to me, said, "Before we go, I'd really like to make Tracy something special."

I nodded. "So would I. If Charles is covering our last night, and since we'll probably leave in a couple of days, then let's plan to cook tomorrow night. How about if I make dinner and you make dessert?"

She quickly agreed, saying she had the perfect dessert. "That will give me time to get what I need."

"Me too," I added. "We can go shopping together."

"What are you going to cook?" she asked.

I hadn't thought that far ahead, but since Tracy was only ten feet away, I motioned her over and asked what she wanted for a thank-you dinner.

"You know what I'm really missing?" she purred.

Before I could answer, she said, "Chili dogs."

I wasn't expecting that. Vee had stopped walking to take a selfie so I asked her, "Will you and the others eat a chili dog?"

Her expression answered my question.

"That's what Tracy wants for a special dinner," I said apologetically.

"Can you at least make turkey chili?" Vee asked.

"I have a great recipe," I replied, smiling.

After Vee walked away to tell Candy, Bev, and Dreamgirl they'd be eating turkey chili dogs tomorrow night, Angie whispered, "A chili dog is the last thing I would have expected her to want for a special dinner."

"She's nothing if not unpredictable."

CHAPTER 33

We had another productive day on the water. Both boats were running really well. I didn't anticipate any problems. If something minor did go wrong and we were unable to repair it while underway, it could wait until landfall in Puerto Rico.

Pat expressed her concern about the mismatch in speed. Much to their chagrin, Vee and Angie agreed to reef *The Aquaholic's* mainsail, at least for a little.

Angie and I excused ourselves and went grocery shopping. I used our time alone to ask if her mom was sideways with Pat. By the look in her eyes, I knew I had hit a nerve.

"Bonnie, Ashley, and Donna all told me how sorry they were for what Captain Rick did to me. I have no memory between Oscar's death and waking up in my cabin."

That was good. She didn't remember the repeated assaults.

"I remember you being there and then going to get Bonnie. Thank you for taking care of me and being there when I woke up."

I nodded and then mentioned her mom and Pat again. She sniffled.

"I called Mom before we reached Bermuda and told her Oscar had been killed but that I was okay." I did remember her using *The Lady Anne's* satellite phone a few times.

"Anyway," she continued, sniffling again, "Mom saw the news story that mentioned my name and the names of the other women who had been sexually assaulted."

I grimaced, thinking my idea to go on the offensive with reporter Brenda had backfired.

"When I told Mom everything that had happened, she was furious with Captain Pat that she had Captain Rick at her mercy and let him go. . . Go on to do what he did."

"Is she mad at me and Tracy too? After all, it was a committee decision."

She wiped her runny nose and then moved closer and lowered her voice. "If you would have known what that monster was going to do, you obviously would have done something differently."

She was right. I would have pushed him into the water and watched the sharks feed.

"But you didn't know and you made a decision and it was the wrong one. I'm not mad at any of you. I'm thankful you rescued me and the others. Give my mom time; she'll get over it."

No more was said. We finished our shopping and returned to the boats. She then went aboard *The Aquaholic* to make her dessert. I cooked onboard *The Lady Anne*. We agreed to serve drinks, appetizers, and dinner onboard *The Lady Anne* and dessert on Angie's boat.

Cocktail hour found everyone in good spirits.

Vee and her crew had changed from their uniforms back to their party dresses. Except Marta, who seemed happy wearing spandex and a sports bra.

I noticed Angie, Pat, and Tracy changed clothes when they saw what Vee was wearing. So did Charles—from his sailing clothes to slacks and a sports jacket. Tiring of rum, I decided to make margaritas. I had a really good recipe: one part good tequila, one part Grand Marnier, one part sweet and sour, and one-half part lime juice—all blended with crushed ice.

Even with plastic glasses and unsalted rims, the margaritas were a hit. As expected, Candy, Bev, and Dreamgirl passed on the alcohol. "Wasted calories," as Candy bluntly put it.

Appetizers were skewers of blackened shrimp. They were a hit too.

Dinner got a lot of laughs when I announced it was self-service chili dogs. I had made my award-winning spicy beef chili and also made a pot of black bean turkey chili. I had three varieties of hot dogs, including kosher hot dogs for Mo. Toppings consisted of shredded cheddar cheese and diced green onions.

After people started eating, the laughs turned to praise.

Everyone loved the chili. Marta especially enjoyed the spicy chili, quickly helping herself to seconds. My beef chili was hotter than normal, probably due to buying unknown varieties of hot peppers. I for one was sweating but kept eating. Thankfully the margaritas helped cut the heat.

Marta stood up and looking directly at me, proposed a toast. "There are three things you've got to do if you're a real woman."

She paused and I waited, along with everyone else, for what could possibly be next.

Marta raised her chili dog to me and continued, "Roll your own tampons. Kickstart your own vibrator. And eat three bowls of Reid's chili."

I took that as a compliment and started laughing. Everyone laughed. Surprisingly, even Jane laughed. That was the first time I saw that she had a sense of humor. That also confirmed that Angie might have been right. Jane wasn't mad at me. She was wrong to blame Pat alone for what happened to her daughter. If I got the chance, I'd make sure she understood that.

Tracy laughed so hard I thought she was going to be sick. Judging by Dreamgirl's and Candy's chortling, they had never heard that before either.

I helped myself to another chili dog and made a point to sit by Jane. I hadn't talked to her very much and wanted to learn a little about her. I told myself not to bring up Angie's ordeal, unless she did first.

"Thanks for making the turkey chili mild," she told me. "Spicy food doesn't agree with me."

"First time to Bermuda?" I asked.

"Yes. I know all about it but it's wonderful to finally be able to see it."

"Are you a travel agent?" I asked.

"No, no, not at all. I just have a voracious appetite for learning."

Angie spoke up. "Reid, you don't know my mom's background. She's a retired museum curator and a former *Jeopardy* champion."

"*Jeopardy*? I'm impressed. That show is really hard," I confided.

"In fact, my mom used some of her winnings to buy Oscar and me *The Aquaholic*."

"Geography is a cinch category, so if you're going to compete on *Jeopardy*, you better know every country, their borders, their capitals, all rivers, lakes, mountains, all islands, and past and present rulers."

"What's a cinch category?" I asked.

"Categories that are highly likely to come up, like geography, history, politics, science, music, and literature."

"Mom, tell him something about Bermuda," Angie said.

Jane took a breath, glanced to the left, refocused on me, and then said, "Bermuda is a self-governing British Overseas Territory founded in 1609 by survivors of an English shipwreck. It is located only two hours flying time from the United States. The major language is English and the two forms of currency are the Bermuda dollar and the US dollar, which are currently exchanged at par."

She drew another breath and continued, "Bermuda has a subtropical climate. Contrary to popular belief, it is not a Caribbean island, the white roofs catch rainwater, and Bermuda has more golf courses per capita than any other country in the world. Its capital is Hamilton and the town of Saint George is over four hundred years old."

I was impressed and I told her so. She smiled. So did Angie.

"If you're going to play on *Jeopardy*, you have to know everything your competitors know, but you have to be faster than they are." Then she added, "It helps to find the daily doubles, and if you're really lucky, final jeopardy will be a runaway, meaning you can't be caught, regardless of wagers."

I thought of a joke I heard a comedian use once so I told Jane that I knew every capital.

"What's the capital of Liechtenstein?" Jane asked. Her expression betrayed her belief that I would probably not know the answer.

I looked her straight in the face and succinctly answered, "*L*." She and Angie paused for a second and then started laughing.

"It's really Vaduz and your answer would not have been accepted, but that's pretty funny," Jane said.

After a little more light laughter, Jane said, "Okay, now I have a joke."

Intrigued as to what kind of joke she would tell, I said, "Fire away."

She nervously glanced around and, satisfied nobody but me and Angie were listening, told her joke. "What do you get when you cross an insomniac, an agnostic, and a dyslexic?"

I had no idea. I was positive I had never heard that one before and those weren't words I bandied about as easily as she had. Almost immediately I shook my head no and turned my palms up.

She smiled and said, "A person who lies awake all night and contemplates the existence of . . . dog."

That made me laugh. I knew I would never remember it, but the more I thought about it, the funnier it got. It was also very politically incorrect in these crazy times and it made me look at Jane a little differently. She might not be as uptight as I figured. And hopefully Angie had been right and her mom would get over her issues with Pat in time.

I could see she was pleased I had understood and enjoyed it.

We finished eating, cleaned up the galley, and then followed Angie over to *The Aquaholic*. I was pretty full but anxious to see what Angie had made with only a handful of ingredients. For no reason, I brought along my trumpet.

On the way over, Dreamgirl, Bev, and Candy told me my turkey chili was the best ever and asked if I would mind sharing my recipe. I told them I made it from memory but I'd be happy to write down the ingredients.

Once aboard *The Aquaholic*, after Tracy had taken her seat, Angie announced she had something to say.

"On behalf of myself, Mo, Gert, Reid, Pat, and several others that aren't here right now, I want to thank Tracy. What she did saved our lives. I am eternally grateful."

Those of us who had witnessed Tracy's selfless act broke into spontaneous applause. I noticed Charles had a questioning look, but he applauded as well.

Vee, Candy, Dreamgirl, Bev, and Marta didn't clap, but they did exchange questioning glances.

Then Angie excused herself for a moment, beckoning me to follow.

"I saw you brought your trumpet. Do you know 'For She's a Jolly Good Fellow'?" she asked quietly.

I nodded.

"Then go get ready," she whispered as she opened the fridge. "You'll know when."

I did as instructed and waited off to the side.

Angie entered the salon, carrying a large cake with a single burning candle. She nodded at me and I began playing.

After Tracy blew out the candle to more applause, Angie served her cake. It was really something to behold and she patiently waited while several of us took pictures.

Angie had made a two-layer cake from a package mix. She spread the canned frosting really thick. She then arranged KIT KAT bars around the outside, like a picket fence, using the thick frosting as glue. The candy bars stood higher than the cake, so she filled in the top depression with toffee pieces and M&M's.

As good as it looked, it tasted even better. More candy than cake really, considering she had mixed more M&M's in the frosting between the layers. Bev, Candy, and Dreamgirl shared a small slice. Vee and the rest of us ate a slice each. Marta ate two. Angie smiled, happy her "Angie food cake," as she called it, was a total success.

CHAPTER 34

After one more day of mixing up the crews and sailing both boats, we decided we were good to go. A quick check of the weather forecast promised good weather.

We refueled both boats on the way back to the pier. As there was no water supply on the pier, Chet had ordered some five-gallon jugs of drinking water. Mo and Pat carefully filled both boats' water tanks. Chet had also arranged for all of the empty propane tanks to be filled. Marta and I carried the full tanks from the pier to their storage lockers and secured them.

Charles took a moment to inform everyone we would have the services of a professional weather routing service all the way to Hawaii. For those of us who didn't know what that was, he explained, "A professional weather routing service has one or more meteorologists that use technology to supply extremely detailed weather information to your vessel, whether it is one hundred miles offshore or one thousand."

"Is that what *The Lady Anne's* weather fax is for?" Pat asked.

"I have a person I use for passages and I've already given him our intended route. I've also provided details about *The Aquaholic* and our crew composition. He will track both vessels around the clock and let us know if we're sailing into any bad weather."

I hadn't thought about hiring one of those companies. Fortunately Charles had us covered again.

"Wouldn't email be easier than fooling around with faxes?" Pat asked.

"Unlike land-based Wi-Fi, satellite email has limits on file size. Given the complexity of a detailed weather map with all of its notations, a fax is just a better tool for the job," Charles replied.

Everyone decided to sleep aboard that evening and get an early start for Puerto Rico in the morning.

Dreamgirl, Angie, and I went shopping for groceries. I took a stack of the folded cardboard moving boxes with us. Elouise decided to accompany the others back to the hotel in case there were any problems checking out. She gave me more than enough money to cover grocery expenses.

When the three of us returned from the market, the others were already onboard, unpacking their clothing and putting away their sailing stuff. All available storage space in the salon was filling with binoculars, VHF radios, PFDs, tethers, chart plotting instruments, flashlights, handheld GPS units, phone chargers, etcetera. Apparently they had not coordinated who would bring what and there was a lot of duplication.

Dreamgirl and Angie started carrying their boxes to *The Aquaholic* but Marta soon took over and finished for them. She then helped Pat and me carry ours to *The Lady Anne*. She told us she needed the exercise. I had purchased enough groceries for thirteen people for ten days and filled every box, plus several cases of drinks, mostly nonalcoholic.

As Pat, Gert, and I put our groceries away, Tracy made an inventory sheet, logging each item onboard *The Lady Anne*. I had forgotten Ensure, instant oatmeal, chewable vitamins, and a few other items, so Chet, Elouise, and Mo made another quick shopping run. I took all of the empty boxes off the boat.

I took a few minutes to call the police detective to tell him we would be leaving Bermuda in the morning. He regretfully informed me there had been no sightings of Pincus. In his professional opinion, Captain Daniel Pincus had fled Bermuda undetected. With my departure, he was moving the case from pending to inactive. I thanked him for his time and effort.

Pat and Tracy weren't thrilled to hear that Pincus had escaped again, but took comfort in the fact that this time tomorrow we would be at sea, miles away, safely onboard *The Lady Anne*.

Charles informed us he had made dinner reservations at a top seafood restaurant. He then went to tell the others. We all got dressed to go to dinner, waiting only for Chet, Mo, and Elouise to return.

A while later, we arrived at a nice restaurant and made our way to the private room Charles had reserved. We were seated at two tables, coincidently choosing to sit with our own ship-mates. Elouise sat with us and Chet sat at the other table, surrounded by women.

I quietly mentioned to my group to go easy on the alcohol or anything fried, greasy, rich, or creamy. When I got ques-tioning looks, I reminded them we'd be at sea for at least five days straight, maybe more, and the first day would seem brutally long if anyone got seasick.

As we enjoyed our fine meal, I asked Charles where he had found Vee. He replied that he had delegated the job of locating an all-female crew to a trusted assistant. With the short deadline and the long passage, he was given only one possible prospect—Captain Veronica Kline and her associates.

His assistant ran a criminal history check, checked to see if Vee's company was registered with the Secretary of State's office, and found no complaints on file with the Better Busi-ness Bureau. He verified that Vee had her captain's license and then interviewed her over the phone. Her references were impeccable. Based on what he found, he concluded she had the background, knowledge and sailing capability Charles and I were looking for. It made his selection really simple.

In between courses, Candy came by and asked me if I would tell her a joke. Everyone at my table stopped chatting and looked at me, waiting.

"What did the fish say when it swam into a rock?"

She said she didn't know so I told her the answer—"Dam." She laughed.

"Don't get him started," Tracy warned.

But it was too late, I was ready to tell some more.

"Why do seagulls fly over the sea?" Nobody at our table said anything. I noticed that even the crew at the other table had stopped talking, apparently overhearing me, and were now waiting for the answer.

I let the suspense build, and then I smiled and said, "Because if they flew over the bay, they'd be bagels."

Mo laughed so hard I feared he would rupture something.

Of course I was ready with another. "What do sea monsters eat for dinner?"

I paused and then finished it. "Fish and ships." Pat groaned, looked down, and shook her head from side to side.

Vee stood up and said, "My turn. This guy walks up to the bartender and orders three martinis."

Before she could continue, there was an outburst from Candy, Dreamgirl, and Bev. Nearly simultaneously, they yelled, "Stop!"

Bev glared. "You cannot tell that joke. Not here, not now, not ever again."

"You know she's right," Candy added. "That joke is worse than your other one."

"If you tell that, none of the men in this room will ever look at you the same again," Dreamgirl confirmed.

Now I really wanted to hear it but Vee sat down, looked

away, and didn't say any more. I made a mental note to have her finish it later, in private.

"Reid," Candy said, looking at me. "Do you have any more jokes?"

"I better stop," I answered, looking at Tracy, who was shaking her head.

"I have a joke," Charles said, taking me by surprise.

"Is it any good?" Tracy asked.

"I like it," he replied.

I wondered what kind of a joke he would tell, but I didn't have to wait very long as he stood up and said, "How do you get twenty sweet, kind, polite, quiet, dainty, elderly women to suddenly cuss and swear like sailors?"

That was another one I hadn't heard. Charles waited a moment and then finished it. "Have number twenty-one yell 'Bingo.'"

I visualized that scene happening in a church basement or gymnasium and started laughing.

Tracy and Pat laughed. Even Jane laughed. Everyone laughed. I repeated it to myself. That was a joke I could use again.

We finished our meal, did a little mingling, and then said our goodbyes to Chet and Elouise. They said they'd be back in the morning to see us off. Chet drove Elouise back to her hotel and the rest of us headed back to the boats.

I was glad it was my last night tied up to the pier. I wasn't going to miss the noise of the generator, the smell of the portable toilets, the chattering of workers, or the barking of the guard dogs.

Charles and I each took a forward cabin. Pat and Tracy had offered Charles the owner's suite but he declined, insisting they continue to use it. Mo and Gert were very happy to return to the crew's quarters.

While Tracy and Gert took Buster for a walk, Charles, Mo, and Pat reviewed each leg of my intended route selection, plotted course lines, and distance and time calculations from Bermuda to Hawaii. Pat took notes and then went over to *The Aquaholic* to make sure Angie and Vee were on the same page.

It had been a frenzied month of preparations and I was feeling a little tired. Charles thanked me for my hard work. I thanked him for footing the bill.

Once everyone was back aboard, we agreed to get up early and then said our goodnights. I made a quick visit to the toilet. When I returned to my cabin, Tracy was already there. She was wearing her new black lingerie and looked sexier than ever.

She posed a bit, bending and stretching provocatively, smiling the whole time. Finally she switched off the light, moved in close, leaned against me, and in a sexy voice asked if I wanted to do a little horizontal swashbuckling.

I suddenly realized I wasn't that tired after all.

CHAPTER 35

The next morning, we got an early start. There was a fax from Ralph Clark, Charles's weather routing person. Ralph's heading to Puerto Rico matched our course line. His fax confirmed we were good to go, weather wise. I wondered if the fax machine running was what Buster had barked at briefly last night.

Chet had been waiting by the guard and joined us once he saw Buster come topside. He didn't have anything to do repair wise. He just wanted to wish us safe travels. He was a nice man and I was glad I had gotten to know him.

I kept expecting Elouise to show. Charles offered to call her but I told him to let her sleep, that she had earned it. I also told him she had done an exceptional job coordinating dozens of payments and handling a myriad of details over the last month. He smiled and told me he'd pass along the compliment.

Tracy and Gert made a simple breakfast: toast spread with peanut butter, some fruit, and coffee. Mo and Gert split an Ensure.

Pat and I made one final inspection above decks. *The Lady Anne* was ready to go. She was sound mechanically and electrically, fully fueled and provisioned, and her crew was experienced and anxious to get started on the long journey that awaited.

Pat confided that this would be her longest trip at sea ever. She looked a little nervous. I made her grin when I said, "Mine too."

"Are the three of us still good?" she asked.

"If by still good, are you asking if I'm still in love with the two sexiest women alive?" I asked, keeping my voice low.

"I don't think we can compete with the women Charles hired. Those women are drop-dead gorgeous."

"Maybe they are." I paused, knowing she was hanging on to hear what I was about to say.

I suddenly pulled her closer and kissed her. As the kiss ended, I whispered, "But they're not kryptonite."

She smiled and squeezed my hand.

I called a final captain's briefing alongside *The Lady Anne*. While I only expected Pat, Angie, Vee, and Bev to attend, everyone else, including Chet, gathered close, forming a semicircle.

"We all know our intended course and we're heading to

Puerto Rico, but first we'll stop at the customs office to check out of Bermuda and retrieve our firearms, ammunition, and flare guns," I said.

Everyone nodded so I continued, "I propose that while we're motorsailing until the wind comes up, we stay close together. Once we have wind, *The Aquaholic* can take point."

Vee grinned, knowing the catamaran was faster.

"Don't get more than a mile or so ahead and keep your radio on and tuned to channel sixteen."

Vee's grin went away.

While I enjoyed competition between sailboats, we had hundreds of miles of open water to cover and I didn't want to get separated by much. I mentioned that we should keep each other in sight just in case anything broke or failed.

I then added, "When we sail through the night, I want us to stay really close. And don't forget to switch on your navigation lights. We should also conduct a radio check at the beginning of every night watch."

"How close is really close?" Bev asked.

"No more than a few hundred yards apart," I answered.

She nodded. So did Angie and Vee.

"My weather router is on the job and today is a good day to leave Bermuda in our wake," Charles added.

"But we'll keep an eye on the clouds, just in case," I continued.

"I also have to insist that PFDs be worn at all times unless you're safely belowdecks or in *The Aquaholic's* main salon."

I told *The Lady Anne's* crew to use the lantern with the red lens in the main salon at night to preserve our night vision. Angie mentioned *The Aquaholic* didn't have one. I silently cursed myself for not having Tommy order one, but it was no big deal.

I added one more thing. "Remember that we'll lose cell phone service around fifteen miles offshore, so once we do, all we will have are the radios."

"Is that statute or nautical?" Bev asked.

"Nautical miles," I replied. "But we might lose service sooner; I don't know for certain."

Pat reminded everyone that *The Lady Anne* did have a satellite phone. I wondered if I should have gotten one from Tommy Kraft for *The Aquaholic*. That would give us communications between vessels, albeit an expensive phone call. I told myself it was an unnecessary expense, that the radios would be perfectly adequate.

I asked if anyone had any questions. Hearing none, I announced last call for the toilets.

Before we disbursed, Pat said, "May we have fair winds and following seas."

"All the way to Hawaii," Charles added.

"All the way to Hawaii," I seconded.

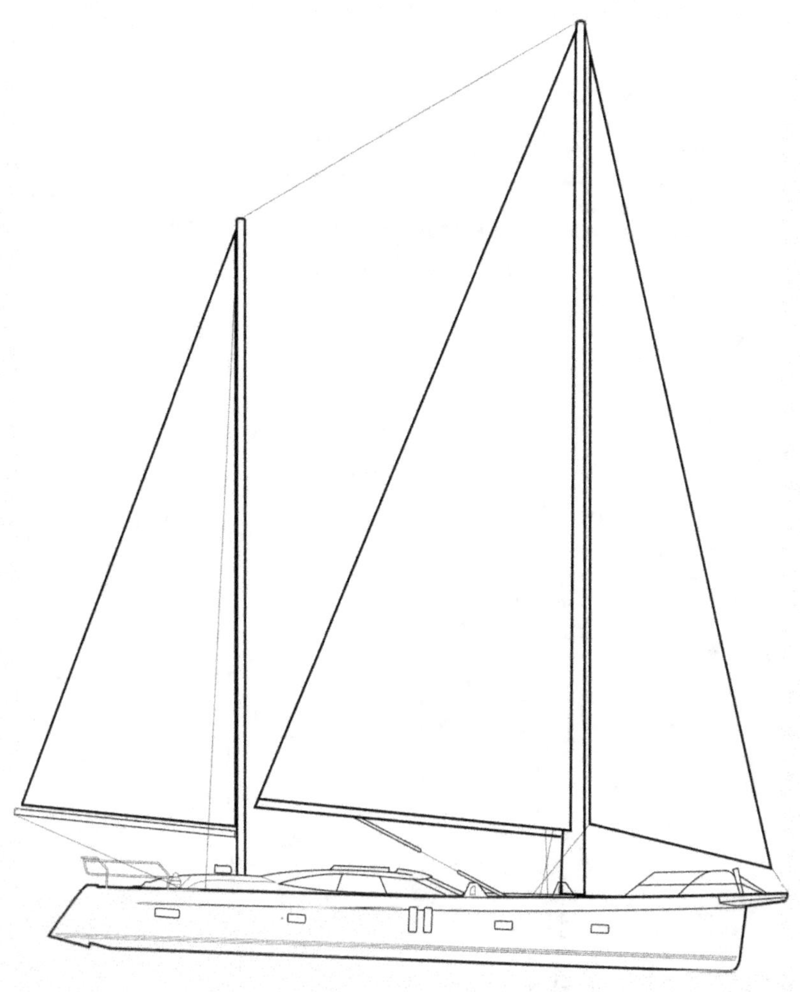

THE LADY ANNE
VESSEL OVERVIEW
NOT TO SCALE

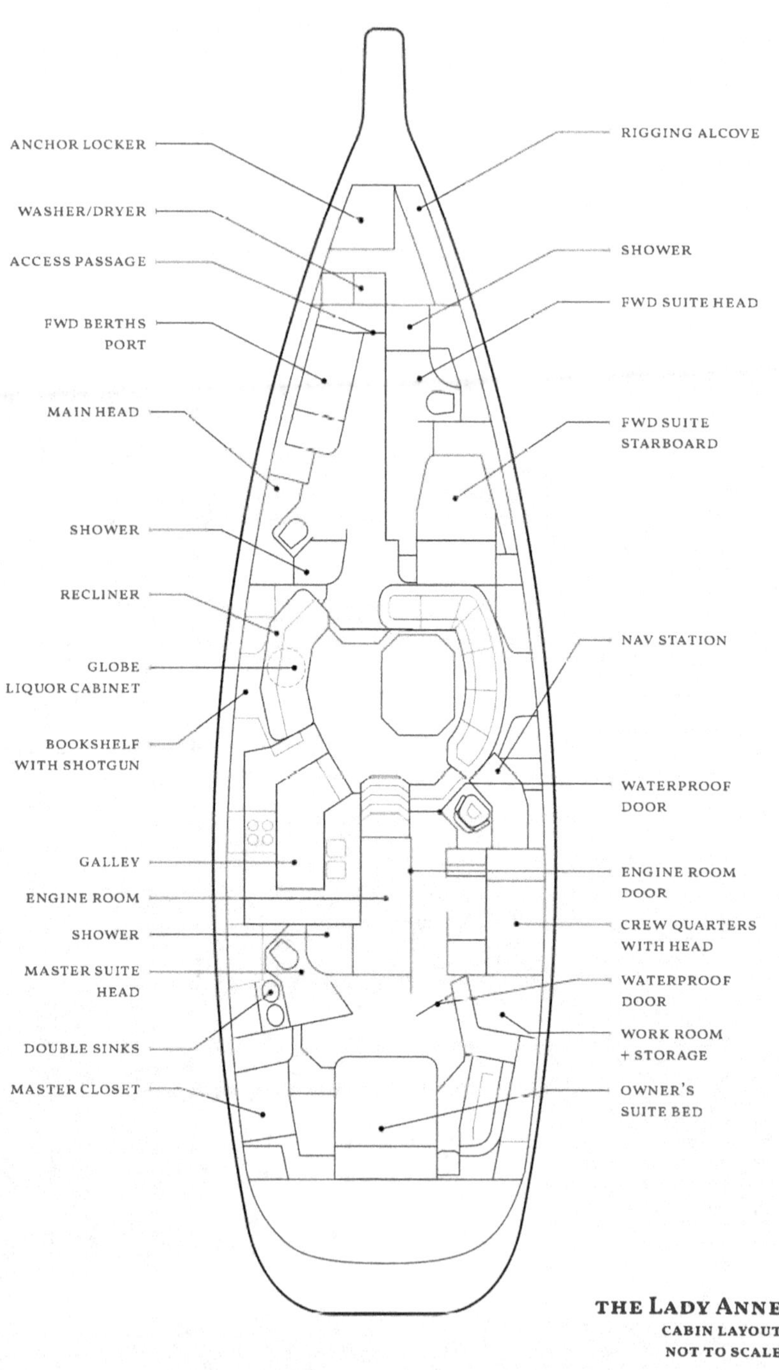

THE LADY ANNE
CABIN LAYOUT
NOT TO SCALE

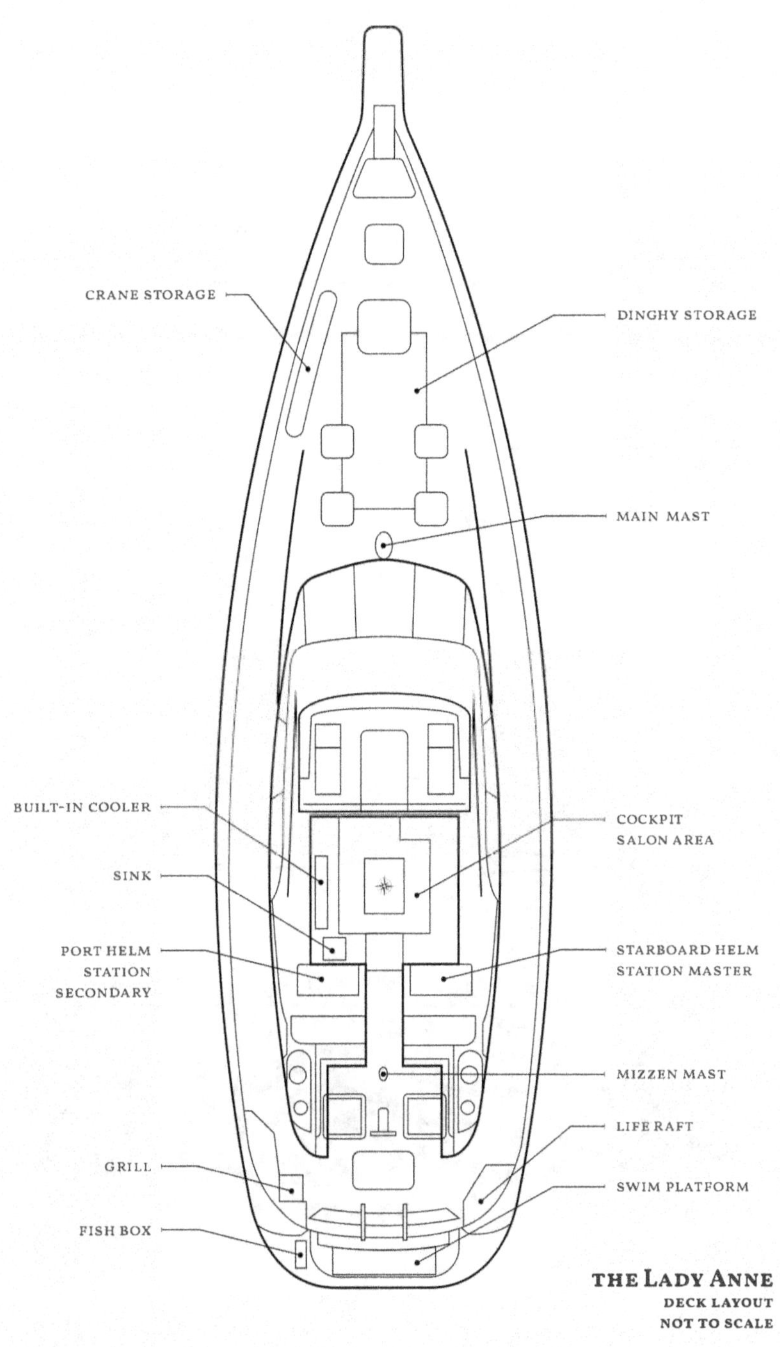

CRANE STORAGE
DINGHY STORAGE
MAIN MAST
BUILT-IN COOLER
COCKPIT
SALON AREA
SINK
PORT HELM
STATION
SECONDARY
STARBOARD HELM
STATION MASTER
MIZZEN MAST
LIFE RAFT
GRILL
SWIM PLATFORM
FISH BOX
THE LADY ANNE
DECK LAYOUT
NOT TO SCALE

THE AQUAHOLIC
VESSEL OVERVIEW
NOT TO SCALE

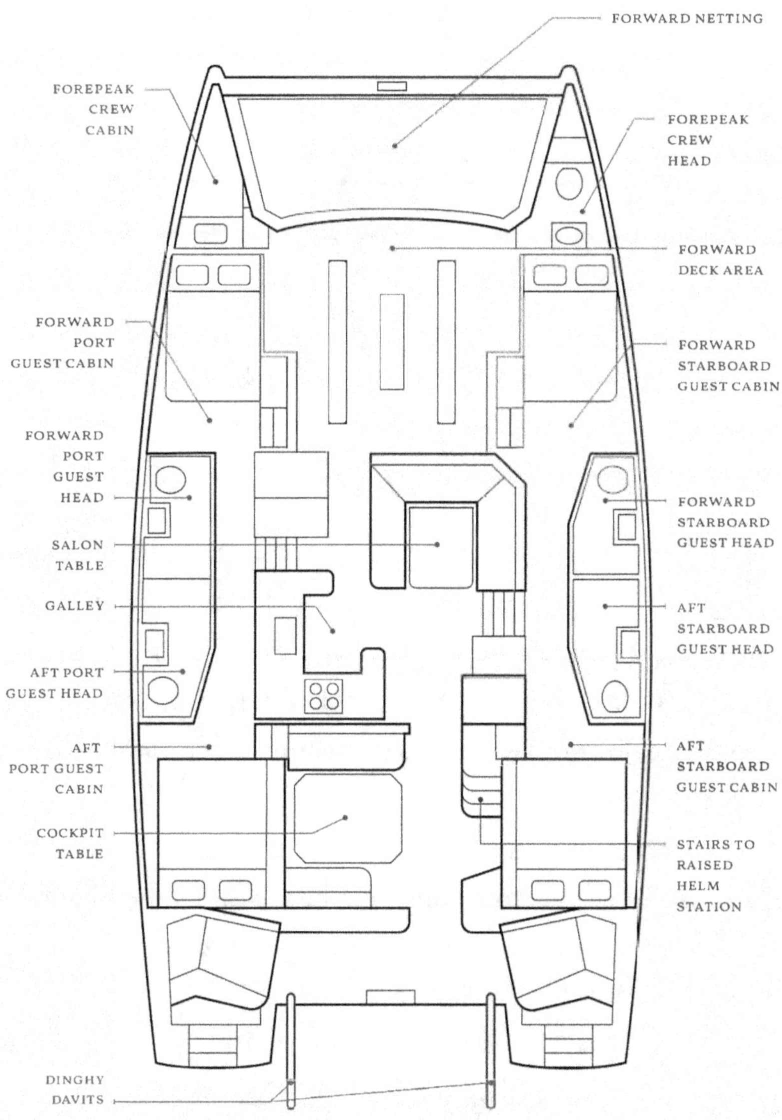

THE Aquaholic
CABIN LAYOUT
NOT TO SCALE

Chet helped us cast off the dock lines and then shouted "Bon voyage" as we motored slowly away from the pier. Tracy took the helm with Charles standing close by.

We didn't put the fenders or the lines away since we would need them when we reached customs. *The Aquaholic* stayed right behind us.

Clearing customs was fast and our firearms were returned with no issues. Before long, we had cleared the channel and were motorsailing. As instructed, *The Aquaholic* took up position on our starboard side and paced us.

Tracy gave Charles the helm and then busied herself raising the pirate flag she had purchased in the Turks and Caicos. Pat was more practical and stowed Bermuda's flag, the fenders, and the dock lines. She also made sure all overhead hatches were closed and dogged shut.

As Ralph Clark predicted, the wind came up, so both vessels hauled out their sails, shut down their engines, and continued on course under wind power alone. *The Aquaholic* quickly pulled away but stayed in sight.

We lost cell phone service twelve nautical miles from Bermuda, a little sooner than I expected. Angie radioed they had no service either.

Tracy and Mo were below, putting *The Lady Anne's* shotgun and Mo's survival rifle away. The flares and flare guns were also returned to their proper place.

The VHF radio's static was replaced by silence. I waited to hear who was speaking but there was no conversation. Mo adjusted the sensitivity but the channel remained in use but silent, like someone was transmitting without speech. He tried changing channels but with the same result.

"Are you guys using the radio?" I hollered to Tracy and Mo, who were still below.

"No," Tracy replied.

With someone trying to transmit, we in effect had no radio. I tried transmitting over the dead signal but *The Aquaholic* didn't respond. I didn't see any other vessels. Had there been any, I would have guessed somebody's radio had accidentally been switched to transmit mode.

A few minutes later, the radar began displaying a bunch of intermittent contacts. The contacts were flashing in and out. First they were there, then they weren't. It then displayed us moving right into a large landmass. That would have been terrifying, especially had it happened at night. The problem was there was nothing ahead but open water.

"What's going on?" Pat asked.

I wasn't exactly sure but replied with the first answer that crossed my mind. "There must be a short in the wiring somewhere. Hopefully it will fix itself."

Pat turned the radar off and then back on but the ghost signals remained.

As if no radio and faulty radar weren't bad enough, Mo hollered up that the GPS coordinates had changed. I went below and confirmed the displayed coordinates were vastly different from where they should be. I tried to find the new coordinates on my chart. They weren't there.

I got a larger chart and was finally able to mark our location. According to the GPS, we were about fifty miles from Myrtle Beach, South Carolina. That was clearly impossible.

Mo stared over my shoulder at the location I had just plotted. He started saying, "No, no no. This can't be."

Pat came below, leaving Charles and Gert at the helm. I showed her the GPS coordinates I had just plotted.

"Do you suppose the aliens have returned?" I asked quietly.

"I hope not," she answered just as quietly.

Mo spoke up. "This isn't an electrical short, this isn't faulty wiring, and this isn't the aliens."

"So what's going on?" I asked. I was getting concerned but tried to mask my anxiousness with calmness.

"Our radio is being jammed, our radar is receiving false

signals, and our GPS system has been spoofed," Mo stated much more calmly than I expected.

"What's spoofed?" Pat asked. I didn't know that term either.

Mo explained, "GPS spoofing occurs when simulated satellite signals are powerful enough to override the real satellite signals, hence tricking the receiver into displaying the wrong coordinates."

"How is this possible?" Pat asked before I could.

"Go get the binoculars," Mo quickly replied. "There's got to be another vessel, or a spy plane, or a drone, or something with sophisticated antennas nearby."

Pat, Mo, and I headed topside, leaving Tracy below. She glanced toward the head and said she'd be right up.

Our presence on deck was greeted by Charles saying he believed something was headed toward us. He pointed forward in the direction of *The Aquaholic*.

The binoculars confirmed a small boat was indeed headed right at us. Judging by their wake, they were coming pretty fast.

I saw Tracy appear at the hatch and told her to go back below and get the shotgun.

"Really?" she exclaimed. "I just put it away."

Mo joined her, saying he was going to get his rifle ready too, just in case.

Charles handed off the helm to Gert, who immediately

relinquished it to Pat, and then tried his phone. But we were out of range of any service.

"Fall off a little," I told Pat as I headed for a winch. "We're on a collision course."

She steered a new course and I trimmed the genoa accordingly. Gert trimmed the other sails. The powerboat adjusted its course slightly. I guessed it would soon slow down and come up on our windward side.

Charles lowered the binoculars and turned to face me. "You're not going to believe who's in that boat," he said.

Judging from his tone, I suspected he had bad news. And one name came immediately to mind.

"Pincus?" I asked.

"In the flesh," he replied.

I felt my heart rate increase. This was not going to go well. After all, he had watched me kill his brother. Self-defense or not, Pincus had to be seething with rage.

"And he's not alone," Charles continued. "Onion is with him."

I moved closer to the hatch and told Tracy the news.

"What should I do?" she asked, eyes wide.

"Put some extra shells in your pocket and stand by," I replied. "Mo, you stand by as well. Pincus doesn't know we have a rifle."

A thought crossed my mind. Given the illegality of firearms in Bermuda, we should have superior firepower. If Pincus was not armed, any attempt to board would likely be futile. That sounded good but did nothing to slow my now-pounding heart.

The powerboat steered away and then circled until it was on a parallel course.

Pincus was driving a center console, fiberglass, offshore fishing boat. There was a short man I didn't recognize in the bow next to Onion. Onion was smiling. The short man was holding a rifle. So much for firearms being illegal.

Their boat had a black hull and a white interior. No manufacturer's name or model number was visible, but I guessed it to be about a twenty-five footer. It had twin Mercury outboard motors but from this angle, I couldn't see what size. Regardless, that thing could probably do forty or fifty miles per hour, several times faster than any sailboat.

Charles joined me in the cockpit, leaving Pat and Gert at the helm. When the boat was close enough, he shouted, "What in the hell is going on, Daniel?"

"I'm sorry that you're here," Pincus replied. "You're not going to believe this, but I mean you no harm. I can't speak for the others though."

Just then the man with the rifle fired into the air, safely ahead of our bow. But it wasn't a single shot. I made it out to be a three-shot burst, maybe five. That meant he had a fully automatic weapon. Mo's little survival rifle suddenly seemed anemic.

"Drop your sails and prepare to be boarded," Onion yelled, still grinning.

"And have whoever is below throw the shotgun over the

side," Daniel added, also yelling to be heard over the noise of his engines.

The rifle fired again, still in a safe direction. I was pretty certain it had been a five-shot burst. He obviously wasn't concerned about wasting ammo, so he likely had another magazine or two, or more.

"Don't make me ask again," Pincus threatened.

Thoughts flashed wildly. They probably couldn't board us easily as long as we kept sailing. The way *The Lady Anne* was heeled over, they would have had to almost jump up from their boat, which was much lower in the water.

But to keep sailing, the helmsman, or helmswoman at this moment, would be an easy target.

If the man with the gun decided to spray a few dozen rounds across our deck, he would likely kill, or at least wound all of us that were topside.

Onion was probably spry enough to make the jump, and he could drop our sails while his rifleman provided cover.

"What's going on?" Tracy asked from below, looking up at me through the hatch. She was clutching the shotgun. She looked more scared than I had ever seen her.

"Take cover in the galley," I instructed. "And blast anyone coming below that isn't me, Charles, Gert, or Pat."

She backed away. I didn't see Mo but was sure he had heard me.

Charles tapped my shoulder and pointed forward.

The Aquaholic had turned and was headed back toward us. Her sails were down so she had to be motoring. There was another vessel alongside. Judging from its beam and profile, it was big. Big enough to have a lot of armed men aboard.

"Daniel," Charles shouted, startling me. "What are your intentions?"

Daniel shouted back, "I've got some new partners that have been hiding me from the authorities. We intend to take *The Lady Anne's* gold, take you for ransom, take the pretty women for the sex trade, slowly kill Reid Adams for revenge for my brother Sam, kill anyone else that can't generate a tidy profit, and then scuttle both vessels."

Grinning, he added, "I also intend to finish my business with Pat and Tracy. When my new partners and I have had our fill, what's left will be sold with the others."

CHAPTER 38

Pat suddenly brought *The Lady Anne* hard over. Charles and I saw the boom flying across and managed to duck at the last moment.

She steered right at the powerboat. I guessed she intended to ram it. We had enough forward momentum and I thought for a second it might work. If we could hit them broadside, we might capsize them, putting them in the water and possibly regaining an advantage.

But Pincus was an experienced captain and quickly accelerated out of harm's way. As he gunned it, he threw Onion and the small man backward into the center console's windshield, knocking them down.

All Pat had done was buy us a few seconds. Instinctively I ducked, knowing a barrage of bullets was going to be fired in our direction as soon as Onion's friend regained his footing.

Pat brought the bow back across, again swinging the boom wildly. Charles ducked to avoid it and then stayed low, like me. When Pat resumed her original course, the sails went back to where they were trimmed and *The Lady Anne* accelerated.

I smiled at Pat, knowing she had tried something very desperate. But she didn't smile back. She shouted, "Fog ahead."

I raised up and looked. *The Aquaholic* and the bigger vessel alongside were being enveloped in fog.

I knew that fog had to be the work of the aliens, I just didn't know how. I watched as *The Aquaholic* passed through the fog, headed for us. I also noticed the bigger boat didn't emerge.

I glanced at Pincus. He had steered out of range of any future ramming attempts. He, Onion, and the rifleman were looking at the same fog we were.

Pat changed course slightly, away from the fog. Despite making a clear target, I went over to the winch and trimmed the genoa for our new course. Without being told, Charles trimmed the mainsail and Gert trimmed the mizzen sail. *The Lady Anne* accelerated some more, heeling further.

I kept waiting to be fired at, knowing the rifleman had to be aiming, but there were no shots fired.

I watched as *The Aquaholic* headed away from both us and the fog. Her sails were still down, but whoever was at the helm was pounding right through the waves.

I noticed the powerboat had slowed and we were getting further away. I didn't take any comfort in that, because Pincus had a huge speed advantage. "Hell," I thought, "he could probably give us a twenty-minute head start and catch us in five minutes, maybe faster."

"What's happening? Pat said, loudly.

"I don't know but keep going," I answered, trimming the genoa and then the traveler to coax a bit more speed, all the while alternating watching the fog and Pincus.

I thought I saw a flash of light from within the fog bank. That confirmed that the aliens were helping us. I knew that when the fog lifted, the bigger boat would be gone, sent back in time like all of us currently onboard *The Lady Anne*, except Charles, had experienced.

I watched the fog and waited. In less than ten minutes, the fog began abating. A few minutes later, the fog was gone and so was the bigger boat that had been escorting *The Aquaholic*.

I looked back toward the powerboat. It appeared to have stopped and was just drifting.

"Reverse course, back toward Pincus," I ordered.

"Why?" Pat asked, looking puzzled.

"We're no match for their speed. We need to bluff them out of here. How's your poker today?"

I asked Charles to take over trimming duties and I started below to see how Tracy and Mo were fairing.

Before I got very far, the radio blared, "Ahoy, *The Lady Anne*. What have you done?" It was Vee and she sounded frantic.

Pat looked at me, waiting for instructions.

"Don't acknowledge that," I stated. "Whatever you say,

assume Pincus and Onion will hear. Turn the volume down and maintain the illusion of radio silence." Then I hurried below.

Mo was waiting a few feet from the hatch, holding both guns. Tracy was seated at the salon table, holding a bottle of single-malt scotch.

The way she looked at me, it was obvious she was loaded.

"What are you doing?" I asked. As soon as I said it, I vividly remembered Pat telling me that Tracy said she heard alien voices when she drank. It was now clear that Tracy was indeed able to communicate with the aliens. I knew she had asked them for help. I didn't know why they had helped her, but I was very thankful they had.

"I heard what Pincus had planned so I asked my little green man friend for help," she stammered, looking very pleased.

Mo chimed in, "I heard you mention the bigger boat that was leading *The Aquaholic* back here, so I told Tracy to tell the aliens to get rid of that bigger problem."

"Did I work? Is things good?" Tracy blurted out, slurring her words.

"Everything's fine; wait here," I replied.

A plan flashed through my mind. It seemed worth a try so I told Tracy, "Tell your green friend thank you."

She bounced her head up and down, kind of a drunk acknowledgement.

I turned to face Mo. "We're sailing back to Daniel's fast powerboat. When we get close, we'll heave to. There are three men on that boat: Daniel, Onion, and a short man with a fully automatic rifle." Mo nodded.

"The rifleman will probably be standing in the bow. When I give the signal, I want you to drop him. You'll only get one shot, but we have to take out the big gun first. Can you do that?"

"Yes, I can," Mo replied.

He thought for a second and then asked, "Do I have time to get to the stern? I don't want any sails in my way."

I nodded and then asked, "Can you live with it? With shooting another person without giving warning?"

"Yes."

"Are you accurate within fifty feet or so?"

"Deadly accurate."

CHAPTER 39

I glanced back at Tracy. She hadn't moved but took another drink straight from the bottle. I smiled. She smiled back.

I then went topside and told Pat to get within forty to fifty feet of Pincus and then heave to. She repeated my instructions back. Mo crawled from the hatch, through the cockpit, past the helm, and made his way to the swim platform. He stayed low and carefully carried his rifle.

I quickly relayed my plan. Have Mo drop the rifleman and then warn Pincus and Onion to leave before we unleashed *The horror of the Devil's Triangle* and made them disappear like their colleagues.

Pat nodded. So did Gert. Charles asked, "What horror?"

"Trust me on this and don't ask too many questions." My reply was succinct and to the point. I wasn't sure how we could pull this off and not disclose we had alien help, but at the moment, bluffing Pincus into fleeing was my prime concern.

I saw *The Aquaholic* had changed course toward us, but calculated we had time for one attempt at evening the odds.

"Wait," I told Pat. "Wait and keep closing until I signal. You'll know when. You can do this."

She wiped her forehead and then tightened her grip on the wheel.

"When she tacks, don't immediately release the main-sheet," I reminded Charles.

"I know what to do," Charles answered, centering the traveler and then casually moving toward the winch that controlled the mainsheet.

When *The Lady Anne* was about fifty feet away from Pincus's powerboat, I nodded. Without a word, Pat began heaving to, bringing the bow through the eye of the wind. I didn't pay attention to Charles adjusting the mainsail; I kept an eye on the powerboat.

Pincus obviously knew what maneuver we were executing, but Onion and the man with the rifle just stood there and watched. The rifleman was standing clear forward in their bow and had his weapon pointed over the water but not at us. Onion was standing slightly behind him. Pincus was seated at the helm.

I nodded at Gert. She said something I couldn't quite hear but I watched as Mo's head and then the barrel of his rifle protruded from the swim platform.

He aimed in the direction of the powerboat. I exhaled and

waited. I wished I had brought the shotgun up with me. In case Mo missed, I could have started firing.

But Mo didn't miss. When the angle was right, he fired one shot and the man holding the rifle fell backwards. He must have squeezed the trigger as he was falling because his weapon suddenly began firing.

Onion ducked and put his hands over his head. The gun fired until it was empty. Mo came up the steps, leaned the barrel over the stern rail for support, and prepared to fire again.

But Pincus didn't stick around for Mo to shoot Onion and then fire at him. He gunned his engines, dumping Onion backwards again, and headed around our bow, using *The Lady Anne* to block Mo from a second shot.

The powerboat sped away in line with our bow. Mo started forward, but by the time he was at the bow pulpit, Pincus was out of range.

We watched as Pincus altered course. Pat compared his course to our compass and said, "He's headed back to Bermuda."

Then she repeated it, with a cheer this time. "He's headed back to Bermuda."

Gert rushed to Mo, hugging him and saying he was her hero.

I called for Tracy to come topside. That it was over.

Charles didn't say anything. I knew he was going to start asking questions.

But at the moment I didn't care. The threat was neutralized. We were safe. I felt at ease and relaxed.

Vee's voice startled me. I hadn't been watching *The Aquaholic* and now it was only thirty or forty feet away.

I knew that Angie would have known what happened but wasn't sure how to explain to Vee, Bev, and the others what they had just witnessed.

But Vee wasn't cheering.

"What just happened?" she yelled.

"We got rid of your problem escort," I replied.

"Where did that boat go?" I noticed Bev, Dreamgirl, and Candy were at the cat's stern, waiting for my response.

"Don't worry about them; they won't bother us again."

"Where are they?" Angie and Jane appeared at the stern next to the other women. They looked upset as well. I didn't understand how all of them could be this freaked out when we had just vanquished our attackers, saving us from who knows what.

"What's wrong?" I asked.

Vee had a wild, almost crazy look on her face. "Elouise and Marta were onboard that big boat when it vanished."

CHAPTER 40

My knees went weak as my adrenaline drained. I sat down on the deck.

"Let's get these sails furled," Pat ordered. "I'm calling an emergency meeting. Vee, prepare to raft."

I just sat there, feeling helpless. Tracy came topside, looked around, wobbled a bit, and without saying a word, sat down next to me.

In slow motion, the boats rafted together. It seemed surreal. My only thought was that I was to blame for Elouise and Marta's disappearance back in time, trapped with men who had bad intentions to begin with and who now would surely make their lives a living hell.

I watched as Vee crossed over to *The Lady Anne*. I knew she was going to yell at me. I deserved it, and I was too numb to care and too powerless to do anything about what had happened.

"Are they dead?" she asked, her face a foot from mine.

I managed to shake my head.

"Where are they?" she hissed, grabbing my shoulders and shaking me.

"We can't tell you where they are," Pat answered, loosening Vee's grip.

"Did you somehow sink them?" Vee pressed, glaring.

I regained a bit of my composure, looked right back at her, and replied, "They're not here and they're not dead and that's all I can tell you."

She blinked. I could see she was processing. She still looked very intense but remained silent.

Bev knelt beside her. "You said Marta and Elouise are alive but not here. Is that right?" Her face was stern but her voice was calm.

"Do you know where they are?" she asked, keeping her emotions under control.

"Yes, but I can't tell you," was my reply.

"Can we go get them?"

That was an interesting question I hadn't thought of or expected.

"What did you just say?" Pat asked.

Bev turned and looked at her, but Vee kept her eyes on me. Bev responded to Pat's question. "I asked if we can go get them. I mean if they're not here and they're not dead, can we just go and get them?"

Pat and I made eye contact. I could tell she was thinking the same thing I was. We both looked at Tracy.

Tracy stared right back at us. I wondered if she understood the question.

"Can you excuse us for a few minutes?" Mo asked.

Bev pulled Vee away from me and Pat helped me stand up.

Mo motioned me, Pat, and Tracy below. When Gert tried to follow, he held up his hand. She stopped and then turned to face the others, in effect blocking anyone else from going below.

The four of us took a seat at the salon table. In lowered voices, we discussed the possibility of returning through time in a rescue attempt. Pat and Mo both pointed out we would have to be returned to a time before the other boat emerged from the time portal, otherwise we'd be outnumbered and outgunned.

Pat speculated that if we accurately timed our passage through the portal, we could affect our rescue while the other boat's people were still unconscious from the time passage.

Mo agreed that if we could be returned ahead of the other boat, there would be a short window during which our opposition would be unable to resist.

It sounded very risky and I needed more information. Rather than ask Vee, I asked for Angie to come down. She joined us at the table.

"Could you please tell us about the big boat that vanished in the fog?" I asked.

"After we got ahead of you, we were on course, minding

our own business, when we saw another vessel approaching from the side. Bev reported it was a powerboat so Vee held our course, knowing that sailboats generally have the right-of-way over powerboats.

"As it got closer, maybe one mile out, the radio stopped working. Then the radar gave screwy images, and finally I noticed the GPS coordinates were way off."

That all matched what *The Lady Anne* had experienced.

"The boat pulled alongside and matched our course and speed. There were five or six men and they all had guns. Another short man brought Elouise out where we could see her. They had kidnapped her from her hotel the night before. He pointed a gun at her head and said he was going to count to sixty."

I waited, having a good idea where her story was headed.

"He warned us that if our sails weren't down by the time he reached sixty, he would shoot her in the head. He sounded serious. Elouise was crying and begging him not to kill her."

"So you dropped your sails, didn't you?" Mo asked.

Angie nodded. "After we furled our sails, a taller man with a bandaged finger went over to Elouise. He was carrying a big knife. He wanted the woman that had sprained his finger to exchange herself for Elouise."

I knew he was referring to Marta from the episode at the party.

"He said he was going to start counting and if that woman didn't come onboard their vessel, he was going to cut off one of Elouise's fingers every fifteen seconds. He started counting."

"Marta didn't wait for us to talk about it. She surrendered, jumped in the water, and swam over to their boat. They pulled her out but then refused to release Elouise, instead ordering us to follow them back to where you guys were."

"Where did the fast powerboat come from?" Mo asked.

"They lowered it into the water right after the radio went out. I watched it speed toward you."

"What kind of boat took Marta and Elouise?" I asked.

Angie thought for a moment and then said, "It looked like military surplus but not a warship, some kind of service vessel. It was probably a little longer than *The Lady Anne*. It was steel and rusting badly. It had a lot of old-style satellite dishes pointing in all directions. It had a tall mast that was probably some kind of antenna."

The satellite dishes and antenna made sense and corroborated Mo's jamming and spoofing theory.

"How many men were aboard?" Pat asked.

"Eight or maybe ten, I'm not sure."

"How high from the water did she ride?" I asked.

"Not real high."

That wasn't very helpful so I rephrased my question.

"If *The Aquaholic* was alongside and I wanted to jump to their deck, would I have to jump straight across, jump up a little or a lot, or jump down a little or a lot?"

After a moment's thought, Angie answered, "Jump up a little. Why? What are you thinking?"

"Can you give us a few minutes?" I asked her.

Angie got up and headed topside. Before leaving the salon she turned and said, "Whatever you're planning, count me in."

When the four of us were alone, Pat took over. She asked Tracy if she could reestablish communications with the aliens. Tracy nodded.

Then Pat said that if the aliens would return us to a time just before the ship emerged from the time portal, we could rescue Marta and Elouise while everyone was still unconscious. Then we could return to our time before the bad guys even knew what had happened, leaving them stranded 25,700 years in the past.

"Good thinking," I praised her.

"We'll have to allow time for us to wake up after transiting the portal," Mo stated.

"We'll need to ask Angie if we can borrow her boat for the trip," I said. "*The Aquaholic* is more maneuverable than *The Lady Anne*."

"That's a lot for me to remember to ask, especially when I have a few more drinks," Tracy said.

Pat smiled. "I'll write it down for you."

CHAPTER 41

Without offering an explanation, I asked everyone to please leave *The Aquaholic* and board *The Lady Anne*. The looks I got made me sure a barrage of questions was about to follow but Mo stepped up and asked them to hold questions until later. Pat added that if they wanted to see Elouise and Marta again, they needed to hurry.

Once *The Aquaholic* was empty, Pat, Mo, and I prepared her for another trip through the time portal. That entailed closing the valves on the propane tanks, preparing to disconnect the batteries, removing the batteries from the GPS units, portable radios, and flashlights, and tightening down the shipping screws on all the compasses.

I had Angie show us where she kept her shotgun. I also asked Vee and Bev to move *The Aquaholic's* dinghy over to *The Lady Anne* temporarily. I was sure we wouldn't be needing it.

By the time we were finished, Tracy informed Pat and me that she had asked her little green man friend for assistance in retrieving the two female passengers that had been transported through time. Tracy explained the women had been taken against their will and if left alone with their captors, the women would be killed, or worse. Mr. Greenman, as Mo called the alien, had agreed to help us.

We gave Tracy our cell phones since we wouldn't be needing them and they weren't working anyway. I didn't want anyone to accidentally take pictures back in time and incur the alien's wrath.

Vee said that she or one of her crew was going to accompany us, explaining that Marta was her responsibility. I told her no. She didn't accept my answer.

Mo explained that what we were trying to do was set for a party of three, not four. Vee argued that she take his place.

Initially Tracy wanted to accompany us back, making an argument that she should come along in case we needed to communicate with the aliens. Pat, Mo, and I were in agreement that she not come back with us.

We insisted she stay onboard *The Lady Anne*. In the event we didn't return within a reasonable time, she could ask the aliens what happened.

Now Vee was pressing to be part of the mission and wasn't taking no for an answer. I didn't want to divulge what was going to happen after the fog bank. I finally just looked at her and told her that we appreciated her offer but it wasn't possible that anyone besides the three of us attempt this. I asked her to trust me. She gave me a dirty look but backed away.

The three of us said our goodbyes and then Pat, Mo, and I got *The Aquaholic* ready to depart and stood by, waiting.

We didn't have to wait long. A fog bank appeared a few hundred yards away. As soon as we were clear of *The Lady Anne*, I slowly motored *The Aquaholic* toward the fog.

I glanced behind us and saw Tracy, Angie, Charles, and the other women watching. Angie, Gert, and Tracy were the only ones waving goodbye. They were the only ones that fully understood what was happening.

I was sure everyone else doubted that we would recover our missing shipmates by disappearing in a fog bank. But the truth was, they didn't have any other option but to trust us.

The instant we entered the fog, I shut down the engines, and Mo and Pat disconnected the starting and house batteries. We then met in Angie's cabin and prepared for the electrical disturbance, freaky light show, static electricity, overpowering ozone smell, the silver glow, unbearable noise, and eventual loss of consciousness. . .

I awoke to Pat gently shaking me. My head ached. Once I moved, Pat focused on waking Mo. Within a short time, we headed for the forward deck area. There was a patch of fog about five hundred yards away.

Thanks to Mo having a watch without a battery, he knew the time. It was eight thirty. Based on the sun's brightness, it had to be a.m.

I located *The Aquaholic's* first aid kit and gave everyone some Tylenol.

Then we reconnected the batteries and test-started the engines. Quickly, we got the flashlights and portable radios working, deployed the fenders on both sides, got all the bow and stern dock lines ready, partially unfurled the mainsail, and got underway.

While Mo and I worked, Pat went about cleaning the slippery time-portal residue gunk off the decks. She couldn't find any degreaser onboard but did find a bottle of deck cleaner. It was a foaming type cleaner and worked pretty well.

She felt bad for polluting the pristine ocean with the foamy suds—we all did—but the label said it was biodegradable.

I took the helm first and sailed back and forth outside one edge of the fog bank. There was a light breeze blowing and all I had to do was tack, sail, tack back, and repeat.

We unfurled a partial jib to make tacking easier. Ordinarily we wouldn't have reefed the sails in light air, but we needed to stay close to the fog and speed wasn't necessary at the moment.

I kicked myself for not reinstalling the old sails before we went into the fog, but there hadn't been time. *The Aquaholic's* brand-new sails were now charred around the edges, courtesy of the time portal's electrical discharges.

All of her new metal fittings were blackened as well. So were her new dinghy davits. I felt bad until Pat reminded me everything could be replaced or buffed out, again, at the next marina.

After a couple dozen tacks, I handed off the helm to Mo. He took over the now monotonous elongated figure-eight loop until it was Pat's turn.

We stayed hydrated and even made some sandwiches and raided Angie's fresh fruit. Pat used one of her breaks to wash her hair. The static electricity had left her short hair a mess. Mo and I didn't care about our appearance, but she did.

As long as the fog held, our routine of sail, tack, sail, tack back was pretty easy and pretty boring.

At 4:42 in the afternoon, our routine was finally interrupted by the changing fog. It got progressively heavier until it lifted. In its place was the vessel Angie had described.

CHAPTER 42

I guessed the ship to be close to one hundred feet long. Angie had been right; it looked like some type of decommissioned military service vessel.

It was steel, and judging by the peeling paint and excessive rust, it was badly in need of maintenance. The mast Angie had described was actually an antenna tower. There were, as she had said, several satellite dishes pointing in various directions.

We sprang into action, knowing the passengers were unconscious but not knowing how long they would stay that way.

Mo was at the helm and started the engines while Pat furled our sails. I retrieved *The Aquaholic's* shotgun and went forward.

Mo switched places with me, insisting I handle rafting the cat. I agreed and pulled alongside.

Pat and Mo easily stepped across and secured us. Pat warned me to watch my step; the metal decks were slippery. I traded places with Pat and told her to leave the engines running. She nodded and kissed me. "For luck," she said.

The raised, enclosed bridge was forward and there was a lower structure aft which I guessed was engine room access. I gave Mo the shotgun and motioned him toward the stern. "Go slow and don't slip," I whispered as I headed forward.

The bridge was elevated, and trying to hold on to the rails and not slip while climbing the ladder was tricky. Inside were two men, passed out and motionless. They were small men and looked Asian, maybe Chinese. I wasn't certain. Next to them were four rifles and an old coffee can full of extra magazines.

There was no way to keep them from waking up but I could take their weapons, so I did, making two trips back to Pat. She took the weapons and coffee can from me. She looked concerned at the number of weapons but didn't say anything.

I then made my way aft. I noticed all the metal was blackened. Some of the more rusted areas were really blackened.

Mo had to have gone below, so I followed and found him in the engine room. There were two more Asian men, also passed out. I didn't see any rifles. Mo came close and whispered so as not to wake them.

"There are two large Caterpillar diesels for propulsion plus two more smaller ones. Based on their configurations and connections, my guess is one of the smaller diesels is for refrigeration and the other is for generating electricity."

I agreed. Even in the low light I recognized the engines' distinctive yellow paint. Based on their size, I guessed the main engines were a thousand horsepower each, maybe bigger.

He gestured toward an electrical panel behind the furthest engine. It was loaded with switches and meters. Of course nothing was working. There were several conduits coming out of the top, running forward.

We left the engine room and returned topside. Behind the bridge, I had spotted access belowdecks so that's where we went next.

"Angie thought six to eight, maybe ten men were aboard," I said quietly. "I found two and you found two so that's four. Keep your eyes open for the others."

Mo nodded.

We descended another ladder and opened a watertight door. It was pitch-black and we waited a few minutes for our vision to adjust.

I remembered that Charles, Pat, and Tracy had all been impressed when I told them pirate captains weren't usually blind but used an eyepatch to preserve their night vision when fighting belowdecks with a cutlass. If Mo and I had been wearing eye patches, we wouldn't have wasted precious time.

I led the way with the shotgun. I had a fifty-fifty chance of finding them so I headed aft. Mo followed with both flash-lights, keeping one of them pointed in front of me.

We passed several racks of electrical equipment, all connected by conduits. It smelled of burnt wiring. Then the passageway ended near some large coils. "Refrigeration system," Mo said softly, smiling. "All that electrical equipment must generate a considerable quantity of heat."

I exhaled and turned around, retracing our steps. We were wasting time locating the others.

Just past the ladder heading topside was the boat's head. It was empty, reeked, and was littered with assorted dead bugs. I chuckled, thinking that if Tracy thought the toilets on the pier were gross, she would have had to find a new word to describe this one.

Next was the smallest galley I had ever seen. It was barely big enough for one person. There was a dirty, two burner stove, a small cupboard, and about two feet of dirty counter space. Again we spotted a lot of dead bugs, compliments of the alien's policy of sterilization.

We followed the narrow passageway, stepping over one man passed out, his rifle lying next to him. I motioned for Mo to take his gun. He did, slinging it over his shoulder.

The passageway ended at another watertight door. It squeaked as I opened it, freezing us in place. Mo moved close and shined both lights inside. It was empty and appeared to be some type of cargo hold. He shined his light lower, its strong beam probing the blackness.

Toward the far end of the compartment, sprawled on the deck between four men, were Marta and Elouise.

CHAPTER 43

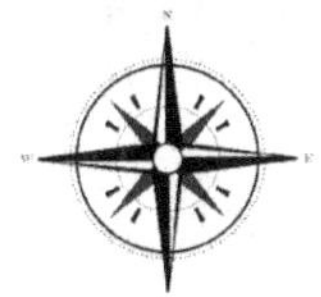

Both women were clothed but their wrists were bound. There were more guns scattered around. I motioned for Mo to move the rifles back to the passageway. He took my shotgun and handed me a flashlight. Then he began moving the rifles, taking two at a time.

The women were tied with heavy cable ties. Trying to saw through the hard plastic with a rigging knife was tough, especially while holding a flashlight. I cut Elouise loose, and then Marta, being extra careful to not accidentally cut or wake either of them. I was also careful not to shine my light in anybody's face, lest I risk waking them. We didn't need another set of problems. I did notice the man closet to Marta had a bandaged finger.

"I'm not sure I'm strong enough to carry one of the women," Mo whispered.

"No problem. I'll carry the ladies, one at a time."

"Which one first?" Mo whispered.

I handed him my light and picked up Elouise. That was harder than I expected since she was completely limp. Once she was safely in my arms, Mo handed me back my flashlight and then led the way back to Pat. On the way, he slung another rifle over his shoulder.

I went topside as quickly as I could, being careful not to smack her head or hanging limbs on the steel bulkheads. When I carried her limp body outside, I feared the sunlight would wake her, but thankfully she never moved.

Mo helped me pass her over to Pat. Once Elouise was onboard the cat, we gave Pat Mo's rifles. She looked very formidable holding a Soviet AK-47 fully automatic assault rifle.

I had been exposed to that rifle in basic training years ago but hadn't seen one since. I gave her a ten-second lesson in how to fire it.

But there wasn't time for small talk; we had to get back for Marta.

I could see Mo breathing hard. I was breathing faster than normal as well, probably due to the stressful situation. Neither of us complained. We both knew we were flirting with disaster should any crew members awake.

We hustled back below but had to wait a few more agonizing moments for our night vision to return. I wished this vessel would have had working red lights below, or we would have had a flashlight with a red lens. That way we could have saved time. But we had neither so we waited.

When we finally entered the hold, Marta was sitting up. Mo and I both froze, not wanting to startle her and have her start screaming.

I shined my light on Mo. When he shined his light on me, I put my fingers to my lips. She hadn't screamed yet, so I shined my light at my mouth, illuminating my signal for her to be quiet.

We slowly made our way over to her. She was watching us, all the while rubbing her wrists. They had to be pretty sore from being tied so tightly.

Keeping two fingers pressed over my lips, I offered her my other hand. She took it and I pulled her up. I waited until she seemed stable and then leaned close and whispered, "We've got to get out of here but we need to stay absolutely silent. Nod if you understand."

She nodded. I quickly shined my light over the unconscious men lying about so she could see where not to step.

I led her by the hand toward the exit, walking very slowly, trying to stay completely silent. Mo followed.

When we reached the passageway, I thought about closing the watertight door behind us and wedging it closed with something, in effect trapping half of the crew. But it had squeaked so loudly when first opened I couldn't risk the shrill noise waking anyone.

Mo stopped to gather the rest of the weapons and then we

proceeded toward the exit, me carrying the shotgun and one flashlight this time.

When Marta stepped over the unconscious man lying in our way, she noticed he had a large knife on his belt. She stopped, bent down, and quietly took it. I didn't say anything.

She followed me up the ladder and we exited into the bright sun. She sneezed once, quickly covering her mouth. It was a loud sneeze and I hoped it hadn't woken anyone.

"Almost there," I said softly, pointing toward Pat and *The Aquaholic*.

"Can I borrow your flashlight for a minute?" she asked, looking at me while shielding her eyes from the sun. Her hair was sticking straight out like Elouise's. But the white streak in Marta's black hair gave her a kind of *Bride of Frankenstein* look.

"Why?" I asked, though I thought I knew what she had in mind.

"I've got some unfinished business below," she replied, turning her knife blade over and then back. "It will only take a minute."

I was right. Did she mean to go back below and kill the man with the bad finger, or maybe kill them all?

I thought back to the decision Pat, Tracy, and I had made to release Captain Rick instead of killing him when we had the opportunity. Rick had gone on to commit a triple homicide and violently rape the three widows. I could have prevented that. If Marta had been violated, did I have any right to deprive her of her revenge?

"Can I borrow your light or not?" she repeated, speaking slightly louder.

CHAPTER 44

I wasn't sure whether to agree. Thankfully, Mo intervened and said, "We are here on a rescue mission. Nothing more."

She looked at him.

He continued on his trajectory, "This is a rescue mission only, not a raid, not an assassination. The objective was to retrieve you and Elouise. To that end, we have succeeded."

I took over. "If we change the parameters of the mission by allowing you below with that knife, we may jeopardize our ability to. . ."

I stopped mid-sentence. I had almost mentioned our ability to return to our own time.

Marta looked confused by what we were and weren't saying.

"We need to leave now," I told her firmly. "If we don't get the 'f' out of here right now, we may not be able to."

She was listening but didn't say anything.

"I know you don't know me or Mo very well, but Marta, you have got to trust us."

She slowly lowered the knife and exhaled, relaxing slightly. However, she did take one of the rifles from Mo. Her expression as she glanced back said clearly if any of her captors should be unlucky enough to show themselves, she would not be taken again. She'd shoot.

I led the way back to *The Aquaholic*, telling Marta not to slip and being careful not to slip myself. Marta followed close behind me, and Mo followed her.

"What's going on?" Pat demanded as we approached. "What took you so long? Elouise is awake. We have got to go. Now." She pointed toward open water. I could see that the fog had reappeared probably a half a mile away. That had to be the alien's way of displaying our exit.

Marta easily climbed aboard *The Aquaholic*, not wanting or needing any help. Mo and I passed over the rifles and then Mo joined her. "Go to the helm," I instructed Pat as I began untying us.

Once loose, I gave a push and stepped aboard. Pat backed away, but she angled too quickly and bumped into the other vessel. The thud reverberated loudly, and I feared the worst. I used my foot to push us away a little further. "Straight back," I told her. "Don't cut it until the bow is clear."

Once we were clear a safe distance, Pat shifted into

forward, brought the bow around, and slowly motored toward the fog. I kept watching the deck of the other vessel, waiting to see if anyone appeared.

Mo joined me, followed by Elouise and then Marta, still holding a rifle at the ready. We were all watching. I was hoping our stealth rescue could be completed undetected by the enemy forces. I wasn't sure if Marta felt the same. The way she held the rifle showed she had experience. I wondered if she would take a shot if the bandaged-fingered man showed his face.

One hundred, two hundred, three hundred yards. We were almost out of range. None of the rifles I had seen had scopes or optics. I hoped we had secured all the weapons, but I couldn't be one hundred percent sure. Now we were nearly safe from all but a skilled marksman or a lucky shot on the chance we missed any.

Four hundred yards. Five hundred yards. I glanced toward the fog. It was getting closer by the minute. I glanced back at the other boat. Still no signs of movement.

"Marta and Elouise, go below and take the batteries out of these flashlights please," I said. "Mo, would you go prepare to disconnect the batteries as soon as we enter the fog?"

He nodded.

"What's happening?" Elouise asked.

"We're going back through the same electrical disturbance as before. Once through, your captors will never bother you again." I kept my voice calm. I knew I wouldn't relax until we were safely back in our time, but I didn't want to alarm

Elouise or Marta. I wasn't sure exactly how bad their captivity had been but I was positive they needed all the compassion I could muster.

"Going back through to where?" Elouise asked again. She looked nervous, scared, and anxious.

"We can't tell you exactly what happened," Mo said, trying to sound reassuring. "But trust Reid. We will all get through this without a hitch."

I could see both women were unsure and I wondered if they thought we were crazy.

After maybe twenty seconds of staring at us and each other, they finally started moving.

I followed as the three of them went inside the salon. I went over to Pat at the helm and told her the moment we were inside the fog bank to cut the power, shut down the engines, and then go help Mo finish disconnecting the batteries.

She acknowledged but asked, "What are you going to do?"

"Get rid of these weapons," I responded.

Pat gave me a puzzled look, so I clarified. "Once we're inside the fog, the bad actors can't hurt us. We don't need a bunch of military-grade weapons showing up and giving Brenda Bishop a story about guns showing up in Bermuda with serial numbers belonging to missing criminals aboard a missing vessel."

She smiled. If she was as nervous as I was, it didn't show. I smiled back, remembering she was a consummate poker player.

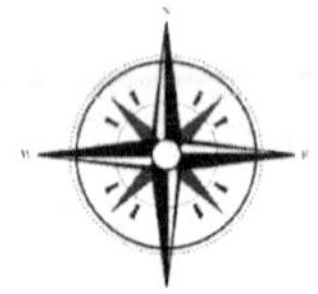

CHAPTER 45

I awoke to being gently shaken by Tracy. "You're back. Can you hear me? Reid, wake up. Can you hear me?"

As if reading my mind, Tracy said, "Pat already woke up. She's fine. So are Mo and Marta. Elouise woke up a few minutes ago. You are the last one."

After a little rest and some Tylenol, I told Tracy to be sure and thank the aliens for returning us. She promised she would the next time she got loaded.

It seemed an unusual way for our two species to communicate, but considering Tracy was tipsy when she originally talked to the alien image on the sphere, the aliens must have assumed that an elevated blood-alcohol level was her normal state. I didn't say anything as I followed her topside.

The Aquaholic and *The Lady Anne* had rafted together. The masts were staggered and lots of fenders were deployed.

Whoever had directed the rafting procedure, he or she had done it properly.

I found out that Tracy, Gert, and Angie had come aboard *The Aquaholic* as soon as it reappeared. They insisted the others wait aboard *The Lady Anne*.

I followed Tracy to the stern area. Marta and Elouise were already there along with Pat, Angie, Gert, and Mo. All of those women, save for Angie and Gert, had frightful hair.

Marta and Elouise had some serious bruising on their wrists. Thinking back to when I cut them loose, the plastic cable ties had been really tight. Pat, Mo, and I had some bruising as well. Mo's bruising was the worst, probably due to his weight loss and semi-frail condition.

My chief complaint was my headache. After four trips through the portal, the resulting headaches weren't getting any easier.

I noticed that all of the persons remaining aboard *The Lady Anne* slowly congregated aft. That location provided them the best view of us. I knew they probably had a million questions and I had a pretty good idea what most of the questions would be about.

"What did they do to your nice clean boat?" Jane asked, looking at *The Aquaholic*, and then Pat, and then her daughter.

That was one of the million possible questions I hadn't expected.

"Angie's vessel has the same charred sails and blackened rigging it had when I first saw it in Bermuda. What happened?" Charles said.

"What in the world did you do to your hair?" Dreamgirl asked Marta.

"What kind of slime is covering the decks?" Vee wanted to know.

The questions were coming so fast, none of us had time to answer.

Charles raised his hands and cleared his throat until everyone else got quiet. When he had our attention, he said, "I have four questions. One: What happened to the other vessel that sailed into a mysterious fog bank but was gone when the fog lifted? Two: How can a vessel emerge from a fog bank with charred sails and blackened rigging that wasn't there before. Three: What exactly is the *horror of the Devil's Triangle* that you referenced earlier? Four: Why did Tracy say she hears alien voices when she was drinking at the luau?"

Charles had managed to address nearly every aspect of our alien secret. And he had done so in front of Vee and her crew, Angie's mom, and Elouise, his employee. I felt my heart pounding again.

I looked at Pat. She looked perplexed. I looked at Angie. She looked away. I looked at Mo. He looked up, then down, then right back at me. Gert was also looking in the other direction. "How convenient," I thought.

At that instant, I made a split-second decision to tell a lie. I really didn't have a lot of options considering I had been warned by the aliens to not tell the truth about our previous encounter, ever. I moved to where *The Lady Anne's* passengers had a clear view of me.

"When we first sailed off the grid, we were declared missing. But we weren't missing. We had accidentally wandered into a parallel dimension. The doorway back and forth between dimensions lies behind a fog bank.

"We met an alien who was stranded on our planet over fifty of our years ago. The alien spaceship encountered an unexplained difficulty. He ejected in an escape pod. The escape pod was not capable of leaving our planet, but it did have enough working technology onboard to see that his spaceship had crash landed."

I saw a lot of blank stares and some rolling of eyes but I continued, making it up as I went.

"The alien discovered his dead companions had been found by military forces. He calculated the crash site as somewhere near Roswell, New Mexico. Due to a heavy military presence, he was unable to retrieve their bodies or his wrecked spacecraft."

Vee exchanged glances with some of her crew but remained silent.

"He used his remaining technology and power to initiate and control the dimensional doorway. The alien has been hiding, in his escape pod, on the other side of that doorway ever since."

Jane looked at her daughter. Angie kept a straight face.

I took a breath. "I can't tell you how, but Tracy accidentally communicated with that alien. He allowed us to pass back and forth between dimensions. I can tell you that Tracy and the alien have had subsequent communications. I cannot divulge any more than that."

I had their complete attention, disbelieving looks or not. I decided it might be a good time to end the tale.

"Tracy was warned not to talk about it so I am imploring you, all of you, to forget what you have witnessed and never speak of it again."

Having delivered my spur-of-the-moment lie, I waited for what I assumed would be an incoming barrage of questions.

But no one said anything. They looked back and forth at each other, looked at Tracy, and then looked back at me, but they all remained quiet. I purposely avoided eye contact with Pat, Tracy, Mo, Gert, or Angie. I didn't want one of them to grin or wink and risk losing my composure.

Pat added to my tale, saying, "The three generally accepted dimensions of space are length, depth, and width. There is also a generally accepted fourth dimension—time."

Mo continued where she left off. "But according to string theory, there may be nearly a dozen dimensions operating in the universe. These include futures, pasts, realities, and inter-dimensional space, both microscopic and gigantic."

Jane surprised me by saying, "There is agreement that something did happen at Roswell that was much more than a reported weather balloon."

"So there's an alien surviving in a parallel dimension and he helps Tracy when she drinks and communicates with him?" Charles said. His tone was firm but not confrontational.

"That pretty much sums it up," I replied. Pat and Mo

nodded their agreement. He didn't have a follow-up question. Neither did anyone else. They just looked at me, waiting for something.

I remained silent. My lie had been told, sworn to, and accepted. I had nothing more to add.

So what's next?" Dreamgirl finally asked, breaking the uncomfortable silence.

My heart was still pounding, but I felt a great sense of accomplishment having just told the whopper of the century.

"We get *The Aquaholic* cleaned up and resume course for Puerto Rico," I replied.

CHAPTER 46

We arrived in Puerto Rico six days later. Except for the obvious, it had been an uneventful journey. Both boats and crews had performed well. Ralph Clark routed us around two weather systems and we had great conditions the whole way. Thankfully, nobody mentioned the incident.

Angie thanked Charles several times for providing such a competent, all-female crew. She was extremely pleased with their sailing skills, knowledge, and attention to safety at sea.

I was grateful to have Charles aboard. He was extremely skilled at sailing *The Lady Anne*. He even insisted on taking a turn at the night watch. That made it easier on Tracy, Pat, and me since Mo and Gert weren't super keen on sailing the boat at night when everyone else was sleeping below.

Mo spent some time each morning at *The Lady Anne's* weather station, taking readings. He made notes. I asked him why once and he replied that he was trying to replicate the weather router's professional forecast. Sometimes he was accurate, sometimes he wasn't. His NASA background had given him a cursory knowledge of meteorology and he enjoyed testing his skills.

Gert would bring him a glass of Ensure and watch patiently as he wrote in his notebook. It was obvious to anyone who saw them that they were very happy together.

Elouise continued on the trip with us. We offered to take her back to Bermuda, but she wanted to stay onboard and not cause any more delay. Charles argued but she wouldn't budge her position.

She didn't help with sailing the boat but didn't get seasick either, so that was good. She had contacted Chet by satellite phone and arranged for him to clean out her Bermuda hotel room, especially the stack of currency in her room safe. He gave her luggage to one of Charles's men who was going to fly it to us in Puerto Rico.

Chet offered to come to Puerto Rico, but we agreed that having him see the condition of *The Aquaholic* would do nothing but invite questions. Charles took Elouise to meet up with his plane. She was really happy to have her own clothes to wear, not borrowed ones.

Since she was already here, she decided to stay with us until we departed on the next leg of our passage. Charles assigned two of his men to stay with her at all times.

Marta kept thanking me, Pat, and Mo for rescuing her. I told her that thanks weren't necessary. I discreetly asked if she needed any medical attention. She declined my offer and whispered that she had been roughed up but not violated.

I was extremely relieved to hear that. I asked her if she'd tell Mo and Pat when it was appropriate. She nodded and then thanked me again. Her gratitude was almost embarrassing. I was glad it hadn't been worse.

I wasn't sure if I should tell her that she and Elouise had been sterilized by the aliens when passing through the time portal. Maybe it would be best if Pat, Angie, or Gert told her that. I decided that discussion could wait.

Pat had given Elouise and Marta a small jar of her aloe cream. It had helped with her bruises from Pincus's attack. She was sure it would help the bruises on their wrists too.

Charles offered to contact Tommy Kraft and have new parts and sails shipped to us but I argued against that, raising concerns about a bunch of questions. We went with a local supplier instead.

There was no way to get new sails that fast, and since the old ones were working fine, we ordered new sails for *The Aquaholic* to be shipped to either Aruba or Cartagena, depending on lead times and our schedule.

I was positive Vee, Bev, and the other female crew members, especially Marta, would jump ship at their first opportunity. I was sure that hearing a story about an alien helping us from a parallel dimension would send them running. But they didn't. Evidently the dimensional doorway story hadn't been a strong enough reason to forfeit the money Charles was paying.

We spent four days at the San Juan Bay Marina. Pat, Tracy, and I had been there before and liked it well enough to return.

It was hard work replacing the blackened metal onboard *The Aquaholic,* but working with a bunch of sexy women wearing shorts and bikini tops made it not seem like work. If anything couldn't be replaced with readily available items, we simply painted over the blackened metal.

Mo and Gert offered a hand with the repairs when needed but mostly helped Jane with meal prep. When they didn't have any chores to do, some or all of them ran errands, with or without Elouise. I noticed that Jane and Pat kept their distance as best they could.

Angie, Bev, Tracy, Pat, Gert, and I made two trips to Costco. Pat seemed happy pushing her flatbed cart up and down each isle. We purchased enough food for a four-month passage to Hawaii. We got as much fruit, produce, dairy products, and meat as we could keep cold or frozen and supplemented the rest of the menus with canned, bagged, jarred, or boxed food.

We also bought toiletries, an embarrassing amount of feminine products (which would not be used by Pat, Tracy, Angie, or Marta, a fact Marta didn't know yet), pain relievers, sunscreen, more clothing, more alcohol, dog food, dog treats, and even a stack of books. Tracy added some DVDs to the pile. Bev added four cases of chocolate milk pouches for Marta. Tracy bought two cases for herself.

Putting everything away filled up both vessels. Tracy inventoried what *The Lady Anne* now held. She suggested someone aboard *The Aquaholic* do the same. Having used the totes from Bermuda, we didn't have many cardboard boxes to dispose of.

Mo surprised me with a gift. He had gone shopping on his own and presented me with a waterproof field watch that didn't use a battery but needed winding every day.

I liked it. It was thin, had large, easy-to-read luminous hands, was marked for both twelve- and twenty-four-hour time, and was rated water-resistant to one hundred meters. I offered to reimburse him but he wouldn't hear of it. He said it was the least he could do. I decided not to argue.

When Pat complimented me on my "handsome, new, practical timepiece" as she called it, he handed her one as well. I thought it a bit masculine for a woman, but she absolutely loved it. He did the same for Tracy. Gert smiled and showed us her wrist. She also had one.

"If we get stuck back in time again," he said with a grin when the five of us were together, "at least we'll all know the time."

Tracy joked that Pat's homemade sundial had been replaced by technology. We all laughed. Mo reminded us to wind it every day but not to overwind it.

She then joked that his barometer made from a can and a condom had been replaced by a modern weather station. We all laughed again.

I noticed that Jane returned once carrying what appeared to be a musical instrument case. She quickly went aboard *The*

Aquaholic without saying a word as she passed by. I made a mental note to ask her about it sometime.

Charles quietly informed me that one of his men had gotten *The Aquaholic* another survival rifle just like Mo's. He and I debated the pros and cons of buying more substantial firepower.

Eventually we decided against it. Hiding a shotgun and a collapsible rifle was one thing. Hiding semiautomatic rifles with large magazines or bulky, large-caliber sniper rifles with scopes and bipods was way too risky.

My real concern was having to anchor one or two times before getting around Puerto Rico and setting course across the Caribbean Sea for Aruba. It felt like we would be sitting ducks when we switched on the anchor light.

Charles said he'd take care of it but didn't elaborate.

I was thankful he was on top of it. I wasn't convinced we had seen the last of Daniel Pincus.

I joked to myself, "Who needs guns when you've got Tracy and her connections."

CHAPTER 47

As before, Charles put us on notice that he would be buying dinner for our last evening in San Juan. Nobody argued. We were all tired from working hard to get *The Aquaholic* cleaned up.

And leaving San Juan didn't mean leaving Puerto Rico. I calculated we still had two or three more days of sailing to reach the southwest corner of the island.

From there, it was four hundred nautical miles to Aruba. Then it was another six hundred fifty nautical miles to the Panama Canal, allowing for a stop in Cartagena.

In between last-minute things like groceries and fuel, on our last afternoon in San Juan, Pat and I found time to be alone. Quietly, we made love. Compared to Tracy's raucous orgasm sessions, the slow pace with Pat was refreshing.

We finished, cleaned up, kissed some more, and then tried

to look innocent as we waited for everyone else to get ready for Charles's dinner party.

Dinner that evening found me seated next to Jane. She talked a little about being a museum curator and then a little more about winning on *Jeopardy*.

"Is there a Mr. Smith?" I asked.

"I'm divorced," she answered.

"I'm sorry."

"I'm not," she replied. "I'm glad to be rid of fuckhead and the kumquat."

I was taking a drink of my beer when she said that and I coughed and nearly spit up. I couldn't believe the words that she had just said. Of all of the people at the table to drop an f-bomb, Angie's mom, Jane, was the last one I would have imagined.

I wasn't the only one who was surprised. Our entire banquet table had just become silent, everyone else obviously hearing what I had.

"That's a sore topic," Angie added, looking directly at me.

As if Jane's outburst hadn't been bad enough, Dreamgirl repeated it. "Who's fuckhead and the kumquat?"

"Fuckhead is my ex-husband," Jane answered, lowering her voice a bit but still speaking with enough volume to make me appreciate there were no servers present at the moment.

"And the kumquat?" Candy asked, trying to suppress a giggle.

"That's the nineteen-year-old waitress he left me for."

"Why do you call her a kumquat?" Candy asked.

"Yes, why a kumquat?" Tracy wanted to know.

I waited for the explanation too. I had heard women called many names, some very derogatory, but I had never heard a woman called a kumquat.

"It's a code word I use that's a cross between cunt and twat," Jane replied.

I tried not to laugh but couldn't help it. Gert turned red and Mo looked away, but everyone else chuckled.

"He left me for a waitress." Jane sighed. "My God, she wasn't even old enough to serve liquor."

There was a brief moment of silence. I felt sorry for her and figured everybody else did too.

"You know, I once uttered a Freudian slip to fuckhead," Jane said calmly.

"What did you say?" Charles asked.

"I said 'you're ruining my life, you fucking bastard.'"

More silence. I was pretty sure her profane outburst would not have qualified as a Freudian slip. I grinned and wanted to laugh but restrained myself.

Pat cleared her throat. "What time should we get started in the morning?" she asked, changing the subject.

"I'd like to be out of here by seven a.m.," Charles replied.

During the rest of the evening, Jane never brought up her ex or the waitress again. I fought hard to keep from breaking into laughter every time I thought about it. Jane's description was probably one of the funniest I had ever heard. It was even funnier because it was so out of character for her to use language like that. I now had a new word to call female drivers that cut me off in traffic. I also hoped I would never have cause for a "Freudian slip" like she had.

I have a joke," I said, tapping the rim of my glass.

"Oh, goody." Candy giggled.

"This isn't lame, is it?" Tracy asked, looking serious but finally smiling.

"A blonde walked up to the librarian and said, 'I'd like a hamburger, fries, and a diet Coke.' The librarian looked at her and said, in a lowered voice, 'Young lady, this is a library.' The blonde whispered, 'Oh, excuse me. I'd like a hamburger, fries, and a diet Coke.'"

Tracy rolled her eyes. "You're pretty brave to tell a blonde joke," Vee said. Her tone was stern but she had laughed along with everyone else, so I did what I do best: I told another joke.

"This blind man went into a bar and ordered a drink. After a few minutes, he called the bartender over and asked if she minded if he told a blonde joke. 'I'll have you know I'm blonde,' the bartender replied, 'and I have a shotgun within reach, underneath the bar. The woman on your left is blonde and she's a deputy sheriff who is carrying a firearm. The woman on your right is blonde and she's an FBI agent who is also packing. The woman on her right is blonde and she teaches self-defense classes for women. Are you sure you want to tell a blonde joke?' After a few seconds, the blind man replied, 'No, I guess not. I don't want to have to repeat it four times.'"

Every woman at the table looked around at each other and

then back at me. When the laughter erupted, I admit I breathed a silent sigh of relief.

Charles tapped the rim of his glass to get our attention and then stood. "I have a few parting comments I'd like to leave you with."

I turned slightly and gave him my full attention. We all did.

"First, I want to thank you all for agreeing to let me sail with you to Hawaii." There were a lot of nods and then a round of applause.

"Second, I want Mo to know that I'm in a position to replace his airplane if the insurance company refuses to do so." Mo was speechless and wiped away a tear.

"Third, I want Gert to know that her two mortgages and her credit cards will very shortly have zero balances." Gert went over and gave him an awkward hug. When she turned back, she was also wiping away tears.

"Fourth, I want Angie to know that *The Aquaholic* is now hers, free and clear. I have also arranged for her insurance payments to be made until her charter business gets established." Angie also gave him a hug. She began crying.

"Fifth, I want to propose a final toast."

We all raised our glasses and waited. His generosity had completely overwhelmed everyone, and I had no idea what he was going to propose next.

"To my new friends. Fair winds and following seas."

I had just taken a sip when Gert said, "I have a question."

"Yes?" Charles asked. He looked right at her but remained standing.

"Please don't take this the wrong way, but I need to know why you are being so generous."

I took another sip, curious to see what his answer would be. He waited a moment, and I could see he was formulating his response.

Finally he said, "The unexpected passing of my wife has given me pause to reflect on my own mortality. I have accepted that my wealth could not save her any more than it can save me."

Pat, Tracy, and I exchanged silent glances.

"When my time comes, my estate will be divided amongst my heirs. Many of them don't really know me, other than they've probably heard I'm very wealthy."

He took a sip and then continued. "When the estate is divided, all of my properties will be distributed as I have outlined. I predict a frenzy of greed, sort of like kids fighting over the property titles in a Monopoly game."

He took another sip. The room was very quiet as everyone waited to see where this was going.

"There's an old saying that you can pick your friends but your relatives you're stuck with." A few of us nodded, having heard that, or a variation thereof.

"Rather than have a bunch of shirttail relatives that have never taken the time to get to know me inherit my lifetime of accumulation, I have decided to put my money to use amongst a small number of people I am privileged to call my friends."

Pat, Tracy, and I exchanged glances again.

"I would like to see my money enjoyed while I'm able to, so that, Ms. Gertrude Kohler, is why I'm being so generous."

Gert had nothing further to say. None of us did.

CHAPTER 48

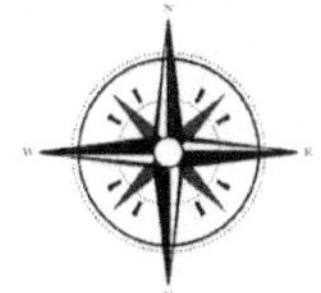

We departed the next morning, on schedule, bound for the far corner of Puerto Rico before crossing the Caribbean Sea. Elouise didn't come with us on this leg, preferring to stay on land and use a vehicle to meet up at the Marina Pescaderia on the west shore when we got there.

Charles's men could legally possess firearms in Puerto Rico so he assigned one man to each vessel. We were assigned Tony. He was of medium height and build. He didn't say much more than that he was a former Airborne Ranger who did private security work for Mr. Williams. I smiled. Charles certainly had taken care of it.

He stowed his small duffel bag in the cockpit, lashing it under the table. Pat offered to show him possible accommodations below but he politely refused, saying he would be staying mostly topside until his assignment was over.

"Are you sailing with us all the way to Aruba?" Pat asked.

Tony shook his head. "Only until your last stop in Puerto Rico."

"I'll keep out of your way," he replied to Tracy's inquisitive look.

I got Tony a PFD. He thanked me.

I had read in the cruising guide that firearms were illegal in Aruba and figured that might have been the reason he wasn't sailing there with us. I also wondered how Angie would feel with a man aboard, changing the composition of an all-female crew. I didn't say anything.

"Strictly a precaution while the boats are anchored close to shore," Charles informed us.

I suppressed a grin, thinking the man aboard *The Aquaholic*, the only man for that matter, would enjoy the scenery.

Everyone onboard *The Lady Anne* was in good spirits. We were fully fueled, fully provisioned, and ready to get going. Judging from the upbeat radio conversations, *The Aquaholic's* passengers were in good spirits as well.

Both boats cleared the harbor and then headed west along Puerto Rico's north shore, still sailing in Atlantic waters. As per usual, Captain Vee and *The Aquaholic* got out to a quick lead and stayed ahead.

We passed a lot of fishing boats and even some dive boats. Some of the waters were clustered with locals in small craft, blaring salsa music for all to hear.

Occasionally Tony would radio Lance, who I learned was his counterpart onboard *The Aquaholic*. Judging from Tony's side of the conversation, I guessed Lance to be retired military also. I noticed Tony used an earpiece with his own portable radio. He also had his own tactical binoculars hanging from his neck which he used to observe all vessels passing close by.

I wanted to discuss how he would have handled the situation when Elouise and Marta had been taken onboard a faster vessel with superior numbers and firepower, but I didn't. I sensed Tony wasn't overly talkative.

We pressed on until late afternoon and then anchored for the night. We were the only two sailboats in a small anchorage packed with powerboats. I wondered how long we'd be subjected to the other boat's loud music but just before the sun went down, the anchorage emptied out.

The powerboats started up and then exited en masse, their music finally fading. Mo and Gert came topside and commented on it now being peaceful. Buster did his business on the swim platform. Tony watched and, smiling, radioed something to Lance, but I couldn't hear what he said.

The Aquaholic unloaded her dinghy and Angie motored over, bringing Marta with her. Earlier Tracy had radioed I was going to be grilling ribs tonight and asked if any of them wanted to join us.

Angie and Marta accepted. Angie had marinated ceviche all day using local red snapper and brought over a batch for an appetizer. It was really good.

Tracy didn't understand how raw fish could be chemically cooked in lemon and lime juice and be safe to eat without using any heat. I let Pat explain it to her.

"It's the acid in the juice," she said. "It *cooks* the fish."

I'm not sure Tracy got it, but once she tasted it, I don't think she cared.

I grilled six racks of ribs, low and slow, basting frequently. I would have preferred making sauce from scratch but didn't have the time so I used two bottles, one traditional and one spicy.

I had planned on grilling Mo a hamburger if he didn't eat pork ribs. He thanked me for thinking of him but whispered he didn't keep Kosher.

We had salad, ribs, and baked beans from a can laced with a little bourbon and stolen packets of brown sugar. The meal turned out to be a hit even with bottled BBQ sauce. Tony joined us briefly. He ate half a slab and asked if we would send the other half back for Lance.

I served a whole pie for dessert. I was glad to get it out of the way. Tony laughed as he asked for a slice for Lance. Marta sacrificed and finished the last two pieces.

"So how are you managing to work out onboard *The Aquaholic*?" Tracy asked her in between bites.

"I do push-ups, pull-ups, sit-ups, calisthenics, isometrics, martial arts' forms, stretching, yoga, Pilates, stairsteps, and planks," Marta replied.

"Any weights or other cardio?"

"A gallon jug of water weighs eight pounds and there is a spare anchor and propane tanks if I want heavier. As for cardio, I just do a few hundred burpees three or four times a day. Those get my heart rate up."

A few *hundred* burpees? I was impressed. No wonder she could eat the way she did.

"If you catch a big fish, you'll get a serious workout reeling it in," Tracy added, winking at me.

"We haven't done any fishing yet, but I'll remember that," Marta replied.

Marta and Angie left for *The Aquaholic*, taking a doggy bag for Lance.

We cleaned up topside and then everyone retired below except for me and Tony. He told me he and Lance would split the night watch and not to worry.

"If the anchor alarm sounds, or if it looks like any of the anchors are slipping, or if the wind shifts, wake me immediately, regardless of the time," I told him.

"Yes, sir. I will," he replied.

"You don't have to call me sir."

"Okay, Mr. Adams," he said, grinning.

I followed the others below, knowing we would be safe from any potential boarders as long as Tony and Lance were on duty.

CHAPTER 49

We raised anchor the next morning. Tony pulled Charles aside and whispered something. Charles then motioned me over. He looked concerned.

Barely speaking above a whisper, Tony told us we had had visitors after midnight. He explained that he saw a small boat row out from shore. He waited for them near the stern.

"Who was it?" I asked, matching his low volume.

"Punk teenage girls probably looking for anything they could steal quickly. They were never a threat."

"What happened?" I asked. I was a very light sleeper when at anchor but hadn't heard a sound last night.

Tony looked at Charles. He smiled and said to go ahead and tell me.

"I surprised them when I shined my tactical light on their little boat and motioned them away. One of the older girls held up a ball bat. I drew my weapon, put the laser dot on her chest, and motioned them away again."

"And then?" I asked, knowing he hadn't fired or the gunshot would have certainly awakened everybody.

"I politely asked them to return to shore and not bother us further." Tony saw my smirk of disbelief and clarified. "I believe my exact words were '*Vaya con Dios, puta.*'"

"Which means?"

"Go with God, whore. They got the message and rowed away so fast you could have water-skied behind them."

I forced myself not to laugh at his choice of Spanish phrases. Drawing a firearm and pointing it an unarmed person, a teenage girl no less, was very serious. I envisioned that girl dropping the bat and peeing herself. She was probably still shaking, expecting to loot an empty cockpit by the dim light of the anchor light and then finding the red dot from a laser sight on her chest. In any language, the meaning of that red dot was clear—death, or at least getting shot and hit.

Tony said he was going to take a quick nap in the cockpit. I offered him my cabin but he refused, saying a few short naps was all he needed. I let him be and we continued along the coast, trying to be quiet so he could rest.

Tracy told me she had managed another contact with the aliens last night. "Really?" I asked.

"I guess I drank more than I thought and I heard them speaking with me in my head."

"What did they say?"

"They told me what happened to the big boat we rescued

Marta and Elouise from."

"What?" I asked. I hadn't thought about it, but it seemed logical that if the aliens were moving back and forth between time periods to observe development on Earth, observing that vessel would be perfectly normal for them.

"They told me that vessel got caught in a storm and blown out to sea. It was powerless, adrift for four days, until it could get its engines started."

"Why four days?" I asked.

"I asked them that and they said their solar panel took that long to charge their batteries."

That was a good answer and matched what we had almost gone through, except we were able to manually start our generator.

"Please continue," I told her, intrigued.

"The ship was only ninety miles from the alien transit point we call Atlantis."

I smiled, remembering how positive Mo was that Atlantis existed.

"But. . ." I said.

"But they didn't know it was there and turned back west, toward North America."

"Where are they now?"

"They are headed toward land but have run out of food and water and are drinking rum."

"That's not good," I said.

"I told the aliens I had no sympathy for anyone aboard that ship after what they did to our friends, and the aliens replied they suspected the survivors would resort to cannibalism before reaching landfall."

Her last words left a gruesome image in my mind so I thanked her for finding out but told her it might be best to keep that a secret. She nodded.

As both vessels turned south, we stayed as close to shore as practical, wanting to skirt the edge of the Mona Passage.

The Mona Passage is the waterway between the Dominican Republic and Puerto Rico that connects the Atlantic Ocean to the Caribbean Sea. It is a major shipping route between the Atlantic and the Panama Canal and is renowned for being very crowded with large cargo ships. It can be quite challenging for small craft or sailboats. It also had a bad reputation for having very unpredictable weather. Ralph had made a notation on the morning weather fax to avoid the Mona Passage today.

Mo did his daily weather station work but couldn't confirm the Mona Passage had unsettled weather. He explained his calculations to Pat, wondering if her engineering background would catch something he had overlooked. She reviewed his work but didn't find any errors.

They only confirmed that despite Mo's best efforts, given the limited weather equipment onboard, his wind and storm predictions were nowhere near as accurate as those of a professional weather router. Again, I was glad that Charles had hired Ralph.

We worked our way south, *The Aquaholic* staying closer than usual, both vessels keeping a reasonable distance offshore.

The radar displayed lots of contacts inside the Mona Passage. There was indeed a lot of shipping. We could see some of the closer ships with the binoculars. Most of them were either container ships or tankers.

As large as they were, they appeared to be moving slowly, but I knew better. Most of those ocean-crossing container ships could sustain speeds of twenty knots. The oil tankers were a little slower, maybe fifteen knots. Both were faster than us.

I was glad to keep our distance. Running into the wake from one of those monsters would bounce us and throw everything around, passengers included.

We passed a cluster of very small sailboats following one another. I guessed them to be a sailing camp or possibly a kid's sailing school.

We sailed hard straight through the day, not even slowing for lunch. Our destination was the Pescaderia Marina located in Puerto Real Bay just south of the town of Mayaquez.

The next fax from Ralph warned of possible storms and no good way around them except stopping and waiting. We informed *The Aquaholic* and then pressed on.

We ran right smack into a brief thunderstorm. It came out of nowhere, poured rain like a car wash for nearly an hour, and then the sun reappeared. There was some thunder but thankfully there was no lightning close by. As a precaution, we reefed the sails during the rain but the wind never increased much.

Late in the afternoon, we arrived. The marina office staff

was very friendly and directed us to a dock where we could tie up one behind the other. We got the shore power connected and then scoped out the amenities.

Besides being a full-service marina, there was a shopping center, a supermarket, a highly recommended bakery, several highly recommended seafood restaurants, a pharmacy, a bank, an art museum, and even a movie theatre all nearby, and most within walking distance.

Tracy was hosing the salt residue off of the deck when Elouise arrived. What had been a scenic drive for her had taken us two days.

She visited briefly with Charles, and then Tony, and then went over to *The Aquaholic* and chatted with Lance. Another of Charles's men came over carrying four big shopping bags. Elouise called everyone to the dock saying she had gifts.

She explained she had taken the Barcardi rum factory tour, which she described as basically a big gift shop with a free drink. I sensed she was disappointed.

But she had purchased T-shirts for everyone. There were different colors and sizes. They all had the Bacardi logo and some of them had Bacardi's trademark—a red circle with a large bat.

I didn't figure Charles to be much of a T-shirt man but he graciously accepted, finding one with a bat in his size.

"For your use in the galley," Elouise said, handing Angie and me an apron, a wood cutting board, and a lime squeezer.

She had even gotten a bag full of sunglasses straps and baseball caps. All of those were quickly taken.

And as if that weren't enough, Elouise had one bag of local Puerto Rican candies for each vessel. I noticed Marta kept an eye on the bag Angie was holding. Her final gift was two bottles of rum for each boat: one light, one dark.

I helped Tracy finish hosing the deck while everyone took their purchases, thanking Elouise profusely. We changed clothes and then went for dinner.

Another of Charles's men showed up and two of them accompanied our group, leaving Tony, Lance, and Buster to watch the boats.

We had a nice meal of locally caught seafood, expertly prepared. Mo and Gert shared an entree but everyone else seemed to have a good appetite. Pat commented that Mo and Gert were so cute, sharing a plate. Elouise ordered to-go boxes for Tony and Lance, which was nice.

We returned to the marina. Elouise offered to come back in the morning to see us off. She was continuing on by plane. Charles, Vee, Bev, Pat, and I had a quick meeting. We decided to keep Tony and Lance's services through the night but let them go after that.

From where we were to Aruba was basically a straight course of 200 degrees magnetic. Having to drop them off would require another landing, or at least a dinghy ride ashore. Since there had been no sign whatsoever of Onion or Pincus, we all agreed we'd be fine on our own after tonight. Even Elouise felt comfortable enough not to require extra security in the hotel.

Charles told Elouise to be back early in the morning. If we

left before she arrived, she'd find Tony and Lance waiting for a ride to the airport. She agreed and said good night and goodbye in case she missed us in the morning.

Dreamgirl took a load of laundry to the marina laundromat. Gert went with her, taking a community load and all of our new T-shirts as well. *The Aquaholic* didn't have a washing machine, and although there was one aboard *The Lady Anne*, it was easier to do laundry ashore.

Jane and Angie came over and joined us in the cockpit. Jane was carrying the musical instrument case I had seen earlier.

"Angie tells me you can really play the trumpet," she said, opening her case.

I nodded.

She removed a violin and checked its tune.

"You brought your violin along on this trip?" Tracy asked.

Jane shook her head. "No. I bought this in San Juan. Why should Reid be the only one making music?"

"Are you ready?" Jane asked Angie, putting the violin into position and brandishing the bow.

"Which one?" Angie asked.

"Hank Snow's nineteen sixty-two hit."

"Really?" Angie asked, looking uneasy.

"You sing it very well," Jane soothed.

Jane began playing and Angie joined in. After the intro, Angie rattled off about fifty places in rapid succession. She paused only to grab a breath. I wasn't a big country music fan but I had heard "I've Been Everywhere" before.

It was amazing that Angie could sing places that fast, and from memory. Jane was accompanying her daughter beautifully but Angie was stealing the show.

The ending was met by thunderous applause, not only from those of us onboard our two boats, but from every other boat berthed nearby.

I hadn't noticed the number of people that had come topside and were listening until they all started clapping in unison.

Jane played another—Jessie Colter's "I'm Not Lisa." It was a slow number and very dramatic, and Angie sang it beautifully, accompanied by her mom. I glanced over at Dreamgirl, thinking about her looking like my ex-girlfriend. She didn't notice.

I went over to Jane and complimented her playing ability. "How's your 'Dueling Banjos'?" I whispered, referring to the hit from the movie *Deliverance*.

"I can fake a duet if you're offering to get your trumpet," she whispered back.

I ducked below and emerged with my trumpet.

I took Angie's place, smiled at Jane, and started playing, waiting patiently for Jane's violin to answer. We had never practiced together but judging from the applause when we finished, we had done a great job.

I'm not sure that piece had ever been played by a violin and a trumpet before. Lots of people were shooting video with their cell phones and I wondered if our strange duet might eventually go viral.

CHAPTER 50

Midmorning found us out of sight of Puerto Rico and on course for Aruba.

Elouise had arrived before we left the dock, even bringing a box of donuts. Charles bid his men farewell until he would see some of them again in Aruba, without firearms. The three departed and we set sail.

Both vessels were now in the Caribbean Sea. We would be in open water until we spotted the California Lighthouse on the northwest tip of Aruba.

The wind was favorable but the sea was rougher than expected. Gradually the bird life diminished, leaving only our wake to keep us company. Besides an occasional cargo ship, we had the waters to ourselves.

We stayed as close to compass course 200 degrees magnetic as the winds would allow.

A large, white motor yacht quickly overtook us from astern. I got nervous enough to go and get the shotgun from its hiding place, but the yacht altered its course and gave us a wide berth. Once the yacht was out of sight, I put the gun away.

Pat suggested we use our signal flags to alert each other if we suspected there might be trouble. Angie and Vee thought that was a good idea. If *The Lady Anne* flew the flags *Sierra* and *Golf*, we were indicating *Shot Gun* and that meant trouble.

The Aquaholic didn't have a set of signal flags, so they agreed to fly Angie's white flag with a red martini glass. Instead of indicating cocktail hour or a party onboard, the use of that flag would now signify distress.

We sailed all day following the watch schedule. Gert served sandwiches for lunch with chips and grapes. She even spread some peanut butter on the bread heel for Buster, a treat he eagerly accepted.

Ralph Clark had us change course to keep in the most favorable winds. For nearly four hours we were on course 180 degrees magnetic. Being on that heading made Pat, Tracy, and me a little melancholy.

We had more sandwiches, toasted this time, for dinner and then sailed through the night. I read the log before my two to four a.m. watch and saw that Charles had reported seeing two cruise ships, both traveling east, both a safe distance away.

I had no log entries except for plotting our position every hour on the hour. My new watch was easy to read by the dull glow of the instruments.

The Aquaholic stayed right with us. Vee, Bev, Candy, or whoever was at the helm knew how to sail. I was very impressed with the crew Charles had hired.

At ten fifteen a.m. the next morning, we were all topside except for Pat, who was sleeping after her watch. Our last fix put us nearly halfway to Aruba.

Twenty minutes later *The Aquaholic* hoisted its happy hour flag. Despite there being no vessels in sight or on radar, that flag made us all very uneasy.

Then *The Aquaholic* hailed us, telling us they were testing their flag and warning that we would soon reach a large patch of floating plastic. We reached it and then sailed through it for over two hours.

There were massive ribbons of plastic garbage that seemed to snake off forever. We identified bottles, bags, cutlery, and food packaging. There was also a lot of floating crud we couldn't identify.

While both boats had gaffs, neither had a net, so there was no way to retrieve any of it. Plus there were miles of floating garbage so pulling out a few bags full would have had zero impact. Tracy took one picture and then deleted it, saying she didn't want a reminder of man's total disregard for nature's beautiful oceans.

I felt bad too. There was quite a bit of plastic garbage floating off the Southern Californian coast, but this was the worst I had ever seen, ruining the beautiful, turquoise-blue Caribbean waters.

Another day passed without incident and another night.

This time Tracy logged seeing a cruise ship on her watch. She noted it was several stories of white lights.

My watch was uneventful but I knew better than complain and risk angering the sea gods. I used to tell my sailing students that sailing was ninety-five percent boring, punctuated by five percent sheer terror. I told myself to get used to it. That we still had many weeks to go.

Early the next morning, Gert was the one to shout out, "Land ho."

She had been watching it approach on the radar and patiently waited until it was in sight to give the cry. We had reached Aruba. Again Pat missed the excitement, sleeping after her watch ended.

Both boats adjusted course slightly and headed for the northwest tip of the island. Our landmark would be the California Lighthouse.

Just before noon we rounded the point and followed the coastline south, later changing course to the southwest. Our destination was the Varadero Aruba Marina & Boatyard in Oranjestad.

Charles's men had flown in the day before and were waiting for us. It was convenient that Charles had given them the codes to track *The Lady Anne's* whereabouts. They knew exactly when and where to find us. Ralph Clark also had the codes so he would always know *The Lady Anne's* exact position.

Charles had arranged for a customs broker to help us clear immigration and customs. He helped us complete the required paperwork, including the certificate of registration for all high-dollar items we already owned.

The paperwork Charles had given me earlier worked fine for clearing Buster. And since it takes advance approval through the Netherlands Embassy in Washington DC to bring guns or ammunition into the country, we agreed to lie about having firearms.

Once cleared, we made our way to the marina, where I learned that Charles's men had already reserved us two slips.

We got the boats hosed off and then a few of us took naps while the others went exploring.

I was resting in my cabin, silently debating whether to take a quick nap or not. Pat quietly let herself in, grinned like the devil, locked the door, and began taking off her clothes slowly.

That ended my debate.

CHAPTER 51

Candy produced a brochure of tourist activities. Most of them involved the water, but one looked interesting: a pub crawl in an open-air bus.

"Let's go," Dreamgirl said after Candy had read the details.

"And why don't we all wear our Bacardi shirts and hats?" Tracy added, giggling.

Mo and Gert decided to pass, but everyone else seemed up for a break from the boats. The way Mo and Gert looked at each other made Pat and me wonder if they were going to use the time alone to make love. Pat was so happy that Mo and Gert were so much in love.

A brightly painted bus picked us up and took us to three different clubs. We all got one free drink upon arrival and subsequent drinks were discounted.

I'm sure that the patrons thought Charles, Jane, and I were the managers of a woman's softball or soccer team.

The local men asked the women to dance. Judging from the smiles and laughter, a night out on the town was just what we needed.

By the time we left the last stop, we were all slightly intoxicated. Feeling pretty good, I thought about telling some more jokes but decided against it.

The bus took us back to the marina. Pat tipped the driver with American dollars, beating Charles to it. It must have been a good tip because he told us to call him if we wanted to do this again.

Our respective crews went back to their boats. Tracy headed straight for the owner's suite. Pat looked around and then gave me a very seductive smile.

Mo and Gert were seated at the salon table but caught Pat's look and excused themselves, going to their cabin. They looked innocent enough, like nothing had happened. In fact they looked a little bit too innocent, so I was sure they had fooled around. If so, I took that as a sign they were feeling better. Charles bid us good night and adjourned below as well.

Pat and I took Buster topside and then kissed at the stern, letting the anticipation of what was coming grow. Soon we returned below.

Tracy was at the cockpit table, writing feverishly in a spiral notebook. Buster was lying near her. She didn't seem to notice us and said nothing as Pat followed me into my cabin.

For the second time that day, Pat and I made unhurried

love. It was the perfect ending to a perfect day in another tropical Caribbean paradise.

As I drifted to sleep, it suddenly occurred to me that we were just fifteen miles from Venezuela, the nonextradition country that Pincus would have fled to after stealing *The Lady Anne's* gold.

But we weren't in peril from Captain Daniel Pincus. I glanced over at Pat, asleep with a smile on her face. I was in ecstasy from Captain Pat Taylor.

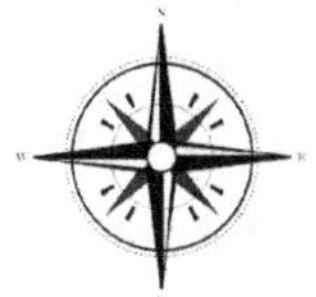

CHAPTER 52

I got up first and headed for the galley. Tracy was slumped over the cockpit table. She hadn't changed clothes and I suspected she had fallen asleep there.

Mo and Charles were examining the spiral notebook she had been using the night before. When I approached, Charles pointed topside, signaling with a finger to his lips for me to be quiet.

Charles went first, followed by Mo. Just as I was preparing to head topside, my cabin door opened and Pat appeared.

She gave me a smile and said, "Good morning."

"Shh," I whispered, motioning to the still sleeping Tracy. Then I pointed topside and whispered, "Follow me. And good morning to you."

Charles took a seat at the cockpit table. Mo sat next to

him and motioned for Pat to sit next to him. I stood behind Pat, watching.

Mo opened the notebook. There was a very neat drawing of a corkscrew-shaped, geometric figure on the first page. He slowly turned the pages. There were several more drawings of various shapes and some diagrams, all very neatly drawn.

"This is the last page," he said quietly. That page had several blocks of writing and no pictures.

"What is this?" Pat asked, flipping back to the first page.

"As best I can tell, these are the drawings for a special magnet," Mo replied.

"What kind of a special magnet?" I asked.

Charles flipped back to the last page. "A magnet that will attract plastic I believe."

Pat swiveled to look at him. "Where did you get this?"

This time, Mo answered. "It was underneath Tracy's sleeping head."

"Are you telling me Tracy drew these?"

"It certainly appears so," Mo said, pushing the notebook directly in front of her.

Pat studied the first drawing for a moment and then said, "Tracy knows accounting, not mechanical engineering. There is no way she could have drawn this."

I gently took the book from Pat and thumbed through it. I had no idea what I was looking at, but one thing struck me as very odd.

"Tracy was pretty hammered last night, right?" I said.

"Yes, she was," Pat acknowledged.

"Then how could she have done this, in pen yet, without one single smudge or correction?"

Charles looked at the pages. "Reid's right. There are no corrections. Nothing crossed out. Each drawing is technically perfect. The level of detail is astonishing."

Pat shook her head. "These drawings contain references to organic polymers, quartz crystals, electromagnetic fields, palladium, and rhodium. The first sketch is a perfect helix." She paused, eyes on the notebook. "Now, I know Tracy pretty well and there's no way on this Earth she drew these sketches." She sat back, folded her arms across her chest, and looked defensive. "I don't know where they came from, but it wasn't Tracy."

"Good," Tracy said, coming topside and startling all of us. "You guys have my notebook. I thought I lost it and I didn't want to have to redraw all those pages from memory."

If she heard Pat's last remark, she didn't acknowledge it.

"Where did you get these drawings?" Pat asked.

"I drew them last night," Tracy said, rubbing her eyes. She held out her hand. "My notebook, please."

Pat handed the notebook over, the skeptical look still on her face.

"What is this supposed to be exactly?" I asked.

"These are the plans for a plastic magnet," Tracy said matter-of-factly, holding the notebook against her chest.

"There's no such thing," Pat said.

Mo tilted his head. "How did you come up with those drawings?"

Tracy glanced around and, satisfied the five of us were alone, winked and said, "Mr. Greenman told me."

There was a moment of silence before Charles asked, "Who is Mr. Greenman?"

Tracy giggled and held the notebook even tighter.

"Why would Mr. Greenman give you the plans to construct a magnetic device that would attract plastic, of all things?" Mo asked.

"Because I told him I was sorry that we humans were polluting the earth's beautiful oceans with a bunch of floating plastic shit."

Pat must have seen where the conversation was headed because she said, "When you say Mr. Greenman, you are referring to the alien that guards the doorway between dimensions, right?"

Like an attorney, Pat was definitely leading the witness.

I hoped Tracy caught on before Charles started in with twenty questions.

She did.

"That's him," Tracy answered, still grinning.

"Are you telling me the alien you can communicate with when you are drunk gave you the plans to a plastic magnet device that we can use to clean up our oceans?" Charles asked, a look of disbelief in his eyes.

Tracy nodded.

"I'm hungry," Tracy said then. "Is there anything to eat?"

"I'll make breakfast," I said.

"Would you mind leaving the notebook?" Mo asked, looking very intrigued.

"Yes, please leave the notebook," Pat added. She sounded part interested, part skeptical.

"Don't hurt it," Tracy said, surrendering the notebook to Charles. "I'd hate to have to redraw everything from memory."

He placed it on the cockpit table and carefully opened it. The three of them, Mo, Pat, and Charles, gathered around it. I followed Tracy below.

Gert was in the galley and the two of us made breakfast while Tracy took a shower and changed clothes. I carried three plates topside with bagel sandwiches with one fried egg, melted cheese, and peppered turkey bacon. The rest of us ate below at the salon table.

"Those three sure like my drawings," Tracy said, smiling in between bites. When Gert gave us a puzzled look, I quickly explained Tracy's notebook of drawings.

"This turkey bacon tastes great. What did you do to it?" Tracy asked.

"He sprinkled freshly ground black pepper over each piece as it was cooking," Gert answered for me.

I couldn't believe we were talking about turkey bacon. I wanted to get more information from Tracy about her encounter with the alien, but she didn't seem inclined to talk about it or to join the others topside. Instead she helped clean up the galley. Only after she fed Buster did the three of us go topside.

None of the three breakfast plates had been touched. I'm not even sure any of them noticed us join them. They were totally engrossed in Tracy's drawings. Tracy sat down beside Pat.

Gert and I let them be and walked over to *The Aquaholic*.

We ran into Bev, who was preparing to board. She had wet hair and was carrying a towel, a small bag, and the gate key.

"How were the marina showers?" Gert asked, reaching her hand out for the key.

When told they were fine, Gert left us, saying she was going to shower and that she'd be back soon.

"So what's the plan for today?" I asked.

Bev stepped aboard. She ticked items off on her fingers.

"Vee wants to make sure the propane tanks are full along with the ice chests. She wants to see if we can buy dry ice here to keep our ice longer. She wants to stock up on more drinking water. She wants some spare fuel cans for gas and diesel. She also wants to make a run to the fuel dock."

"What about Angie and her mom?" I asked.

"Angie has more shopping to do and I suppose Jane will go with her."

Angie appeared at the stern. She held a tray with several cereal boxes, bowls, protein bars, chocolate milk boxes, and a pitcher of milk. She placed it on top of the closest ice chest.

"Shopping for anything in particular?" I asked.

"I need more groceries and I want to see what a couple of sea kayaks would cost."

"Why do you want sea kayaks?" I asked. We had a schedule to maintain that didn't allow a lot of time for sight-seeing or paddling about exploring coves, caves, or deserted beaches.

"If we were becalmed and completely lost power, a kayak would be easier to paddle than the dinghy," Angie replied, looking surprised that I had questioned her.

While I didn't believe we would ever completely lose power, she had a valid point.

I chatted with Vee, Bev, Candy, Dreamgirl, Angie, and Jane while the women prepared their breakfast. Marta had gone to the forward deck area and was exercising. I purposely didn't mention Tracy's notebook. I didn't want to have to answer any questions about Mr. Greenman. I hoped that Mo or Pat wouldn't slip and accidentally tell Charles what had really happened.

Marta finished her workout and took three protein bars and two chocolate milks below.

Gert returned, handing Vee the gate key. Vee, Marta, and Candy, grabbed their toiletries and headed for the showers. Bev went with them to keep them company. Angie and Jane left to go shopping. Gert went back to *The Lady Anne*. That left me alone on *The Aquaholic* with Dreamgirl.

CHAPTER 54

"We've got a little time alone." Dreamgirl smiled. She placed a hand on my arm. "I notice the way you look at me. What's on your mind?"

I had seen that smile before and, knowing that we were alone, knew it could be trouble. "You look like someone I used to date." I paused. "But you do know that I'm engaged, right?"

"To two women." She laughed. "That's probably not legal, even here in the islands." She stepped closer, letting her breasts press against my chest.

I took a step back. "I'm very flattered, Ms. Penelope Porter, but I'm not interested."

She stopped cold, her seductive smile vanishing, instantly replaced by a look of bewilderment. "How did you find out my name?"

"I saw it on the paperwork Pat got when we cleared into Aruba."

"I hate that name."

"Why? What's wrong with Penelope Porter? Didn't you go by Penny or something?"

"Penny. Nickel. Dime. Want to make a quarter?" she said mockingly, backing away.

"What?"

"That's what I heard all through school. I was tormented by all the other kids, boys and girls."

"I'm sorry," I said, trying to be comforting but keeping my distance. "But why Dreamgirl?"

"I had a one-night stand in college and that's what the guy called me the next morning. I liked it and have used it ever since."

She turned on the charm again. "Sure you wouldn't like to see how I earned my name? You can close your eyes and pretend I'm someone else. I'll never tell."

I told her I'd keep her real name secret, but thinking that discretion is always the better part of valor, I beat a hasty retreat back to the safety of *The Lady Anne*.

Pat was below, gathering what she would need to take a shower at the marina's facilities.

"Any comments on Tracy's drawings?" I asked.

"Imagine a large corkscrew, but instead of being made of metal, this one would be made of melted plastic debris from the ocean."

"Okay." I nodded but I wasn't really sure I knew where this

was headed.

"At equal distances inside the corkscrew, there are a series of lenses. But instead of glass lenses, they would be made out of slices of quartz crystals."

I nodded again.

"Now in the center of each crystal would be three very small holes, a little larger than a human hair. Passing through each hole would be an ultra-small diameter wire made of palladium. Using both frequency and electricity generators, a field would be generated that would cause the corkscrew to attract the very materials the corkscrew was constructed from. In this case, plastic debris from the ocean."

"Do you think it will work?" I asked.

"It might," she replied.

"What about Mo? What does he think?"

"Mo thinks the design is sound."

"And Charles?"

"He believes that if Mo and I both believe it could work, he will fund the construction of a prototype."

"Can we build it here or on the way to Hawaii and test it the next time we pass through a floating garbage pile?" I asked.

"No. It will take some pretty sophisticated design and production techniques to replicate the device pictured in Tracy's drawings."

"Charles might make a fortune with a patent on something that attracts floating plastic."

As soon as I said that, Pat starting laughing.

"What's so funny?"

"There's a sentence on the last page that says that no one can profit from the device."

"Does Charles know that?"

"After Tracy pointed it out. But he still intends to go forward with funding."

"That's very magnanimous of him," I stated.

"I think he felt as bad as all of us passing through that floating plastic refuse pile. He's eager to help make it right."

CHAPTER 55

Bev returned later that day with a small bag of dry ice. Mo happened to see her putting the pieces in *The Aquaholic's* cooler that held blocks and bags of ice. She told him what she had paid for the dry ice and he walked away shaking his head.

Later Mo and Gert returned from a quick trip to a fire extinguisher supply company. Mo had four CO2 fire extinguishers, two for each boat. He also had two pairs of heavy leather welder's gloves, one pair for each boat, and some safety glasses.

He called Bev over. Pat assisted as he discharged one of the units into a pillowcase. Wearing the welding gloves, Pat reached into the pillowcase and retrieved small chunks of dry ice. She put them in *The Lady Anne's* cooler to keep our ice frozen longer.

"And that's how we can make our own dry ice whenever we need it," Mo stated, high-fiving Pat.

"That's all there is to it?" Bev asked. I had the same question. What he and Pat had just done looked pretty simple.

"Just make sure you have carbon dioxide only fire extinguishers. You don't want any added fire-retardant chemicals," Mo explained.

"You also want to wear safety glasses, closed-toed shoes, extra heavy gloves, long pants, and a long-sleeved jacket," Pat added. "Dry ice is so cold it can be dangerous if basic safety precautions aren't taken."

I had noticed the safety glasses, gloves, and the jacket. I hadn't noticed she had put on long pants, nor had I paid attention to her closed-toed footwear.

Shortly after the dry ice making demonstration, a delivery man arrived and wheeled a bunch of plastic gas cans over to *The Aquaholic*.

"Why the different colors?" Tracy asked.

"Red is for gasoline, yellow is for diesel," I replied as we watched Candy and Marta lash the cans to the forward deck. "Standard color scheme for the storage of flammable liquids on small marine craft." The way they were handling them made it obvious the cans were full.

Bev opened each can and took a gentle whiff. "Just checking to make sure we weren't ripped off with cans of saltwater," she reported.

Just when I thought *The Aquaholic's* clean look had been

compromised by the addition of extra fuel storage, it got worse. Angie and Jane arrived lugging a two-person sea kayak down the dock.

"There's more gear in the parking lot," Angie hollered.

Dreamgirl, Pat, Tracy, and I brought the second kayak and four double-ended paddles down to *The Aquaholic*. Angie thanked us as she passed, going to pay the driver.

With the kayaks secured along the lifelines, *The Aquaholic's* decks were now crowded.

"She certainly has changed," Charles said sarcastically, gazing at *The Aquaholic*. "Between the black-and-white razzle-dazzle paint job, yellow and red fuel cans, different colored ice chests, one blue kayak, and one green kayak, she looks like she's been outfitted by someone who was color blind."

His comment was funny but sadly true. *The Aquaholic* now looked . . . tacky. Practical, but tacky.

Pat pulled me aside and asked if I thought we should get sea kayaks for *The Lady Anne*.

Tracy overheard and added she thought the sea kayaks looked like they would be fun. But I knew that walking past all of that stuff lashed all over the decks would be challenging, especially at night in rough conditions.

But, then again, having another source of transportation independent of fuel might be a good idea. Pat and I agreed to think about it.

Tracy then asked if we were going to buy a bunch of cans of gas too.

"Vee knows *The Aquaholic* doesn't have the tankage, and consequently doesn't have the range of *The Lady Anne*," Pat answered.

"They are trying to turn *The Aquaholic* into a floating gas station, but unless they exchange those five-gallon cans for fifty-five-gallon drums, they'll never match our range under power," I added.

Later, Charles informed Angie, Vee, Pat, and me that he had received an update on *The Aquaholic's* new sails. The sails would not be ready by the time we left Aruba. They probably wouldn't be ready when we reached Cartagena either, but we might be able to get them delivered to Panama and pick them up there.

Angie and Vee went back to inform the others. Pat said she needed to ask Charles a question. The way she said it made me suspicious, so I lingered close enough to hear.

"Do you remember the night of our infamous poker game?" she asked.

"I will never forget it."

"When the hand was finished but before you left, you placed something in the dealer's hand, remember?"

He nodded and began to smile.

"Was that a gold coin for a tip?"

"You are very perceptive," he said, still smiling.

"I've been thinking about this. So here's my question. Was that a tip for dealing a hand with an . . . unconventional wager? Or was that a payment for cheating? Rigging the hand so Tracy and I would win?"

I waited to hear Charles's answer. Pat was staring right at him, waiting as well.

He didn't reply. He just walked slowly away. Eyebrows raised, Pat and I exchanged glances.

CHAPTER 56

The next day Tracy reminded me that she and Pat had taken a scuba diving course and asked if the three of us could go diving somewhere. The cruising guide listed numerous dive spots, ranked by difficulty. I suggested a shallow dive in protected waters. They agreed. Charles overheard our plan and asked if he could join us. After all he had done for us, he didn't have to ask.

The site we picked was a bit far for the dinghy, so we told Vee we were taking *The Lady Anne* diving and that we'd be back. Two of Charles's men accompanied Charles, Pat, Tracy, and me.

We took *The Lady Anne* and anchored in a secluded bay. Pat had forgotten to tell me she had purchased three entry-level dive computers and sheepishly handed me one. While it might have been a basic model, it would keep track of the depth, dive times, and ascent rates, and that was all we really needed.

The Lady Anne had equipment for four, so we were all able to go diving together, leaving Charles's men onboard to watch the boat.

The water was warm, the current was negligible, and the visibility was good. There weren't a ton of fish, but the ones swimming around were brightly colored. Besides some small reef fish, we saw a few larger angelfish, one spotted eel, and one small octopus but no sharks or barracudas.

We surfaced and refilled our tanks. After some snacks, we made one more dive in the same place. This time we saw barracuda in the distance, but they weren't very big.

No one had any problems, and although the diving was mediocre by my standards, it was a nice break from being at the marina. Pat and Tracy had me sign their logbooks. They were very happy. Elated, we returned to the marina without incident and Charles thanked his men for coming with us.

We left Aruba when Ralph Clark told us the weather forecast was promising and set course for Cartagena. We stayed well offshore and covered the three hundred fifty nautical miles in less than three days, sailing straight through.

Thankfully the seas were moderate. We had the current and winds behind us, and for the first time since leaving Bermuda, *The Lady Anne* easily stayed ahead of *The Aquaholic*.

We were flying our spinnaker for hours at a stretch while

The Aquaholic had to reef her mainsail and tack downwind because she didn't have a spinnaker.

Angie mentioned she had never considered it worthwhile to buy one since *The Aquaholic* was a charter party boat that sailed close to the islands, not a passage maker. Neither Ed, Chet, nor Tommy had suggested one either.

Sailing downwind was dangerous for a catamaran because she risked slamming her bows into the wave trough, or she risked pitchpoling—flipping stern over bow. A catamaran completely upside down would not be able to right herself. With no escape hatches in the bottom of the hulls, anyone unfortunate enough to be belowdecks when the catamaran flipped end-for-end would face drowning.

Vee and Angie talked with Pat, Charles, and me about sailing closer to shore where the wind and seas should be calmer. Consulting with the weather router proved her hunch to be right. We ultimately decided against it, though, having heard horror stories about well-armed guerrilla pirates who preyed on vessels that got too close to the coast.

To keep the boats closer together during the night, both vessels cut their speed by reefing their sails.

We sailed through at least one squall every afternoon, but they passed by quickly and were usually over before the helmsman could change into their rain gear. We passed a lot of ships but had no close calls. The night watches were uneventful, but our log of radio calls showed that both Vee and Bev did the majority of the night sailing.

Again, those two sailed very efficiently. Maybe even a little more efficiently than our night watch did.

Tracy had purchased a Tortuga Caribbean Rum Cake at the marina store so I served it for dessert one evening. When I cut open the packaging, the smell of rum invaded the galley. The recommended serving suggestion was to serve it warm with vanilla ice cream.

I served it room temperature with berries and slices of an ice cream sandwich since we didn't have any vanilla ice cream. The cake was very moist and you could really taste the rum. Mo and Gert shared one piece while the rest of us easily finished it.

Had I known that cake was saturated with rum, I probably wouldn't have served it until we had docked in Cartagena, but the alcohol didn't appear to adversely affect anybody.

Pat commented the cake was so strong it probably was flammable but she didn't test her theory. Tracy laughed and said she had three more, of different flavors, for later.

When we were one day from Cartagena, we made reservations at the Club de Pesca marina. The marina office connected us with a maritime agent to facilitate our entry into Colombia.

The following day, we sailed into the Bay of Cartagena via the Boca Chica Channel. Our new agent met us at our slips and helped us complete the required paperwork. We had to lie about having firearms as they were restricted throughout Colombia, ironic for a country plagued with drug wars.

We were glad to see the marina had twenty-four-hour security, gated piers, and there were lots of cameras placed about. Nearly all of the employees we met were bilingual.

The office assigned us two nearby slips at the floating docks. There was electricity and fresh water. The marina had Wi-Fi, a laundry room, a fuel dock, and a wastewater pumpout station. The bathrooms were air-conditioned and the showers were clean. As a bonus, the marina we picked happened to be pet friendly. There was an onsite convenience store and a restaurant.

After the normal hosing the salt off the decks, everyone took it easy for the rest of the day. We were tired from the passage from Aruba. Angie brought over a loaf of homemade banana-nut bread. It was so good we just left the knife in the bag. We had some much-welcomed showers, changed clothes, and then met for dinner at the marina's restaurant.

The next day Vee, Bev, Angie, and Jane excused themselves to go shopping for a spinnaker for *The Aquaholic*. As usual, Marta went where Vee went. Vee apologized for not insisting on one back in Bermuda. It was obvious she felt bad for slowing us down.

I almost asked if they wanted me to come along but decided against it. Nearly all of my spinnaker experience was on monohulls, not multihulls. I was sure they could handle it, and I didn't want to imply that they couldn't. I was also fairly certain they were unlikely to find one of the proper size and design just sitting on a shelf.

Mo and Gert stayed aboard, saying they were tired and

they would watch Buster. Candy stopped by. She had been assigned to do their laundry, and offered to do ours. Gert said she'd help her. Charles stayed aboard *The Lady Anne,* too, to check emails, make some calls, and check on the sails.

The rest of us decided to go explore the old walled city.

CHAPTER 57

I had checked the cruising guide and seeing the old walled city neighborhood of Cartagena was highly recommended. It appeared to have something for everyone—from well-restored colonial architecture to stunning hotels; from numerous boutique shops to street vendors; from bright pink balconies to women balancing baskets of fruit on their heads. But what really caught my attention was the mention of many of Colombia's best restaurants, a "foodie's paradise."

Pat, Tracy, Dreamgirl, and I had a nice morning exploring the shops. I didn't need anything but enjoyed watching the three women darting in and out of shops, trying on this and that. To my inexperienced eye, some of the goods seemed pricey. As lunchtime approached, we viewed the posted menus at several restaurants.

We wanted to try a local place, but none of us spoke

Spanish and we couldn't read any of the menus. Dreamgirl told us that Bev and Candy both spoke Spanish, but Candy was doing laundry and Bev was hunting for a spinnaker.

We ended up at the Hard Rock Cafe. Dreamgirl had a salad, Pat had a steak, and Tracy and I had burgers and split a milkshake. It was American comfort food and we all enjoyed it. Pat insisted on paying for lunch and then she bought us each a hoodie at the gift shop.

When we returned to the marina, all hands were onboard *The Aquaholic*. They had found an asymmetrical spinnaker that didn't require a spinnaker pole. Vee was supervising as Angie, Charles, Mo, Candy, and Bev rigged the necessary lines to control their new sail.

Vee told me the local sail loft had one that a customer had ordered two years ago but had never picked up. It was two years old but unused and was the right size.

Bev asked me to send Chet a text thanking him for replacing the two spinnaker halyards, even though there was no spinnaker sail onboard. Having those halyards in place had saved a ton of time rigging the new sail. I sent a text right then so I wouldn't forget.

Vee hoisted the sail inside its sock, and when the sock was raised, behold, *The Aquaholic* had a spinnaker, a blue and yellow one with a large white plus sign in the center.

"Where's the pole?" Tracy asked. "*The Lady Anne* has a pole for our spinnaker."

"The hulls are so far apart they act as the pole," I replied.

"What's with the big tube sock thing?"

"That's a device to make deploying and retrieving an asymmetrical spinnaker easier. It's technically called a dousing sock or a spinnaker sleeve."

Vee ordered the sock pulled down over the sail and collapsed the spinnaker without much effort. Both Pat and Tracy agreed the sock was pretty cool.

"You might not stay in front the next time we have the wind behind us," Vee said, looking directly at me and laughing. I didn't respond, knowing she was probably right.

Candy and Bev agreed to be our interpreters at a local restaurant for dinner. We left for dinner early so those that had missed the shops earlier could browse a bit before cocktails and dinner. We all agreed to wear our Bacardi shirts.

"Will we see where *Romancing the Stone* was filmed?" Vee asked. "I really liked that movie."

"Actually, *Romancing the Stone* was filmed in Mexico and the United States," Jane answered.

"It wasn't filmed in Colombia?" Vee questioned.

"Filming a big-budget Hollywood movie in Colombia today, or even in the 1980s, would be problematic. There was, and still is, an unstable political climate, widespread violence, and drug trafficking."

A few minutes later Pat quietly showed me her phone. She had Googled *Romancing the Stone* and sure enough, it had been filmed where Jane said, not in Colombia.

"It might be handy to have a *Jeopardy* champion around when we don't have internet," I whispered. Pat put her phone away and nodded grudgingly.

We found a place for dinner, and after translating some of the menu for the rest of us, Candy and Bev made reservations. The hostess seemed excited to be speaking Spanish to gringos.

We browsed the wares of the street vendors for an hour and then returned for dinner. Having Bev and Candy available to translate was helpful. Evidently we had picked a local spot that didn't get a ton of tourists. The place was clean, the drinks were generous, the server was attentive, and the food was delicious.

Charles had asked for the bill as we were seated and the server left it with him. He was adamant to pay. Mo and I offered to split it three ways but Charles politely laughed and wouldn't relinquish the check.

He also insisted on reimbursing Angie for the sea kayaks and the new sail she had purchased. Jane tried arguing, saying she wanted to purchase those items for her daughter, but Charles wouldn't budge.

Inside, the walled city seemed a thousand miles away from the skyscrapers that dotted Cartagena's skyline. I don't believe any of us, with the possible exception of Jane, expected Cartagena to be such a modern city.

On the way back to the marina, we passed some clubs that were blaring Latin music and had waiting lines of well-dressed, muscular men and attractive women wearing short skirts and high heels. I grinned, thinking of my old saying about high heels and single women.

While there were lots of younger people milling about, we were careful to stick to the main well-lit streets. I was sure there was safety in numbers, but I didn't want any trouble. It was interesting that Marta kept glancing around, especially behind us.

Jane told us a little about the history of the walled city. Cartagena was under Spanish control and served as a major port. After pirates robbed the city of a large quantity of gold, the Spanish had stone walls erected.

Again Pat discreetly showed me her phone. Jane's story was right on.

"What was the last question you missed on *Jeopardy?*" Pat asked Jane. It was probably a valid question, but Pat's tone reinforced there was still friction between them.

Jane answered that in Final Jeopardy, the category was US currency. The question was: This President is pictured on the $100,000 gold certificate. She didn't know, so she guessed Herbert Hoover. The correct answer was Woodrow Wilson. Her wager would have been enough to win but she missed the question and lost.

I watched to see what Pat's response would be. She didn't say anything. I hoped that would be the end of whatever was going on between them but knew it was something deeper.

Tracy wanted a closer look at some of the clubs but agreed with Charles and me that it might not be safe to stay out too late. We made our way back to the boats.

I entertained Tracy that evening in my cabin. As her first orgasms subsided, she said, "Pat won't join us for a three-way, but I'm pretty sure Dreamgirl would, if you're interested."

The way she said it caught me by surprise. I wondered if

she had come up with that observation on her own or if Dreamgirl had said something. I looked into her eyes, searching for the right thing to say.

"Just think about it and let me know," she said as our love-making resumed.

I tried not to think about having sex with Dreamgirl, but I couldn't help myself. There was an obvious physical attraction there, but I didn't want to stress the already unusual romantic triangle by adding another woman into the mix.

"Since you brought up the topic of a three-way," I said. "Can I ask you a very personal question?"

"Go ahead."

"Are you bisexual?"

The way she started laughing made me sorry I had asked, but you can't unring a bell. I waited for her to say something.

"I want to have a three-way for your benefit. Isn't having sex with two women every man's fantasy?"

"You, Tracy my dear, are every man's fantasy. I can barely manage to keep you satisfied. If I had another woman to pleasure at the same time, I'd probably . . ."

"Probably what? Have a stroke? A seizure? A coronary?"

"Probably die from having too much fun."

CHAPTER 58

After we finished breakfast the next morning, the women of *The Aquaholic* stopped by. They were going to get haircuts and asked if any of us wanted to join them.

Mo, Charles, and I stayed aboard while the women went to find a salon. Mo went back to studying Tracy's drawings. He was fascinated by them. Charles pulled me aside.

"Ashley and Donna wanted me to tell you that your rental property, your bank account, your apartment, your credit card, your vehicle, and your taxes and insurance are all in great shape and not to worry."

"Please tell them thank you," I said.

"I will."

"By the way, how are they adjusting to Hawaii?"

"They are absolutely loving it. And they are glad to have

work to do to keep themselves busy. They said the long-distance management was challenging but therapeutic."

"Thank you for what you did for them," I told him, shaking his hand.

He smiled and then went over and told Mo that Ashley and Donna had his stateside affairs, along with Gert's, in order during their absence and not to worry. I assumed he had the same news for Tracy and for Pat. He really was a generous and thoughtful guy. He also mentioned the new sails weren't ready yet, but they should be ready to pick up when we reached Panama.

After the women returned from their salon experience, Angie, Jane, and Pat went grocery shopping. The fact that Pat went with them made me hope Jane and Pat's situation was moving toward neutral, perhaps. We would soon be departing for the canal, and most of us wanted to spend time ashore. I had no problem staying aboard alone. It was nice to just relax.

We all ate aboard *The Lady Anne* for dinner. Angie and Gert made a buffet line of pizza toppings, using pita bread as the crust. Each person would custom make their "pizza" and then bring their creations topside for me to finish on the grill.

Charles acted as the bartender, having purchased some local spirits to augment *The Lady Anne's* inventory. The red wine I tried tasted spoiled. It wasn't even worth cooking with. Yet the local beer was pretty good, so I stuck with that.

Dessert was fresh fruit, which seemed to please all of the women, and some world-famous Colombian coffee. I was hoping for a piece of local artisan chocolate, but seeing how careful the women were about what they ate, I settled for the fruit instead.

After dinner was finished and everything cleaned up, there were numerous requests for music. "What's the national dance of Colombia?" I asked, figuring it was respectful to play something local.

Before anyone could reach for their phone, Jane responded it was the cumbia, music similar to salsa.

I didn't know any cumbia songs and neither did she so she played "Jealousy," a tango. Then I played "It had Better be Tonight" in Samba tempo.

For our encore, we decided we could manage to fake a duet through "The Prayer." For not having music or having rehearsed even once, we rendered a passable duet that was well received.

Jane asked if she could play another so I moved out of the way. She played Led Zeppelin's "Stairway to Heaven." In my opinion, that was the one of the best rock songs ever recorded. I have probably heard it a thousand times and know all of the words. I had even played it at trumpet recitals when I was younger.

But I had never cried when hearing it; that is, I had never cried before tonight. Jane's masterful rendition of that classic rock song brought tears to my eyes. Her performance will be imprinted on my brain forever. She played it that well.

We all applauded and cheered, as did a number of other crews on nearby boats that we hadn't even noticed were listening. I was glad to see that Pat was applauding.

A knock on the hull startled us, including Buster, who started barking. A uniformed marina guard was on the dock. He beckoned Jane over. I tensed, figuring we were in trouble for violating some rule about loud music. I wondered how long he had been standing there.

But instead of chastising her, he shook her hand and took a selfie. He asked for her and my permission to post the video he had taken. Apparently he had heard her tango, walked over, and then recorded everything that followed. She was embarrassed yet flattered and she agreed. I gave him my permission as well. I wondered why he didn't offer to take a selfie with me. I could see Pat watching me and interpreting the look on my face.

She came over. "Don't be too sad," she whispered. "Look who's standing right behind Jane."

I did. Dreamgirl, Bev, and Vee were clearly in the background.

Suddenly, I didn't feel so bad.

It concerned me a little that the guard had been there for at least fifteen minutes, shooting video, and none of us, not even Buster, had noticed him. We needed to be more vigilant.

"Your turn." Jane smiled, nodding toward me.

There was no way I was going to follow her performance so I politely declined. The guard looked disappointed but then glanced at his phone and grinned, waved goodbye, and then walked briskly back down the dock.

CHAPTER 59

We departed early the next morning for Panama. After clearing customs, we headed out through the main channel, avoiding the larger ships. Once clear of the congestion, we plotted a course for the San Blas Islands on the way to the Panama Canal.

Rather than follow the coast, which would have calmer water but add many miles and considerable time, we headed west, cutting straight across to Panama. That shortened the passage to just over two hundred nautical miles but took us through open water.

As Cartagena disappeared from the radar, the sailing conditions rapidly deteriorated. As Ralph Clark's latest weather fax outlined, we were in for some heavier weather, but nothing he felt we couldn't handle.

As usual, he was right. The winds had shifted, so instead of sailing downwind, we were now sailing upwind. Flying *The Aquaholic's* new spinnaker would have to wait.

The winds were averaging between fifteen and twenty knots, gusting to thirty-five, and the waves were three to five feet, maxing out at about ten. The conditions were too rough for the autopilot so we hand steered. It was a rollicking sail through the rolling, frothy seas.

Charles spent a lot of time at the helm. Based on his gigantic smile, he was really enjoying himself. Tracy put the dog below and then rejoined the rest of us topside. Without me saying anything, I noticed that everyone was tethered to the boat. I also noticed that Vee didn't get very far ahead this time, keeping *The Aquaholic* closer than usual.

As the day wore on, as Ralph had predicted, the winds died down a little and the waves gradually subsided. Although we were still sailing upwind, the seas were flatter and the wind was less. Once we were able to reengage the autopilot, we all felt a bit more relaxed.

I awoke at three thirty a.m. the next morning, just in time to take over the helm from Charles for the early morning watch. I read the previous log entries to see if anything inter-esting had happened.

Tracy had reported seeing several container ships and two cruise ships. She noted having to alter course to avoid a colli-sion with the second cruise ship. I smiled, thinking she had transformed very well from a beginning sailing student to an experienced night helmswoman.

The San Blas Islands came into view before lunchtime.

Pat had been reading a cruising guide for Panama that Tommy Kraft had provided. She reported the area looked fantastic and the guide included detailed charts that would enable us to safely avoid the numerous reefs if we decided to stop.

Charles used the satellite phone to check on the order status of *The Aquaholic's* new sails. They still weren't ready. We could either spend a few days cruising this area or we could push on to the Panama Canal and wait for them there. If the sails still weren't ready, we could continue waiting or we could keep going without any new sails and hope the old ones didn't fail.

Charles was happy to delay here for a few days but checked with Ralph. Ralph thought that was a good idea as the weather ahead was unsettled and would be for a few days as a front passed.

Tracy told Charles that a layover would increase his costs for Vee and her people but he dismissed her reminder as inconsequential. A brief radio conversation with Angie sealed the deal; we would stop and explore and wait for better weather ahead.

We anchored in a protected area between three small islands. They had white sand beaches, were overgrown with palm trees, and appeared deserted. The sandy floor below was clearly visible in the clear turquoise waters. *The Aquaholic* anchored nearby.

After lunch, both vessels launched their dinghies. *The Aquaholic* also launched her kayaks. Charles and I swabbed the deck while Tracy, Pat, Gert, Mo, and Buster took our dinghy and went ashore.

Candy and Dreamgirl paddled their kayak over. Candy showed us the starfish she had found floating before paddling toward the shore where the others had landed.

When they were out of earshot, I had a question for Charles. "Is it just me or is Dreamgirl one of the sexiest women ever?"

His grin answered my question.

"Maybe we should invite her over to play some poker," I said, grinning too.

"Maybe we should," he replied. But then he started laughing and I knew he wasn't serious.

"You know, that Dreamgirl woman is an eleven," I said. He gave me a puzzled look, so I finished the line. "That's a ten that doesn't get a headache."

When our crew returned, Pat broke out the snorkeling gear and Charles joined her in a lazy swim over to check the anchor.

Tracy said the beach was full of driftwood and she wondered if we could build a fire that evening. I suggested we have a beach barbecue. She radioed Angie, who said that sounded like a great idea.

Pat and Charles returned and reported the anchor was securely buried in the sand. She was sad they didn't see a lot of fish, but she reported the water was warm and there were starfish all over the bottom.

There was no campfire grate onboard either vessel, and

rather than take our grill apart, I suggested that Angie make salad and dessert and I would make the main course. Tracy was curious what I was going to cook without a fire grate. So were the others. I told them it was a surprise.

Watching Pat shower on the stern was more arousing than usual, so when I handed her the towel, I whispered that she should meet me in my cabin. She grinned and we were screwing five minutes later.

Dinner consisted of quesadillas wrapped in foil and heated in the coals. They were easy to make, cook, and serve. I made some vegetarian and used lunchmeat in the others. Angie had made potato salad, and for dessert, everyone made their own s'mores.

The sunset was beautiful as it sank below the horizon. Later we turned around and watched the moonrise. Seeing both so close together was pretty cool.

Marta made sure the fire was out and then we went back to our respective vessels. Tracy shared my cabin that night. I bent her every which way and she begged for more. A thought flashed through my mind that perhaps thinking of a lewd poker game with Dreamgirl earlier had been more arousing than I realized.

CHAPTER 60

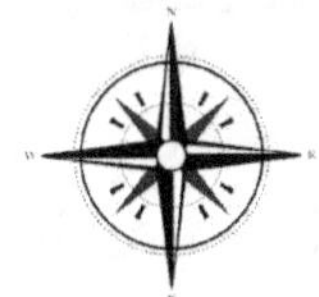

We spent two days in the San Blas Islands, exploring and relaxing. It was tricky sailing around the reefs. We saw eight or nine shipwrecks. We posted lookouts on both vessels, not wanting to add to those numbers. The sheer number of wrecks, some of them looking to be fairly recent, explained why no bareboat charter companies operated in the area.

Most of the sailboats joining us in the area were catamarans, but there were a few monohulls. There were also a lot of powerboats, some of them quite loud between the music and the engines.

Having a minority of monohulls made sense. Generally speaking, both catamarans and powerboats could navigate shallower water than a comparably sized monohull. Had *The*

Lady Anne not had an adjustable bulb-keel, she would have been very limited in anchorage choices.

Once, when we were anchoring for lunch, another cat motored over close and complimented *The Aquaholic's* paint job. They were even more impressed when Jane told them it was her great-great-aunt Luverne's original design.

Another cat stopped by and asked where we arrived from. When told we sailed over from Cartagena, they wanted to know if we got seasick on the crossing. Gert was happy to respond that we hadn't. The way the woman asked the question made me figure she hadn't been as fortunate and probably ran into some heavy weather that we missed. I didn't mention we had really come from Bermuda.

We were also approached by the local Kuna people selling live lobsters, coconuts, and weed from small boats. We bought enough lobsters for dinner and a few coconuts. We all passed on the weed. I half expected a local selling fresh fruits and produce to come by but none did.

I grilled our lobsters and Angie boiled hers, but everyone agreed they were delicious.

Once when crossing fairly open water between two of the larger islands, I spotted dark clouds closing in rapidly. Pat had read in the cruising guide there were sudden, unpredictable storms called the *Culo de Pollo.*

Figuring that was what was bearing down on us, I ordered the engine started and the sails furled. Charles radioed *The Aquaholic* to do the same.

Within five minutes, the previously tranquil seas got

choppy and the wind came from all directions. It lasted less than an hour and then abated just as quickly as it had arrived.

I noticed we had received a weather fax from Ralph telling us to keep our eyes open. I showed it to the others and joked that his warning was better late than never.

The storm was no problem for our engine and bare poles, but if a sailor had been caught with their sails up and been anywhere near a reef, they might have had a serious problem.

I noticed it rained quite often, but the rains were short and everything dried very quickly.

Besides the ubiquitous starfish, we saw barracuda, several fairly large sea turtles, and even a few manta rays.

Our last night at anchorage was bad. The little cove was pleasant enough, but just before ten p.m., a large, double-decked powerboat arrived and anchored right by us. The music was booming and the passengers were loud and drunk. I debated taking the dinghy and asking them to be quiet but we didn't want any trouble. Neither did Angie, so we tried to ignore them, figuring they had to stop at some point.

We weighed anchor early the next morning, passing that big boat on the way out. Several of the partiers were passed out on the deck. One young woman was squatting near the rail, peeing or worse. She was naked and just stared at us as we motored past.

A uniformed crew member was watching her. He waved, grinning. I returned a different gesture. So did Pat. So did Tracy. Even Gert flipped him off.

I was glad to have seen the San Blas Islands. They were

very beautiful in a desolate sort of way. The Kunas were friendly. The lobsters were cheap. The starfish were happy. The palm trees were nice. Even though there was no diving, if I passed this way again I would probably drop anchor.

But a couple of days was enough and I was anxious to transit the famous Panama Canal, which was now less than one hundred nautical miles away.

CHAPTER 61

Pat's cruising guide listed the available marinas on the Caribbean side of the canal but Charles was most insistent we use the Shelter Bay Marina. That was fine with us onboard *The Lady Anne* and also with Angie and Vee onboard *The Aquaholic.*

We radioed when we were close and were quickly assigned two slips. Pat had read that the harbor entrance could be challenging, especially at night or in rough weather, but we stayed alert and didn't have any problems.

I had just finished securing my dock line when someone tapped me lightly on my shoulder. It was Elouise. She had been waiting at the onsite hotel for us to arrive. I was glad to see her.

"That's why Charles wanted us to stay here," Tracy said,

coming over and giving her a hug. "He knew you were waiting."

I nodded. I also noticed that Tony, Lance, and another large man I hadn't seen before were waiting a discreet distance away. "No harm will befall her with Charles's men on duty," I thought.

Elouise had gotten us a transit agent. We met with him later that afternoon. He was very friendly and had been assisting private sailboats with their Panama Canal transit for over fifteen years.

In a nutshell, we had to do four things: get measured, make payment, get organized; follow instructions.

He explained that until our vessels were officially measured and payment was received by the local bank, we would not be assigned a transit date. Once we had a date, he would arrange for everything, including an advisor and line handlers.

He said that we might not get a transit date for five or six days, maybe longer, maybe shorter. Talk about a definite maybe.

Both vessels were measured the next morning. The Panama Canal Authority official found both vessels to be slightly longer than the builder had specified, even allowing for *The Aquaholic's* new dinghy davits. However we quickly learned that his official tape measure was the final word.

Elouise handled the payment. She wouldn't tell me how much everything had cost but just smiled and said not to worry about it. She did mention our agent had accompanied her to the bank, along with a security guard and two of

Charles's men. She was slightly nervous but had no problems.

Tracy spoke with her in private later and found out the transaction was several thousand dollars and included transit tolls, cruising permits, and a bond to cover any additional transit charges.

Elouise had also left a substantial amount of cash to cover other charges, like line and fender rental, water taxis, pilot boats, etcetera.

"Wow," I told Tracy. "This is more involved than I imagined."

"Me too," she said, shrugging.

But then she smiled and added, "If we didn't have Mr. Charles T. Williams along to subsidize Elouise to pay the bills, Pat would be cashing some more coins."

Our agent stopped by later with a transit date. We were to meet at the Flats anchorage, near Port Cristobal, at nine thirty a.m., four days from today. Our two vessels would likely raft together but it was possible another vessel would join us.

Before leaving, he told us we would get our lines and fenders the day before transit. We were also expected to furnish meals, snacks, and beverages for the advisors and line handlers.

Angie, Vee, Bev, Charles, Pat, Tracy, and I had a brief discussion over whether we should do some or all of the line handler's work by ourselves or hire it out. We agreed to hire five line handlers, two for *The Aquaholic* and three for *The Lady Anne*.

Our rationale was that if Vee and Angie were at the helm, Dreamgirl, Candy, Bev, and Marta should be plenty to work two of the lines. The two hired line handlers could manage the other two. That left Jane to manage snacks and incidentals.

As for us, if Tracy and Charles took the helm, Pat and I should be able to easily manage one of the lines, leaving the three hired people to manage the other three. Pat didn't want Mo and Gert to have to do anything more than be in charge of food.

Our agent agreed with our decision. He told us it would be no problem to get more line handlers on day two of the transit if they were needed.

Just as I thought we had an agreement, Charles changed his mind and ordered eight professional line handlers, four per boat. He wanted us to be able to enjoy the transit and not have to be working the entire time. Pat and I glanced at each other and shrugged.

Charles did have a good point. The others probably saw his wisdom because nobody tried to argue.

I was relaxing topside after dinner with Tracy, Gert, Charles, and Buster. Mo and Pat were below, looking over Tracy's drawings—again. I didn't see any of Charles's men but was pretty sure they were watching the boats from somewhere.

An older, bright-blue sailboat maneuvered into position to back into the slip next to us. It was a steel ketch with a pilot-house, maybe fifty feet long not counting the bowsprit. Based on the design, I guessed her to be from the late fifties or early sixties. For being a classic, she appeared to be in surprisingly good condition.

There were no hands on deck. The man at the helm waved as he began reversing.

"Let's go give him a hand," I said to Tracy. "He looks like he's solo."

We hustled over and offered our assistance with the dock lines. He eagerly accepted. The name on the stern was *Rusty Knot, Baja California Sur*.

The tires hanging on the sides and the long blue lines loosely coiled fore and aft were a dead giveaway that this boat had just come through from the Pacific side.

"Nice boat," I greeted.

He smiled and nodded.

"Are you alone?" Tracy asked.

"I started with four crew but we had an accident."

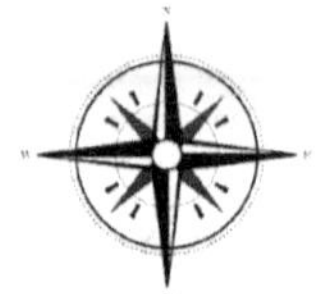

CHAPTER 62

Charles, Gert, and Buster made their way over and everyone introduced themselves. His name was Roger Wilson. He was single and a full-time cruiser. He was tall and skinny and maybe in his late forties or early fifties. I guessed he might have been a basketball player before succumbing to the call of the sea.

"So tell us how the transit was," Charles said.

"They had an accident," Tracy responded.

"What kind of an accident?" Gert asked, looking concerned.

Roger told us how he had bought *The Rusty Knot* in San Diego but had been sailing her in the Sea of Cortez. He wanted a change of scenery so he decided to move her to Grenada. Since he had recently broken up with his last sailing partner, he was in need of crew.

He had met some bareboat charterers at the marina in LaPaz and convinced four of them to come back for an extended passage to Grenada, at his expense, to help him with *The Rusty Knot's* relocation.

Everything had been going well until the Miraflores locks. They had rafted with one other sailboat but got crooked due to the sudden current from the locks and the wake from the larger ship ahead of them.

Their advisor ordered the stern line loosened, and the crewman doing that didn't respect the tension on that line. When he loosened the line from the cleat, his hand was violently pulled into the winch. He didn't lose any fingers, but his hand was pretty mangled. As the raft started to rotate, the other two crewman grabbed for the line. They managed to get it cleated but it ripped the flesh from their palms in the process.

After the raft was under control, they continued through the locks but stopped briefly in Miraflores Lake. The three injured crew left for a Panama City hospital and the fourth crew member packed up all of their gear and left with them.

Roger's entire crew had quit without notice, literally jumping ship. He was able to hire line handlers for the rest of the transit.

"Don't underestimate the load on those lines," he told us after he had finished his tale. It was quite a dire warning and made me appreciate that Charles had insisted on hiring professionals.

During sailing lessons, I always emphasized being super

careful around winches. This was just another unfortunate incident to reaffirm that practice. I envisioned the crewman operating the winch wearing sailing gloves but the two that grabbed for the line weren't.

"Where did the line handlers go?" Tracy asked. "Wouldn't they have helped you dock here?"

"As soon as we were through the Gatun locks, they and the advisor left on a pilot boat. I wondered how I'd manage to dock her by myself with the stiff breeze, but then you two came over and did all of the work."

"What's your plan now?" Charles asked.

"Hang out here until I can hire another crew I guess."

"What do you do for income to support being a full-time cruiser?" Tracy asked.

I was wondering that too since he looked a bit young to be retired but I wasn't brazen enough to ask. However I had learned that Tracy had a limited filter and just said what was on her mind.

"I'm able to cruise full time because I matched five numbers in the lottery and had bought the multiplier."

I was impressed to have actually met someone who had won the lottery.

He continued, "For a three-dollar ticket, I won a million dollars times the multiplier, which was four."

"Was it a quick pick?" I asked.

He chuckled. "I played the numbers on the back of the fortune cookie. I never play the lottery, but something told me to play those numbers. That win enabled me to quit my real job and here I am."

After he excused himself to complete the marina paperwork, I went below. Mo and Pat were still engrossed in Tracy's drawings.

I told them about Roger Wilson, *The Rusty Knot*, the fortune cookie's lucky numbers, and what had happened to his crew. Mo echoed Pat's gratitude to Charles for hiring line handlers.

"Why wasn't his crew wearing their gloves?" Pat asked.

"You'll have to ask Roger," I replied.

Pat grinned up at Charles. "I'll have to tell him sometime about how I happened to win *The Lady Anne*. Now *that* was a lucky number!"

Everyone else came below except for Tracy. Charles said she went over to *The Aquaholic* to tell them what had happened.

Tracy, Candy, Angie, and I went shopping the next day. I wasn't overly impressed with Colon. The city seemed dated and poverty was evident. Tracy took pictures of the pigs that were wandering about. Our taxi driver offered to stay with us while we shopped. He said the city was "mostly safe."

We accepted his personal guide services. I could see where parts of Colon might be a bad idea for tourists after dark. However the people we met were all friendly. A few of them spoke passable English. Angie and Tracy enjoyed negotiating prices for fresh produce, with Candy translating.

I was able to buy some thick leather work gloves. In case

the line handlers needed assistance, I wanted to have something more substantial than my regular sailing gloves.

I also bought some heavy canvas tarps to cover the solar panels. Tracy had found that piece of advice on another sailboat's blog about transiting the Panama Canal. Their solar panel had been damaged.

To get the rented lines from the boat to the shore, the shoreside personnel threw a lightweight messenger line from the shore to the vessel. It had a heavy "monkey fist" heaving knot tied to one end. The process was for the boat's crew to then tie that messenger line to a large loop tied in one end of the heavy rented lines. The shoreside line handlers would then haul both lines back ashore. Apparently the monkey fist used was tied around a metal weight, and when it accidentally hit the boat's solar panel, the panel shattered. The blog implored readers to pad their solar panels.

Our driver convinced us to take a side trip to the sixteenth-century Fort San Lorenzo. It was about an hour's drive, each way, so we bought some food for a picnic lunch. Taking a break from the boats seemed like a good idea.

We took a bridge over the entrance to the Gatun locks. Then we had a scenic drive, seeing both coast and jungle. We spotted some wild monkeys. The fort's ruins weren't in good condition, but it was cool to see the old cannons sitting about.

When we returned to the marina, Tracy eagerly told the others what they had missed. Mo, Gert, Pat, Charles, and Jane decided to engage our driver for a repeat trip the next day.

Again, I was glad to see that Pat had included herself on a tour with Jane.

Vee, Marta, Bev, and Dreamgirl passed on seeing either Colon or the fort. I sensed that perhaps they wanted some time for themselves.

A couple of days later, Bev and Candy invited me to go shopping with them. We didn't really need anything, but since they asked me to come with them, I accepted.

I had been concerned about not being able to tell them apart, but after getting to know them, apart from their figures and their blonde hair, they really weren't all that similar.

Our driver dropped us off at the far end of a long street lined with local shops and we slowly made our way back.

We hadn't gone very far when Bev leaned close and said, "Don't look now, but we're being followed."

CHAPTER 63

I followed her instructions and didn't look back.

"Is it Pincus or Onion?" I asked. I kept my voice calm but I was starting to tense.

"No," Candy answered. "I don't recognize him, but a lone man has been shadowing us since we got out of the taxi."

I was nervous and curious, wondering how they were so sure.

"It's broad daylight and the streets are fairly busy so we should be okay, right?" I asked. I still hadn't looked back, trusting that they were right, somehow.

"Let's go into the next shop," Bev said softly. "When you reach the door, look back casually. You'll see a man wearing a straw hat about two stores back. That's him."

I did as instructed and saw the man as described. He was a

small man. I didn't recognize him but I didn't get a very good look.

Once inside the shop, Candy said we'd slowly leave and cross over the street. If he followed, we had a tail. If he didn't, we might still have a tail.

"Who in the world could possibly be tailing us in Colon?" I asked.

They looked at each other but neither answered. I wasn't really scared, but I was beginning to get nervous.

We left as planned and headed across the street. We were almost across when a shiny black Mercedes screeched to a stop about five feet away. The doors opened and two men got out. They were carrying pistols. One headed toward Bev, the other toward Candy.

Bev and Candy didn't move, so neither did I, but I noticed people fleeing down the sidewalks on both sides.

My heart started pounding. I wondered who in the hell these guys were. I then wondered how Bev and Candy knew we were being followed. I then wondered if we were going to be shot, or kidnapped, or both.

The man on the left advanced toward Bev and said something in Spanish. His last word was *puta* which, thanks to Tony, I knew meant "whore." He raised his weapon and pointed it at her head. I was expecting him to shoot and knew he couldn't miss at that range. A thought flashed through my mind that I was going to watch Captain Beverly Thompson die.

But Bev wasn't ready to die. She leapt toward him, grabbing his gun hand and whirling him around. When his pistol was pointed at the other man on the right, she put her finger over his and fired off two rounds.

They hit the man on Candy's side in the chest. He immediately collapsed. Then Bev pivoted her man some more and fired three more rounds at the car's windshield. The bullets went right through, leaving small holes, but the glass was tinted and I couldn't see if she had hit anyone.

Candy dropped down and snatched up the pistol the man on her side had dropped. She crouched low, aimed at the man in the straw hat, and fired one round.

I had forgotten about him but saw he was pointing a handgun toward us. But he never got the chance to fire. Candy's shot hit him right in the forehead and he crumpled.

I glanced back at Bev. She repeatedly slammed her man's hand into the car's hood until he dropped the gun. Then she got in behind him, grabbed the back of his head, and pounded it into the hood. After the fourth or fifth slam into the now-dented hood, she let go. He fell, his face broken and bloody.

I still hadn't moved but did so now. I picked up the gun he had dropped and looked at Bev.

"If anyone gets out of the car, drop him," she said, her voice surprisingly calm. She looked at Candy and motioned toward the car with her head. I pointed the pistol at the car and moved my finger over the trigger. I was ready.

Without being told, Candy pulled open the driver's door and pointed her gun inside. She fired one round and then moved toward the back door.

Bev reached her hand to me for the gun. Controlling the barrel's direction, I carefully handed it to her.

Bev said something in Spanish. An answer, also in Spanish, came from inside the vehicle. It was a man's voice and it sounded angry. I didn't hear *puta* this time but had no idea what was being said.

Candy answered him. Then Bev added another few sentences. Her tone was firm. There was more Spanish from the man in the back seat. He sounded really pissed.

Without saying anything further, she and Candy opened the back doors simultaneously. I expected gunfire to originate from inside the car. When there was none, I assumed the occupant must have been unarmed or injured and unable to fire.

Bev and Candy both pointed their pistols inside and then looked. Bev said something in Spanish. Candy backed away.

Bev fired two more rounds into the back seat. I saw the muzzle flash through the darkened windows. The boom reverberated. She said something else and then glanced up and down the street. Candy looked around as well. Satisfied there were no more threats, they concealed their pistols into their shorts and moved back toward me.

"Let's go," Bev said.

"Walk with purpose but don't run," Candy added. "And don't look back.

I did as instructed.

We quickly got away from the Mercedes. A few people

were looking at us, but they moved out of our way and didn't say anything. Before long, we were a block away.

"Sorry to cut the shopping trip short but we better get out of here," Candy said. Again, I didn't argue. I hadn't done much during that attack but my heart was pounding.

"Are you okay?" Bev asked. I couldn't believe she asked me that. I should have asked them that. Her question momentarily stumped me.

"What do you mean am I okay?" I finally answered. "Are you okay?"

"We're fine," she answered.

"What the hell was that?"

Bev gave me a wink and said, "Disgruntled relatives."

CHAPTER 64

We went three more blocks. Our pace was quick and purposeful. We turned into another shop and I noticed that both women got a good look behind us.

"We're clear," Candy announced.

"Are you going to tell me what just happened?" I asked. My heart rate was up from the brisk walk but at least it was no longer pounding.

We exited the shop and crossed the street. We went a little further and then turned into a coffee house. Bev motioned me toward an open table and Candy went up to the counter. About that time I heard a siren. I knew where it was headed.

I glanced around. There were a few locals seated about. None of them paid us any attention. Candy joined us a few minutes later. She placed a cup of coffee in front of me.

I took a moment to relax. I had a million questions, but keeping my voice down, I said, "You two are obviously way more than an attractive all-female sailing crew." They exchanged glances.

"Would you like to tell me what just happened?"

Candy answered first. "We used to do things we can't talk about for a government agency we can't mention."

Then Bev spoke. "The last time we were in Colon was to take care of a really bad person."

"That bad man's brother was the one in the Mercedes. He must have spotted us and tried to get even back there," Candy said.

I started to say something, but Bev reached over and put her hand on top of mine. She said, "Reid, dear, it would be best if you forgot what you think you just saw."

Candy took my other hand and squeezed it, saying, "We have retired from that life."

I looked back and forth between them. They were calm. Too calm for having just shot four people and beat the crap out of number five. I wondered how many other people they had shot or beat up. "Did Vee and Dreamgirl work for the same . . . company?" I asked.

Bev nodded.

"How about Marta?"

"Marta took an early retirement from Interpol a few years ago," Candy told me, lowering her voice and releasing my hand.

"So she's a spy like you two?"

"Your words, not ours." Bev smiled.

"Don't tell Mo or Gert. Don't tell Angie or Jane. Don't tell Charles. And especially don't tell Pat or Tracy," Candy warned. It wasn't a threat but it was very clear that I was to keep silent about what had transpired that morning.

I took a sip of my coffee. It was really hot.

My head was spinning. I couldn't come up with a single thing to say that would put what just happened to us in context. Suddenly, I blurted the first thing that popped into my head.

"So how did you get into sailing?" I asked.

Bev let go and sat back. Candy moved closer and answered, "We were all tired of doing despicable acts in hostile places for unclear reasons we didn't always agree with."

Bev continued, "We took an *early retirement* and reinvented ourselves as sailors."

"And Marta?" I asked.

"She helped us do something we can't talk about and negotiated citizenship for herself as a bonus."

"We all sleep much better at night now," Candy added, smiling.

"There's nothing like the sea to make you forget your past and your problems," Bev said.

I nodded. Some of my friends found sailing boring. I found it peaceful. I had often wondered where the line was between boring and peaceful. Obviously, these women found the sea therapeutic.

"Now finish your coffee, tell us a joke, and let's go." Candy smiled, leaning in close. "We've got to wipe down and dispose of these weapons and we had better arrive back at the boats with some packages."

For the first time I can remember, I couldn't think of a single joke.

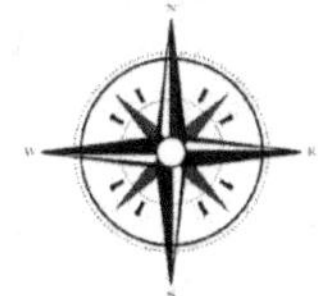

CHAPTER 65

The day finally arrived for our transit through the Panama Canal. As our transit agent had promised, our lines and tires had been delivered by water taxi the day before.

I was really anxious to leave Colon. I hadn't said anything and told myself not to, ever. But I did view Vee and the others in a different light. Whenever they laughed or giggled, I wondered if they were cleansing their minds of their former lives.

I tried to focus on their sailing prowess, not on their past lives. They seemed very happy aboard. I told myself that part was real and they deserved peace wherever they could find it. Those women had a major secret, but I knew it would be safe with me.

The Aquaholic's decks were cleared of the sea kayaks by

storing them with the dinghy. Her gas cans had been temporarily moved below. All the solar panels had been covered.

As per a tip from the marina personnel, we purchased a case of Coca-Cola for each vessel's line handlers and advisor. Both vessels were also well stocked with plenty of food for snacks and lunches.

Everyone was in great spirits. Elouise had paid the marina's bill and we were ready to go.

Vee, Bev, Candy, and Dreamgirl were wearing their nautical white uniforms and looked as hot as ever. I wondered if part of their previous job description had been seduction. If it was, and if they were as good at it as they were at handling dangerous situations, I had no doubt they seldom failed. Marta was wearing her normal workout attire. She looked more intimidating than sexy.

I dismissed the seduction thought as quickly as I could.

Elouise and Charles's men bid us *bon voyage* and said they'd be waiting for us in Panama City. We shoved off, making our way to the Flats anchorage, a waiting area near Port Cristobal.

We were supposed to meet up with our advisors and line handlers at eight a.m. We were expecting them to be timely because we were, but they were late.

While we were waiting, Tracy pulled me aside. She told me Elouise had asked Pat if she should be concerned about missing her period.

"What did Pat tell her?" I asked, very curious.

"Pat told her the trip to the parallel dimension had messed with the women's systems. None of the women who had visited the other dimension had their periods and it was surprisingly convenient at sea."

"She didn't mention you'd all been sterilized?"

"No," Tracy replied, shaking her head. "She explicitly didn't mention that."

It was nearly ten thirty a.m. when a water taxi arrived with our advisors and line handlers.

We were informed it was just going to be our two vessels making the transit, so we made our way toward the Gatun locks. While waiting for a large ship to pass, we moved out of the way and rafted *The Lady Anne* and *The Aquaholic* together. Between our regular fenders and the rented tires, both boats were well cushioned.

The line handlers tied large loops in one end of the rented lines. After the large ship had passed, we motored into position. We were behind a ferry full of tourists.

The canal workers threw their monkey fists. Nobody got hit and neither did our solar panels. The workers tied the messenger line to the large loops and the canal personnel pulled the transit lines up to them.

Our advisor gave orders concerning engine speed and line tightening/loosening as he determined appropriate. He communicated his actions with his counterpart aboard *The Aquaholic* by radio. Our raft made it through all three locks without incident, gaining eighty-five feet of elevation by the time we reached Gatun Lake.

Once we got started, the entire process through the Gatun locks took less than four hours. The way the lake water filled the locks to raise the ships to the next level was nothing if not a spectacular feat of engineering.

The advisors and the line handlers had obviously done this several thousand times and we had no issues. Our snacks and lunches were well received and devoured.

A pilot boat met us on Gatun Lake and picked up our passengers. We had been instructed where to moor for the evening and where to meet in the morning for the second leg of the transit.

We unrafted and made our way, single file, to an unused mooring. The mooring was a gigantic concrete caisson that would have held a really large ship. We tied on opposite sides.

We watched the steady parade of ships pass, yet we were fairly close to the jungle. Buster was very interested in the noisy monkeys and kept barking. Pat pointed out there were small crocodiles in the lake, prompting Tracy to immediately put Buster below.

We all celebrated a successful first transit day with two bottles of French champagne. We then ate the leftover snacks as appetizers. After, Angie, Jane, Vee, and her crew walked across the concrete caisson to *The Aquaholic*.

I grilled some steaks and skewers of peppers and mushrooms for *The Lady Anne's* contingent. Charles selected a very good red wine. Mo and Gert were happy to share a steak.

Tracy laughed that they were eating salads aboard *The Aquaholic*. She opened another of her rum cakes for our dessert. She and I had a different type of dessert later that evening in my cabin.

CHAPTER 66

As instructed, we were ready to go at precisely eight a.m. the next morning, but nobody showed up. We passed the time watching the constant flow of vessels crossing Gatun Lake.

We saw more small crocodiles, lots of birds, one monkey, and even a sloth.

At ten forty-one a.m., a pilot boat brought our advisors and line handlers out to us. Both of the advisors and most of the line handlers were different than yesterday.

One of the line handlers was a very young woman, one of the few we had seen working the canal. She was short and skinny and her name was Lupe.

Now, I freely admit I've never been good at guessing women's ages, but this gal looked like a teenager. Our advisor told us it was her third day.

Both vessels made their way across Gatun Lake, passing lots of islands and numerous other ships. We were extra careful to watch the buoys and stay in the marked channel. We were told there were lots of old tree trunks outside of the channel. That seemed logical, considering Gatun Lake had once been nothing but jungle.

On the way, our advisor told us that construction of the fifty-one-mile-long canal had taken thirty-two years. It was completed in 1914. Over 75,000 men and women worked on the canal. There were 28,000 deaths from malaria, yellow fever, other tropical diseases, mosquitos, and accidents.

We stopped before entering the Gaillard Cut and waited for a container ship to emerge.

While we were waiting, our advisor shared some history of the Cut. It was a narrow section, dug out through the rocks of the Continental Divide by over fifty-eight hundred men using 30,000 tons of dynamite. Sadly, there were a lot of unnecessary deaths during the blasting because inexperienced workers used fuses that were too short.

We were all fascinated by the story of the canal's construction. The engineer in Pat asked some good questions, but our advisor was very knowledgeable. His pride at working here showed.

Once the container ship exited the narrow section, we rafted together and proceeded to the Pedro Miguel lock. This time we were behind a luxury yacht. When that yacht accelerated through the lock, our raft momentarily got caught in their wake.

But unlike *The Rusty Knot,* our line handlers reacted quickly and we didn't have any issues.

I found it amusing that when anybody gave Lupe some instructions, it sounded like they were saying "You pay."

When we cleared the final Miraflores lock, we had been lowered down to the Pacific Ocean. Our transit was complete.

We unrafted and proceeded under the Bridge of the Americas. We dropped off the advisors, the line handlers, the lines, and the tires before proceeding to the Flamenco Marina in Panama City where Elouise had reserved us two slips.

She met us as we docked, smiling and waving. Next to her was a dock cart holding *The Aquaholic's* new sails. Angie was thrilled. She and Vee decided to continue using the old sails, but they were both glad to have replacement canvas.

It was a nice-looking marina with numerous amenities. Elouise told us there was twenty-four-hour security, gated piers, and the entire staff was bilingual.

Tracy inquired about what we should eat if we wanted to eat like locals, not tourists. She was steered toward a local place and told not to miss the *sancocho,* which was chicken and beef soup; the *ropa veija,* which was shredded beef; the *empanadas,* which were chicken-stuffed turnovers; and the *carna guisada,* which was cubed beef.

Both crews cleaned up the decks. I helped Vee remove the kayaks from the davits and she retied them along the lifelines.

Everyone relaxed, cleaned up, and changed clothes. Leaving two of Charles's men to watch the boats, we took three taxis to an early dinner at the restaurant Tracy had been told about.

The place was small but clean and not crowded. With half of us wearing our Bacardi T-shirts, we were obviously tourists. Using Candy's translation services, Elouise immediately asked for the check. Under my breath I said with a chuckle, "You pay. You pay."

Then I flashed back to Candy saying Spanish to the man in the back seat of the Mercedes. I wondered what she had told him, but I knew I could never bring the subject up again.

CHAPTER 67

The next morning we had an impromptu meeting at the marina's restaurant. Ralph had advised us the weather was favorable for continuing our passage, but it seemed foolish to be in historic Panama City and spend all our time at the marina.

We decided to take one day off and explore the city. We would spend the next day making sure both vessels were ready for the passage to Hawaii via the Galapagos Islands. Assuming that Ralph's weather forecasts remained favorable, we planned to depart the day after.

Charles, Jane, Mo, Gert, Vee, Marta, Candy, and Elouise booked a city tour departing early afternoon. Tracy, Pat, Angie, Dreamgirl, Bev, and I hired a minivan to drive us around town and show us the highlights. That gave each party their own translator if needed, courtesy of Candy and Bev.

My group of women wanted to go shopping but not at a mall or at outlet stores. They didn't want souvenirs or local crafts either. Bev told our driver what we wanted, or rather what we didn't want, so he took us to the local fish market.

We snacked on ceviche by the cup as we wandered around, surrounded by fresh fish. There were so many choices it was intimidating. Angie bought sea bass fillets; I finally decided on tuna steaks.

The prices were the cheapest I had ever seen, so we bought as much as we thought we could keep cold. The fish looked fresh and more importantly, it smelled fresh. The fishmonger cut our selected fish for us and packed it on ice. Bev told us he was offering us the heads at no charge. Angie and I grinned but both politely declined.

Bev acted completely normal, as if having forgotten what transpired on the streets of Colon. I still stared at Dreamgirl occasionally. Her looking like my old lover combined with my assumption she had been a spy like the others gave her an intriguing quality.

Pat caught me staring and lightly elbowed me in the ribs, saying, "Kryptonite, remember?"

I remembered and looked away.

There was a separate area selling fresh fruits and vegetables so Angie and I took advantage of that as well. Angie even bought a basil plant, saying she wanted the fresh leaves on the long passage to Hawaii. That was a good idea, so I got one too.

Bev and Angie were a few stalls ahead of us when I heard a screeching loud whistle coming from their direction. I looked and saw Bev taking her fingers out of her mouth. She had whistled. I didn't have to wonder why for long because I watched as a young boy bolted away from her, carrying Angie's purse.

He was running full tilt right at us. Before I could react, Dreamgirl dropped down low and did a leg sweep, knocking the boy's knees right out from under him. He crashed into the ground and Angie's purse skidded away from him, toward me.

I picked the purse up and Dreamgirl picked the boy up by the arm. Bev came over and read him the riot act in Spanish. The kid, who was maybe twelve or thirteen, looked horrified. I wondered if it was because his latest purse snatch attempt had failed miserably or from being yelled at by a beautiful blonde woman. Or maybe it was because some of the patrons were clapping for what Dreamgirl had done.

Anyway, Bev turned him over to one of the security guards who had come to investigate the ruckus and we all headed back to our vehicle. Angie was very thankful to have gotten her purse back. The way Dreamgirl and Bev worked as a team left little doubt they had special training.

The only one who didn't seem impressed by what had happened was Pat. Instead, she quietly told me that Bev's damn whistling had hurt her sensitive ears.

Back on the road, Angie had Bev ask our driver if he knew where we could get freshly laid eggs. He took us to a roadside stand.

"Why fresh eggs?" Tracy asked. "Aren't you worried about getting a baby chicken?"

"Fresh eggs will keep for three to four weeks before needing refrigeration," Angie replied. We split ten dozen.

On the way back, Pat asked if they had Costco in Panama. It turns out there was a sister company called PriceSmart. We dropped the fish, eggs, basil plants, and produce off at the boats and then had our driver take us there.

Pat's Costco membership card was accepted, so we grabbed flatbed carts and, knowing Pat as well as I did, began over provisioning.

Angie bought bread flour, sugar, salt, yeast, and olive oil, all in mega-sized packages.

"Are you going to be making bread?" I asked, knowing full well the bread flour was a dead giveaway.

She nodded.

"Will you share?" Tracy asked, grinning.

Angie nodded again.

Most of our purchases were canned or packaged food that didn't require refrigeration. I knew we had way too much but knowing what had happened to us before, I kept quiet.

Pat looked at me for approval as she added a case of this or that to the cart. I smiled and nodded each time.

Dreamgirl and Bev both objected when Angie picked up a whole case of Spam. Angie didn't say anything as she loaded it onto her cart.

I asked her if she'd spare a few cans and she said yes. While Spam may have had a limited following, it was very versatile if fresh meat was not available.

"Why shouldn't you open any emails from Hormel foods?" I asked.

Not getting an answer, I said, "Because it might be Spam."

Pat groaned. So did Tracy, saying, "That's not a sailor joke."

"Sailors eat Spam, Hormel makes Spam—sailor joke," I replied.

Angie laughed and told me she'd be using that when she fried it for a hot breakfast on a chilly morning.

On the way back we passed a small grocery store. Angie asked the driver to stop. She and Bev went in and soon came back with several boxes of cake mixes and instant pudding.

"For desserts at sea," she said, smiling as she climbed back in.

We returned to the marina with all of our purchases. The others had returned from touring. Marta carried the totes from the van to the boats. I offered to get some dock carts but she insisted on carrying the totes by herself.

We had a nice meal of fresh fish and produce. The others had enjoyed their tour. Charles mentioned some of the architecture was first rate. Mo and Gert excused themselves right after dinner. We finished off the wine Charles had selected and made jokes about buying too much food at PriceSmart. Pat joined me in my cabin that evening.

The next day was spent cleaning, refueling, and basically getting the boats ready for the nine-hundred-nautical-mile passage to the Galapagos Islands.

Every time I noticed a man staring at me, I thought about

the man in the straw hat and got a little nervous. I wondered if this was going to be the new normal.

At Charles's request, Elouise had already hired an Ecuadorian agent who had requested the necessary permits. While there were no marinas in the Galapagos, there was limited shopping and limited fuel available. There was also an airport if we needed Charles to have supplies or parts flown in.

We planned to spend six to eight days touring the islands before setting course to our final destination—Hawaii, a distance of roughly four thousand nautical miles.

Had we included Easter Island like Tracy originally wanted, that detour would have added nearly two thousand more nautical miles.

Angie, Mo, Pat, Vee, and I calculated fuel usage and determined we had enough to make it to Hawaii without refueling as long as we were under sail most of the time.

If we were able to refuel in the Galapagos, our safety reserve would be larger. Ralph provided an extended weather forecast that looked promising, and we planned to take full advantage of the Equatorial Currents.

Angie mentioned she wanted a few more propane tanks, just in case. I didn't see how she could possibly use as much propane as she already had onboard between here and Hawaii but I didn't argue.

Elouise, Marta, and I got two more tanks from the marina. "You pay. You pay," kept flashing though my head as Elouise paid the charges with cash.

CHAPTER 68

We checked out of the Flamenco Marina right after a light breakfast the next morning.

Charles told Elouise and his men that he'd see them in about six weeks in Hawaii. We cleared customs and left Panama City, with its tall buildings, in our wake.

The Aquaholic stayed right behind us as we motorsailed offshore, picking our way through the large number of anchored cargo ships waiting their turn to transit the Panama Canal.

A multi-decked ship, possibly some kind of sightseeing boat, stayed a few miles behind us. I doubted they were going to the Galapagos Islands and just waited for them to change course and head back to Panama.

Our most recent fix put us sixty miles offshore. We were under full sail and the knot meter showed our speed right at eight knots. *The Aquaholic* had passed us and was maybe one-half mile ahead. We were on course for the Galapagos Islands.

Gert and Tracy were at the helm with Buster. Mo and Charles were talking at the cockpit table. Pat and I had cleaned up the lunch dishes and had managed to sneak in a quiet quickie. We returned topside and made our way aft.

"Is that larger ship closing in on us?" Pat asked after a few moments of discreet hand holding.

I had almost forgotten about it until she mentioned it. I retrieved the binoculars and took a look. Sure enough, despite its size, it was rapidly closing in. I guessed their speed to be close to fifteen knots, nearly twice our speed.

"They're really gaining," Pat said, reaching for the binoculars. "I wonder what's up."

Tracy saw us looking and stated, "Since we're under sail and that vessel is under power, we are the stand on vessel and they have to give way."

She had recited one of the navigation rules perfectly. She could have used the other rule about the vessel overtaking staying clear of the vessel being overtaken, but I didn't say anything.

I couldn't see any passengers, which seemed odd. All of the other sightseeing ships we had passed had people waving like crazy at us. This one seemed strangely empty.

Mo and Charles joined me at the stern.

"What's going on?" Charles asked.

"Not sure," I replied.

"That tour boat seems a long way from anywhere," Mo added.

"Put the dog below," Pat said, "I've got a bad feeling about this."

I took Buster below and shut him in my cabin. I retrieved the shotgun from its hiding place and made sure it was loaded and ready. I didn't expect trouble, but I wanted to be prepared.

I returned topside, placing the gun just inside the cockpit, out of sight.

I then got the *Sierra* and *Golf* signal flags. I knew that if I hoisted them from the mizzen mast, *The Aquaholic* wouldn't see them since she was ahead of us. I made my way forward on the windward side and tied them to the bow pulpit. I hoped someone onboard *The Aquaholic* would notice them. I then made my way aft back to the others.

The tour boat overtook us on our port side. As it did, it slowed to match our speed. She closed to within fifty feet or so. The decks were empty. I couldn't see the bridge. The name on the bow was "*La Princesa del Pacífico*. I didn't need Bev or Candy to translate—Pacific Princess.

She stayed alongside for several minutes. Pat tried haling her but there was no response. Vee radioed, asking what was happening. Pat replied that we didn't know exactly.

I saw *The Aquaholic* raise her martini glass flag. That reassured me that the women onboard would be retrieving their weapons and getting them ready in case they were needed.

Mo sent Gert below for safety. I had Tracy alter course away. *La Princesa del Pacífico* altered course and stayed with us.

Mo, Charles, Pat, and I were all waiting, watching *La Princesa del Pacífico* intently. Charles suddenly pointed at the second level.

"Movement," he said. "Someone's moving. Just behind the bridge."

I spotted a person pointing a rifle in our direction. Before I could say anything, the gun fired. I heard the boom as Charles whirled and fell down.

"Take cover," I yelled as I ducked and moved toward Charles.

Pat and Mo headed for the cockpit. I reached Charles. He was holding his arm. I helped him crawl back to the cockpit.

The radio squawked, "Was that a gunshot?" It was Vee.

Tracy had altered course away and wasn't able to respond.

"What's going on?" Gert hollered, peering out from the hatch.

"Someone is shooting at us," Pat said. "Get back below."

I grabbed the shotgun and moved back toward Charles. Our situation was grim. The shooter, whoever he or she was, had the high ground and a clear advantage. They also had a rifle, but since there had been only a single shot, it probably wasn't an automatic weapon.

La Princesa del Pacífico maneuvered alongside again. A moment later there was movement, followed by another blast.

Mo screamed that a bullet had just missed his head. He heard it whiz by.

Vee radioed again. Tracy had ducked and radioed back that we were being shot at. Her voice shook.

CHAPTER 69

We were sitting ducks. The shooter had all the advantages: elevation, superior firepower, and a faster vessel that could also be used for ramming.

With the shooter's elevation advantage alone, we were in danger of being picked off one by one. Even if I began returning fire with the shotgun, the shooter was keeping out of sight and not presenting much of a target.

Charles had managed to crawl below. Mo went with him, telling me he was going to get his rifle.

Just then a voice came over *La Princesa del Pacífico's* PA system. "Drop your sails and prepare to be boarded."

I recognized it immediately. Pat and I exchanged looks. She did too.

It was Pincus.

"Drop your sails and prepare to be boarded," he repeated. "Don't make me tell you again."

I stood up and walked back to the helm. On the way I gently placed the shotgun on the cockpit table, in full view of Pincus. Tracy was kneeling for cover, shaking and sobbing. I took her hand and helped her stand.

"Go below with Pat," I said softly. "I'll take over here."

She wiped her eyes. "What are you going to do?"

"I want you both to go below," I said quietly, slowly turning my back to Pincus. I was positive he couldn't hear me but I didn't want him reading my lips. Before either of them could argue, I continued, "We don't have cell phone service, so use the radio. Call Vee and tell her to get *The Aquaholic* the hell out of here."

"He'll hear the radio," Pat said, frowning.

"Pincus wants *The Lady Anne* and her gold. *The Aquaholic* is not his primary target. Once he secures the gold, he may want to eliminate witnesses, but the others might be able to get away."

"What about us?" Tracy asked.

"Yes. What's your plan for all of us onboard *The Lady Anne*?" Pat asked. Before I could answer, her gaze shifted up and then back to me.

"Don't look now but that Onion man is with Pink-Ass," Pat said, using their old slang for Pincus. Ordinarily her mispronunciation would have made me chuckle. Not this time. My mind was racing, trying to figure out how to answer Pat's question without scaring them even more.

Tracy confirmed that Onion had emerged from the bridge and was looking at us.

"Use the radio and broadcast a Mayday. Give our position and say we are under attack by pirates. Then use the satellite phone and tell Ralph Clark what's happening and to send help."

"Pirates!" Tracy exclaimed. "Really?"

"Yes, pirates," I answered. "They didn't charter that vessel. They stole it." She looked at me and nodded.

Pat moved closer and said, "Belay that. Help will be an hour away if we're lucky. Pincus isn't going to wait for the cavalry to show up and save the day. He's going to board us and take what he wants. I know what he wants from me and Tracy."

Her message was grim but probably accurate.

If Pincus was armed, Onion probably was as well. If Mo and I started shooting, they'd start shooting back. I couldn't risk Pat, Tracy, or Gert getting hit by stray bullets. Charles was already wounded. I didn't want anyone else wounded, or worse. I vividly remembered Pat pinned and Pincus seconds away from raping her. Tracy would have been next. Trying to survive long enough for help to arrive, especially help from a foreign country, seemed futile.

Then I had a vision of Bev and Candy turning their would-be assailant's weapons against their attackers and basically executing the man in the back seat of his black Mercedes. That image vanished when I realized that neither Bev or

Candy were close enough to offer their special kind of assistance.

I focused my thoughts on our options. If we surrendered, Pincus would take Pat, Tracy, and the gold. Then he would certainly kill me, Charles, Mo, and Gert. Surrender was not an option.

If we fought back, we'd probably lose. The enemy had every advantage. Had Pincus been alone, it would have been a little different since he couldn't shoot and drive at the same time. But having Onion with him strengthened their position, not ours. Fighting back was not a good option.

If we waited for help to arrive, Pat was probably right. We'd be dead long before help could possibly get to us. While *The Aquaholic* was only minutes away, she carried no heavier firepower than *The Lady Anne* did. Even if we kept them between us, in a cross fire, shotgun blasts and small caliber rifles were no match for Pincus and Onion with rifles aboard *La Princesa del Pacífico*.

Even if Bev, or Candy, or one of the others had sniper training, the little survival rifle onboard *The Aquaholic* was the wrong tool for the job. Trying to take out the bad guys would only put the women in danger.

We could make a run for it. *La Princesa del Pacífico* was faster but less maneuverable. Having been *The Lady Anne's* former captain, Pincus was well aware of our capabilities, both under sail and under power. Whoever was at the helm would be in a perfect position for target practice. Plus Pincus could easily disable *The Lady Anne* by ramming her.

I shook my head and said, "This is bad. Surrendering, fighting back, waiting for help, or making a run for it are all going to end badly for us."

That left one option.

I could see that Pat was thinking about what I had just said.

Tracy looked scared. I wasn't sure what to say to comfort her. But that one option was all we had.

"Go below," I said softly to Tracy. "Go below and start drinking."

She looked at me and wiped away a tear.

"We need alien help," I told her. "Pat, you go with her."

I could see in Tracy's face the moment it registered what I wanted her to do. "Okay, I'll try," she said.

"Walk slowly. Don't give Pincus a reason to shoot."

As soon as Tracy and Pat were safely below, I began furling the sails, starting with the genoa. I didn't start the engine but planned to do so before furling the last sail.

I worked steadily but slowly. I knew that Pincus and Onion were both watching. They were using their vessel's steel structure for cover. The way they were positioned, it's highly unlikely Mo would have had a decent shot. Onion waved at me. I kept working and didn't wave back.

If either of them thought I was deliberately stalling, no one called me on it. I furled the mizzen sail, started the engine, leaving it in neutral, and then furled the mainsail. I glanced over at *La Princesa del Pacífico* but Pincus and Onion were both out of sight.

"Unload the dinghy and then transfer all of the gold to her," the PA system blared.

I acknowledged by waving.

As I moved forward toward the crane, I saw Pat standing below the hatch, out of sight of Pincus.

"How's Charles?" I asked, keeping my voice low.

"He's in shock but he should be okay. The bullet just nicked him," Pat replied.

"Is Tracy drunk yet?"

"She's working on it."

"Let me know if the aliens will help us," I said as I passed.

"Will do."

I unfastened the dinghy as slowly as I thought I could get away with. Then I got the crane set up. I knew that Pincus knew the process. I suspected that if I deviated too much, I'd probably get shot at.

The fact that he grazed Charles and missed Mo made me hope he might miss me if provoked enough to fire. After all, he was an athlete and a captain, not a person with tactical firearms training like Bev and Candy. Still, it was a huge gamble.

I was ready to connect the dinghy to the crane when I heard tapping coming from right below me.

"Yes," I said softly, "I'm listening."

It was Gert's voice. "The aliens have agreed to help us."

I changed my position, enabling me to look around without being obvious. I didn't see any fog. But *La Princesa del Pacífico* was partially blocking my view.

If the fog was coming from behind her, I might not see it in time to motor away a safe distance. I had no desire to be transported back through time again.

There was nothing I could do but continue with the unloading process and wait for a clear signal.

"Have the others gotten the gold ready to load?" The PA system blared and cracked.

I walked back to the hatch and said, loudly enough for Pincus to overhear, "Have you got the gold loose yet?"

"What?" Gert replied. Her voice was low enough that Pincus could not have heard her.

"Let's go, let's go," I said, equally as loud.

Then I turned to face *La Princesa del Pacífico* and shouted, "They're about halfway."

"I've got Vee on another channel," Pat said, poking her head up by the hatch. "She wants to know what we want them to do."

"Tell Pat and Tracy they'll be driving the dinghy over," Pincus said before I could reply. I could hear the meanness in his voice even through the slight distortion of the PA system.

I turned away from Pincus and said, "Tell Vee to radio the instant she sees fog."

Pat didn't acknowledge. I could only hope that she had heard me and understood and not been freaked out by Pincus's last order.

The crane had lifted the dinghy off of its cradle when Mo came up from below. He came forward to help me. I didn't see his rifle.

"Vee sees fog forming. Let's get out of here."

I lowered the dinghy back on its cradle and then headed aft to the helm, motioning for Mo to follow.

As we passed through the cockpit, I told Mo to get below and tell the others to hang on.

Once he was clear, I zigzagged to the helm, keeping low. I threw the motor into reverse and backed away at full throttle.

Waves smashed over the swim platform, soaking the stern, but I didn't slow down. I turned the wheel, keeping our bow pointed at *La Princesa del Pacífico*. Had I simply motored away, Pincus would have had a clear shot at me. This way, there was a lot of deck and a mast between us.

I ducked down and waited for enemy fire.

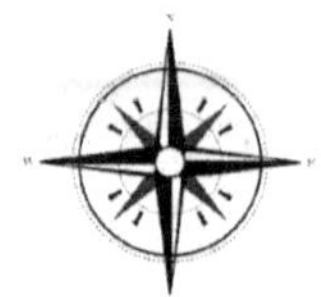

CHAPTER 70

I watched Pat crawl through the cockpit toward me.

"It's not safe here," I told her, making a space for her to partially conceal herself behind the helm's seat.

"If we're going to die, I want to die next to you."

She squeezed my hand. I squeezed hers back.

"Why isn't he chasing us or shooting?" she asked, leaning in close.

"I don't know."

Cautiously, I peered over the helm. *La Princesa del Pacífico* was headed slightly toward us, perhaps trying to outrun the alien's fog.

I took a seat at the helm and turned the wheel. I slowed the engine a little more.

A minute later we were in neutral but still moving backwards. I shifted into forward, straightened out the wheel, and waited to begin making way.

The Lady Anne slowed, slowed, and then stopped ever so slightly before beginning to move forward. I increased the throttle until the engine's RPMs were at maximum.

The Lady Anne responded, picking up speed. Pat sat next to me. I steered away from Pincus. His vessel was faster but much larger and, theoretically, less maneuverable. At least it should be.

La Princesa del Pacífico changed course toward us. I turned back toward her.

"Don't tell me we're playing chicken," Pat said, quite concerned.

I answered her question by veering away.

He was gaining on us, but the fog was now visible and was closing in on him. I changed course again, crashing through our wake. *The Lady Anne's* bow hit the waves hard but I didn't slow down.

I was running out of maneuvers when the fog overtook *La Princesa del Pacífico*. She went out of sight, completely obscured.

I kept our speed, determined to get as much distance as possible.

But the fog bank had stopped moving. It had swallowed Pincus, Onion, and *La Princesa del Pacífico*. I slowed to a reasonable speed and altered course for *The Aquaholic*.

Mo came topside and looked around. When he didn't see

any other vessels except for *The Aquaholic*, he smiled and came back to the helm.

"The aliens came through for us again, didn't they?" he asked.

Pat nodded.

"Unless we meet them back in time, I believe we have seen the last of Captain Daniel Pincus and Mr. Dwayne 'Onion' Outerbridge," I said.

"Do you suppose those two were alone on that ship?" Pat asked. "You don't think they had taken any other hostages, do you?"

"I sincerely hope they were alone," I replied. "Any hostages would be in a really bad way being stuck back in time with their captors." I took Pat's hand. "He likely stole that boat from wherever she was kept. There was probably minimal security because a boat like that is too big to be considered much of a target."

"After all," Pat added, "who in their right mind would steal a passenger tour boat? I mean, where are you going to go and not be immediately spotted with an albatross like that?" She looked up at me. "How do you suppose Pink-Ass found us here in Panama?"

"It's probably my fault," I answered. Then I explained that I had found Onion's phone hidden onboard The Lady Anne. I also told her that I had been talking to Buster when I plotted the courses we would be on between Bermuda, Hawaii, and ports in between. If Onion had been listening, when he joined forces with Pincus, Pincus would know what Onion knew—which was basically everything.

"After their failed attack south of Bermuda, all they had to do was make their way to Panama and wait for us to transit the Panama Canal. Then they could intercept us in the lonely waters between there and the Galapagos."

Pat squeezed my hand and said, "This is not your fault. Pincus is an evil man. Badly intentioned and very smart. If Onion wouldn't have overheard you, Pincus no doubt had contacts at marinas all over the area. His lust for the gold wouldn't have ended until he found us."

I squeezed her hand back.

We caught up to *The Aquaholic* and radioed Vee to prepare to raft.

Mo helped me retract the crane and then he and I deployed our fenders. A few minutes later, we were rafted.

There weren't many questions, which was a relief. They had seen what had happened. Even from a distance, it was clear *La Princesa del Pacífico* had disappeared in a fog bank.

Pat told them about Pincus and Onion while I went below.

Charles was leaning against the salon table. He looked a little pale. His shirt was off, and despite the heat, he was shivering. Our first aid kit was open and on the table next to him. Gert was just finishing taping a large bandage to his upper arm. I got a blanket and told him to relax and take some deep breaths.

Tracy was seated at the other end of the table. A new

bottle of Palmera soursop rum from Aruba was in front of her. The way she squinted at me, I could tell she was hammered.

"Good girl," I told her as I kissed her cheek.

She didn't say anything.

"How bad were you hit?" I asked Charles.

"Daniel's bullet barely grazed me. Just a big scratch really," he replied, trying to flex his arm but wincing slightly from the pain.

"It cleaned up pretty good," Gert said, smiling as she put the bandages back in the first aid kit.

CHAPTER 71

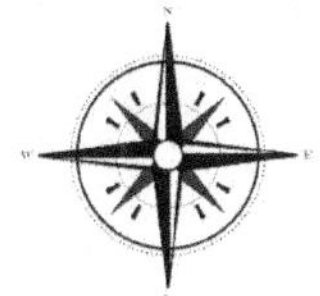

While we were waiting for Tracy to sober up, Mo, Pat, and I thoroughly inspected *The Lady Anne*. Charles wanted to join us but listened to Gert and remained below.

There were no bullet holes anywhere to be found. I took a moment to put the shotgun away. Mo disassembled his rifle and put that away also.

Ninety minutes later, we had a meeting of all personnel aboard *The Aquaholic*.

Charles did not want to go back to a Panama City hospital. He was adamant he was able to continue. Vee and Dreamgirl thanked Gert for what she had done but checked his wound anyway. They inspected the wound and agreed he would be fine. They rebandaged it for him, using plenty of antiseptic. Then Dreamgirl sort of ordered him to take a seat and just relax. She got him two bottles of water and told him to stay hydrated. He didn't argue.

I decided to express my concerns about the most recent piracy attempt. I told them that had it not been for Tracy, the encounter would have ended terribly.

"If Pincus and Onion told anyone else about us and our expected course to the Galapagos Islands, we could still be in jeopardy," I stated.

"Why don't we just plot a new course and head directly for Hawaii?" Pat asked.

"I would have liked to have seen the Galapagos Islands, but given we've had two attempts at being boarded, I'm okay with not going there," Tracy said, sipping on a bottle of water.

Angie retrieved a large paper chart of the Pacific Ocean and spread it out on the table.

She pointed to our approximate position and then to the Hawaiian Islands.

With her, Mo, and Vee looking over my shoulder, I studied the chart, looking specifically for the currents.

I pointed out which direction the currents generally ran. I showed them that if we sailed south until we were clear of Panama and then headed due west, we'd be sailing against the North Equatorial Current.

"If we skirted the coast, staying one hundred miles or more offshore until reaching nine degrees north, we could turn left and have that current with us all the way," I stated, drawing on the chart with my finger.

A brief discussion determined that any stops in Panama

or Costa Rica might expose us to being spotted by anyone who was actively looking for us. There was a lot of information online. Once we left a paper trail, be it customs, or permits, or visas, or even fuel receipts, we were vulnerable to discovery.

"Avoiding all harbors, marinas, and landfalls will greatly minimize the possibility of another attack," Pat said.

"We are fully fueled and provisioned," Charles stated. "I propose that we tell Ralph of our new plan and then set sail to Hawaii, nonstop."

There were no arguments.

Vee, Bev, and Angie plotted our course on a more detailed chart to nine degrees north latitude, keeping us a minimum of one hundred miles off the coast of both Panama and Costa Rica.

I then copied their calculations to *The Lady Anne's* chart. Pat and Mo double-checked my work. Gert sat close to Mo as he worked. Pat smiled her approval.

Vee and I loaded our course into the autopilots. Bev and Mo checked our inputs. We unrafted and resumed course.

Vee insisted that Bev sail with us aboard *The Lady Anne* since Charles was injured. She acknowledged that would leave them one person short, but she said they'd adjust their watch schedules accordingly. That seemed reasonable, so none of us argued.

Charles sent a fax to Ralph informing him of the new plan and asking for new weather forecasts.

During the sail, nobody had much to say. I knew everyone

was grateful that another piracy attempt had been thwarted, but the mood aboard *The Lady Anne* was somber.

We passed several large cargo and container ships. I got a little nervous each time one showed up on the radar.

We sailed through the night, keeping each other in sight. We took shifts as before. Using the red light belowdecks made the transition between the salon and topside much easier on the eyes. Both vessels made hourly radio checks. Both watches made hourly log entries. Bev's log entries showed she sailed very efficiently. I was glad to have her aboard, in more ways than one.

The next morning, Pat was tired from her shift but waited patiently for Tracy to wake up. I could see something was on her mind but puttered around in the galley, making a light breakfast.

When Tracy finally came into the galley, Pat handed her a cup of coffee and said, "I want to talk to you about how you communicate with the aliens."

CHAPTER 72

"What's on your mind?" Tracy replied, sipping her coffee.

"Getting drunk is very inefficient," Pat told her.

Tracy looked at her but didn't speak. We could both see she was thinking. Finally she said, "I agree, but they seem to think that's normal for me since that's how I was when we first communicated."

"I can see why they might assume that," Pat replied, finally smiling a bit. "But you need to tell them they're wrong. Tell them that you don't want to elevate your blood-alcohol levels to communicate with them anymore."

"Okay," Tracy said. "How do you suggest I contact them without getting drunk?"

"During my watch I had a lot of time to think about it, so here's what I propose."

Tracy and I listened as Pat outlined her plan. Tracy would have a few drinks and communicate with the aliens in her normal way. This time she would tell them she no longer wanted to be drinking alcohol to communicate. She would ask them for another way to signal them she needed to talk.

Tracy would also tell the aliens that Pat needed to communicate with them too, because she had several questions about the drawings for the plastic magnet.

Tracy thought that to be a very doable plan. So did I. We agreed she would try after lunch.

We sailed through the morning and then rafted for lunch. Bev went back to *The Aquaholic* and was replaced by Candy. Angie gave us a loaf of French bread that looked like it had come from a bakery.

While Pat and Tracy went below, I asked about her bread.

Angie explained she had a dough hook for her hand mixer and used a special baker's knife to make slashes in the loaf.

"How did you get the crust so golden brown?" Gert inquired, taking a whiff and admiring the loaf.

"Throw some ice cubes in the bottom of the hot oven when you add the bread. The steam does the rest," Angie smiled, proud Gert had noticed.

"Most of your crew doesn't eat bread, do they?" I asked.

She chuckled and replied, "They eat this bread."

I went below to get the fixings to make sandwiches. Tracy was seated at the salon table, an empty glass in front of her. Her eyes were closed. Pat was seated alongside and motioned for me to be quiet.

I got what I needed and returned topside. I had just finished making sandwiches when Candy pointed aft and shouted, "Fog."

Fog was forming astern, maybe fifty yards away. Compared to the previous alien fog banks, this fog bank was pretty small, not much larger than a big house.

I started below to inform Pat and Tracy what was happening when Pat met me at the bottom of the ladder. Tracy was standing behind her, wobbling.

"Launch the dinghy," she told me. "Tracy and I are going for a ride."

Since *The Aquaholic* was on the same side as our crane, I told Vee to launch their dinghy. She gave me a questioning look but did as instructed.

Pat got their dinghy started while Marta and I helped Tracy get aboard.

"Are you sure you know what you're doing?" I asked as I shoved them off.

"Wait here," Pat said. Then she motored slowly toward the fog. My heart was pounding. I noticed that everyone was aft, watching.

I couldn't imagine that Pat and Tracy were going to be sent back through time. There was no way they would survive the electromagnetic portal in an open dinghy. That would be certain electrocution.

Plus they had no supplies, not even water. Even if they survived a transport through time, they would certainly face a slow and agonizing death adrift at sea in a barren dinghy.

I watched as the dinghy entered the fog. My heart pounded faster. I steadied myself against the bulkhead.

There had to be something else happening. I just didn't know what it might be.

CHAPTER 73

I watched and waited for a time before finally crossing back over to *The Lady Anne. I* forced myself to relax. The fog stayed put despite the breeze that was blowing. Our raft was slowly drifting away from the fog but was still well within the dinghy's range.

Gert brought Buster over and told me everything would be okay. Charles joined us, saying the same thing. There wasn't anything to do but wait. I wondered how long they'd be gone, but it really didn't matter. I wasn't leaving. If our raft got too far away, I'd just motor back closer.

I was in the cockpit, keeping one eye on the fog and thumbing through our log. Buster was resting next to me. Charles and Gert were below. Mo was casting off the stern. He hadn't caught anything. I suspected he was burning off some nervous energy.

Twenty minutes had passed since I had motored our raft toward the fog, stopping about fifty yards away. Now it was just more waiting.

I heard the dinghy's motor start. A moment later the dinghy powered out of the fog. Pat was driving and Tracy was in the bow. I jumped up, accidentally knocking Buster off of the cushion.

Pat changed course back to us. She waved. I waved back and scrambled over to *The Aquaholic*. I was glad to see them approaching and curious about what they had to say.

Tracy threw me a line and I pulled them in. Marta helped them aboard. Vee asked Pat if she was done with the dinghy. When Pat said she was, Vee told Bev and Dreamgirl to put it back in the davits.

"Should we debrief now or later?" I asked.

"I'll tell everyone what happened. It was really cool," Pat replied.

I rang *The Lady Anne's* brass bell. That brought everyone on both vessels topside.

Pat waited until the dinghy was secured and then thanked us for waiting, apologizing for being gone so long.

"Tracy can now talk to our alien friend without having to drink first. So can I."

That's all she said. Tracy didn't add anything else. I waited to see if there was more but there wasn't. Pat and Tracy returned to *The Lady Anne*. Pat said, "Let's resume sailing."

"Aren't you going to tell us what happened in the fog?" Jane asked.

"We can't talk about it now," was Tracy's short reply.

I hoped that at least one of them would talk to me about it later, but I kept quiet.

We unrafted and resumed course. Bev switched places with Candy, who took over the helm. Charles, Mo, and Gert stayed topside. I followed Tracy and Pat below. Tracy said she was tired and went to lie down.

I cornered Pat in the galley. "What really happened?" I asked.

"The sphere appeared like before, only it was smaller. Tracy told it that she wanted to be able to talk to them without drinking any alcohol. I told it that I needed the ability to communicate with them because I had questions about the plastic magnet."

"Then what happened?"

"We were both immersed in light. There was no speaking but I could 'hear' them in my head. They told me how to concentrate to be able to contact them."

"And?"

"And I asked them my questions."

"Did they answer?"

"Sort of," she said. "The alien voice in my head told me how to answer my own questions. It said to state the problem, state the constraints, state the positives and the negatives, and then list all options to counter or minimize the negatives. The explanation made perfect sense."

It did? It seemed confusing to me, but I kept listening.

"Using that exact methodology, the alien walked me

through the process to answer my own questions. It is actually pretty simple once you accept thinking outside of the conventional box."

"So do you think you can build a plastic magnet?"

"Well, I can't build it here," she answered. "But I can work with the right manufacturer to build one. Once it's tested, it can be mass-produced, so yes, I think we can clean up the Earth's oceans eventually."

"What about sending would-be boarders back through time? Did they tell you how to do that?"

"I asked them that very question. They refused to answer."

"Did they tell you why?"

She met my eyes. "Too dangerous. They said that kind of power would only serve to corrupt me."

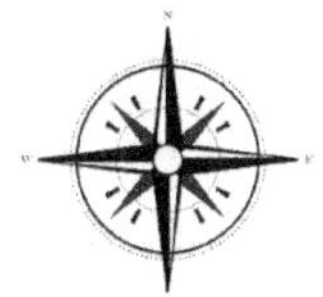

CHAPTER 74

We covered the waters to nine degrees north and turned left. We were now headed due west. We rafted every day, using the opportunity to exchange crew and to run the engines.

While the engines were running, we had power to recharge the batteries, run the water makers, cool the fridge, make hot water, and occasionally run *The Lady Anne's* washing machine.

Angie kept making bread, each loaf as perfect as before. She also sent over a "poke cake." Underneath the frosting there were holes filled with pudding. She explained she used a skewer to poke holes throughout the cake and then pressed the liquid pudding in the holes. While the pudding was setting, the frosting covered it all up. She was very clever, and the "poke cake" was the moistest cake I had ever tasted.

When our speed was slow enough to fish, we did a little

trolling. I gave Bev, Candy, and Dreamgirl lessons in how to operate the reel and position the lure so it splashed through our wake.

Finally Dreamgirl hooked something. She started hollering like a little kid, she was so excited. I moved in behind her to help her steady the rod until we could get *The Lady Anne* heaved to.

Just then the fish got off, the line went slack, and Dreamgirl fell back into my arms. With her face about an inch from mine, she thanked me for catching her.

Pat cleared her throat. She looked agitated that Dreamgirl was in my arms. I quickly helped her regain her balance and took over the fishing pole. Pat didn't say anything but turned her back on us and went back to helm duties.

One day Vee came across to take a turn on *The Lady Anne*. Surprisingly, Marta didn't come over with her. That was one of the few times I could remember them not being together.

During dinner, Charles asked her to tell us about herself and how she got into the professional crewing business.

She changed the subject. It was obvious from her expression that topic was unwelcome. I knew a little about Bev's and Candy's pasts and assumed Vee had a similar background. I kept the conversation going on the new topic.

"So when did you get your captain's license?" Charles asked later.

She brightened. "When I retired from a job I didn't like, I found I really enjoyed being out on the water. I studied boating and dreamed of owning my own charter boat one day."

Tracy smiled when she heard that and looked at Pat. "Sound familiar?"

Pat nodded.

"Anyway," Vee continued. "I studied really hard, took classes online and in person, accumulated enough hours at sea, and eventually passed the Coast Guard exam, which is brutally hard by the way."

I smiled.

She smiled back. "You know about that, do you?"

I nodded.

Vee went on. "So, I recruited some qualified women, started my own business, and here I am."

CHAPTER 75

A few days later, Pat told me she would be ready to start overseeing production of a plastic magnet prototype when we reached Hawaii.

She also said she thought she might be able to generate fog in a controlled laboratory environment.

Between using the alien's methodology for problem-solving and being able to actually ask the aliens questions, she said her knowledge had expanded exponentially.

The one thing she was determined to pursue was the alien's ability to generate a time travel field. She didn't know enough about the mechanics of time travel to even know which questions to ask.

She told me how she had tried to work through the time travel process, even enlisting Mo's help, but neither of them could make any progress. Time travel was just way beyond their abilities to even theorize.

But we agreed that being able to generate the time travel field had saved us before. It had gotten us away from Onion's pirate friends near Bermuda, it had enabled us to rescue Elouise and Marta from their captors, and it had sent Pincus and Onion away, permanently.

Pat thought it to be a worthy self-defense tool. I foresaw its military applications. It would be as much of a game changer as gunpowder or the atomic bomb.

I believe the monotony of crossing so many thousand miles was getting to everyone, but especially to Pat. It was wave after wave, followed by another wave, and then some more waves.

Anyone aboard could see how much in love Mo and Gert were, but no one more than Pat. She commented how they held hands at the helm, how they shared Ensure with two straws, how she helped him with his weather forecasting while he helped her in the galley. She always seemed to direct her comments to me, as if pointing out the shortcomings in our relationship. If I asked her directly, she'd deny that's what she was doing. It didn't help that our days had become long and boring. Once our boats turned west, the limited birdlife we had been seeing became virtually nonexistent.

We had seen a few whales, but none within the last week or so. Compared with the sea life that we sailed through 25,700 years ago, this voyage could be classified as barren.

We hadn't even had a decent rain for over a week. At least that broke up the routine.

The fishing had been lousy. There had been a few strikes but nothing had been landed.

One morning when we had rafted for breakfast and a crew change, Dreamgirl did a little casting off the stern. She got her lure caught in the rigging and I had to help her get it loose. Judging from Pat's expression, it was pretty obvious she considered Dreamgirl a threat and didn't like me in her proximity.

I couldn't tell anyone, but my feelings toward Dreamgirl stemmed not only from her being sexy, but also because she looked so much like my ex-lover. She was easy to be around, and I guess I enjoyed it when she flirted with me.

You know you're bored when the most exciting thing that happens all day is a container ship goes by. When we were lucky, they would hail us on the radio.

The women onboard *The Aquaholic* played games when we had a radio contact by speaking in all different languages. Listening to the awkward responses on the other end was pretty funny.

Just as we were tiring of Angie's French bread, she switched to making those big, soft, German pretzels. Until we ran out of mustard, those pretzels were a welcome treat. But Buster didn't care. He devoured them plain.

Pat became very concerned about our last encounter with Pincus and Onion. She still had nightmares about Pincus raping her, but now Onion was helping hold her down. Sometimes she'd wake up screaming, waking me up thinking something had happened to *The Lady Anne*.

I didn't think that Angie had nightmares from her ordeal at the hands of Captain Rick since she was unconscious the whole time. I did suppose that Ashley and Donna still had demons from their bondage.

I wondered how Bonnie and her kids were doing back in Texas. I was surprised that we never heard from them. I figured Bonnie might need someone to talk to who understood what she had been through.

One morning, Pat told me she had news of Pincus and Onion. I got nervous until she explained she had communicated with the aliens and had simply asked about them in an attempt to make her nightmares stop.

The aliens told her *La Princesa del Pacífico* had been slammed into a rocky shore by a storm. It was damaged beyond repair. The two survivors had located fresh water and were foraging for food ashore in the area that we would know as Costa Rica.

Neither of us felt any sorrow for Captain Daniel Pincus. He deserved what he got. I did feel a little bad for Onion. He was a good worker and had seemed like a nice man, but he needed to pick better friends.

I plotted our current position on the chart every day. Our progress was slow but steady. Some days we'd cover two hundred miles, some days the wind was uncooperative and despite Roger's best weather predictions, we couldn't even manage one hundred.

Mo had been very generous in giving Pat and I celestial navigation lessons. Obtaining your position by using only the celestial bodies might have been a very old method, but it was completely new to Pat and me. Tracy tried it a few times and decided it wasn't for her.

Mo showed us how to adjust our calculations if we found ourselves 25,700 years in the past again. It was challenging for me, even with detailed notes.

But with Mo's patience, I could usually get a fix that was within five miles of what the GPS showed as our current position. Pat was better at correcting for variables and her fixes were usually within two miles. I consoled myself that a two to five-mile error was more than acceptable, especially out in the middle of nowhere.

The boats chewed up the miles, getting help from the North Equatorial Current. The swells were quite large but not spaced very close together. Ralph usually routed us through winds that were very consistent, enabling us to stay on the same long tack for days at a time.

Sometimes Mo's onboard weather calculations would have dictated a course change to those winds, but usually he couldn't predict the low-pressure systems until we were nearly right on top of them. Tracy watched his calculations a few times and wasn't interested in learning anymore. She was happy with Ralph's weather faxes.

We had covered over twenty-eight hundred miles and were only a day or two from our final course change to the northwest. That heading would take us into Hawaiian waters.

Changing course was highly anticipated. It would signify we were on our final one-thousand-mile leg.

One afternoon, Pat and Tracy had an argument.

Pat wanted to ask the aliens to give us a device to activate the time travel defense on our own.

Tracy said they wouldn't give us that kind of power and we didn't need it anyway. There was nothing between us and Hawaii but water.

Pat finally convinced her that if we got in a bad way, initiating the time travel portal might be our only escape.

After a few days or badgering, Tracy finally agreed to let Pat ask.

Pat told me not to disturb her and then went below, into her cabin. I kept Tracy topside with me at the helm.

Forty-five minutes later Pat emerged to rejoin us. Her face was expressionless.

CHAPTER 76

Tracy and I waited for Pat to tell us what had happened.

After several minutes, she told us the aliens had agreed to help us, sort of.

Slowly, she explained that the aliens would send their equivalent of an underwater drone device to shadow *The Lady Anne*. That device would be able to initiate the time travel portal when activated.

It could be activated by receiving a signal from a device that could be constructed from materials that were currently onboard.

Once activated, the target vessel would become engulfed in fog and the electromagnetic portal would be opened to the past.

Pat was ecstatic. I was surprised the aliens would put that kind of power in our hands.

She then got some paper and made a drawing of how to construct and operate the signaling device. Like Tracy's earlier drawing of the plastic magnet, Pat's drawing was surprisingly detailed. Pat told me she could see the images in her head and just drew what she saw.

Once Tracy and I had finished looking at her handiwork, she took her notes and headed below.

Tracy looked at me and shrugged, saying, "I hope that wasn't a mistake. I hope we never have to use it."

Candy was on loan that day and smiled as we passed. She asked me if I had kept their secret, and when I nodded, she gave me a hug.

Charles's wound had healed and no longer required daily dressing changes. He had a small scar.

Mo's celestial navigation lessons had ended. He said we were good to go with what we knew. I think he knew Pat could do it with the math skills she had from her engineering degree. I also think he was impressed that I stuck with his lessons and didn't give up.

Buster had eaten something which made him throw up. I cleaned it up.

Later that day, Pat returned topside, carrying a cardboard box. She was smiling. I didn't think we had any cardboard boxes onboard, but it was obvious she had found one. From her expression, it was also obvious that she had finished building the signaling device. She motioned for me and Tracy to meet her at the cockpit table.

Charles was at the helm. Mo and Gert were below, resting

for their next watch. I wasn't sure where Candy was but didn't see her.

Tracy and I opened the box simultaneously.

Pat had cut the wooden cutting board Elouise had given me in half the long way. To that piece, she affixed three of our portable radios, their antennas all pointing in the same direction.

Covering each antenna was a funnel-shaped piece of aluminum foil, attached by a rubber band. That was it. It looked pretty simple.

"So how does this work?" Tracy asked, being careful not to touch anything.

"The radios are set to three different channels. Point them at the target, turn them on, and then key the transmit switch for the proper interval, in the proper sequence."

She placed her drawing from earlier on top of the radios. It showed the sequence and duration.

"The alien's underwater device will pick up the signals and start the process." She beamed, obviously pleased.

"Do you suppose the alien's device is already close to us and waiting to be activated?" Tracy whispered.

"There's one way to find out," Pat answered. She looked intense, almost scary.

"Please put that away where it won't accidentally be found," I told her, closing the lid.

We agreed not to discuss it further. I wondered if getting access to that kind of technology was a good idea, or a bad one.

CHAPTER 77

When it was time to change course, Charles announced a little celebration was in order. He told us there would be a party onboard *The Lady Anne* later that afternoon. He laughed, saying the dress code was business casual. He relayed that information to *The Aquaholic*. They accepted.

We made our course change. We would be leaving the North Equatorial Current but would pick up the tail end of the westbound California Current instead. That current would stay with us all the way to our destination. Charles insisted on making the log entry. He was excited at having come so far, pirate attacks and Pincus notwithstanding.

I radioed Angie and we coordinated the menu. She still had lots of tortillas left, so she offered to bring quesadillas and fish tacos. I had what I needed for nachos. Drinks would consist of one-half potency margaritas. Angie insisted on bringing dessert.

We agreed that a Hawaiian-themed party was more appropriate, but we were out of pineapples and coconuts. My leis had been thrown away long ago. She laughed and said that a basil plant wasn't a very tropical centerpiece. I agreed and signed off.

We rafted later that afternoon. Vee and her crew were wearing their nautical white uniforms. Marta was wearing her usual workout attire. Those that had been to Hawaii were wearing tropical shirts except for Charles. He was wearing a sport coat but, thankfully, no tie. I was wearing my cleanest nautical-themed shirt. Mo and Gert were sporting clothing that had previously belonged to Charles and his late wife.

Everyone looked happy. All that was missing was the cruise ship.

The party was a great idea. It was nice to take a break from sailing and just let our raft drift.

My margaritas were intentionally weak but popular. Angie's food was a hit; so were my nachos. For dessert we had homemade chocolate chunk cookies made with Toblerone candy bars.

I insisted that as *The Lady Anne's* captain, Pat make a toast. Tracy seconded that idea. Everyone stopped talking and looked at her.

Pat raised her glass and said, "The meek will inherit the earth. The brave will get the oceans."

It was well received.

Apparently I was the only one who had heard it before.

Charles had two announcements. First, he had spoken with Elouise via the satellite phone and asked her to check online for any news of the disappearance of *La Princesa del Pacífico*. He was pleased to report that while the ship itself had been reported as missing, there was no mention of missing crew or passengers.

Second, he reported that Ralph Clark had made a notation at the bottom of the last weather fax to let Captain Pincus know *The Lady Anne* had nearly completed the passage to Hawaii without incident.

I blinked, but before I could say anything, Charles told us that he immediately called Ralph for an explanation. It turns out that Pincus had told Ralph that he wouldn't be making the voyage but wanted to be kept informed of our progress.

Charles apologized for never informing Ralph that Pincus no longer worked for him. That explained how Pincus knew where we were.

There was an awkward silence until Pat finally said, "Well, it doesn't matter now; that guy is toast."

"Pink-Ass toast," Tracy chimed in. Everybody laughed.

Jane talked to Angie for a moment and then went and got her violin. Angie sang the Charlie Daniels hit "The Devil Went Down to Georgia" while her mom accompanied her.

Angie then announced she was going to sing an original song she had written titled "The Old Dappled Gray." She sang it while Jane accompanied.

Based on the first verse, I was expecting a kid's song about carousel horses racing around in a circle. Imagine my surprise when it turned out to be a love song. I was impressed, as was everyone else.

Jane then played the "Orange Blossom Special" at Charles's request.

Jane pulled me aside and hummed a movie theme, asking me if I'd accompany her with my trumpet. I recognized it and agreed.

She played the lead violin part of the theme from *Young Frankenstein*. I added the horn part.

When it was my turn, I played the only Hawaiian song that came to mind—Don Ho's "Tiny Bubbles."

Mo spoke up, saying he had an announcement. We all listened as he professed his love for Gert. That shouldn't have surprised anyone who had seen how affectionate they were toward each other. What was surprising is when he asked Pat, as *The Lady Anne's* captain, to marry them.

After Pat stopped crying, she agreed. Vee asked if she and Bev could co-officiate to make it legal since Vee and Bev were both licensed captains and Pat wasn't.

Mo and Gert agreed. They gave Pat the vows they had written. She read them aloud, then Pat, Vee, and Bev said a few words, pronounced them married under nautical law, and announced them as Morrie and Gertrude Morris. They kissed to thunderous applause.

Charles immediately poured French champagne for everyone. I played the first wedding song that came to mind —"Here Comes the Bride." Tracy gave me a strange look at my timing. Jane played Elvis Presley's "Love Me Tender." She got a standing ovation.

Most of the women had moist eyes. I had a lump in my throat. Marta videoed the whole ceremony with her phone. It was very sweet. Angie laughingly scolded them for not telling her so she could have made them a wedding cake. Mo and Gert both laughed. They were the happiest I had ever seen them.

After the party we unrafted and resumed course. Vee forgot to leave someone onboard *The Lady Anne* so we were back to our original contingent.

It didn't matter. Charles had been taking a full shift for quite a while and Mo and Gert were covering any shift as needed.

We kept sailing toward Hawaii. Our plotted positions on the chart kept inching closer and closer. The party had brightened everyone's mood. Spirits were still high.

Aside from our nearly exhausted supply of fresh fruit, dairy, and produce, our supplies and fuel were good. By my rough calculations, we had plenty of food, fuel, and propane left. As long as there was power for the water maker, we could have sailed past Hawaii and, with Ralph's guidance, made it all the way to Japan, no problem.

At three hundred miles south, southwest of Hawaii, at ten twenty-seven a.m., a blip appeared on the radar. Vee confirmed the contact. I watched as the blip closed in on our position.

CHAPTER 78

In less than thirty-five minutes, a naval ship was clearly visible. I was at the helm and just held my course, announcing that we had company.

Everyone came topside except for Mo and Gert, who were resting. Bev was our guest sailor today and she joined me at the helm.

"What's going on?" she asked, looking through her binoculars.

"Not sure," I replied.

Vee radioed, asking if there was something she needed to be aware of. Bev told her there was a destroyer closing on us.

The navy ship turned and maneuvered to a position midway between us and *The Aquaholic*. It slowed to match our speed and just motored along, maybe five hundred yards away.

She was flying a US flag. There were two helicopters on

the stern deck. There were lots of sailors watching us. The number on the bow was "998." I guessed her to be about four hundred feet long but Bev corrected me, saying it was an Arleigh Burke class destroyer and was five hundred nine feet long.

The fact that she knew that made me guess that her previous employer might have either been the US Navy or the Department of Defense. Of course I knew better than to say anything out loud.

"What are we going to do?" Tracy asked anxiously.

"Until we hear differently, we're going to just hold our course," I replied, keeping my voice calm.

"What do you suppose the navy is doing way out here?" Pat asked.

"My guess is they are checking to see if any vessels matching our description have been reported stolen or missing."

"What's your plan?" Bev asked, still looking through her binoculars.

"Stay on course and wait to see if they do something, I guess," I replied. "Why don't you radio Vee and tell her to do the same?"

After fifteen minutes of being shadowed, I motioned Charles over. "Did you arrange for a naval escort?"

"I have absolutely no idea what is going on," he replied.

I looked directly at him. He didn't flinch. I believed him.

I tried hailing them and they immediately responded, identifying themselves as *The USS Fields*. I asked if everything was alright. They replied they were conducting an exercise and they would be in the area for a while.

Bev rolled her eyes when she heard that but didn't comment.

I noticed *The Lady Anne* was being impacted by their wake. I explained that and asked if they would mind moving away a little.

They said they would. A few minutes later they changed course, angling out another five hundred yards before turning to parallel us again. That solved the wake problem and I thanked them. They signed off.

I watched them through the binoculars for over an hour. I observed that all of the sailors on deck were wearing helmets. Several of them were armed. It was also a little odd that none of them were waving. The other ships we had passed this close had at least a few of the crew waving.

Their presence was a little perplexing. I knew we didn't warrant a private escort. I didn't really believe they were conducting any exercises because there wasn't much movement on deck. *The USS Fields* was a warship. I wondered if they were looking for drugs or contraband.

I radioed Vee, knowing that our conversation was being monitored. I told her it was probably best not to raft for dinner. She agreed. We decided to sail right on through the night.

Just before six p.m., Tracy took a GPS reading and stated we were only two hundred fifty miles from Hawaii. As she was making the log entry, I heard sirens blaring from *The USS Fields*.

The ship turned toward us.

Mo was at the helm and I joined him, telling him to hold his course. He looked nervous. I know I was.

The ship closed in and then their PA system blared. "This is *The USS Fields*. Heave to and prepare to be boarded."

Mo switched places with me and worked the lines while I heaved to. Everyone rushed topside. Bev reported *The Aquaholic* was furling her sails. That made sense because it's hard for a catamaran to heave to.

"Now what?" Pat asked.

"Beats me," I replied.

Tracy looked through the binoculars and reported, "They've got guns." She sounded scared.

The Lady Anne was quickly hove to and slowly oscillated back and forth.

We watched as *The USS Fields* lowered two dinghies over the side. Some of the sailors were armed. The machine gun in the bow was manned. Something had obviously happened to have spooked them. I had no idea what, but I was certain we would find out shortly.

All any of us could do was watch as one dinghy headed toward us and the other toward *The Aquaholic*.

CHAPTER 79

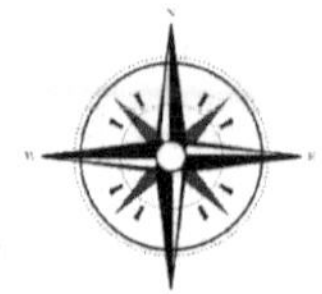

Their dinghy pulled up to our stern and three armed sailors stepped across to our swim platform. The fourth, a lieutenant, followed them. One man wearing a suit followed him. An air force colonel brought up the rear. I was surprised to see an air force officer coming from a naval destroyer. Judging from Bev's puzzled expression, so was she.

Two sailors remained with the dinghy. One of them was at the helm. The other was manning the machine gun in the bow.

Pat was waiting at the stern rail and asked if she could help them.

The man in the suit flashed a badge. "Agent Hill, NSA, National Security Agency."

Agent Hill was probably in his forties. His face was tan. He was clean-cut and about my height. He was wearing dark sunglasses, a dark gray suit, and black-soled shoes. I had a fleeting thought that I hoped his shoes didn't leave scuff marks on our clean white fiberglass deck. Had he been a sailing student, I would have asked him to change his footwear for the next lesson.

"With me is Colonel Wolf, United States Air Force." Agent Hill gestured. Colonel Wolf was about six feet tall. His uniform fit snugly. His hat and mirrored aviator sunglasses obscured his face. He was wearing a sidearm.

Agent Hill nodded at the lieutenant but didn't say anything. The lieutenant pointed forward, then pointed below, and then tapped the grill.

The armed sailors moved as directed. One went forward to the cockpit, one went below, and the third moved over by the grill. They didn't say anything, they just took up position as their lieutenant had indicated.

Agent Hill produced a portable electronic metal detector like airport security sometimes uses. He asked Pat if she would please extend her arms out to the side. She gave him a puzzled look but did as instructed. He ran the metal detector up and down and around her body. It beeped at her watch and her PFD's metal fittings but he didn't say anything. When it beeped at her pocket, she sheepishly removed her rigging knife. He noticed the pointy marlin spike but didn't comment.

The lieutenant produced a grocery-sized plastic bag and Pat put her knife in the bag.

Charles moved next to Pat. "My name is Charles T. Williams and I need to remind you that we are United States citizens onboard a US flagged vessel in international waters. By whose authority are you boarding our vessel? By whose authority are you searching us?" Charles was firm and perhaps a bit confrontational.

"This is a matter of national security and I'm checking for concealed weapons," Agent Hill replied. If Charles's tone had irritated him, it didn't show. "Now would you mind extending your arms?" Charles didn't move. Agent Hill said, "Please?" Charles exhaled and complied.

The armed sailor returned topside and reported there was nobody below. He kept his position near the hatch. When Buster barked at him, Tracy picked up her dog.

One by one we were all checked. The lieutenant collected my rigging knife and several cell phones. Tracy had the fishing pliers in her pocket. She surrendered those as well. Mo reluctantly parted with his multi-tool.

Agent Hill hesitated a bit when he got to Beverly. He looked her up and down. "Are you Thompson or Glover?"

"Thompson," Bev replied. Despite the gravity of the situation, I was silently amused that he couldn't tell Bev and Candy apart. I thought back to when I first saw them and thought they were twins.

When Agent Hill was satisfied that we weren't armed, he asked if we would all mind taking a seat at the cockpit table. Everyone except for Pat and I complied. While there was still room at the table, I felt more comfortable standing in case I needed to adjust our hove to position. I figured Pat did too.

"Would you mind telling me what is going on?" Pat asked.

"We need to ask some questions. Ms. Patrica A. Taylor, please take a seat," he replied. His tone was firm.

"How do you know my name?" she asked, sitting down.

"We know who all of you are," Agent Hill answered. Then he pointed at each of us, one by one, and called us by name. I noticed he used our formal names. I had a bad feeling that his agency had a file on each of us.

"What kind of questions?" Tracy asked. She looked nervous.

"All things in time, Ms. Palmer."

"Mr. Adams," the lieutenant said, looking at me, "since you're a sailing instructor, would you mind dropping the sails?"

"Why?" I asked, knowing we were hove to perfectly, as instructed.

Agent Hill replied before the lieutenant could answer. "Because the sailing catamaran *The Aquaholic* will be joining us shortly. We want everyone together, and this vessel looks large enough."

I looked toward *The Aquaholic*. Sure enough, she was motoring right toward us, accompanied by the second dinghy.

"What kind of a national security matter is this?" Charles asked.

"I'll explain everything soon enough. Please remain seated."

Bev spoke up. "I'm sure whatever reason you have for being here involves me and my friends aboard *The Aquaholic*. Is there any reason to involve everyone?"

"More reason than you know," Agent Hill replied. Then he looked at me. "I believe you were asked to lower the sails. Now do you want to comply or should I just have them cut down?"

I did as instructed, with Pat's assistance. The lieutenant watched us closely.

With her sails furled, *The Lady Anne* began to drift. I wasn't concerned since *The Aquaholic* was now very close. I asked the lieutenant if he wanted us to raft and he nodded.

Pat deployed our fenders while I got the dock lines ready. Candy, Dreamgirl, and Angie did the same aboard *The Aquaholic*.

After we were rafted, Agent Hill motioned for the women to come across to *The Lady Anne*.

A new face followed the women over. He introduced himself as Agent Washington, CIA, Central Intelligence Agency.

Agent Washington could have passed as a stunt double for Will Smith. Except for his thick-framed black glasses, he looked just like him, but maybe a little shorter. His suit was black, his tie was black, and he had the same black-soled shoes as Agent Hill. The thought of encountering *The Men in Black*, like the movie, flashed momentarily. Given our alien connection, I forced myself to keep a straight face.

"Are the women clear?" Agent Hill asked.

Agent Washington displayed another metal detector and nodded.

There were three armed sailors watching us from *The*

Aquaholic. Agent Hill told them to return to their dinghy and wait. He then told our lieutenant and his men to do the same.

The lieutenant carried the bag of our metal objects below and then he and navy personnel left. They took both dinghies about twenty yards out where they slowly circled our raft. *The USS Fields* kept her distance. Angie and her mom joined Mo, Gert, Tracy, and Bev at the cockpit table. The rest of us gathered around, waiting.

The colonel and Agent Washington stood behind Agent Hill. I felt cornered.

CHAPTER 80

Agent Hill repeated his name and agency for the benefit of *The Aquaholic's* passengers. The colonel didn't say anything.

Agent Hill glanced at Agent Washington, glanced at Colonel Wolf, looked at the dinghies that were circling, straightened his tie, put down the metal detector, and then retrieved a small, well-worn notebook from his jacket pocket.

"I'm going lay out the facts as we know them," he began. "Please hold your questions and please don't speak unless spoken to." He looked serious.

"Fact number one," he said, turning to the page he wanted. "Numerous vessels and one plane were reported missing in the same general area." Agent Hill spoke slowly and deliberately. I had a feeling this was going to take a while.

"Number two: none of these vessels were spotted, despite numerous search efforts.

"Number three: two of the missing vessels arrived in Bermuda, a long way from where they went missing in the Caribbean."

I felt pretty good. So far he was just stating the obvious.

"Agent Washington, would you like to tell them what your agency saw on the Bermuda television news?"

Agent Washington took over. "The CIA monitors newscasts all over the globe. When we heard about different passengers, from different missing vessels, all ending up on two vessels, we did some investigation."

I knew there was no proof of aliens but I was curious what the CIA's investigation had uncovered.

"The CIA did two things. One, we got copies of the recordings the customs office made. Two, we got pieces of blackened metal from the trash."

I didn't know what the others had told the customs officers but I knew we had all agreed not to mention anything even remotely concerning the aliens. As for looking through our trash, I wondered what blackened metal rigging and fittings would indicate, besides an electromagnetic storm. I also wondered if the CIA rummaging around the trash bin in Bermuda was what had spooked the guard dog one evening.

Agent Washington continued, "The CIA contacted Colonel Wolf in Colorado and coordinated testing on the blackened metal from both vessels."

"You're from Colorado?" Tracy blurted out. "Where?"

"I work at Cheyenne Mountain," he replied.

"The Cheyenne Mountain Zoo?" Tracy asked, looking confused.

I tried hard not to snicker. I, and probably most everyone else, knew he meant the military facility located deep inside Cheyenne Mountain, more commonly referred to as NORAD.

But Pat couldn't contain herself. "Not the zoo, dummy. NORAD."

Tracy looked really hurt. I felt bad that Pat had called her a dummy. Tracy was a lot of things, but a dummy wasn't one of them.

The colonel smiled and said, "The North American Aerospace Defense Command, or NORAD for short, is one of several agencies based in that facility, and yes, Tracy, I've often called it a zoo myself."

Agent Hill got everyone back on track. "Tests were conducted and it was determined that the blackening of the metal salvaged from these two vessels"—he gestured—"could not have been caused by conventional lightning."

"Uh-oh", I thought. "This is going to be bad."

"After analyzing the recordings, the CIA determined the adults that were interviewed were telling a rehearsed story. There were just too many matching sentences for it to be anything else," Washington said.

"So we did what we often do." He paused.

I waited, wondering who had been visited for a subsequent

interview or interviews. Probably none of the people onboard or I would have heard about it.

Then he dropped a bombshell. "Unlike the Bermuda customs officials, we interviewed the Buckman kids."

I tensed up. Pat glanced over. So did Tracy. My bad feeling was getting worse.

"Let's just cut to the chase," Agent Hill said, closing his notebook. I took a deep breath.

"It's funny what people, especially kids, will say when they get frightened. All it took was a visit from the Federal Bureau of Investigation to their school."

"This isn't so bad," I thought. "I mean, who's going to believe the words of young boys?"

"For instance," Agent Hill said, maintaining his gaze upon Tracy, "they both swear that you were talking to an alien image, a little green man."

Tracy looked uncomfortable.

Agent Hill continued. "We had them separated yet they gave nearly identical stories of being sent back in time, and then going through a time portal again to return to the present time. They even drew surprisingly similar pictures. The FBI agents that questioned them believed them to be telling the truth."

Colonel Wolf took over. "We got permission to park a satellite over *The Lady Anne* and instituted surveillance."

I had never suspected any such surveillance, but why would I?

"The CIA saw reports about Captain Daniel Pincus from the Coast Guard, the Saint Thomas police department, and the Bermuda police services," Washington said, changing the subject. "Then coincidently, four of our retired operatives and one retired Interpol agent, who unconventionally negotiated citizenship, show up in the very same place where Mr. Adams killed Pincus's brother, allegedly in self-defense."

I wanted to respond to his implication that it hadn't been self-defense, but held my tongue. I did notice that was the first time he had specifically referred to Vee's and her friend's pasts. I also noticed a trace of contempt, or maybe sarcasm, when he referred to Marta.

"Then Kowalski gets into it with criminal felons at a party and sends one of them to the hospital."

Remembering what Marta had done to that man's finger made me suppress a grin.

"Captain Pincus and those same felons were seen boarding a vessel later. That vessel is owned by known Chinese agents. They have been suspected of interfering with satellite communications."

"Now when I see the crew you have hired, I have to wonder, why them?" Agent Washington asked. "Of all the people you could have hired to sail to Hawaii, why would you have chosen four retired CIA operatives and one former Interpol agent? It makes me question if they are truly retired or if they have found another employer? A Chinese employer perhaps?"

Vee shook her head. So did Candy. I hoped that he was way off base with that logic. I just couldn't see Vee, or Bev, or any of them retiring from the US Government and then working for a foreign power.

"Back to the Chinese vessel. It disappeared in the first of three mysterious back-to-back fog banks. After the first incidence of fog, Pincus and Outerbridge escaped the area and returned to Bermuda. Outerbridge was one of the workers who refurbished the boats. We learned he was fired. Checking with his supervisor found the termination reason was listed as 'association with shady characters.'"

Washington looked around and knew he had our attention. "After the second incidence of fog, *The Aquaholic* was gone from the area. But it returned after the third incidence. Very suspicious."

I swallowed. They were fitting the pieces together.

"When *The Aquaholic* left Bermuda, she was in pristine condition following her refit," Colonel Wolf said. "But when she arrived in Puerto Rico, her sails and metal parts were blackened as before. As Agent Washington stated, satellite imagery confirms there was fog in the immediate vicinity. It did not indicate any storms, much less lightning strikes. Not that lightning strikes would have caused that type of damage to metal anyway."

Agent Hill spoke. "In Panama City, Captain Pincus and Outerbridge were caught on camera stealing *La Princesa del Pacífico*. Subsequently *La Princesa del Pacífico* disappeared in another mysterious fog bank. The fog appeared when weather conditions shouldn't have allowed it to form. Although these two vessels were in close proximity to the fog, neither of them suffered any more damage."

They were really focused on the appearance of fog and the disappearance of vessels. Thankfully they hadn't mentioned the electromagnetic disturbance, just the blackened metal on *The Aquaholic*. I guessed it was because the fog somehow obscured the electromagnetic portal from the nosy satellites.

Agent Washington added, "And I need to point out that neither *La Princesa del Pacífico* nor the Chinese vessel have been seen since."

"Ms. Palmer," Colonel Wolf said, "if you are able to communicate with an alien species, how do you do it? Why are aliens here? What happens in the fog? Please tell me so I can understand."

Tracy didn't respond.

Agent Hill produced a pen and reopened his notebook. "There are too many coincidences and too many unanswered questions for me to be comfortable with what we have uncovered. I intend to find out what's going on, now, no matter how long it takes."

He looked right at Tracy. "Tracy A. Palmer, let's start with the colonel's first question. How are you able to communicate with an alien species?"

She looked at him. He frowned back. I watched intently. I had no idea what Tracy A. Palmer was going to say.

She paused, rubbed her temples, and said softly, "I want a lawyer."

"Me too," Gert added.

"So do I," Jane echoed.

"No lawyers," Agent Washington replied. Tracy, Gert, and Jane all looked at him with a look of surprise on their faces.

"Are you depriving us of our right to legal counsel?" Charles asked. His tone indicated it wasn't really a question.

"He's saying you're all this close to being categorized as enemy combatants and taken to a military prison, forthwith," Agent Hill roared back.

He had raised his voice and was losing his composure. Or maybe those two were going to play good cop, bad cop. I wasn't sure.

I couldn't believe the government I had served for twenty years could even consider classifying me as an enemy combatant and send me to Guantanamo Bay like a dangerous terrorist.

Vee moved close to Agent Washington. He tensed up but didn't retreat. "You and I both know that the CIA doesn't have the kind of power to classify us enemy combatants based on two kids' testimonies, a bunch of circumstantial evidence, and an intermittent fog bank."

They stared at each other, neither going to be the first to yield.

Bev moved in close to Agent Hill and hissed, "Either cuff us or leave us alone."

"Off my boat, now," Pat said, raising her voice. "You didn't request permission to come aboard, you just boarded us. You searched us without probable cause or a warrant. Now you're making threats to send us to prison without due process. I thought people were innocent until proven guilty. Like Charles said, we're in international waters and flying a United States flag. Get off of my boat."

"Mine too," Angie added, raising up.

Dreamgirl moved behind Agent Washington. He moved away, watching both her and Vee. He slowly moved his right hand toward his waist. From my angle, I couldn't see a weapon.

Candy moved toward Colonel Wolf. He put his hand on his sidearm.

I wondered if Candy would attack if he drew his weapon. Knowing what she was capable of, for his sake, I hoped he wouldn't draw. Thankfully he didn't. He retreated and waved for the dinghies.

One dinghy pulled right up to our swim platform. The other dinghy stopped about ten feet behind them. As the closest dinghy lightly bumped into the swim platform, the colonel stepped aboard. Agent Washington was right on his heels.

As those two moved out of the way, Agent Hill got ready

to join them. Vee touched his shoulder. He whirled around, nearly losing his balance.

"Stick this somewhere." She smiled, handing him his metal detector.

We all gathered at the stern and watched as the dinghies motored back to *The USS Fields*.

CHAPTER 82

I was speechless. The consequences of being classified as an enemy combatant engulfed me like a death sentence. I looked at Vee. She was the leader of her group. Except for Marta, they were all retired CIA operatives. She must know what was coming.

"What's next?" I asked her.

Vee looked at Bev. Bev shook her head. So did Candy. "We've got about twenty minutes before the shit hits the fan," Vee replied. "Hill and Washington are going to make their case to classify us as enemy combatants and if they are successful, we are fucked, totally fucked."

I could feel the gloom drifting over me.

"We're not fucked yet," Pat said.

Before I could ask her to explain, she hurried below.

While she was gone, Charles grabbed my shoulder.

"What's this about time travel? I thought the alien was in a parallel dimension?"

"You've probably got questions for us, questions about our past," Vee said. "But now we have questions for you. Questions about time travel, for instance." I could feel everyone looking at me.

"Now what?" I thought. I had no desire to compound a lie, but the questions probably weren't going away by themselves. These people all wanted answers. They wanted the truth. My thoughts flashed back to the alien warning not to discuss what had happened. I hesitated, trying to calculate my options.

Mo came to my rescue. He gently put his hand on Charles's shoulder and said softly, "One thing at a time. We were not entirely truthful when we said parallel dimension, but the aliens had forbidden us to discuss what really happened."

All of us were at the stern watching the dinghies off-load their passengers to *The USS Fields*. I glanced around for Pat but didn't see her. Assuming she was still below, I resumed watching.

"Can they really do what they said," Tracy said, "and send us to a military prison?"

"Not when my lawyers get done with them they can't," Charles answered. I watched the four women for a reaction. Of all of us, they probably knew exactly what the CIA could and couldn't do.

The four of them exchanged glances but didn't speak.

Finally, Vee said, "The kids' testimony wouldn't stand by itself, especially if they were questioned without a parent being present." The way she said it, I figured more was coming.

"The fact that Colonel Wolf was able to redirect a satellite for surveillance implies this is top secret and they have high-level permission to investigate. That might hold up."

"Enough to classify us as enemy combatants?" I asked.

Before Vee could reply, Mo pointed toward *The Fields* and shouted, "That's fog." A second later he added, "Where's Pat?"

Mo was right; a large bank of fog was bearing down on *The USS Fields*. I whirled around and looked for Pat. I didn't see her. I rushed below, calling her name on the way. There was no response. A quick search below confirmed Pat wasn't there.

"She's on *The Aquaholic*," Angie hollered down.

I rushed topside. Angie, Tracy, and most of the others were looking at Pat. She was seated at the cockpit table, holding her drawing. The alien signaling device was sitting on top of the cardboard box. The foil-wrapped antennas were aimed directly at the navy ship.

Pat smiled as the fog engulfed *The USS Fields*.

Bev moved into position where Pat could see her and shouted, "There are over three hundred men and women on that ship. What have you done?"

Pat put her contraption back into its box and replied, "I'm not going to prison." She put her drawing inside the box and then came back aboard *The Lady Anne*. She calmly returned the box below. She didn't seem fazed by what she had done.

"Sending bad people who would board our vessel and do bad things to us back 25,700 years in time is one thing," I thought. "Sending all those innocent sailors and officers back in time is just plain wrong."

Pat returned topside. She looked at all of us staring at her. I glanced back at the fog. It was still there but the navy ship was no longer visible. I knew that when the fog dissipated, *The USS Fields* would be gone.

"I see the looks you're giving me," Pat said, "and I don't understand why I'm suddenly the bad guy here. Those bastards were getting permission to incarcerate us without any respect for our rights. Get over it. I just did what most of you were probably thinking."

I hadn't been thinking that, but she did have a point. The others remained silent. Their expressions said they were thinking about her logic.

"Now what?" Tracy asked, turning around to watch the fog.

"When that ship disappears and ceases communications, the navy will start looking for it," Pat stated. "In a few hours, this area is going to be crawling with naval ships and planes."

"Not if their mission was top secret," Mo interjected.

"Meaning?" Pat asked.

"Meaning we probably have more than a few hours," Vee answered.

Tracy turned back around. "So?" she said.

"So. . . We should probably get out of here," Pat replied.

CHAPTER 83

Angie went back to her vessel. Jane followed her daughter. Vee, Candy, and Dreamgirl followed Jane. Marta followed Vee. Bev stayed with *The Lady Anne*. We unrafted and resumed course.

Both boats sailed hard through the night. Except for Mo and Gert, none of us could sleep. We were all too wired from what had just happened.

Bev and I alternated helm duties all night. Pat, Charles, and Tracy trimmed the sails in the moonlight, trying to coax every knot of speed from *The Lady Anne*. None of us spoke about what Pat had done. The lack of conversation was disquieting.

I kept asking myself if I had it to do over, would I have stopped her? I kept giving myself different answers. Sometimes what she had done felt entirely wrong. Maybe we deserved the consequences of using alien technology to repel boarders.

Other times her action seemed justifiable. I was sure that nobody aboard either vessel wanted to wind up in a military prison. Especially without any due process or a trial by a jury of our peers.

I found myself going back and forth between being angry with Pat and being grateful.

The winds and the seas cooperated and morning daybreak found us nearly one hundred miles from where Pat had dispatched *The USS Fields*.

Bev and I were fairly certain the skies would be filled with planes once that destroyer failed to report in. But no planes ever appeared. We both wondered if their mission was indeed top secret, like Mo had suggested. If so, being out of radio contact for a few hours, or more, might not be immediately noticed or reported.

Around noon, Vee radioed that we should raft. We furled the sails and motored into position. Both vessels took advantage of engine power to run their water makers.

Bev immediately went over to *The Aquaholic*. Angie came over to *The Lady Anne* to discuss lunch plans. She and Pat went below to talk to Mo and Gert about eating.

It all seemed so normal.

Vee finished talking to Bev. She motioned for Tracy, Charles, and me to come over. I wondered what she had to say but there was only one way to find out. The three of us crossed over. We were directed to the cockpit table and took a seat.

Around the table were Bev, Candy, Dreamgirl, Marta, and Jane. Vee remained standing. I figured she was going to run the meeting, if that's what this was. Tracy squeezed my hand lightly. She looked nervous. I squeezed back.

"I'm not sure we can go to Hawaii," Vee stated.

That came out of nowhere. Of all the things I imagined her saying, that wasn't one of them.

"Why not?" Tracy asked. "We're almost there."

Vee glanced at Bev and then continued. "Because if we simply sail into Hawaiian waters after the navy ship that was sent to intercept us vanishes without a trace, we are. . ." Her voice trailed.

"We are what?" I asked, both curious and nervous.

Vee gathered her thoughts for just a second and then answered. "Whatever Agents Hill and Washington had planned for us will seem like a pillow fight when the navy gets done with us."

"What does that mean?" Tracy asked. Her voice indicated she was getting scared.

Bev answered, "It means that having a suspected Chinese communication's vessel and a stolen tour boat strangely disappear in a mysterious fog bank will be viewed as inconsequential compared to *The USS Fields*, an Arleigh Burke class destroyer with a complement of over three hundred personnel, vanishing in another mysterious fog bank without a trace."

"You were in the marines," Candy said, looking at me. "You know interrogation basics."

"I wasn't a real jarhead that stormed the beaches and took

prisoners. I played the trumpet." My remark caught her off guard, but not for long.

"Well, we were with the CIA and have witnessed firsthand things that we won't ever forget, the things nightmares come from," Candy said. "We all know what's going to happen the instant we show up at a marina." Her words were ominous.

"I assume you have some kind of a plan?" Charles asked, beating me to it.

"Here's what I propose," Vee answered. She looked serious.

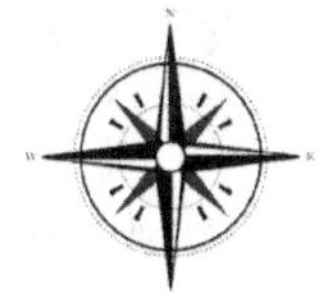

CHAPTER 84

Vee looked at Charles. "Any chance you could borrow a motor yacht for a couple of weeks and have it meet us while we are still in international waters?"

"I might be able to do that," he replied. "Why?"

"The five of us"—Vee gestured to her four comrades—"would live aboard until we can get another sailboat."

"Why do you need another sailboat?" I asked, not following her at all.

"So we can get lost when the investigation of *The Lady Anne* begins. Between the navy, the CIA, the NSA, the FBI, and NORAD, it's going to be the most involved investigation that people will have never heard of." Vee looked at me, waiting.

"What kind of sailboat?" Tracy asked.

"We know where there's a Clarriage ninety-five for sale,"

Bev answered, smiling. "We delivered it to Vancouver ourselves."

"Are you asking me to buy you a Clarriage ninety-five?" Charles asked. He looked surprised by his own question, but by the way he looked at Bev, it was obvious he wanted an answer.

"We've got that covered," Vee replied.

To the questioning looks, Vee explained. "When CIA operatives recover contraband, they turn it in, or at least they are supposed to." She looked at the others and then continued. "But who is to know if a suitcase contained 27,000 carats of diamonds, or only 23,000 carats?" She winked at Bev.

"Four thousand carats is almost two pounds," Jane said, doing some math with her fingers.

"Only one-point-seven-five," Vee corrected her, smiling.

"You've got one-point-seven-five pounds of diamonds you stole from the CIA?" Tracy asked, her eyes suddenly wide.

"Not anymore," Marta answered. "I arranged for the sale and now the proceeds are nice and safe in a Swiss bank account."

"One benefit of recovering merchandise from dead bad guys is the dead bad guys can't testify as to how many diamonds, exactly, the suitcase actually contained," Candy added.

"We've got access to plenty of cash," Vee stated. "We don't consider ourselves thieves; we just saw an opportunity."

"The CIA sold those diamonds to finance more covert ops," Bev explained. "Our bosses were happy with 23,000 carats. They never suspected anything was amiss. It was the perfect crime."

Dreamgirl smiled. "We considered it severance pay. A way to make up for the things we had to do. Things that a thousand showers can't erase."

"Think of it as two wrongs making a right," Marta said.

I didn't judge them. Given their situation and the things they were no doubt asked to do in the name of "national security," who was I to judge?

Charles looked at Vee and said, "So you want to live on a motor yacht for a couple of weeks, out here in international waters, until you can buy the big Clarriage that's in Vancouver. Is that right?"

"Yes," Vee answered, holding his gaze.

"And then what?" Tracy asked. "What are the five of you going to do with a Clarriage ninety-five?"

"We're going to get lost," Candy replied.

"Maybe the Marshall Islands, the Gilbert Islands, or the Solomon Islands, for starters," Bev replied.

"I'm not as good with geography as Jane is." Tracy smiled. "But aren't those islands out in the middle of nowhere?"

"Which is exactly why they're perfect," Bev answered. "Remember Colonel Wolf has satellite surveillance on *The Lady Anne*. Not on this boat."

"So the five of you are going to disappear, living on that big Clarriage?" I asked, wanting to confirm their plan.

"Not exactly," Vee answered. "That boat has ample room for seven full-time, live-aboard cruisers."

Before I could ask who the other two were, she told me. "We want you and Tracy to join us. Ditch Pat; she's nothing but trouble. Let Charles get lawyers for Mo, Gert, Angie, her mom, and himself. They'll all be on US soil and safe behind an army of lawyers."

Cruising the South Pacific for an indefinite period aboard a bigger Clarriage surrounded by beautiful women had to be a dream. But I wasn't dreaming. I was sitting at the cockpit table of *The Aquaholic* listening to the craziest proposal I had ever heard. "What about Pat?" I asked.

"Fuck her," Bev replied rather loudly. "That bitch should have asked us before she made *The USS Fields* vanish. She did that on her own and now she can deal with the aftermath. If Charles wants to get her legal counsel, that's his call. The five of us all agree we should leave her behind."

I felt overloaded and blindsided. I hadn't seen any of this coming.

I tried to put myself in Pat's shoes, tried to think like she would. For her to take such drastic action without any discussion, she would have had to have thought the situation was hopeless.

I tried to remember what Vee had said as the agents were leaving back to their ship. It was something about being "totally fucked."

Vee had credibility having been with the CIA. If she thought the future was . . . bleak, Pat would have reasoned that any action was worth a try. Since we were likely to be denied access to legal counsel, she used the only tool she had available—dispatch your problem back in time, courtesy of the aliens.

I knew she hadn't had an opportunity to test her alien signaling device. She was taking a big gamble that it would even work. But it did work. It worked so well *The USS Fields* was now gone without a trace.

But that didn't mean our problems were over. It dawned on me that Pat's action may have only made things worse. But could I leave her behind? That was the 64,000-dollar question.

Dreamgirl interrupted my thoughts when she lightly grasped my hand. I looked at her. "Now what?" I thought.

"Are you thinking about our proposal?" she asked.

"Well, I'm thinking about considering it," Tracy replied before I could answer. "I'd rather go sailing with you five than go to prison."

Tracy's reply only added to my confusion. I really was in love with two women. How could I choose which one to stay with? Using some of Pat's engineering logic, it was a no-brainer—go with Tracy and be free instead of staying with Pat and being imprisoned. But that would mean Pat and I would be separated. Was I ready for that?

"Anything?" Dreamgirl asked, still holding my hand.

"Say something," Tracy said, taking my other hand. "Don't overanalyze this the way Pat would."

I wasn't sure what to say. Part of me wanted to go with Tracy. Part of me wanted to stay with Pat regardless. I felt like I needed to come to Pat's defense and verbalize some of my earlier thoughts. But I didn't have any right to talk Tracy into something that went against her initial decision to split with Vee. I finally accepted this was truly a no-win situation.

"So how about it, Charles?" Vee asked, interrupting my thoughts again. "Can you get a motor yacht for us to stay on until we can get the Clarriage ninety-five purchased and delivered here from Vancouver?"

"If that's what you want, I can help," he replied, nodding.

"When a yacht comes out for them"—Jane was looking at Charles—"can its crew help Angie and me get *The Aquaholic* back to Hawaii? And can you get my daughter and me a lawyer?"

Charles nodded again.

"How about you two?" Vee asked, looking directly at me and Tracy. "Will you ditch the bitch and join us as we explore the South Pacific on our gently used Clarriage ninety-five?"

I didn't respond right away. I felt pressured into making a decision with serious implications. I could go with Tracy, Vee, and her crew. Doing that might or might not keep me out of prison. It was likely the two agents and the colonel would simply be replaced and the investigation into the mysterious events involving *The Lady Anne* would resume, albeit with different players and perhaps in a different location.

Without getting new identities, how long would it be before my passport's use was recorded and tracked? These women thought they could run, or more precisely, they thought they could simply sail away and blend in with hundreds of other sailboats.

Deep down, I didn't really want to be involved with the

five women. But I didn't want to say goodbye to Tracy either. Or say goodbye to my freedom.

I thought that maybe I should just cooperate, tell the agents the truth. But then, I didn't want to incur the aliens' wrath and be vaporized either. My head hurt. Maybe I was totally fucked, like Vee said. Maybe I had nothing to lose. Maybe everything. I looked at Tracy.

"If we'll be sailing in the South Pacific, can we go and see a Komodo dragon?" Tracy asked Vee. "I've always wanted to see a dragon."

"Absolutely," Vee replied.

"You know that a Komodo dragon isn't really a dragon," Jane stated. "It's a big monitor lizard with toxic saliva."

Tracy didn't acknowledge Jane's comment. Instead she looked at me, a twinkle in her eye.

"I'm game if you are," she replied. "Your call."

"I'll see that your affairs are managed while you're . . . away," Charles added.

"You won't regret coming with us," Dreamgirl said, squeezing my hand.

I had no idea what to do. This situation was crazier than helping two former students deliver a sailboat they had won in a poker game. Even crazier than being sent back in time by aliens for taking their picture.

I made eye contact with Tracy. She smiled and said, "Let's do it.

CHAPTER 85

Pat cleared her throat. I had been so engrossed in my thoughts that I hadn't noticed her topside on *The Lady Anne*; none of us had. But there she was, close enough to have overheard Vee's plans. She looked really pissed.

"Uh-oh." Tracy snickered. "The other woman."

In a flash, Dreamgirl let go of my hand. She looked guilty. I stood up and moved to the stern. Tracy got up and followed. Vee moved out of our way.

Pat started quivering. Her face contorted with rage.

She moved close to the lifeline and started shrieking at me. "So you and Tracy are going to 'ditch the bitch' and join those sailing floozies on a Clarriage ninety-five? Really?"

I didn't reply. She obviously had been listening. Except she didn't know my decision. How could she? I didn't even know what my decision would be. I sensed she wasn't finished.

"I figured you and that top-heavy kumquat were fooling around. Now you two are holding hands, in broad daylight no less. Typical man."

"What did you just call me?" Dreamgirl asked, raising her voice as well.

Pat looked right at her and shouted, "I called you a top-heavy kumquat. Ask Jane what it means, or maybe I should write it down for you."

Pat was pissed. As mad as I had ever seen her. But before I could say anything, she redirected her fury at me.

"And you, Mr. Innocent, do you even notice the way you two look at each other?"

To tell the truth, I guess maybe I was guilty, maybe a little. "But guilty of what?" I asked myself. "For thinking about a past lover?"

Pat continued at full volume, "It is so cute the way Mo and Gert follow each other around. They fell in love and I married them, right over there." I looked where she pointed, not following her analogy.

She saw I didn't get it so she explained it to me. "You two follow each other around the exact same way. Admit it. You two are falling in love. How long before you're fucking, if you're not already?"

"I am not fucking Reid," Dreamgirl shouted right back at her. "Though I bet I could if I wanted to."

I looked at Dreamgirl. Now was not the time to antagonize Pat. I held up a hand, but before I could say anything Pat was screaming at us again.

"Do you really expect me to believe anything that a woman who calls herself 'Dreamgirl' says?"

Pat might have suspected that there was something going on between Dreamgirl and me, but I knew that I hadn't slept with anyone except the two women I was engaged to. Pat seemed determined not to let me talk.

She took a deep breath, wiped her eyes, and continued, still shouting at full volume. "Now my fiancé and my best friend are going to leave me to face the CIA and run away and hide. You are a bunch of ungrateful fucks. I saved your asses from prison and this is the thanks I get? Really?"

I didn't see Mo, Gert, or Angie around, but there was no way they weren't hearing this. I hoped that Buster was below and that Pat's screaming wasn't scaring him. I know it was scaring me.

Tears were streaming down her face. I knew I needed to say something, try to calm her hysteria. I watched her but kept quiet. She was out of control. This was not the time to try and soothe or console her. She wouldn't hear it.

And besides, I still hadn't made my decision to either stay with Pat or go with Tracy and the others.

"You don't understand—" Tracy started.

But Pat didn't let her finish. "Not a fucking word, you oversexed tramp. I see you have no problem sharing Reid. I saw the three of you holding hands. I'm sorry I ever met you. I hope you die in a ditch."

Tracy was speechless. We all were.

Pat untied her gold coin engagement pendant and deliberately threw it past my reach into the water. I heard it splash and watched it sink.

"Go fetch, you bastard," she screamed. Her face was red and she was shaking.

Pat wiped at her tears and then began untying the boats. She slammed the lines down and pushed the boats apart with her foot. The vessels began drifting apart. She then stormed below, flipping us the bird on the way.

I wasn't concerned that our raft was untied. The fenders were still out and I knew we could retie quickly if needed. I was disappointed she was mad enough to pitch her pendant overboard. It was way too deep to dive for it, so it appeared that my engagement to two women was officially over.

What bothered me the most was that Pat wasn't being rational. She had jumped to a wrong conclusion about my infidelity with Dreamgirl. She hadn't even let me try and explain the hopelessness of our situation. Hell, maybe both boats could have bypassed Hawaii and we could have bought ourselves some time to think about a viable solution.

"She'll cool off," Tracy told me, rubbing her pendant. "I'm not tossing mine."

Vee took a look at Tracy's pendant and complimented my workmanship. She was trying to change the subject, redirect my thoughts away from Pat's maniacal tirade and behavior. I didn't respond. My thoughts were running wild. My head was pounding. I would have rather faced a hurricane that have to face what I was facing now.

Mo came topside. He shrugged and headed to the helm. I

watched as he shifted into gear and applied just a bit of throttle. *The Lady Anne* motored away.

Pat re-emerged topside a few seconds later. She was concealing something behind her back, but I couldn't tell what it was. I hoped it wasn't a shotgun or Mo's rifle. Was Pat mad enough to shoot me? I hoped not. Fortunately, she was nearly out of shotgun range.

When the boats were maybe fifty yards apart she yelled, "Roses are red. Violets are blue. I'm a bitch. Fuck you."

Tracy started laughing. I noticed that Vee, Bev, Dreamgirl, Candy, and Marta were suppressing laughter. Charles might have been holding in a laugh as well. I wasn't sure about Jane.

But I wasn't laughing. Pat wasn't a bitch. She had just stepped on a proverbial landmine. If she moved left or right, forward or backward, she'd blow up. If she stayed put, the mine would go off in time. I thought that it wasn't Vee who was "totally fucked." It was all of us.

I looked back at Pat. She was getting further away by the minute. I wanted to say I was sorry. I needed to. But she was aiming something at us. I wasn't sure what it was, but she was definitely pointing something in our direction. At first I was thankful it didn't look like a firearm.

But then I saw the fog approaching.

I knew what she had done.

The End

(For now.)

Book three on the horizon.

Nautical Glossary

Aboard	On a vessel, or to go onto a vessel.
Adjustable keel	The ballasted structure on the bottom of the vessel's hull that can be raised or lowered to suit conditions.
Adrift	Moving on the water but not under power or control.
Aft	At or toward the stern.
Aground	Stuck on the ground in shallow water.
Ahoy	1. A nautical greeting. 2. A shout used to attract attention.
Amidships	Area in the middle of the vessel, either front to back or side to side.
Anchor	A device, usually deployed from the bow, used to secure the vessel to the bottom to keep the vessel from moving away. Anchors come in different shapes and sizes to optimize holding in different bottom compositions (mud, sand, rock, etc.)
Anchor alarm function	A device using GPS to monitor the vessel's position and sound an alarm if the vessel moves outside of a preset boundary.
Anchor light	One or more white lights shown at night when a vessel is at anchor. Sailboats often have this light atop the mast.

Anchor storage compartment / Anchor locker	A compartment where the anchor and associated tackle are kept. On a dinghy, this is often in the bow. On some vessels, there are provisions for a freshwater rinse of the anchor and its chain/line.
Anchoring	A process of deploying or retrieving the anchor.
Astern	The area behind the stern (back) of the boat.
Autopilot	A device of various designs to automatically keep the vessel on a preset course.
Backstay	A support, often made of cable or rod, that leads downward and aft from the upper part of the mast. It is used to support the mast and to control sail trim.
Bare poles	Not having any sails deployed. The masts are "bare."
Bareboat charter company	Companies that allow sailors to charter (rent) sailboats/yachts with or without any crew for a few days or a few weeks. Those persons chartering the boat will need to prove they are qualified to sail and operate the size boat they are chartering.

Bareboat Chartering class	Instruction to take the Bareboat Chartering test, an advanced-intermediate level of certification to be able to charter (rent) sailboats, between 30 - 50 feet in length, for sailing in moderate wind and sea conditions, within sight of land, during daylight hours. The prerequisite is usually the Coastal Cruising certification or equivalent. There is normally textbook, classroom, and on-the-water instruction, including an overnight sail.
Basic Keelboat class	Instruction to take the Basic Keelboat test, a beginning level of certification that demonstrates the ability to prepare the sailboat to sail, get away from the dock, raise sail, perform basic sailing maneuvers such as tacking and jibing, and get the boat safely back to the dock. There is usually no prerequisite as this is a beginning level course. There is normally textbook, classroom, and on-the-water instruction, including learning several knots.
Beam	The widest part of the boat.
Becalmed	A condition that exists for a sailboat when there is no wind whatsoever.
Belay that	A command to cancel the previous order.
Below	The area beneath the deck.
Bermuda Triangle	An area loosely bordered by points in Florida, Puerto Rico, and Bermuda where dozens of ships and planes have disappeared, some under mysterious or unexplained circumstances.

Berth	1. A sleeping space aboard a vessel. 2. A vessel's allotted space at a dock.
Bilge	1. The lowest, deepest part of a vessel where the bottom curves up to meet the sides. 2. The water (often dirty and smelly) that collects in the bilge.
Blip	See Radar blip.
Board / Boarding / Boarded	To get on, to be getting on, or to have gotten on a boat.
Boat	A small vessel propelled by oar, paddle, sail, pole, or an engine. Rule of thumb: a boat will fit on the deck of a ship, but a ship will not fit on the deck of a boat.
Boom	1. A long spar of various materials protruding out from the mast, holding the foot (bottom edge) of the sail. The boom can be released (eased) to swing from side to side. 2. The last sound you hear when you are unexpectedly hit in the head by the boom. This can be very dangerous, even fatal.
Bow	The front of the vessel, also called the pointy end.
Bow line	A dock line used to secure the front of the boat to the dock.
Bow pulpit	A railing, usually metal, at the bow of the vessel. It sometimes extends forward past the deck. On some larger vessels, it may hold the anchor.

Bowline knot	A temporary, nonslipping loop. The bowline can be untied easily, even when wet, as long as there is no load (tension) on the line. (Pronounced like "colon," with a B.)
Bowsprit	A spar or pole protruding forward from the bow to which sails or rigging can be attached.
Brass bell	The ship's bell, made of brass or bronze, used to signal the time or produce required sound signals. They are normally engraved with the vessel's name and can be quite ornate.
Bridge	The dedicated area of a ship, usually with a good view or immediate access to such a view, from where the ship is commanded.
Broadside	The side of a ship above the waterline.
Bulb-keel	A specific type of keel, ballast filled and usually teardrop shaped.
Bulkhead	A support or dividing wall between compartments to strengthen the vessel.
Buoy	An anchored float, normally used as an aid to navigation or to display warnings or mark dangerous areas.
Cabin	An enclosed area on a vessel that may or may not be tall enough to stand up in. The nautical equivalent of a room.
Capsize	To turn over or upside down in the water.

Captain	The person in charge of the vessel and responsible for its safe operation and the safety of the crew and passengers.
Cat	Abbreviation for catamaran.
Catamaran	A vessel with twin hulls running parallel to each other.
Celestial navigation	The process of finding one's way by observing the positions of celestial bodies (the sun, the moon, and/or the stars).
Channel	1. A navigable length of water, often marked with buoys or other aids to navigation, connecting two other, often larger bodies of water. 2. A specific band of frequencies used in radio or television.
Channel 16	A specific VHF radio frequency primarily designated for international distress and safety calls.
Chart	A nautical map, paper or electronic, used for navigation. It usually shows the water depth, land features, markers (buoys), traffic lanes, distances between islands, the method to convert magnetic to true north, etc. Charts are marked in degrees latitude and longitude. The depth can be shown in feet, meters, or fathoms (6 feet in a fathom).
Charter boat	A vessel for rent or hire, normally located in island or coastal destinations.

Clarriage 68	A fictional luxury sailing yacht, 68 feet in length, designed to cross oceans and then live aboard for extended periods in complete comfort.
Clarriage 95	A fictional luxury sailing yacht, 95 feet in length, designed to cross oceans and then live aboard for extended periods in complete comfort.
Clarriage Yachts	A line of fictional luxury sailing yachts designed to cross oceans and then live aboard for extended periods in complete comfort.
Cleat	A normally metal object upon which a line can be fastened.
Cleat hitch knot	A type of knot, resembling a figure eight, used to secure a line around a cleat.
Cleating / Cleated	The process of securing a line to a cleat.
Coastal Cruising class	Instruction to take the Coastal Cruising test, an intermediate level of certification that adds to the Basic Keelboat instruction. Advanced topics include reefing, anchoring, heaving to, docking under power, and additional proficiency with knots. The prerequisite is usually the Basic Keelboat certification or equivalent. There is normally textbook, classroom, and on-the-water instruction.

Cockpit	The location of the controls on a vessel, normally outside the pilothouse/deckhouse and often recessed slightly into the deck. There may be a separate helm station on some designs.
Crew	The person or persons who assist in the operation of the vessel.
Crew's quarters	A spartan but efficient living space to offer the crew some privacy. Somewhat self-contained and may or may not have minimal galley facilities.
Crewed charter boat	A boat for charter (rent) that comes fully equipped (food, drinks, dishes, linens, towels, fuel, captain, cook, crew, etc.) so all the guests have to do is bring personal items and relax.
Cruisers	1. Those that sail from place to place, living aboard for extended periods, for pleasure. 2. Vessels designed specifically for cruisers. 3. Those persons who repair their boats in exotic locations.
Cruising	What cruisers do—sail from place to place and fix their boat in exotic locations.

Cruising guide	A publication, either hard copy or electronic, dedicated to a specific area, giving various levels of information and details about the area. May include information such as marina locations, yacht clubs, approach/departure routes, monitored radio frequencies, facilities, lodging, shopping, marine repair, sightseeing, dining, fishing, customs information, etc. May also include chart excerpts for specific locations.
Current	The movement of water usually caused by tides, winds, or flow.
Current position	Accurately obtaining the vessel's location by electronic or other means. Caveat: If the vessel is moving, the position you obtained and noted may be several minutes old.
Cutlass	A short, broad sword sharpened on the cutting edge. They could be straight or curved and were a common weapon during the age of sail.
Deck	A floor-like surface permanently covering one or more level(s) of a hull or compartment and serving to strengthen the hull.
Diesel engine	The most common engine in sailboats over 25 ft. long. Compared to gasoline fuel powered engines, diesel fuel powered engines offer higher torque, higher available horsepower, lower maintenance costs, no carbon monoxide production, and less sensitivity to moisture. But, diesel engines are heavier, noisier, and more expensive, initially.

Diesel generator	An additional mechanical device to provide electricity other than using a diesel engine. Diesel fuel is safer to store than gasoline because diesel fuel doesn't vaporize as easily and is less combustible.
Dinghy	A small open boat, often carried on or towed behind a larger vessel. A dinghy can be used as a tender (transport) for recreation or even as a lifeboat. Dinghies can be rowed, sailed, or motor driven. Their hull can be inflatable or rigid.
Dinghy davits	A crane-type mechanical device used to raise, lower, or support the vessel's dinghy.
Distress signal	1. Any of various internationally recognized indicators (either visual or audible) signifying a vessel is in danger. 2. A request for assistance.
Dock cart	A wheeled, wagon-type carrier used for moving supplies to or from the vessel when docked. Some dock carts fold for compact storage aboard.
Dock line	A specialty line used to secure the vessel to the dock. Dock lines often have a factory spliced loop at one end, are water and fade resistant, and provide some stretch. They vary in size, load rating, and length, depending on application.
Dock(s)	Man-made walkway(s) in the water from which to access boats. Many docks are floating to allow for tides or fluctuating water levels.

Docking Certification class	Additional instruction to practice safely and efficiently maneuvering and docking an engine powered sailboat.
Dogged	To close something (watertight door, porthole) and securely latch it closed.
Downwind	The direction the wind is blowing.
Drifting	At the mercy of the wind or current, having no means of directing the motion of the vessel.
Drogue	An external device attached to the vessel's bow or stern and used to slow the vessel down in a storm. They are designed to keep the hull perpendicular to the waves. Also called a sea anchor.
Duffel bag	A type of bag, traditionally cylindrical in shape and closed by a drawstring or zipper. The bag got its name from Duffel, a town in Belgium where the cloth was first made. Duffel bags are preferred by sailors because unlike a suitcase, they can be collapsed when emptied, thus saving precious space.
Ease	To slacken, let out, decrease tension, or pay out slightly.
Electronic chart overlay	Using GPS and an electronic chart, an electronic method to synchronize the vessel's autopilot to keep the vessel on a predetermined course.
Emergency Locator Beacon	See EPIRB

Engine compartment	A usually limited space to access the vessel's engine. On sailboats, the engine compartment is often located behind the ladder (steps) leading below decks. The ladder is removed to access the front of the engine and then additional panels can be removed to access the remainder of the engine.
Engine room	A specific compartment or large area dedicated to housing the vessel's engine(s). There is usually comfortable and well-lit access to all sides of the engine for inspection or maintenance purposes. The engine room is normally well insulated to reduce the engine's noise.
EPIRB	An Emergency Position Indicating Radio Beacon (EPIRB for short) is a distress beacon used by mariners worldwide to alert (using satellite technology) search and rescue forces that the mariner/their vessel is in distress.
Eye of the wind	The direction where the wind is coming from.
Fair winds	1. A nautical blessing for a safe journey. 2. A favorable wind blowing in a desirable direction of travel for the mariner.
Fall off	To turn the sailboat away from the direction of the wind.
Fender	A bumper placed outside the hull, used to prevent damage to the vessel. Fenders are often deployed when docking or rafting two or more vessels together. Fenders can protect both the vessel(s) and the dock.

| Ferry | A specially designed boat or ship to carry passengers, vehicles, and/or limited cargo across a normally small body of water at regular intervals. |

| Fittings | Mechanical devices to connect various components together, i.e., sailing hardware. |

| Fix | 1. See Position. 2. Repair. |

| Floorboards | The floor of the vessel, also called the sole. It is often made of long pieces of a species of wood that is resistant to water damage, such as teak. Some floorboards are removable to access the space(s) beneath them, such as the bilge. |

| Flying the spinnaker | Having deployed the spinnaker sail. (See also spinnaker.) |

| Following sea | Waves coming from behind the vessel. |

| Fore | See forward. |

| Forepeak | The furthest forward area/compartment in the vessel's hull. |

| Forestay | A support, often made of cable or rod, that leads downward and forward from the upper part of the mast. It is used to support the mast and the headsails. (See also standing rigging.) |

| Forward | At or toward the bow. |

| Fuel dock | A fixed or floating structure (dock) used to dispense (sell) fuel (gasoline or diesel) to boats while in the water. Fuel prices at marina fuel docks are often considerably higher than traditional, land-based gas stations. |

Full sail	When all of a sailboat's sails are set, raised, hauled out, unfurled, or deployed.
Furl/Furled	To roll a sail over itself by using the roller furling mechanism. Opposite of Hauled out, def. # 1.
Gaff	A handheld hook, often attached to a rigid handle of various lengths, used for holding or lifting heavy fish. The hook can be barbed or not and is often fairly sharp and pointy.
Gale	A strong sustained wind. A gale at sea is accompanied by large waves and regular whitecaps. There may be blowing foam or churning seas. It is stronger than a breeze but weaker than a tropical storm.
Galley	The kitchen area aboard a boat or ship.
Gated pier	A locking gate, often made of metal, across the entrance to a pier or dock, controlling access.
Genoa	A sail set near the bow that does extend aft of the main mast. A genoa is larger than a jib.
Give way vessel	As per the navigation rules, the vessel that is required to keep out of the way of another vessel.

GPS	A satellite navigation system (Global Positioning System) used to determine the ground position of an object. The GPS receiver uses multiple signals from orbiting satellites to calculate a fairly accurate position using the process of triangulation.
Grab rail	A safety device, often in the shape of a railing or bar, used to provide the sailor with a strong and convenient handhold while moving about the vessel.
Hail	An attempt to establish contact by various methods, including a radio call, to see if anyone is listening.
Halyard	A line that raises a sail (or flag) up or down.
Hand bearing compass	A handheld magnetic compass, capable of one-handed use.
Handed off the helm	1. Literally, to not let go of the wheel or tiller until your replacement has a hold of it. 2. To relinquish control of the helm to a replacement.
Harbor	A place on the coast where vessels may find shelter. Harbors are usually protected from rough water by land, piers, jetties, sea walls, or other artificial structures.
Hatch	1. An opening in the deck leading to a lower level through which cargo, personnel, and even air can be passed. 2. A covering for such an opening.

Hauled out	To deploy a sail that has roller furling by pulling it out by the clew (one of the corners on a triangular sail). Also called unfurling the sail.
Head	1. The bathroom on a vessel. 2. The top corner of a triangular sail.
Heading	A direction or course to steer.
Headsail	Any sail set forward of the most forward mast.
Heave to	A technique for (nearly) stopping a sailboat by positioning the sails to counteract each other. The vessel will oscillate slowly from one direction to another and then back again, over and over and over.
Heavy weather	Strong winds and large waves. May or may not be accompanied by rain, thunder, and/or lighting.
Heel/heeling	The angle the boat sails at. The more the boat is heeled, the steeper the angle.
Helm	1. The tiller or the wheel that controls the angle of the rudder. 2. The area of a sailboat from which the boat is steered.
Helmsman/ Helmswoman	The person who steers/drives the vessel.
Holding tank	A container, usually metal or plastic, in which wastewater is temporarily held prior to its proper disposal.
House battery	The battery that provides power to run the vessel's lights and electrical equipment but is not used to start the engine.

Hove to	Past tense of heave to. A sailboat that has "heaved to."
Hull	The main body of a vessel, including the bottom and the sides.
Jib	A sail set near the bow that does not extend aft of the main mast. A jib is smaller than a genoa.
Jibe	A maneuver to bring the stern of the boat through the eye of the wind.
Jibe ho	A command issued (normally by the helmsman) while jibing, just prior to the boom swinging across to the other side.
Keel	An extension of the hull that goes deep(er) into the water and provides stability from heel and sideways resistance to the wind.
Ketch	A type of sailboat having two masts. The aft (rear) mast (the mizzen mast) is generally shorter than the forward mast (the main mast).
Knot	1. A measurement of speed at sea equal to one nautical mile per hour. 2. Used to fasten (tie) a line to itself or another object.
Knot meter	An instrument, normally electric or electronic, that measures the vessel's speed through the water.
Ladder	What steps on a ship (not a cruise ship) are often referred to as, due to their steepness.

Land ho	An expression shouted by the vessel's watch to inform the crew that land has been spotted. After long passages at sea, "Land ho" was very comforting to hear.
Latitude	The angular distance, measured in degrees, minutes, and seconds, running north or south of the equator.
Leeward	1. On or toward the side sheltered from the wind. 2. The side sheltered or away from the wind. (The side opposite windward.) (Pronounced loo ward, like "steward" with an L.)
Life jacket / Life vest	A flotation device designed to keep the wearer afloat in the water. They are available in different styles and are designed for various purposes and sea conditions.
Life raft	A smaller boat used in emergencies, often inflatable. Some life rafts provide a cover that can be used as shade. Some life rafts are designed to be difficult to sink or flip in rough seas.
Lifeline(s)	A wire or cable that runs along the outside of the deck, designed to help restrain passengers (or crew) from falling overboard.
Lifeline gate	A section of the lifeline that can be unhooked/unfastened to allow easy access on or off the boat without having to step over the lifeline.
Light air	Wind with a very low speed.

Line	Rope or other forms of cordage that have come onboard a vessel. Lines with specific uses may be called by other names.
Log	1. A book in which all matters concerning the vessel are notated. 2. To make a notation of an event worth recording. (Similar to an entry in a journal.)
Long tack	A sailing vessel being on the same tack (point of sail) for a long period of time.
Longitude	The angular distance, measured in degrees, minutes, and seconds, running east or west of the prime meridian running through Greenwich, England.
Macerate	The act of using a machine to grind solids (including sewage and food waste) in wastewater into small pieces so they can be discharged directly into the sea (normally when a minimum of 12 nautical miles offshore).
Magnetic north	A compass bearing relating to the magnetic poles rather than the true north and south poles.
Main mast	The primary, usually the tallest, mast aboard a sailboat.
Main salon	The primary indoor guest area on a vessel.
Mainsail	The primary source of power for a sailboat. The mainsail is attached to the main mast and the boom.

Mainsheet	The line that controls the mainsail, bringing it in or letting it out, from side to side.
Making way	A vessel moving through the water.
Marina	A normally sheltered or protected commercial area where yachts and small vessels can dock, refuel, and get repairs and supplies.
Marlin spike	A pointy tool used in marine rope work. It may be a separate tool or one item on a specialty pocketknife.
Mast	A tall upright spar of various materials and designs, erected vertically, generally along the centerline of the vessel. On a sailboat, the mast(s) carry the sail(s).
Mayday	The international distress signal that a vessel uses to declare they have a life-threatening emergency.
Messenger line	A light line used to haul a heavier line between vessels or to the shore.
Mizzen mast	The mizzen mast is aft of (behind) the main mast. It is usually shorter than the main mast.
Mizzen sail	A sail affixed to the mizzen mast. The mizzen sail is usually smaller than the mainsail.
Mizzen sheet	The line that controls the mizzen sail, bringing it in or letting it out, from side to side.

Monkey-fist knot	1. A knot in the category of heaving knots tied to the end of a line serving as a weight, making it easier to throw. 2. An ornamental knot. (It is so named because it resembles a bunched fist or paw.)
Monohull	A vessel with a single hull.
Motorsailing	The act of a sailboat using engine power while keeping the mainsail up (for stability).
Multihull	A vessel with two, three, or more hulls running parallel to each other. (All catamarans are multihulls but not all multihulls are catamarans.)
Multihull Certification class	Additional instruction to learn how to safely sail a catamaran. This class is for those that already have experience sailing monohulls.
Multi-tool	A versatile hand tool that combines several individual functions (screwdriver, knife, pliers, etc.) into a single unit.
Nautical mile	A unit used for measuring distances at sea. Historically it was equal to 1 minute of 1 degree of latitude. Now it is equal to 1,852 meters, 6,076 feet, or approximately 1.151 statute (regular) miles. It is abbreviated "nm."

Nautical uniform / Nautical white	A clothing style borrowing from naval officer's designs. Uniform will be white in color, not blue. Shirts will have epaulet straps. Epaulets (an ornamental shoulder piece) may be plain or striped, with or without an insignia. Pants are often a solid color and may be pleated. Belt may have nautical themed designs, possibly signal flags, and the buckle may have an insignia. Hats are captain's style, with or without gold striping, insignias, and/or scrambled eggs (leaf shaped embellishments) on the visor.
Navigation station	A dedicated area of a vessel that houses the navigation tools and equipment. On a sailboat, it is usually below deck, often near the radio and the electrical circuit breaker/switches. Also called the Nav station.
Night watch	A lookout during the night or a person(s) keeping such a lookout.
Ocean crossing	1. The passage of passengers (and/or cargo) across an ocean. 2. An ocean crossing vessel is designed to handle rough seas and long passages.
Offshore	1. At sea, often out of sight of land. 2. A wind that is blowing away from the land.

Offshore Passage Making class	Instruction to take the Offshore Passage Making test, an advanced level of certification. It is a weeklong (or longer) live-aboard class, consisting of nearly nonstop sailing for a minimum of 600 miles, 250 of which are at least 50 miles from shore. The prerequisites are usually the Bareboat Chartering certification and the successful completion of a Coastal Navigation course and possibly a Celestial Navigation course, or equivalent. This is a capstone class for those wanting serious sailing instruction in real-world conditions. Instructors for this class will be highly qualified.
Offshore rain gear	Foul weather gear designed for consecutive days or weeks of use in extreme conditions. It must be durable, waterproof, highly breathable, and made of heavy-duty, high-quality fabrics, components, and construction.
Outboard motor	A small internal combustion engine with a propeller integrally attached for mounting at the stern of a small boat.
Overhead hatch	A hatch leading to the space above. They can be used for ventilation, light, or if they are large enough, as an emergency exit for personnel.
Overtaking	To come up (on another vessel) from behind.
Owner's suite	Normally the most luxurious accommodation/cabin aboard in terms of size, comfort, location, and features.

Paper chart	A nautical chart printed on paper. They are often laminated or a heavy-duty, smudge-resistant paper. (See also chart.)
Passage	A voyage between points that entails a large number (hundreds or thousands) of miles of boating/sailing in the open ocean.
Passageway	An internal corridor allowing access (horizontally) to different areas or compartments onboard a ship. (The nautical equivalent of a hallway.)
PFD	Abbreviation for a Personal Flotation Device. (See also life jacket.)
Pier	A manmade structure that protrudes from the shore.
Pilot boat	A vessel dedicated to transferring a skilled helmsman (pilot) from a harbor (or river mouth) to a ship that requires steering or guidance (piloting) into the harbor, and vice versa.
Pilot chart atlas	An aid to navigation that depicts historical averages of winds, wave heights, currents, barometric pressure, and other weather conditions broken out per month, per ocean.
Pilothouse	An enclosed structure on a vessel from which the vessel can be steered and navigated by the helmsman. Also called a deckhouse.
Piracy	The practice of attacking, robbing, stealing from, or committing illegal violence against vessels at sea.

Pirate	One who engages in piracy.
Pirate flag	A flag, sometimes displaying a white skull and white crossbones on a black background, originally flown to indicate a pirate ship. The first recorded use of a flag displaying such symbols dates to the seventeenth century. Other pirate flags featured a skeleton and could be black or red. The pirate flag was usually only flown when the pirates wanted to announce their presence, i.e., just before a raid or battle. Now they are displayed for fun.
Pitchpoling	To turn upside down in the water by flipping the stern over the bow.
Plot a course	Basically drawing a line between two points on a chart, calculating the distance between them, and determining the compass heading.
Port	1. The left side of the vessel when aboard and facing forward. 2. Where vessels come in to dock.
Porthole	A round, window-like opening with a hinged, watertight glass cover in the side of a vessel for admitting light and/or air.
Position	Also called a fix, position is the determination of the vessel's location, arrived at by various methods, usually expressed as precise coordinates in degrees, minutes, and seconds of latitude and longitude.
Powerboat	1. A boat propelled by an engine. 2. A fast boat used in racing.

Primary helm station/ Master Helm Station	When there are steering wheels on both sides of the boat, the side where the engine controls are located.
Propeller	A rounded blade that rotates in a circle and moves the vessel forward (or backward) through the water. Can be called "prop" for short.
Propane/Propane tanks	Liquid Propane Gas (LPG) is a flammable fuel, usually used for heating or cooking, that is stored in pressurized tanks.
Propane locker	A vapor-tight compartment enclosing propane (LPG) tanks and some of their associated connections, separated from the interior of the vessel or outside of the vessel in a location where leaking gas will not drain to the interior of the vessel.
Radar	Equipment to, or a means of, sending out radio waves to detect objects in the distance that may be obscured by weather, darkness, are simply out of sight, or difficult to see.
Radar blip	A generic term for a radar echo or radar response from an object displayed on the radar screen or other type of display.
Raft	1. Buoyant materials fastened together to make a floating platform. 2. To tie two (or more) boats together, side by side, while in the water, away from a dock to assist in easily moving between them. 3. Two or more boats tied side by side are said to be rafted.

Railing	See stern rail. See lifeline.
Raise sail	The act of hoisting, hauling out, unfurling, or otherwise deploying the sail(s).
Reef	1. To decrease sail area (make the sail smaller). 2. A ridge of jagged rock, coral, or sand just above or below the surface of the water/sea.
Reefing	The act of making the sail smaller.
Regatta	A rowing, powerboat, or sailing race or a series of such races.
Registration papers	Written documentation providing evidence of vessel ownership.
Repel boarders	Any action used to keep people from coming aboard a vessel uninvited or unwelcomed.
Replacement canvas	Another name for spare sails, even if the sails aren't made of canvas but of another material instead.
RIB	Abbreviation for a Rigid Inflatable Boat. A lightweight but high performance, high capacity boat constructed of a solid and an inflatable hull.
Rigging	1. Standing rigging are the cables, shrouds, and stays that support the mast(s). 2. Running rigging are the sheets, halyards, and lines that control the sail(s) or parts of the sail(s).

Rigging knife	A specially designed knife used to cut heavy lines. It may have a serrated edge for sawing through the line. It may have an extra-heavy blade, suitable for pounding with a mallet, to drive the blade through the line. The folding models often come equipped with a marlinspike for convenience. (See also marlinspike.)
Rigging station / Rigging alcove	A dedicated area in a vessel containing rigging equipment, specialized tools, and supplies, often including an assortment of lines and fittings and perhaps even extra sails.
Right-of-way	As per the navigation rules, the vessel that has the legal authority to stay on (hold) its course.
Roller furling	A mechanism to furl (roll) a sail in or out. It is also used when reefing (making the sail smaller) by furling it in partway.
Rudder	An underwater appendage that controls the direction of the vessel when moving through the water.
Run aground	The act of getting the vessel stuck (on the bottom) in shallow water. (See also aground.)
Running lights	Navigation light(s) is/are a source of illumination on a vessel that give information on the vessel's type, position, heading, and status.
Running rigging	The sheets, halyards, and lines that control the sail(s) or parts of the sail(s). (See also rigging.)
Sail	Material (often a specialty fabric) used on a vessel that uses wind for power to propel the vessel.

Sail loft	An area (often a large room) where the manufacturing (making) of sails takes place.
Sailboat	A vessel that uses wind power to propel it forward through the water.
Sailing certifications	A certification, issued by various sailing organizations, stating the individual has completed progressively advancing levels of training. Proof of certification, including presenting a sailing resume, is often a requirement to charter a sailboat, especially the larger ones. There are also various levels of certifications for sailing instructors.
Sailing gloves	Gloves designed to protect the hands from abrasion and blisters that often occur when handling lines. They are available in different styles, fabrics, and colors, depending on the expected usage.
Salon table	The primary dining table in the salon of a vessel. Some salon tables can convert into a berth for sleeping.
Satellite phone	A telephone that transmits and receives voice (and possibly short messages) from orbiting satellites providing coverage around the world.

SCUBA certification	A diving certification, issued by various dive organizations, stating the individual has completed required levels of training, normally consisting of coursework, pool work, and open water experience. Proof of certification, including presenting a logbook with recent dives, is a requirement to have dive tanks refilled (with air). There are also various levels of certifications for diving instructors. (SCUBA stands for Self-Contained Underwater Breathing Apparatus.)
Scuttle/scuttling	To deliberately sink a vessel, often by making holes in the side or bottom of it.
Sea anchor	See drogue.
Secondary helm station	When there are steering wheels on both sides of the boat, the side that doesn't have the engine controls.
Sextant	A precision astronomical instrument used to determine latitude and longitude by measuring the angular distances, especially the altitude, of the sun, the moon, and/or the stars.
Shakedown cruise	Time on the water to test a vessel's performance. Usually used for new vessels or those having undergone substantial repairs.
Sheet-in	To tighten, bring in, or increase tension on the sail for sailing closer (higher) to the wind.
Sheet(s)	A control line(s) for a sail. Sheets control the sails side to side.

Ship	A large vessel. Rule of thumb: a boat will fit on the deck of a ship, but a ship will not fit on the deck of a boat.
Shipshape	A desirable condition aboard a vessel where everything is clean, neat, tidy, organized, and in good working order or condition.
Shipwreck	1. An accident in which a vessel is destroyed, lost, or sunk, especially by hitting a reef or running aground. 2. The skeletal structure of such an unfortunate vessel.
Shipwrecked	Those persons affected by a shipwreck.
Shoal	A shallow area of rock or coral.
Shore power	The provision of shoreside electrical power to a vessel at berth while its main and auxiliary engines (or generators) are shut down.
Shroud	A wire or cable supporting the mast. (See also standing rigging.)
Signal flags	1. Various flags, used internationally, by vessels at sea to spell out short messages. When used in certain combinations, they may have special meanings. 2. Signal flags were used in military operations to communicate while maintaining radio silence.
Skipper	See captain. Skipper is a less formal title.

Slip	1. The area of water that is between docks, piers, or wharves where vessels can be moored. (A space to park/secure your vessel that has shore access. See berth def. #2) 2. To fall or lose one's balance.
Solar panels	A device used to convert the sun's energy into electricity (or heat).
Solar shower	A device originally designed for campers, it consists of a container that absorbs the sun's direct heat to raise the temperature of the inside water. It will have a hose and showerhead with a valve to regulate the flow and normally a hole or hook from which to hang it.
Sock	See spinnaker sleeve.
Sole	See floorboards.
Spar	A long, cylindrical object made of wood, metal, or composite material, such as the mast, boom, or bowsprit.
Spinnaker	A large, usually colorful, three-cornered sail, typically bulging when full (of wind), set near the bow, used when running (sailing downwind).
Spinnaker pole	A spar used to help support and control the spinnaker. It can also be used with other headsails when sailing downwind without the spinnaker.
Spinnaker sleeve	A device used to make deploying and retrieving the spinnaker sail much easier. Also called a "dousing sock" or simply a "sock."

Squall	A sudden, strong wind gust, often lasting only a few minutes, and usually blowing in excess of 16 knots.
Stanchion	A vertical metal support along the outside of the deck supporting the lifelines.
Stand on vessel	As per the navigation rules, the vessel that has the right-of-way and should hold its course.
Standing rigging	Cables that support the mast, usually braided wire. These have specific names depending on location. The cable in the front of the mast is the forestay, the cable on the side(s) of the mast is a shroud, and the cable at the back of the mast is the backstay. (See also rigging.)
Starboard	The right side of the vessel when aboard and facing forward.
Starter / starting battery	The battery that provides power to start the engine.
Statute mile	A unit of measurement equal to 5,280 feet. (See also nautical mile.)
Stern	The aftermost part of the vessel.
Stern line	A dock line used to secure the rear of the boat to the dock.
Stern rail	A railing, often metal, at or near the stern of a vessel designed to help restrain passengers (or crew) from falling overboard. It is usually more substantial than a lifeline. May also be called the "stern pulpit."

Stiff breeze	Vague term for a moderate wind with a speed of 10-15 knots.
Stow	To put something away on a boat.
Support	See stanchion.
Swells	Big waves that travel over long distances in the open ocean.
Swim platform	A structure on the stern of a boat designed to make getting into or out of the water easier.
Tack / tacking	1. A maneuver to bring the bow (front) of the boat through the eye of the wind. 2. The direction the boat is sailing as it moves through the wind.
Tankage	The capacity and/or contents of a tank.
Teak	The wood from a teak tree. It is strong, durable, resistant to insects and warping, and is frequently used in ship building.
Tender	A small boat used to ferry crew to and from a larger vessel. (See also dinghy.)
Tether	A short lead for a safety harness.
Tethered	The process of connecting your safety tether to something secure.
Tommy Kraft	A fictional person with a fictional line of marine supply stores.
Topside	On or toward the upper deck of a vessel.

Traveler	A track which allows for side to side adjustments of the mainsail (or mizzen sail).
Trim	1. To adjust the sails to be more or less efficient. 2. To pull in or let out a sheet.
True north	North according to the earth's axis, not magnetic north (according to a compass).
UFO	Any unidentified flying object, often associated with sightings of alien ships.
Underway	Moving through the water.
Unfurl/unfurled (the sails)	See hauled out, def. # 1.
United States Coast Guard	A branch of the United States' armed forces, responsible for the enforcement of maritime law and for the protection of life and property at sea.
Vessel	Any boat, ship, yacht, or watercraft.
VHF radio	A common type of radio used in marine applications. VHF (very high frequency) refers to the marine frequency range of 156 to 174 MHz, inclusive. Channel 16 (156.8 MHz) is the international calling and distress channel.
Wake	The waves caused by the motion of the vessel through the water. The wake from a large vessel, like a cruise ship, can be dangerous to small craft getting caught in it.

Wastewater	The product contained by the vessel's sewage system. Numerous laws and rules govern where and when wastewater can be discharged overboard. It is normally referred to as "greywater" when without fecal contamination, such as that from sinks, baths, showers, or dishwashers. It is normally referred to as "blackwater" when having fecal contamination (from toilets).
Wastewater pump-out station	A specific area with specialized equipment to remove wastewater from the vessel's holding tanks. Your nose will usually alert you to the proximity of where such an area is located.
Water maker	A device used to obtain potable (drinkable) water from seawater by the process of reverse osmosis. Also called a "desalinator."
Waterline	1. A line that marks the level of the surface of water on something, usually the vessel's hull but often the shoreline as well. 2. A line marked on the outside of a vessel that corresponds to the water's surface when the vessel is afloat.
Watertight door	A special type of door, found on vessels, designed to prevent the ingress of water from one compartment to another during flooding or accidents.
Wave trough	The low point in the cycle of a wave.
Weather fax	A facsimile machine designed to receive and print high-quality, high-definition weather charts and satellite images.

Weigh anchor	To retrieve the anchor when ready to get underway.
Wheel	Used to steer the sailboat by controlling the rudder. Some wheels fold to save space when not in use.
White light	A type of navigation light used at night by vessels at sea.
Winch	A mechanical, drum-shaped device using gears and a handle (or electric operation) to increase the tension in a line.
Windward	1. Facing the wind or the side facing the wind. 2. The side or direction from which the wind is blowing. (The side opposite leeward.)
Wire cable	See standing rigging.
Workroom	A room (or compartment) containing specialized tools, parts, supplies, and/or equipment for making repairs or building needed things.
Yacht	Any sail or power vessel used for pleasure, cruising, or racing. Conventionally, any watercraft over 40 feet in length will likely qualify as a yacht, but the minimum length to be considered a yacht is debatable. And the category of "mega" or "super" yacht is also very subjective.
Yacht club	A club organized for the enjoyment of sailing (and boating).

ABOUT THE AUTHORS

Jim Schoendaller

Jim Schoendaller is a Certified Sailing Instructor, ironically teaching in the landlocked state of Colorado. He is a retired public-sector employee who is enjoying writing novels instead of contracts. He is an avid traveler, having visited 5 continents so far, and is an accomplished Ballroom dancer.

Jeanne C. Stein

Jeanne C. Stein is the national bestselling author of the Urban Fantasy series, The Anna Strong Vampire Chronicles and most recently, The Fallen Siren Series written as S. J. Harper. There are nine books in the Anna Strong series and two books and two novellas in a series written with Samantha Sommersby under the S. J. Harper pseudonym. She also has more that a dozen short story credits, including the novella, Blood Debt, from the New York Times bestselling anthology, Hexed and The NYT bestselling anthology, Dead But Not Forgotten edited by Charlaine Harris. Her short stories have been published in collections here in the US and the UK. Her latest, an Anna Strong novel titled Paradox, was released in November 2019.